THE EXTINCTION CODE

Dean Crawford

© 2016 Dean Crawford
Published: 13th October 2016
ISBN: 1539722821
ISBN-13: 9781539722823
Publisher: Fictum Ltd
The right of Dean Crawford to be identified as author of this Work has been asserted by him in accordance with sections 77 and 78 of the Copyright, Designs and Patents Act 1988.
All rights reserved.

www.deancrawfordbooks.com

I

Megiddo, Canaan

1457 BCE

They came out of the south.

The first hint of dawn broke across the barren plain like a river of molten metal that spilled along the horizon, banners of torn cloud tiger-striping the glowing heavens to the east above the Jezreel Valley. As Tjaneni stood in the darkness he felt the cool desert wind ripple the fabric of his loose shirt, bringing with it the scents of the distant Mediterranean Sea and the wild, untamed wilderness beyond Mount Carmel.

Atop distant ridges rows of flickering lights illuminated the darkness like stars, the flaming torches of King Kadesh's watching scouts. Tjaneni's young servant, Misha, pointed to them.

'Tjaneni, war is upon us!'

'Calm thyself,' Tjaneni soothed his young friend. 'They will not strike us here on the plain, for we are many.'

Tjaneni turned and hurried inside his tent to dress, knowing that the great King would call for him now that their enemy had been sighted. As the Pharaoh's senior scribe, it was his duty to record and preserve everything that his master saw and to ensure that his great victories were recorded for all time.

Pharaoh Thutmose III was already the most successful King The Black Land of the Iteru River had ever known, extending the empire in a series of daring raids against warrior clans and neighbouring kingdoms with brutal but brilliant efficiency. A revolt in Kadesh, the land of the Amurru, had resulted in the Kadeshi people's attempt to change their vassalage and ally themselves to the Hittites. The Caananite hordes had then allied themselves to the Amurru and the Mitanni, from the region of the two rivers between the headwaters of the Orontes and the Jordan. Worse, the King of Megiddo had joined the revolt. Both cities enjoyed fortress strongholds, but in typical style Thutmose III had responded by leading his army personally to deal with the revolt. Spread across the plain outside Tjaneni's tent were endless flickering campfires, as though the vast starry expanses above were reflected across the sprawling deserts below. Tjaneni knew from his records that the Pharaoh had amassed chariots and infantry numbering more than fifteen thousand men, while the King of Kadesh possessed a tribal force of similar number now encamped beside the waters of Taanach.

Tjaneni knew that his master would need to know what his enemy would do next.

'Gather the seers,' he ordered Misha as they stepped back outside into the dawn light. 'They will be at the oracle, as they always are.'

The younger man dashed away as the huge army came to life before Tjaneni, infantry emerging from their tents and cavalry riders hurrying to prepare their mounts for the brutal battle that would soon come. Tjaneni had seen more than once the terrible sight of thousands of men clashing together amid clouds of swirling sand, the sound of metal upon metal, upon flesh and bone, the screams of fear and agony, the desert stained red with rivers of blood as the Pharaoh's mighty army crushed all who stood before it.

'Tjaneni?'

He turned, and Misha beckoned him to follow. They walked across the side of the encampment to the great hall, a huge enclosure wherein resided the King of Kings, Thutmose III himself.

Tjaneni entered the enclosure on his knees, his hands stretched upon the rugs before him, his shoulders pulled in and his head low, prostrating himself before the God–King. Ahead of him stood ranks of guards, lining a deep red path that ended before the throne upon which reclined Thutmose, surrounded by flaming torches that crackled and snapped on the dawn breeze rippling the walls of the great enclosure.

'Rise.'

Tjaneni slowly stood upright and saw Thutmose watching him with eyes deeply sunk into his skull. His forehead was low, giving him a permanent expression of deep concentration, and his jaw was wide and heavy. His elaborate Pharaonic Nemes headdress fell to his broad shoulders in gold and blue stripes that shimmered in the light from the flaming torches lining the interior of the hall, giving him the appearance of a squat, powerful toad.

'Approach.'

Tjaneni walked to stand before the Pharaoh and immediately got down onto his knees once more, as was the custom. Nobody, not even the greatest warrior in the Kingdom, was allowed to stand taller than the King when in his presence.

'The loathed enemy of the King of Kings awaits,' Thutmose said, his voice softer than one would imagine for such a powerful and feared Pharaoh, but Tjaneni had long ago learned not to underestimate the man–god before him. 'What news awaits?'

Tjaneni spoke softly, kept his head low and his eyes averted.

'The seers are coming, oh King. The oracle will show us the way.'

Behind him Tjaneni heard the entrance into the royal enclosure of the seers, the mysterious sages and mystics who resided in the Temple of Amon–Ra and the House of Life in Memphis. He feared them as all men feared them, for their knowledge was drawn from places where mortals could not tread; the *ipet resyt*, or southern sanctuary.

Tjaneni moved in a low crouch to one side and turned as he watched the six robed figures, their features hidden from view by white veils and hoods, drift like ghosts to stand before the Pharaoh. Worshippers of the goddess Wadjet, or *"Eye of the Moon"*, they spoke of a realm beyond human sight where the past, the present and the future were as one.

Thutmose leaned forward in his throne, his voice the only sound above the crackling flames of the torches.

'Speak of the morrow.'

Tjaneni concealed a flush of dread as he saw the figures kneel before the Pharaoh and slender arms reach up to remove their veils. In the flickering firelight they stared up at the Pharaoh, all of them young girls with their hair tightly braided, their skin smooth as buttermilk, their lips sculptured. Tjaneni swallowed as he looked at their unseeing eyes, pale white orbs that seemed to glow in the firelight, the girls blind from birth. All of them were pure born, their virginity unsullied by menfolk.

'The enemy awaits,' the youngest of the girls said. 'They have seen us and they believe they know our path.'

Thutmose frowned deeply, his dark eyes staring without fear at the young girls. The Pharaoh was one of the few men who could do so knowing that he himself was half man and half deity.

'What do they believe us to do upon the dawn?' he demanded. 'There are three routes into Megiddo.'

'Kadesh believes that we shall advance by way of Dothaim and Yehem, and cross into the Jezreel Valley by Zefti or Taanach,' came the reply from another of the girls.

Thutmose smiled thoughtfully. 'They believe we will take an easy path around the mountains.'

Tjaneni watched as the Pharaoh's senior military commander nodded. 'It is the only way, my King. The route directly through the mountains at Aruna is a ravine only wide enough for four men. If we take that route, the enemy will cut us down with ease as we enter the valley.'

Thutmose nodded, still deep in thought, and then he looked at the oracles before him.

'How do we know which route will be best?' he asked them.

The youngest girl again spoke, for she was the purest of all the oracles and thus the one with the clearest vision.

'When the stars fall from the sky,' she whispered in reply, her sightless eyes staring into oblivion, 'you shall know that Aruna is the path to victory.'

Tjaneni heard the military commanders sigh and scoff in dismay at the girl's bizarre prophecy. Tjaneni himself knew that stars crossing the sky were a rare and much feared event, omens of doom that often heralded great suffering among the ordinary people. But the stars never actually fell from the sky. The chances of such a thing happening here on the plain in the next few hours were almost unthinkably small and…

'The Canaanites are here!'

The cry went up from outside the great hall and Tjaneni saw the Pharaoh stand from his throne and stride without fear past the seers toward the entrance, his military commanders filing in behind him.

Tjaneni followed them out of tent and saw a band of shimmering lights spreading across the horizon to the south, brilliant against the deep blue horizon and far brighter than those of the Kadeshi scouts still lining the hills. Tjaneni had never before encountered the Caananites in the flesh, and the fear that he felt as they appeared bolted shamefully through his belly to weaken his legs with the poison of dread.

'Tjaneni!'

He turned and saw a cleric who had mentored him for so many years shuffle to his side. Ahmen was an old man now, his gait weary and awkward, his eyes rheumy and unfocused, but in the instant the old man saw the lights his expression collapsed first into uncertainty and then into apprehension.

'The Caananites are here,' Tjaneni informed him. 'This is where the battle will be fought, on this very plain.'

Ahmen shook his head slowly, his knuckles white as he clasped tightly the cane on which he supported his aged frame.

'No, Tjaneni,' he replied softly, 'those are not Caananites.'

Tjaneni frowned and turned back to point at the lights and argue that they could not possible be anything other than the army of the enemy hordes, but his words stopped short of his tongue and his eyes widened as he stared at the lights. To his amazement they were no longer arrayed across the horizon like the torches of countless enemy soldiers, forging across the plain with murder in their minds and rage in their hearts. Now, the lights were up in the sky.

'Ahmen,' was all that he could whisper, his throat tight and his voice hoarse. 'What is this? Sorcery?'

Cries of alarm went up across the Pharaoh's encampment, and then the alert horns sounded a mournful chorus that swept across the plain on the growing winds as the fearsome orb of the sun rose as if to do battle with the lights to the south. Veils of sand gusted across the plain as the Pharaoh surveyed the lights that soared upward into the heavens, jerking up and down, flickering and pulsing with vibrant colors that rivalled the glorious sunrise searing the sky to the east.

'What are they?' Tjaneni asked again, barely able to speak.

Ahmen moved to stand alongside his young apprentice. 'The watchers are coming,' he replied simply as he held his cane with both hands and watched the lights climbing into the night sky, 'and they have been here before.'

'You've seen The Watchers before?' Tjaneni asked in amazement, his voice falling to a superstitious whisper. 'Why did you not tell me of this?'

'Would you have believed me?' Ahmen countered.

Shouts from the soldiers emerging from their tents in their hundreds cut the conversation off as Tjaneni turned again, and now true fear wrenched at his heart. The glowing lights were more than thirty in number and were growing in size.

They were surrounded by a halo of light that seemed to pulse as though alive, one moment green, the next blue or orange or a fiery yellow that competed with the brilliance of the sun itself.

One by one, the brilliant lights accelerated across the vault of the heavens, and Tjaneni heard what sounded like the rumble of distant thunder that reverberated through his chest like beating war drums. He realized that he was breathing fast, his fists clenched so tightly by his sides that his fingernails dug into his palms.

'They glow with such beauty,' he said in awe.

'And they strike fear into the hearts of brave men,' Ahmen pointed out.

The lights jerked across the sky, changing direction violently as they zig–zagged, their glow flickering among the high clouds scattered across the heavens. Tjaneni saw the Kadeshi scouts' torches vanish from the distant hills as the enemy fled into the distance toward Megiddo, and then suddenly the lights soaring above them emitted tongues of vivid orange flame as they descended and rushed overhead. Tjaneni heard the horses panic and bolt, heard cries of shock and alarm from among the men as he smelled a foul odor that stung his eyes as the lights thundered by overhead.

Ahmen watched in silence as a large, orange light descended toward a hillside a few miles to the east and disappeared. Tjaneni saw the light vanish behind the hills, and then the remaining lights flew away and with bright flares of white light they rocketed up into the heavens and vanished like dying stars as a deafening crack of thunder split the skies. Tjaneni ducked down, the inside of his ears aching with the infernal noise as he cowered in fear. The lights vanished and the dreadful thunder echoed away into the night on one side and the dawn on the other, as if merely the remnant of some terrible nightmare.

The plain returned to silence as the horses calmed and the terrified infantry slowly stood tall once more, thousands of eyes staring up in vain into the sky amid the slowly fading stars.

Ahmen glanced at the Pharaoh's aides. 'This is a great portent, and one of doom.'

Tjaneni shook his head. 'Pharaoh does not think so, look.'

Thutmose looked down upon the enormous army before him as he raised his flail and his ankh, his voice suddenly deep and melodious as he roared his command across the plain as though defying the universe itself.

'We march for Aruna, for the stars have fallen upon the site of our victory!'

Across the plain the army thundered its response, tens of thousands of men stamping their bare feet upon the ancient earth and thrusting their weapons into the dawn sky. Tjaneni turned toward his tent to gather his parchments, for he knew that Pharaoh would wish it all to be recorded for the End of Days.

Ahmen stayed him with one hand.

'Gather the horses,' the old man said as he looked at the distant hills where the bright light had descended. 'We must travel east.'

Tjaneni felt his legs quiver with fear and awe. 'We cannot. The King shall do battle this dawn, and the realm of The Watchers is no place for men.'

Ahmen smiled.

'But I am old, Tjaneni, and I have little to lose. Would you not wish to learn the will of The Watchers from their own mouths, and not the riddles of the seers?'

Tjaneni looked to the east, the hills now bathed in brilliant sunlight, and he turned to Misha.

'Fetch three horses, as fast as you can.'

***

II

Black Dragon Canyon, Utah

Present day
'Listen up!'

A row of vehicles with flashing hazard lights were packed tight around the entrance to a deep ravine, a rugged fissure that split the canyon wash and rose up toward the dawn sky above. Sergeant Robbie Dixon could see the first rays of sunlight striking the tops of the mesas high above with brilliant golden light as he joined his fellow officers. A dozen of Uintah County Sheriff's Department's finest men were standing around the hood of a patrol car, all of them having driven across the desert in the pre–dawn light from the nearby city of Vernal.

Their commander, Lieutenant Franklyn Bolt, was a towering figure of a man, barrel chested and with a white moustache that drooped either side of his mouth like mare's tails as he spoke.

'We all know who's waiting for us in there, and we all know what they've been doing. They're armed and they're convinced that the end of the world is upon us, so they won't hesitate to shoot once we come through their door. These are not nice people and we know that there are children inside. Your task is to apprehend, and to shoot only if there is no other option.' Bolt took a deep breath, as though his message of restraint to his men was a step too far even for him. 'I want the women and children out alive and unharmed, but if this happens to be the End of Days for Abraham Messian then I won't be shedding a tear tonight.'

A ripple of agreement fluttered like a dark thought among the twelve heavily armed officers and was shared by Robbie Dixon. He had two young daughters at home, aged three and six. Like the rest of the Armed Response Team he had heard the rumors about what had been going on up here in this lonely canyon, miles from Vernon where the apocalyptically minded Abraham Messian had set up his *Messiah's Advent* cult headquarters four years previously.

Although state law prohibited the founding of cults, there was nothing in the legislation to prevent people from building new dwellings out in the Utah wilderness, a fact that held true for most all American states. Modern cults were smart enough to ensure that they complied with the law in order to draw as little attention to themselves as possible, thus allowing their less palatable pursuits to flourish behind closed doors. Out here, deep inside Black Dragon Canyon where an abandoned mining settlement was the local "ghost town" and renowned for supposed hauntings, Messian had created the perfect environment for both seclusion and suspicion.

The first hint of trouble had come when two girls had gone missing from Maesa, Vernal. Vague whisperings that they had been abducted by Messian's cult members had circulated for a while around town but with no firm leads and no probable cause to enter the cult compound deep inside Black Dragon Canyon the police had been unable to obtain a warrant from the District Attorney to search the premises. Time had gone by, the two girls still missing despite television statements from their distraught families and concerned law enforcement officials, but then just two days ago the Sheriff's Department received a call that changed everything.

A body had been found just north of the canyon, that of a thirteen–year–old girl. Robbie's guts convulsed as he recalled that terrible day when he and four other officers had arrived at the scene to find the waif–like teenager's remains slumped in a ravine. Although the desert scavengers had got to her body before the long–distance endurance runner who had stumbled upon the corpse while training in the blistering heat of the Utah wilderness, there had been more than sufficient biological material remaining to identify her as Lorraine Feyer, from Maeser, one of the missing girls. An autopsy confirmed that she had been sexually assaulted, and in a remarkable testimony to modern technology the coroner had been able to extract a small amount of foreign DNA from her loins that had been conclusively matched to one Warren Blaise, a member of Messian's apocalyptic cult. Regardless of whether Blaise had acted alone or in concert with the cult, it was the break the Sheriff's department had been waiting for.

Within eight hours of the autopsy report being filed the Sheriff's team had been assembled, briefed and had drawn weapons from the armory, just in time for the DA to hurriedly sign the warrant that would allow them to finally smash their way into whatever house of horrors Messian had created amid the crumbling ruins of Dragon Canyon's ghost town.

'Three teams of four,' Bolt announced, 'one each at the front and back, the third acting as a sniper team up on the hills for top cover. We'll go in the front and flush them out and the rear team can mop up anybody who tries to get out the back door. Any questions?'

All twelve officers shook their heads grimly, everybody wanting this over with and eager to liberate whoever was trapped inside the insane leader's deranged cult. Robbie checked the magazine on his shotgun, loaded with shot specially designed for close range and minimum spread that would limit the chances of collateral damage. Like everyone else on the team, he knew that this would be close and dangerous. His bullet–proof vest was hot and heavy but he wore it without question: there were no television–style mavericks in real life police enforcement, and those that tried to be were soon either out of a career or lying dead in the street. Robbie wanted to get home to his family that night, and if he and his team did their jobs right perhaps at least one abducted girl might get home to hers too.

'Let's move out!'

Robbie hefted the shotgun into a prone position and followed Bolt's team at a jog as they advanced up the desiccated canyon. There was little sound this early in the dawn and the air was refreshingly cool, so much so that it seemed hard to imagine that within an hour or two the sun would hammer down mercilessly on the desert and temperatures would soar to the high eighties before noon.

Messian's cult hideout was located deep inside one of the canyon's myriad washes that ran down from the high mesas. Although the area received little rainfall, when it did come it was typically torrential, provoking flash floods and dangerous conditions for the unwary. Plenty of folk had been drowned by water rushing down from rainstorms miles away that they may not even have seen or heard.

The sniper team broke off into a rugged gulley to the right and began the long climb to a ridge that overlooked the cult's compound. Aerial photographs obtained by the local police from light aircraft and drones had given the team high resolution images with which to plan their assault, but the limited access to the area meant there was no way for a large force to make the initial attack. Instead, thirty more police and Sheriff's department officers were stationed a short distance behind them at the mouth of the canyon, along with ambulances and fire teams on stand–by, waiting earnestly for news of the armed response team's raid.

Robbie followed Bolt to an outcrop in the canyon where it turned sharply. He knew from memory that the compound was built on the slopes nearby, elevated from the canyon floor but in a good position both to conceal itself and also to collect water run–off. Messian had a strict code of living independently, "of the grid" as many of the *prepper* communities liked to call it. The compound was arrayed with solar panels built into the roof of a long, low two–storey building that looked somewhat like a ranch, and a small custom–built wind farm had been erected on a nearby ridge to take advantage of the brisk winds that moaned across the hot desert. Robbie knew from the briefing that the ranch itself contained at least twenty individual rooms and a large church in the center where Messian preached to his brainwashed followers of the imminent End of Days, which had of course been "imminent" for several thousand years.

'Bravo Team in position.'

Bolt's radio crackled and hissed, but the volume had already been turned down enough to prevent it from alerting any of the slumbering cult's members to their presence.

'Charlie Team in position.'

Bolt turned to Robbie and his two companions as they saw Bravo Team crouching amid dense foliage behind the compound, which was surrounded by gates and chain link fences topped with razor wire. Robbie could see the severed heads of poisonous desert snakes tied in their hundreds to the fences, bared fangs glistening in the dawn light and acting as a grim deterrent. Robbie knew that the cult's members partook in something called "snake handling", believing that their faith in Jesus was more powerful than the serpent's bite. That alone had cost the cult a few members over the past four years, convincing the Sheriff's office that some members must be partaking in the illegal practice and convincing Robbie that blind faith of any kind was a really bad idea.

One of the team cradled a solid metal ram under his arms as he looked at Lieutenant Bolt.

'Ready?' Bolt asked.

Robbie nodded, as did their two companions, and Bolt pressed the safety switch on his weapon to "off" as the other of Robbie's fellow officers hefted a pair of steel croppers in his hands, ready to cut through the chain link fences.

'Go, now!'

Robbie sprinted to the fence alongside his colleague, ready to give covering fire as the officer next to him slid to his knees in the dust and clipped through the fence, tearing a man–sized hole into it and then leaping back out of the way as Bolt and Robbie jumped through, their bullet–proof vests more than a match for the snake fangs. The other two men followed them inside the compound moments later and they ran together to the front of the building.

The officer with the ram dashed up onto the porch of the ranch and hit the front door at full speed, the ram smashing into the locks with a crack that echoed down the canyon like a gunshot. Robbie pinned himself against the wall as he heard shouts and cries of alarm from inside the compound as the ram smashed again and then a third time and the door's locks were finally overcome and the door smashed inward.

'Armed police, get on the ground!' Bolt roared as the team plunged into the building.

Robbie followed Bolt closely and moved to the left as Bolt took the right side of the hall to give the rest of the team a clear line of sight. The interior of the ranch was dark and Robbie almost gagged as the stench of stale ammonia and faeces hit him.

'This is a house of the Gods!' a voice screamed.

Like a vision from hell Robbie saw a half–naked man stagger into the hall, his white bed–shirt undone, a shotgun held in both hands and his eyes wide with rage and terror as he aimed the weapon at the officers rushing toward him.

***

III

Robbie fired past Bolt without conscious thought, an instinctive response to the sight of the rifle being brandished at them. The shotgun blasted with a brief flash of light and the shot hit the man in the chest and hurled him backwards as his own weapon clattered uselessly onto the wooden floorboards at his feet. From outside, Robbie heard the rest of the team open up with their loud-hailers, a deliberate attempt to make the occupants of the cult house believe that there were literally hundreds of officers outside.

'Armed police, get on the ground!'

Bolt staggered to one side, the shot having gone off inches from his ears as Robbie rushed forward. His heart thumped in his chest and he barely noticed the dead man's eyes still wide open, a bloodied wound across his chest as he turned left into a small room and saw two women cowering beneath stained sheets.

'Easy,' Robbie said as he skittered to a halt, his voice hoarse with tension as the rest of the team thundered past in the corridor behind him. 'Show me your hands.'

The two women stared up at him and one of them dropped the sheets to reveal her hands. As Robbie looked at her, the other woman's face collapsed into rage and she lunged at him with a blade that flickered in the weak light filtering through threadbare curtains.

Robbie reacted instinctively as his training took over and he flipped the shotgun over in his grasp. The butt of the weapon whipped up and smashed under the charging woman's jaw before the blade could reach him, and in an instant of time he saw her face twisted with grotesque rage, her eyes wild. The butt cracked loudly as it impacted and the woman's eyes rolled up into their sockets as she flipped over backwards and landed on the thin mattress at his boots, the knife falling from her grasp.

The other woman recoiled away from Robbie and the blade, the role of captor and abductee clear for him to see.

'Stay where you are!' Robbie snapped as he tried to inject some small measure of compassion into his voice.

The woman nodded frantically as Robbie grabbed the blade and then turned, hurrying back out into the corridor as he heard fresh shouts and cries competing with bellowed police orders to *get down* and *stay down*. Bolt and the team stormed out of sight into the darkened heart of the building, and Robbie was about to dash in pursuit when he stopped short and stared in amazement at the wall beside him.

Across its surface were lines and lines of what looked like Egyptian hieroglyphics scrawled in a jagged, uneven hand as though the author of the works were unable to see quite where they were writing. Unlike the orderly patterns

Robbie remembered seeing in text books at school, the hieroglyphics inside the ranch undulated up and down like the waves of some bizarre sea.

Robbie looked ahead into the darkness and saw nothing but shadows as he heard Bolt's booming voice echo through the ranch.

'Armed police, get down!'

'This is a house of the Gods!' another voice screamed in reply.

Then, Bolt's voice once again. 'Get on the ground, don't do it!'

And then the dark heart of the building vanished into a haze of flame as a terrific blast ripped through the corridor and Robbie was hurled aside and slammed into the wall as a wave of heat washed over him and flames billowed across the ceiling above his head. The woman he had liberated screamed as she was thrown back into the room from which she had emerged and Robbie tumbled in behind her and crashed down onto his belly.

A thick pall of smoke billowed into the room, flames flickering like dancing demons in the corridor beyond as Robbie tried to stand upright. His legs felt weak and he could hear nothing but a ringing in his ears. He managed to get up on one knee and sucked in a lungful of air to try to clear his head, but all he got was thick smoke that scorched his throat.

He grabbed the terrified woman and pointed to the building's entrance, where sunlight still penetrated the smoke boiling through the corridor.

'Get out, now!'

The woman staggered away toward the light as Robbie hauled himself to his feet and stumbled out of the room, then turned and headed deeper into the building.

The interior of the ranch had been scorched by the ferocity of the blast, flames roaring in twisting vortexes as though alive and reaching out for him. Heat billowed in heavy clouds toward him, blocking the way to the interior and his colleagues. Massive pillars and timbers collapsed in clouds of spiralling embers riding black waves of smoke as Robbie's eyes filled with tears from the pain and the heat. He staggered backwards against the wall and was about to flee when he heard the crying.

Robbie turned, yanked a kerchief from the pocket of his fatigues and wrapped it around his face as he tried to draw a breath. The flames were rising higher, fuelled by the hot air from outside being drawn in through the funnel of the entrance corridor, the flames reaching out for him like searing fingers that hissed as they wound their way closer.

Robbie felt panic rise up inside him but he mastered his fear and stumbled further into the blazing ranch to see the shattered remnants of what looked like some kind of church, an altar at one end burning furiously. To his horror, amid the collapsed timbers and scattered chairs were countless corpses, the bodies of Messian's followers and fallen police officers, arms twisted and broken, uniforms and robes burning in furious pyres. Robbie moved toward the closest officer but he knew that he could not help any of them, that the blast had done its terrible work in an instant.

The crying attracted his attention again and he turned to see a cage of some kind set into a revetment in one wall, and within it the form of a young girl. Her head was bowed, her hands covering her face as she screamed at the floor, her voice rising desperately above the flames.

'..el….me..'

Robbie turned toward the cage and stumbled toward it, flames dancing around him and up through the shattered roof above as pillars of black smoke soared into patches of blue sky visible between burning rafters as Robbie heard the girl scream again.

'…Ro… me…'

He staggered over the corpse of a young woman, half of her face burned off, the other staring wide–eyed into oblivion. Robbie clambered over the gruesome remains and stumbled on weak legs to the cage, and then he heard the girl's screams clearly for the first time.

'Rob…bie!'

Robbie froze in place, almost superstitious with awe as the young girl's scream reached his ear. For a brief moment in time he wondered how on earth she could have known his name and then a hand reached out of the cage with shocking speed and grabbed his wrist. Robbie looked down at the girl, barely visible in the smoke and the darkness, no more than fourteen years of age, her grip vice–like on his arm as she spoke to him.

'Release me!'

Robbie placed one gloved hand atop hers. 'It's going to be fine honey, just stay there and…'

'Get down!' the girl screamed at him as she yanked her hand away.

Robbie dropped as though his life depended upon it, and as he did so a massive beam crashed down behind him and slammed into the floor, clouds of burning debris and smoke smothering them both. Robbie reached for the cage door, saw the thick padlock keeping the girl entrapped within, and he aimed his shotgun at it.

'Get back!'

The girl cowered in one corner of her cage as Robbie fired twice. The rounds smashed the padlock and he yanked the cage open, the metal warm to the touch. The young girl within launched herself at him and flung her arms about his neck with enough force to almost knock him over, her waif–like legs about his waist.

Robbie caught her and held onto her as he turned and desperately sought a way out of the burning ranch, jerking the shotgun up and down in his grip to pump a fresh round into the chamber. Thick smoke obscured the building around him and he realized that he could not see a way out. To his amazement, above the roaring flames he heard the girl's voice in his ear.

'Follow the star.'

Robbie stared about him in disbelief, wondering what she was talking about. Then to his right he saw a corridor, above which was a five–pointed Star of David etched into the wood itself. Robbie hurried toward it, hoping against hope that he wouldn't break a leg on the debris inside the ranch as he ran with his eyes almost closed against the heat and the smoke, crouching down as much as he could with the girl clinging to him as they plunged into the corridor.

The smoke thinned out, the air a little clearer but the heat still stifling as Robbie followed the corridor through the darkness. He could hear timbers above creaking as they were weakened by flames, could smell the smoke following him as the inferno intensified behind them.

The girl's voice whispered to him as though from a dream.

'Gun, your left.'

Robbie reacted instantly, bringing his shotgun up as a figure lunged out of the blackness toward him from a doorway to his left, a pistol in their hands and a wild gleam in their eye as they aimed the weapon at him.

'This is a house of the...'

Robbie fired, the shot hitting the gunman in his chest. The light of life vanished from his eyes and he collapsed onto his knees, leaning against the wall and staring into the darkness as though he were waiting for somebody, his heart still pumping blood from his wound.

Robbie pushed past the corpse and ran down the corridor, sliding the shotgun through his grasp and pumping a fresh round into the chamber as he moved. Ahead he could see a thin, bright rectangle of light beaming past the jam of a door that must lead out of the ranch and to the rear of the building. He was almost there when the girl's voice whispered into his ear.

'Behind you!'

Robbie whirled and saw in the corridor Abraham Messian, his robes aflame as he staggered toward them with a shotgun in his grasp, his wild hair burning and his skin blistering from countless burns and lesions.

'This is a house of the Gods!' he screamed and took aim.

Robbie, weak from smoke inhalation, hauled the heavy shotgun up single-handedly once more to point at Messian as he heard the girl's voice in his hear.

'Don't shoot! Get away from the exit!'

Robbie ducked to one side and crashed through an open doorway as he twisted aside and Messian's shotgun blasted its rounds past them both as they fell. The door to the outside rattled as the shot hammered into it and punched a few holes through the wood that cast beams of white light into the smoky air.

Robbie slammed down onto his back and saw Messian rush toward them as he aimed the shotgun, and then suddenly a dozen pistol rounds smashed through the ranch door from outside and punctured Messian with enough force to lift the old man off his feet and hurl him onto his back. The shotgun clattered down alongside him, and as Robbie stared in amazement so the ranch door crashed open and four heavily armed troopers dashed in, fire crews following them and running straight past where Robbie and the girl were sprawled on the floor.

'It's safe now,' the girl whispered into his ear, her arms still wrapped tightly about his neck.

Robbie staggered upright and out of the doorway into the brilliant sunlight with the girl still clinging to him, squinting and staggering until he collapsed onto his knees and sucked in a deep lungful of the blessedly clean air. He instantly collapsed in a deep coughing fit as he felt the girl being lifted from his arms. Robbie let himself be helped up by two firemen and a paramedic who had rushed to their aid, and he dimly became aware of a helicopter thundering overhead and the dozens of law enforcement vehicles swarming into the ranch compound as fire teams sprayed hoses of white foam into the building's blackened hulk.

'You okay, pal?'

A paramedic was fussing over him, but apart from his coughing Robbie was beginning to recover. He nodded as he was patted down for injuries, and as he stood there in the bright sunshine so one of the fire crews hurried up to him.

'Hey, how the hell did you get out of there? My men can't get close to that building without risking their necks?'

Robbie gestured to the girl, who was now being laid on a gurney with an oxygen mask over her face as the medics prepared to get her to a hospital.

'She showed me the way out,' Robbie replied, coughing again, 'and saved my life twice on the way. She's sharp as a button, make sure she's well looked after.'

The fireman looked back at the girl and then at Robbie. 'What are you talking about?'

'The girl,' Robbie frowned. 'I didn't find my way out of there, she did. She told me to follow a star on the wall, to duck when the wall came down, told me about the shooter in there and when you guys came blasting in. She saw it all.'

The fireman stared at Robbie for a few moments more and then clapped his shoulder. 'I think you just got real lucky and the smoke's got to you pal, that girl can't see a damned thing.'

Robbie frowned in confusion and then looked at the girl's face for the first time in broad daylight, and he felt the hairs rise up on his forearms and the back of his neck as though insects were crawling on his skin. She was looking right back at him but her eyes were as white as clouds, the girl completely blind.

'She owes you her life pal,' the fireman said, 'know when to take credit.'

Robbie barely heard the fireman as he watched the girl being lifted into the ambulance, and never once did she take her sightless eyes off his.

***

THE GENESIS CYPHER   Dean Crawford

IV

Defense Intelligence Agency,

Joint Base Anacostia–Bolling,

Washington DC

Ethan Warner walked into the south entrance of one of the most secretive intelligence agencies in the world, and although he had been here many times before he felt oddly out of place. Beside him his partner Nicola Lopez looked as though she felt the same, as though they were returning to a house that they had lived in many years before.

Lieutenant General J. F. Nellis, the Director of the DIA, appeared in the building's lobby and strode toward them across the large emblem emblazoned across the floor tiles. Ethan and Lopez moved through two security posts, Ethan getting a brief glimpse of himself and his partner in the monitors nearby; Lopez, diminutive and dark skinned, a Latino with a bad attitude that would put any soldier he had ever met to shame, while he was six–one tall with somewhat unkempt light brown hair and a jaw that was perhaps a little too wide to be considered handsome.

'Ethan, Nicola,' Nellis greeted them with a brief handshake.

'Where's the fire?' Lopez asked.

Nellis smiled but did not reply, indicating that they should follow him. Ethan complied in silence, aware that discussing such delicate matters here in the lobby was not something that a four–star general would be willing to do. Nellis led them to an elevator and they travelled in silence up to the fifth floor before walking to the Director's office. They sat down inside as he closed the door behind them.

'I've got some work for you,' Nellis said as he sat down behind his broad desk of polished mahogany, 'and a few updates.'

Lopez frowned. 'We haven't worked for the DIA since Majestic Twelve was liquidated six months ago. Why drag us out of Chicago now?'

Ethan had begun working for the Defense Intelligence Agency some six years previously, when his former colleague in the United States Marines, Doug Jarvis, had recruited him to go in search of something that he would never have believed possible: the seven–thousand–year old remains of a humanoid creature found in the depths of Israel's Negev Desert. Since then, with Nicola Lopez at his side, they had conducted ten major investigations for the agency involving phenomena that all other agencies had rejected as superstition.

'We're listening,' Ethan intervened, to a dirty look from Lopez.

Although Lopez was dismissive of the DIA since their last investigation had come to an abrupt and violent close over six months before, Ethan was more than happy to listen to what the director had to say. Majestic Twelve, a shadowy and corrupt cabal that had operated within the United States Government for over sixty years had met its demise in South America at their hands. Despite defections from within the DIA in the wake of the victory Ethan and Nicola had considered their task complete and had returned to Chicago, where they had continued their work as bail–bondsmen in relative peace ever since.

General Nellis pulled out a file and opened it before them on the desk.

'Majestic Twelve is no more,' he said, 'long live Majestic Twelve.'

Ethan looked down at a series of photographs taken from automated feature–recognition cameras in airports and hotels, and he instantly recognized the faces upon the first of the images.

'That's Jarvis,' Lopez uttered in shock, 'and Aaron Mitchell. But they're together!'

Ethan leaned back in his seat and dragged one hand down his face. Their boss, Jarvis, had been one of the major DIA defections after MJ–12 were taken down, and had somehow managed to spirit away with him the vast majority of the cabal's thirty–billion–dollar wealth. Now it appeared that he had enlisted the assistance of MJ–12's most feared former assassin, Aaron Mitchell, a towering African American.

'Jarvis and Mitchell are confirmed as working together, but who are these other people?' Nellis asked Ethan, looking at the other images.

'This is Lillian Cruz,' Ethan replied as he pointed to a picture of a woman wearing dark glasses moving through an airport in Sao Paulo. 'Lillian had business with Majestic Twelve some years ago after a series of events in New Mexico, with which I'm sure you're familiar?'

Nellis recalled the investigation clearly.

'Lillian Cruz was born in Montrose, Colorado, in the year 1824. She was the last survivor of eight soldiers of the Union army who took sanctuary in a place called Misery Hole in New Mexico in 1862, just after the Battle of Glorietta Pass.'

Lopez leaned back in her seat. 'So you think Lillian's gone over to the other side? I don't believe that for a moment; she was iron–willed and hated MJ–12 for the way they hunted her and her friends down.'

'While searching for a cure for human mortality?' Nellis surmised.

'She was persecuted by Majestic Twelve,' Ethan confirmed. 'She, her husband and some soldiers had hidden from enemy forces in New Mexico and drank water from a subterranean cave that slowed the ageing process via a bacteria present in the water known as Bacillus permians. MJ–12 killed the other members of the group a few years back, her husband included, but she survived long enough to cut a deal with MJ–12. They got the elixir of life, she got her freedom from persecution.'

'What about this one?' Nellis asked, pointing to a woman in another image. 'She looks far too young to be a member of such a cabal?'

'Amber Ryan,' Lopez identified her. 'Her uncle was a man named Stanley Meyer. He invented a fusion device that could have powered the world for free, but was killed by Majestic Twelve before he could give away for nothing the fusion cage he built, an act that he considered essential to mankind's future, because it would have cost MJ–12 profits from fossil fuel interests.'

Ethan spotted another familiar face among the photos.

'Doctor Lucy Morgan,' he said, 'Jarvis's granddaughter and the woman who got me into this in the first place. She discovered the remains of some kind of humanoid species in the deserts of Israel a few years back.'

Nellis nodded, well aware of the origins of ARIES, the Defense Intelligence Agency's Advanced Research and Intelligence Engineering Section, which Jarvis had headed up before he had decided to cut his ties to the US Government.

Created to support to the work of other agencies such as the NSA, CIA and DARPA, ARIES was tasked with emulating the technology of other nations that had been uncovered by covert overseas operations, for the purpose of finding effective defenses against those technologies. In a world where digital and cyber–warfare was more widespread now than ever, where foreign hackers were capable of accessing everything from the computers of major film studios to even the Pentagon and other defense installations, the need for absolute security had never been more paramount.

Ethan knew that with Jarvis and his companions somewhere on the outside and with a great deal of knowledge of the inner workings on ARIES, Nellis would be keen to reign in their erstwhile former boss and prevent history from repeating itself.

'What do you think he's up to?' Lopez asked as she looked at the images. 'It's no secret that Jarvis and I didn't get along so well, but he's no bad guy.'

'He's not immune from the rule of law either,' Nellis pointed out. 'He walked off with billions of dollars of assets that should have been seized by the US Treasury, so as you can imagine there are some seriously annoyed shouting heads roaming around the Capitol at the moment.'

'Let 'em shout,' Ethan said. 'We shut down MJ–12. They should be putting medals around our necks, not burying what happened to save their own careers.'

'I agree,' Nellis said, 'but we have another problem.'

'We do?' Lopez challenged. 'Ethan and I signed out after MJ–12 got themselves toasted in South America, remember?'

'Yes, but nobody knows Jarvis better than the two of you.'

'He worked for you for almost eight years,' Ethan pointed out.

'And disappeared when he was damned good and ready,' Nellis shot back, 'but not before ensuring that both you and Nicola were safe. Whatever the DIA may think of Jarvis it's clear that he cares enough about you both, and that's his weakness if we're to bring him down.'

'You're actually going after him, after everything that he's done for his country?' Ethan challenged the director.

'Everything Doug Jarvis did for his country was in the name of fighting corruption,' Nellis snapped. 'Deciding to up and off with a few billion dollars didn't exactly endear him to the White House despite his prior record. However, as I said that's not our only problem right now.'

'Our?' Lopez echoed, never missing an opportunity to express her displeasure.

'What's happened?' Ethan asked.

The Director produced another file, this one containing no images at all but filled instead with data that looked as though it may have come from the National Security Agency, the ultra–clandestine cryptographic and cyber–crime unit based not too far away in Maryland, Virginia.

'Over the past two years, the NSA has been intercepting communications chatter among Russian political and military channels. Russia has been flexing her muscles a little too prominently for our comfort lately, especially in Crimea and the Ukraine, and it's been deemed highly important to monitor what they're up to both in the Kremlin and in the field.'

Ethan, like most people across the globe, had witnessed the Russian annexation of the Crimea and its barely–covert involvement in the civil war raging across Ukraine's eastern borders. That its belligerent president was becoming bolder by the month, and that there seemed little the west could do about it without provoking a full–scale third world war, was clear to anybody with the most basic grasp of world politics.

'The Russians are keen to expand their influence and take back what they see as their fair share in world events and markets stolen from them post–Glasnost,' Nellis explained. 'Nobody's quite sure what the Kremlin's true intentions are in the long term, but that there seems to have been a backsliding toward pre–Glasnost politics and subterfuge is clear enough to us. The Cold War is returning and with the consent of the Russian people, too. Like most countries Russia's population is gradually ageing, and the old guard there have developed a hankering for what they see as the "good old days" of the Politboro.'

Lopez raised an eyebrow. 'They're asking to queue for bread again, to re–open the Siberian prisons and for politicians to be beheaded if found at fault?'

'Who knew?' Nellis replied with a shrug. 'For them Glasnost was a moment of weakness, of bowing down to the west and becoming the lap–dog of the United States. The Russian people want a strong leader, a hard man with little compromise, which explains the popularity of their current President.'

'How does all of that affect us?' Ethan asked.

Nellis showed them the folder.

'The Russians, believe it or not, have opened up a unit that is based directly on ARIES.'

'No way,' Lopez smiled brightly. 'You think that there's a Warzinski and Lopchek working out of Moscow?'

'I doubt that,' Ethan replied as he stifled a smile. 'The Russians don't have anybody as good looking as us.'

'They also don't have anybody as humane,' Nellis said. 'The Russians are calling their unit *Mat' Zemlya*, or Mother Earth, which isn't as new age as it sounds. They've been overheard talking about the operation you two conducted in Peru a few years back concerning the Russian, Yuri Volkov.'

'He was searching for ancient alien corpses in Machu Picchu,' Lopez said. 'The only corpse he found was his own when we left him up there in the mountains.'

'It seems that the Russian's interest in all things paranormal has recently gone through the ceiling, and that bothers us here at the DIA.'

'Because they'll find out what we've been up to here?' Ethan asked.

'No,' Nellis replied, 'because that's what got the Nazis started in World War Two. Hitler's obsession with the occult led them to conduct gruesome experiments on human beings that I can barely allow myself to read about. Let's just say that putting monkey heads on human bodies and conducting invasive surgery without anaesthetic only scratches the surface of what those insane lunatics got up to.'

Lopez shifted uncomfortably in her seat. 'You think that the Soviets are looking to catch up some ground they lost after Glasnost, right?'

Nellis nodded, impressed at Lopez's insight. 'Russia lost pretty much everything after Glasnost as its economy collapsed and its military crumbled, the old Soviet Union fragmenting as the states broke away in favor of independence. The old guard's growing influence in Moscow seeks an empire back in power, and for that to happen quickly enough they somehow have to bridge the gap of the last thirty or so years.'

'So they turn to paranormal means,' Ethan figured. 'Trouble is, apart from a pandemic or an open war which they would probably lose, there's only the nuclear option left and we all know that ends with no winners. Even their current president wouldn't be so insane as to hit the big red button and give us all a thousand–degree heat wave, right?'

'You'd hope not,' Nellis replied. 'However, he might be able to get the edge if he knew what we were about to do next.'

Lopez frowned. 'How would he know that? Since we ended Joaquin Abell's campaign in Florida all those years ago nobody can see into the future.'

'That, I'm afraid, is where the Russians would tell you you're wrong.'

***

V

'Say what now?'

Nicola Lopez was watching the General with a keen interest as Nellis gestured to the files before him.

'As you both no doubt already know, one of Russia's most recent forays beyond its borders includes a presence in Syria in support of government troops loyal to Syria's president. The Russians claim that they're fighting terrorism alongside the Syrian Army, when in fact most people know damned well that they're propping up the Syrian government, who are staunch Russian allies and opponents of western interests in the region.'

'The Syrian president is a psychopathic terrorist,' Ethan said. 'How Russia thinks that it can support such a dictator who is accused of war crimes is beyond me.'

'It's beyond any of us,' Lopez agreed, 'but what does Syria have to do with us?'

'The country is irrelevant to ARIES,' Nellis said, 'but what is being done inside that country is of great interest. Put simply, the Russians appear to have been conducting clandestine experiments within Syria at the time the civil war started, and it was only when those experiments were threatened with exposure by the advancing *Free Syria* army that they intervened and turned the course of the war.'

'What kind of experiments?' Lopez asked in an ominous tone.

'The kind you or I wouldn't want to be involved in. Hellerman will brief you in detail, but what we have on the chatter picked up by the NSA appears to concern something called Deep Trans Cranial Stimulation.'

'I've heard of that,' Ethan said, 'electrodes placed around the skull to create electrical discharges used to improve memory, heal certain neurological disorders, that kind of thing.'

'In a medical setting, yes,' Nellis agreed, 'but the chatter we've picked up from the Russians seems to suggest that they've been having some success in using this form of stimulation to provoke seizures in patients, during which those patients experience visions of the future.'

'Seizures?' Lopez echoed. 'You mean Ivan's taken to making people ill in order to get ahead of the United States?'

'We've done similar things,' Nellis reminded her. 'One of your own investigations unveiled the case of the CIA's Project Stargate.'

'Those were remote viewing projects,' Lopez said, 'with willing participants who were mostly military themselves. They weren't wiring people's heads to mains power and cranking the switch.'

'How much success are we talking about here?' Ethan asked, interested despite himself.

'The Russians seem very excited about the prospects,' Nellis replied. 'We have several reports that the Kremlin has doubled the funding and that they are obtaining what they call "viable information" on United States assets and operations in foreign soil. The last transmission suggests they're attaching a high ranking officer to the unit for field operations.'

'Which means, presumably, that they know what we're going to do next?' Lopez speculated.

'It sounds like something from a bad movie,' Ethan said. 'We've already investigated one individual who was able to use technology to get a glimpse of the future, but this sounds like a wild goose chase. Project Stargate was shut down by the CIA because they couldn't get any reliable intelligence from the people involved.'

'Indeed it was,' Nellis agreed, 'but the devil's in the details. You should note that at no time did the CIA suggest that remote viewing did not work. Their issue was that the remote viewers were genuinely seeing things but were unable to articulate with a sufficient degree of accuracy precisely what they were seeing. On at least one occasion during Stargate a remote viewer correctly identified the construction of massive pipes and underground structures which were presumed by the operators of the project to be some kind of new military installation, as that was what the viewers had been instructed to "visit". After much research and money were plowed into investigating this new military site, it was eventually identified as an entirely innocent power station. The viewer had correctly seen a place thousands of miles away but a lack of knowledge of what they were actually observing resulted in that particular sighting being deemed a failure.'

'Okay,' Lopez conceded, 'but why Syria? Surely the Russians could have chosen a location on home soil, somewhere less turbulent and dangerous?'

Nellis's expression turned grim.

'As it turns out a place like Syria is precisely what the Russians needed. Hellerman will explain everything, but right after he's done I want you both to travel to Utah.'

'What's out there?'

'A new case if you want it, that ties in with Russia's brave new world of paranormal investigations.'

'We're busy with bail–runners right now,' Lopez said, ever eager to remind Nellis that they were visiting the DIA at their leisure. 'Why would we want to keep dropping everything we're doing to run errands for the DIA?'

Nellis closed the files before him and took a deep breath before he spoke.

'The Secretary of Defense asked me precisely the same question yesterday morning.'

Ethan raised an eyebrow. 'SecDef knows about us?'

'As does most of the administration,' Nellis confirmed. 'Your work has become highly respected as part of the ARIES team. However, there have been many people asking why we should keep sending you, civilians, on such sensitive expeditions, questions that have arisen many times over the years.'

'So what did you tell him?' Lopez asked. 'And what difference should it make to us?'

Nellis smiled briefly.

'I told him nothing but the truth, that you represent as a team the finest investigative agents that I have here at the DIA. I told him that I wouldn't send anybody else after this, because they either wouldn't have the skill set or they would say the same things as all the other agencies do when confronted with cases like yours; it's a fool's game, superstition, hearsay and so on.'

Ethan smiled. 'And then you show them MJ–12.'

Nellis nodded. 'They shut up real fast when I tell them that it was the two of you, and Jarvis, who exposed and destroyed MJ–12's network. So the deal's changed and the administration knows that the both of you consider your work for this country done and want nothing more than to return to your lives. They respect that, and if you want to leave then they will understand and I will not bother either of you ever again.'

'Get to the main course,' Lopez growled, 'the starter's gettin' cold.'

'One per cent,' Nellis said.

Ethan sat still for a long moment and said nothing as Lopez leaned closer to the general. 'One per cent of *what?*'

Nellis looked her in the eye as he replied, his hands folded calmly before him on the desk.

'One per cent of whatever Jarvis and his companions took from MJ–12, which according to our most basic estimates amounted to some thirty billion dollars of assets.' Nellis leaned forward, his eyes still fixed on Lopez. 'I'm sure you can do the math.'

Lopez seemed frozen in time for a long beat, and then she leaned back in her seat and examined her fingertips. 'One per cent each.'

'Shut up Nicola,' Ethan said as he looked at the director. 'The administration can't just make offers like that. How can they offer Nicola and I millions of dollars when Hellerman and yourself presumably received no such offer? It makes no sense.'

Nellis smiled innocently. 'Who says they didn't make me an offer?'

Lopez blurted out a laugh. 'You sly old dog, what's your cut?'

'None of your business,' Nellis replied, 'but let's just say I'm not looking at retiring to a condo in Florida but a small island instead. The point is that the administration wants all of this to go away and it's a rather convenient coincidence that very few people know about what ARIES has been doing these few years past. Offering a small portion of MJ–12's ill–gotten gains as a sweetener to finish the game and not talk about it to anybody, ever, seemed like a smart move on the part of the White House and I signed up right away. What you do is up to you but it's a one time offer.'

'What's the catch?' Ethan asked, ever cautious.

Nellis's smile slipped slightly.

'To get the money that Jarvis took with him, you have to get Jarvis also.'

'That doesn't sound so bad,' Lopez said demurely.

Ethan nodded, having already figured that the administration would want Jarvis's head on a plate. Thirty billion dollars was a hefty prize, and one per cent each of that was enough money that neither Ethan nor Lopez would ever have to work again.

'Jarvis is up to something,' Nellis went on. 'We need to know what and with whom. The only people who can get close to him are the two of you. You finish the game with the DIA, or you go back to the thankless and never–ending task of mopping up scum off the streets of Chicago.' He shrugged. 'Your call. What's it going to be?'

***

VI

Lopez led the way into the Defense Intelligence Agency's Advanced Research and Intelligence Engineering Section after a swift ride down in the elevator. Neither she nor Ethan had exchanged a word during the journey so far, both of them mulling over the offer that Nellis had made and wondering whether they were looking at a retirement with more money than either of them knew what to do with, or whether somebody in the administration was taking them for a ride.

Lopez sighed wistfully beside him.

'You know that one per cent of thirty billion dollars is...'

'I know what it is,' Ethan replied. 'I'm trying not to think about it.'

'I can't stop thinking about it,' Lopez replied. 'Man, it's our ride out of this. We can't just walk away.'

'That's 'cause you signed up on the spot!'

'I only signed my own name. What you do is up to you.'

Ethan shook his head. 'You know I wouldn't let you do this on your own.'

'Thanks, honey,' Lopez smiled sweetly. 'Look on the bright side: Jarvis hung us out to dry more than once. It's time for payback.'

'Jarvis also saved our assess more than once,' Ethan pointed out as the elevator doors opened. 'Are you really going to send him to a lifetime in a security max prison for one indiscretion?'

'That's called a woman's prerogative isn't it?' Lopez murmured as they walked into the ARIES Watch Room.

The DIA's secretive ARIES section was located below ground level, shielded from prying eyes both beyond and within the agency. ARIES' heart was a giant pool of computer stations arrayed before banks of large plasma screens showing news feeds from around the world with analysts scrutinizing all manner of classified documents, talking quietly into microphones as they worked. Essentially the hub of the DIA's intelligence gathering force, what came into the room rarely left except to be investigated by agents like Ethan and Nicola.

Lopez led Ethan to a small, private office with mirrored windows and closed the door behind them. As they entered the office they were greeted by a slim, bespectacled and bearded young man with an infectious enthusiasm radiating from his gaze.

'Guys, you're back!'

Joseph Hellerman had worked for the DIA for several years and was one of the chief technicians specializing in novel technologies. Ethan considered him something of a 'Q' character from a James Bond movie, but Hellerman's near–genius level intellect had saved them from certain death on numerous occasions.

Lopez embraced the young technician, having developed something of a soft spot for Hellerman over the years.

'We were never far away,' she replied as Hellerman shook Ethan's hand.

'What's all this we're hearing about Ivan poking around in the future?' Ethan asked.

Hellerman gestured to a nearby computer screen mounted on the wall of his office. 'Look at that picture and tell me what you see.'

Ethan and Lopez looked at the screen and saw the image of a young girl, crying and in pain as she ran toward the camera amid the smoldering ruins of a city, smoke billowing from recent explosions behind her.

'War zone,' Lopez replied with a sigh that suggested she had seen far too many such images over the years, 'child victim of a misdirected military strike of some kind.'

'Looks like Russia,' Ethan said, glancing at the Soviet style buildings in the background and barely visible billboards bearing Cyrillic text. 'Maybe Chechnya, or Ukraine?'

'Ukraine,' Hellerman confirmed. 'And this one?'

The image switched to one of a baby swaddled in blankets, also crying and apparently in pain, and on its arm was a crudely carved scar of a Nazi Swastika.

'Jeez,' Lopez murmured, 'enough already, what's your point?'

Hellerman leaned against his desk as he replied.

'Both images are of victims of Ukrainian aggression against Russian forces operating in the defense of their people,' he said, 'at least that's what Russia wants you to believe.'

'Propaganda?' Ethan asked.

'Precisely that,' Hellerman confirmed. 'The crying girl fleeing the destruction is in fact a Russian actress in a staged scene, and the baby was crying for food and doesn't have a swastika carved into its arm – that was added later by Russian computer artists. It's all a part of a war being fought to win the hearts and minds of the Russian people and propel its president into a position of global power that will rival in both method and results what Hitler achieved in the 1930s.'

Hellerman began flicking through images on a computer screen as he spoke, most of them looking like shots obtained by journalists working in war zones around the world.

'Fake images abound on Twitter and Facebook, or its Russian equivalent, Vkontakte. The crying child fleeing the bombs was posed, a direct copy of the real life image of a Vietnamese girl running naked after a napalm attack during the Vietnam War, her body badly burned. It is still believed that single real–life image was responsible for America losing the conflict, as it turned public opinion so strongly against the administration. In Russia, images like these are being posted daily in their hundreds on a pro–Kremlin site called Antimaidan, with allegations that Ukrainian maternity workers disfigured the baby's arm with the swastika to humiliate the mother, a woman from the Donbas region in east Ukraine and the widow of a pro–Russia fighter. In fact the crying baby image is a stock Internet photo that appeared years before on the US website Popsugar, notably without the swastika.'

'How do we know all of this?' Lopez asked.

'From a NATO Colonel in the Soviet army called Aivar Jaeski, an Estonian born career soldier who revealed all of this in an interview with the EUobserver in Riga, where he worked as deputy director of NATO Strategic Communications Center of Excellence, or Stratcom. The principal of the Russian program used to be called propaganda, but is now far more sophisticated and widespread and is referred to as "psy–ops", or psychological warfare.'

Hellerman shut off the images as he went on.

'Jaeski said that the Russian psy–op mission was a campaign to use very carefully selected messages for targeted audiences in Ukraine, inside Russia and in the West which would support the statement made by Vladimir Putin in 2005, that the "greatest geopolitical catastrophe" of the last century was the collapse of the Soviet Union.'

'Tell that to people who used to queue for hours for a loaf of bread,' Lopez replied.

'Russian state TV lies openly to its people,' Hellerman said, 'and uses actors to play various roles in its reports of Ukrainian "war crimes", with the same faces appearing as an activist, then as a widow, then the mother of a deceased soldier, a refugee, or an anti–Maidan participant. It's a wonder that such blatant theatre hasn't been noticed by the Russian people for what it truly is, but somehow it seems to work in generating sufficient outrage and support for Putin among ordinary Russians.'

'Russians don't have the same access to world news that we do,' Lopez replied. 'Just like North Korea or China, the government controls what the people see and doesn't provide or allow any independent coverage from a free press.'

'We get the return to glory message that Putin has been trying to mete out to the people in Russia,' Ethan said. 'What does this have to do with Nellis's briefing?'

Hellerman turned and picked up a bizarre contraption from the desk beside him.

'Know what this is?'

Ethan looked at the device, which resembled a cycling helmet smothered in wires and electrodes.

'Trans Cranial Stimulator?' he hazarded.

Hellerman's eyes widened. 'Well done. You've used one before?'

'It sharpens his brain, if not his wit,' Lopez said, 'and Nellis mentioned them.'

'Remarkable devices,' Hellerman said, 'I've tried it myself. They use mild electrical currents to stimulate specific areas of the human brain to promote creativity and memory function, suppress negativity and so on. There's quite an industry building up around these things already, largely unregulated as ever, and that's causing a few problems as people use the devices to extremes and find themselves suffering issues as a result.'

'What kind of issues?' Ethan asked.

'The seizure kind,' Hellerman said. 'A few notable incidents occurred during the early days of availability of these kinds of devices, and as a result the Russians appear to have taken advantage of that and instigated a program devoted to attempting to provoke "second sight" in subjects. Worse, they appear to be doing it whether the subjects want them to or not.'

Second sight was something that Ethan had heard about before, a supposed ability of some people to predict the future, often only seconds ahead. Although rejected by mainstream science as myth, there were quite a few instances in history of people demonstrating an ability to predict future events, although no incidences of them being able to do so at will.

'Second sight appears to be a transient phenomenon,' Hellerman explained, 'that emerges only briefly and then vanishes again. However, like many paranormal events, they seem to congregate around one particular sub-set of humanity.'

Lopez winced. 'Young girls.'

Hellerman nodded. 'More accurately young girls who are socially awkward, stressed, under pressure and so on. The Russians are fully aware of this and according to intelligence gleaned from the NSA, they've despatched teams into war zones to extract girls who fit the description of individuals who may be capable of second sight.'

Ethan felt a plunging sense of dismay over how low the Russian military had sunk.

'They target orphaned girls,' he said, predicting Hellerman's explanation himself in a somber moment of personal second sight. 'They're troubled, with nobody to protect them and living in a combat zone where if abducted there's nobody left to notice.' Ethan thought for a moment. 'The Russians are working in Syria.'

'Top marks. Syrian children in besieged cities are enduring permanent stress, sorrow and suffering,' Hellerman agreed. 'If you're looking for the kind of girls who can provoke poltergeist activity or perhaps second sight, you couldn't pick a better spot.'

'I take it that we're going to head out there at some point,' Lopez surmised.

'Right after Utah,' Hellerman confirmed. 'Whatever the Russians are trying to do it needs to stop. From what little we can gather they're using these Trans Cranial devices to their absolute limits, and that can't be doing their already psychologically damaged subjects any good what so ever. Your mission for now is simple. Get to Utah and interview a girl there who we think may have some connection with what the Russians have been doing in Syria. This isn't just an intelligence gathering mission: it's a humanitarian one, and any girls out there right now who are being used by the Russians in this way have nobody thinking about their welfare but for the two of you.'

'And Jarvis?' Lopez asked, evidently still thinking about the money.

Hellerman sighed.

'I hate what he did, but I don't think that he should be persecuted the way the administration is doing. They've virtually ordered Nellis to track Jarvis down and apprehend him, and they're offering us all vast sums of money to do it. Something doesn't add up to all of this and I don't like it.'

'Us either,' Ethan said before Lopez could reply. 'We'll stay in touch, and let's keep this little deal they're offering us between ourselves for now, 'kay? If it turns sour, we don't know how far the government will go to keep it secret and I don't think that Nellis will be able to protect us.'

***

VII

Rose Island, Nassau

Bahamas

The golden sands of the beach were warm beneath the Caribbean sun as Doug Jarvis strolled casually toward a sheltered cove and listened to the whispering of the rollers brushing against the nearby shore. There were no tourists this early in the morning, the sun only just up over the perfect horizon and painting the skies with golden hues as though from the brushes of the high cirrus clouds sweeping through the heavens above. As he walked, a single word revolved around in his head in a gentle lullaby.

Billionaire.

Jarvis had always wondered what it would be like to be wealthy beyond avarice, to have more money than one could realistically spend in a lifetime. Now, he knew. For the past six months he and a small band of very fortunate individuals had lived a life that they could barely have imagined before, and all of it funded from the coffers of men who had once believed themselves both infallible and untouchable, the cabal of Majestic Twelve. Now, thanks to the courage and cunning of both Jarvis and a biochemist billionaire by the name of Professor Rhys Garrett, whose father had been murdered by a member of MJ–12, the cabal was no more and the vast majority of its assets had been filtered and laundered through hundreds of companies across the world before being absorbed by Garrett's own immense trading empire and distributed to Jarvis and their companions.

Rhys Garrett had made his own fortune with a series of start–up companies developing advanced genetic profiling kits for hire to the pharmaceutical industry, and then selling the companies one after the other as new start–ups under the banner of his company. He had countless patents to his name, many of which had earned him tens of millions of dollars. Although he had once worked alongside departments of the United States military, his connections and skills in finance had allowed him to make Majestic Twelve's immense finances vanish without trace, a task made easier by the fact that the cabal's ill–gotten gains were already tough to locate and examine, held in countless off–shore accounts to which Jarvis and Garrett had gained access. As a token gesture, they had left three billion dollars in place so that the administration would still be able to provide evidence of a successful mission to eradicate corruption within the military industrial complex, satisfying the media and ensuring that Jarvis and his accomplices could vanish as if into thin air.

'Good morning.'

Several people were waiting for him in the cove ahead, faces that he knew well and trusted with his life, largely because in many cases he had saved theirs.

Rhys Garrett stood and shook Jarvis's hand, as did the other members of the team; Jarvis's granddaughter, the palaeontologist Lucy Morgan; Civil War survivor Lillian Cruz from New Mexico; Amber Ryan, the niece of inventor Stanley Meyer whose fusion cage would have brought down the world's oil industry were it not for him being murdered by Majestic Twelve, and Aaron Mitchell, a hulking African American who had once worked as an assassin for MJ–12 before betraying them and joining Jarvis in the mission to eradicate them from the face of the earth.

The six of them sat down together around a small table in the sheltered cove, and Jarvis happily allowed Garrett to speak first.

'Now that we're all here for our monthly meeting, I'll update you on what's happened since we last spoke. Obviously, our ploy of remaining incognito as much as possible has paid handsome dividends. As of this moment the Defense Intelligence Agency has no idea where we are, what we're doing or where we've been. Although it is possible that they have used technology to watch us, perhaps identified that we're working together, it is unlikely that they have any real leads on our current whereabouts. I represent the only true link to what we've achieved, and there have been no enquiries into my business from any legal or law enforcement agencies in the last six months. It is highly unlikely that any agency will now be able to unravel the money trails that I've created and even if they did it would take several years to follow those trails to any of you.'

Jarvis leaned back in his chair, satisfied with Garrett's work, but his granddaughter appeared less convinced.

'I can't believe that we're as safe as you seem to think that we are,' Lucy said. 'It's been six months and we haven't yet done a thing with all of the money you said we took from Majestic Twelve. I thought that we were here to start saving lives, not sit on gigantic bank accounts and crow about how clever we are.'

Jarvis smiled, admiring Lucy's unwavering sense of philanthropy.

'We can't just go out there and start throwing money at charities,' he explained, 'just as none of you can start suddenly buying mansions. The DIA will make connections instantly, so we have to be careful and especially so when it comes to you Lucy, or your mother Rachel. They know that you could lead them to me and will be watching constantly, because I'm the only person they think ran with the money.'

'I agree,' Garrett said, 'Lillian and Aaron have lived in the shadows for years and are used to maintaining a low profile, but you and Amber both need to continue with your normal lives to avoid raising suspicions.'

'I get that,' Amber replied, 'but we still haven't even begun to work on my uncle's fusion cage. Just that one device could crash the oil and energy sectors overnight, bring down the fat cats at the top and end their seven figure salaries and bonuses.'

Again, Jarvis had the answer for Amber's impatience for her late uncle's free-energy device to reach the common market.

'And lose the jobs of thousands of ordinary workers,' he pointed out to her. 'You really think that those fat cats will let their jobs go before those of the people working for them? Their companies will contract with massive job losses before the fat cats you mention finally surrender to the inevitable, and even then they'll seek bankruptcy protection from the federal government. Before you know it, they'll walk off with seven figure severance deals and the thousands of ordinary people employed by the companies will get nothing. This has to be handled carefully, planned to the last detail to avoid a global economic crash and unnecessary suffering for ordinary people.'

Amber bit her lip as Garrett continued.

'We have to assume that the DIA will continue its mission to track down the remaining finances we took from Majestic Twelve to fund our new mission, and in doing so they will come after us. Our plan to avoid arrest is simple: we make ourselves indispensable to the government.'

'We're going to do what now?' Amber asked.

'We're going to take back the knowledge that they have spent so long covering up,' Jarvis replied for Garrett. 'I spent most of my post–military career working for the government, and I can tell you that the DIA alone has concealed some of the most incredible secrets you can imagine. These are things that could change humanity, that could render the wars of today a thing of the past and yet they're concealed from public view just so that the United States can gain a secret advantage over other nations. That, in a nutshell, is our mission.'

Amber Ryan peered at Jarvis. 'You're going to be a big whistle–blower then?'

'With a difference,' Garrett interjected. 'When we blow the whistle, we also let the cat out of the bag for everybody to see. We're not just going to contact world media and start spilling the beans on the fusion cage or alien autopsies. Our plan is to actually distribute to the people the physical evidence that supports what we're saying.'

Lillian Cruz got it instantly.

'By which means you gain the public trust sufficiently to come out of the shadows once more.'

'Ideally, yes,' Jarvis agreed, 'although it may not happen that way. Vested interests ensure that there will be more than a few people willing to kill to prevent us from achieving what we're hoping to. Corruption and greed are what brought the human race to where it is today, and some are more than happy for the status quo to remain.'

'So what's our first move?' Lucy Morgan asked. 'As I understand it we have around thirty billion dollars to our name but we don't have any access to it and I'm still working in my laboratory five days a week. How are we supposed to achieve anything when some of us are still holding down day jobs?'

Garrett smiled as he replied.

'We have spent much of the past six months figuring that out,' he said. 'You will each have a responsibility, a role within our organization. Lucy, you will be required to apply your scientific knowledge and discipline into the study of artefacts as and when they are found. Amber, you'll be in the field and travelling at will as you have the least level of surveillance of any of us. Your inheritance after your Uncle's death has secured your future, so the government will figure you're unlikely to be involved in a conspiracy such as this. I'll act as your liaison as I too am not under any suspicion from the DIA, who believe that any involvement I had with Majestic Twelve is now over, given their collapse.'

'Why aren't they interested in you?' Lillian asked him. 'You were instrumental in bringing the cabal down.'

'A cabal with whom I was conducting normal business,' Garrett explained. 'Before Jarvis and I cornered the cabal on my island in South America, I bought stocks and shares in their companies as proof of honest investments made before they visited me in Dubai and America. I lost a lot of money when the cabal collapsed, or so the government believes – why would I be involved in their collapse if I stood to lose millions of dollars?'

Lillian looked at Jarvis. 'So you took the fall. They think you've got all the money.'

'It was the only way to divert suspicion,' Jarvis explained, 'and I needed Garrett's help to pull it all off. I couldn't have done any of it without his financial support.'

Lucy Morgan rubbed her temples with one hand. 'So what now?'

Garrett did not reply, but instead looked at Aaron Mitchell. The towering assassin stood and spoke in a soft, melodious voice.

'My connections, formed from my employment with Majestic Twelve, remain intact and I continue to receive a flow of information from former MJ–12 plants within the intelligence community. Many of them were variously bribed or blackmailed into providing information to the cabal, and I have cultivated their loyalty in return for guarantees that neither they nor their families are in danger of being liquidated if they fail to deliver accurate information. It is a compromise that is serving us well.'

'We have a mission,' Jarvis confirmed, 'which you'll be pleased to know is humanitarian in nature.'

Mitchell leaned on the table as he spoke. 'Our target is a human trafficking ring being run by the Russians in Syria.'

'Modern slavery,' Amber Ryan spat in distaste. 'I can think of worse places to start.'

Jarvis smiled. 'It's not the slaves we're looking for,' he said. 'It's the ones they keep behind we're interested in.'

'What the hell good will that do?' Lucy asked.

'The Russians have taken a keen interest in Syria,' Garrett explained, 'not because they want to save the people of the country from civil war but for their own interests, a predictable reason. Most people think that Russia wants Syria's regime to survive the conflict simply because they're pro–Russian, but in fact the true reason is natural gas.'

Jarvis nodded as he took over.

'Oil is falling out of favor in the west due to decreasing demand and the rise in renewables,' he explained, 'but gas is the new wonder fossil fuel and Russia has a lot of it. It wants to protect that reserve and trans Syria pipelines are under threat if the regime is toppled during the civil war. Hence, Russia steps in and bombs anyone and anything that stands in the way of their profits, even if it does happen to be in a civilian area.'

'Once we have enough information I will travel to Syria,' Mitchell said, 'and begin the task of unraveling the Russian influence on the ground while also exposing the traffickers to arrest by international law enforcement.'

'And the human victims they leave behind?' Lillian asked. 'What's that all about?'

'We're not sure yet,' Jarvis replied. 'That's why I'm travelling to DC as soon as I can to find out why the DIA are so interested in what's happening down there. My hope is that Ethan Warner and Nicola Lopez will be despatched to investigate, so that Aaron can locate them and glean more information.'

Lucy Morgan raised an eyebrow at Mitchell. 'Good luck with that. Have you ever seen those two in action?'

'At close range,' Mitchell confirmed, 'but they know me well enough to let me speak. My concern is Lopez, who has always been rebellious.'

'And what about me?' Lillian asked. 'How do I fit into all of this?'

Jarvis reached out and patted the back of her hand.

'You, my dear, will be our eyes and ears on the ground. You're unknown to the government, to anybody at the DIA except Ethan and Nicola. You have no Social Security details, no history, no bank accounts, nothing. You've been a ghost for a hundred eighty years and so you're the only person we can be sure is able to travel freely around the globe. But first, we need to get to the bottom of what MJ-12 were doing.'

Lillian leaned forward on the table. 'How?'

Jarvis smiled, keenly enthused by the degree of control he now had to investigate things that had been ignored by the DIA.

'We're going to get to the bottom of what inspired the creation of Majestic Twelve,' he promised her. 'We have acres of their paperwork in our possession, and I want to know what got them started, when, why and how. Then, we're going after it.'

***

THE GENESIS CYPHER   Dean Crawford

VIII

Glavnoye razvedyvatel'noye upravleniye

Grizodubovoy str. 3,

Moscow

Colonel Anatoly Mishkin walked into the headquarters of the Main Intelligence Directorate in Moscow, keeping his chin high and his stride determined in the hopes that nobody would notice his anxiety. The GRU building was an angular, blocky construction that both departed from the old Soviet style of architecture while somehow retaining its bleak nature. Built from gray steel panels and surrounded by concrete walls topped with vicious barbed wire that glinted in the weak morning sunlight peering through tumbling blankets of cloud, few ordinary Russians ever entered, or wanted to enter, this building. Even the General Secretary of the Communist Party of the Soviet Union needed to go through a security screening to enter GRU headquarters.

The foyer of the building had a floor cast in marble which was emblazoned with a large image of a bat, the emblem of the Spetsnaz Special Forces, the agency's logo mounted on the opposite wall over an image of the earth as though Russia had already laid claim to it. The GRU's official full name was the Main Intelligence Agency of the General Staff of the Armed Forces of the Russian Federation, and it was Russia's largest foreign intelligence agency, deploying six times as many agents in foreign countries as the SVR, the successor of the KGB's foreign operations directorate. Tens of thousands of Spetsnaz troops were also under its command, the agency given the role of handling all military intelligence from sources outside the Soviet Union.

Colonel Mishkin was new to the agency, having previously served within Spetsnaz as both an infantry soldier and then as a troop commander. His time in Chechnya had hardened his heart and his soul to almost anything a theatre of war could throw at him, but now he had realized that this new assignment had put him far out of his depth. Mishkin was no data gatherer. He was a soldier, and this new form of warfare irked him immensely. Cryptography, espionage, surveillance; all of it felt as though it were the work of someone of less stature than a decorated war veteran. He knew that the GRU operated residencies all over the world, along with a dedicated Signals Intelligence station in Lourdes, Cuba and throughout the former Soviet–bloc countries, and that it served an important role in his country's defensive structure, but that didn't make him feel any better about being stuck in an office instead of commanding men in the field.

Mishkin took an elevator up to the fourth floor and followed the signs until he reached the office of the agency's director, General Sergei Olatov. Mishkin checked his watch: ten in the morning in *three, two, one…* He took a breath before he knocked on the door and after a muffled "enter" he walked in, literally arriving on time.

He closed the door behind him and walked to where General Olatov sat behind a large desk which was undecorated but for a laptop computer and a framed photograph of the general's wife and two children. Craggy, white–haired and with his uniform hanging off his wiry frame, the general looked as though he should have retired a decade previously. Mishkin realized he probably would have if not for the president's reliance on an "old guard" to prop up his dreams of a return to former Soviet glory.

'Sit down, colonel.'

No welcome, no preamble, just as Mishkin preferred. He sat down and waited in silence to be ordered to speak.

'You have news of our operations in Aleppo?'

Mishkin replied in crisp, no–nonsense tones, using as few words as possible.

'The Syrian government is making strides against the rebel factions besieging the city, and it is likely that with our continued airstrikes we will break the siege and retake the city within days.'

'How much does the international community know?'

Mishkin knew what the general was referring to. The use of chlorine gas in Saqareb and other weapons banned by the Geneva Convention in retaliation for Russian losses in the region were political hot–points that he knew the GRU could not afford to be brought to account for.

'Not enough for the people of the world to care enough,' he replied.

The general smiled, the phrase a popular one in the GRU. Although world media sought often to demonize Russia for her actions, they did not do nearly enough to elaborate on the corruption that blighted all western governments. In his time at the GRU, Mishkin had learned that the US Government had virtually created *Al–Qaeda* through CIA operations in Afghanistan during the Afghan–Russian war of the 1980s. Arming the aggressive Afghan *Mujahideen* to fight Russian troops, the natives had rebelled when the US withdrew support from them when the war ended, their future leader Osama bin–Laden taking over the financial leadership when he joined them and forming the terrorist group a few years later to unite the tribally fragmented Mujahideen. Likewise, Mishkin knew that US Presidents had close ties to major corporations that had funded *Al–Qaeda*, but when journalists got too close to the truth they mysteriously suffered from fatal "accidents" in homicides every bit as ruthless as any carried out by the GRU or even the KGB back in the Cold War.

'Maintaining an ally in the Syrian leadership is essential to bulwark against American expansion in the Middle East theatre,' the general said. 'As long as the government stands, our mission is a success. Now, what of the other mission?'

Mishkin felt his anxiety rise up again.

'It continues but is under pressure from rebel activity and interest from US Government agencies.'

'Which agencies?'

'DIA,' Mishkin replied. 'We have intercepted communications that suggest American agents intend to deploy in or near Syria with the intention of disrupting or exposing our experiments. The presence of American Special Forces teams in the area training rebel forces is already well known, although of course disputed by the White House.'

The general's cold gray eyes peered up at Mishkin. 'Names?'

Mishkin had memorized the names of their foes upon first reading of them and their history of operations within the DIA.

'Warner, Ethan, and Lopez, Nicola. Both are civilian contractors.'

The general snorted derisively. 'Civilians,' he uttered, as though it were a curse. 'They entrust their foreign missions to gumshoes and bail hunters.'

'You know these people?' Mishkin asked.

The general reached across to a folder that he opened, and Mishkin saw an image of a man he recognized instantly.

'This was Yuri Volkov,' the general said, 'a Russian billionaire who did more to expose the inner workings of the DIA before his death than almost any Russian before him. He was of course a traitor to the Motherland, more interested in his own fortune and power than that of our country.'

Mishkin felt a little of the old anger return at the general's words, his shoulders tensing and his fists clenching where they rested on his knees. Mishkin's parents, honest folk who had toiled the fields north of Saransk, had been the first to suffer when Gorbachev's Glasnost and Perestroika had struck at the heart of the former Soviet Union. The economic collapse of one of the most powerful countries on earth had sent shockwaves throughout the world, and the political turmoil that followed in Russia had seen a near famine in many remote regions of the country far from the assistance of the government. Mishkin's dear parents had both died within three years of the so–called "economic reforms" that had destroyed so many other countries around the world as capitalist consumerism spread its greedy wings. The great glory of the Soviet empire was now just a memory to all but a few loyal souls in the Kremlin, led by their iron–willed president.

'It was our own traitors who brought down the Motherland, for the enemy were too weak,' Mishkin said.

The general nodded, his expression somber. 'None the less, Volkov's work exposed much of the DIA's mission.'

'Which is?'

'Which is connected to our work in Syria,' the general replied. 'I take it that you have read the files concerning *Operation Orakul*?'

'I have,' Mishkin replied, squirming slightly in his seat, 'although I must confess that I do not understand its purpose.'

'That I sympathize with, colonel,' the general said, 'but it is essential that the operation be able to complete its objectives beyond prying eyes, and a theatre such as Syria provides us both with subjects and a location difficult for western media to penetrate. The reluctance of the west to openly engage militarily in Syria further plays into our hands.'

Mishkin decided to push his luck a little. 'May I ask: what is the objective of Operation Orakul?'

The general stared straight at Mishkin and for a moment he thought that he had gone too far, but instead the general spoke frankly.

'The GRU believes that a select number of people may possess an ability to see events deep in the human past, and perhaps a limited ability to predict the future.'

Mishkin stared at the general for a long moment as he considered his reply. He knew better than to scoff, for this was an operation that was clearly important enough for the general to have signed off on it, but even so…

'Have we had any confirmed results yet?'

Mishkin added the "yet" as a sign of willingness to go along with whatever the general had in mind, and it seemed to appease the old man.

'Yes, actionable intelligence that has allowed the Syrian army a small number of recent victories in their battle for Aleppo and the protection of our proposed trans Syrian gas lines. It is early days, but the project has sufficient value for us to support it in Homs.'

'Why Homs?'

'The city is uniquely placed to intercept Syrian refugees fleeing the conflict further north,' the general replied, and then appeared to have a clairvoyant experience himself as he answered Mishkin's next question. 'Refugees are necessary as we require the subjects chosen for the experiments to be, how can I say it, troubled?'

Mishkin nodded, not really understanding but willing to simply go along with the general for now.

'How may I be of service?'

The general smiled briefly, his lips forming what looked like a crack in concrete.

'You will travel to Homs and transport the most capable of the oracles out of the city. There is more to what they have seen than we could have hoped, and if their visions are to be believed, then a grand prize may await us.'

Mishkin waited for further information, and the general did not disappoint as he passed the Colonel a simple, hand drawn image. It was crafted with shaky lines, as though drawn by a tired child, but the image before Mishkin was unmistakeable: a box, almost square, with carrying rods at its base and winged cherubim on its top, facing each other and their wings touching.

'They have actually seen this?' Mishkin uttered.

'They have,' Olatov confirmed, 'more than once, and they fear their visions greatly. If we were able to obtain this artefact, colonel…'

Mishkin nodded, needing no elaboration. If the myths were in fact true, the legends actual historical record…, then it would not just be Russia who would be searching for such a prize.

'The American agents have a long history of interfering, successfully, with major operations. It says in the files that they may have been responsible for exposing and destroying Majestic Twelve?'

The general nodded.

'We have intelligence suggesting that the DIA was involved in that operation. Furthermore, we also understand from a number of Russian billionaires who had dealings with the cabal of Majestic Twelve that the billions of dollars recovered by the United States Government from the cabal after its collapse was only a fraction of its actual worth. We cannot be sure, but it would appear that some members of the DIA absconded with the bulk of the money and that the DIA is understandably keen to recover such vast sums.' The general leaned forward on his desk. 'I too would be keen to see that money recovered for the benefit of the Motherland, along with the artefact. Any officer who achieved such a goal for the GRU would be rewarded.'

For the first time since entering the room, Mishkin smiled. The old general truly was one of the old guard, and willing to bend a rule or two for his own gain rather than see a fortune go entirely to waste in the Kremlin's coffers.

'I take it that this meeting did not occur, general?'

'You have been despatched to Homs to oversee and complete Operation Orakul, Colonel,' the general smiled, 'nothing more.'

'Will I have support?'

'Everything that I can reasonably provide you with, without arousing any suspicions. You will be ably assisted by a former Spetsnaz operative by the name of Gregorie Petrov, who is awaiting you outside. I think you will find him a suitable choice.'

Colonel Mishkin stood, fresh and invigorated as he realized that he would not be sitting at a desk any longer.

'And the agents of the DIA, Warner and Lopez? They may be willing to fight for their own mission.'

'They are civilians,' the general replied, 'expendable to their government and an irritation to our own. If you find them, follow them until you have extracted all that you can about their mission. Then, kill them.'

Colonel Mishkin saluted the general vigorously and then whirled on one heel and marched from the office, barely able to conceal the smile on his features. He opened the door and walked out, closed it behind him, and then turned to find himself face to face with a broad barrel chest.

Gregorie Petrov stood to attention before Mishkin, all six feet five of him. Short–cropped blond hair, cold blue eyes, shoulders as wide as a harbor wall and an inscrutably emotionless expression on his face.

'Gregorie,' Mishkin said as he looked up at the towering man.

'I am at your disposal, Colonel,' Gregorie replied briskly, and then lowered his gaze to look directly into Mishkin's eyes. 'When do we begin the hunt?'

***

IX

Black Dragon Canyon, Utah

'This is it.'

Lopez pointed out of the windshield of the Lincoln as Ethan pulled in to the narrow entrance to a gorge that sliced through the towering rock faces either side of the road. He eased to a stop before a line of police tape as a sheriff approached the vehicle and leaned down beside the window, his rugged features shielded from the blistering sun by his hat.

'Warner and Lopez, Defense Intelligence Agency,' Ethan announced to the sheriff.

'And what brings you folks down here?' the sheriff asked, peering at them with an expression of disdain. 'You think we can't figure out our own investigation?'

'We're not here for your investigation,' Lopez replied curtly. 'We're here for ours and your superior officers were notified hours ago. You gonna lift that tape or am I gonna have your badge by sundown?'

The sheriff raised an eyebrow in alarm and backed away from the Lincoln, then waved to a companion. The tape obligingly lifted and Ethan eased his way through.

'Locals don't like us snooping around I guess,' Lopez said as they drove through the canyon toward the site of the cult compound that Nellis had briefed them on before they departed Washington DC.

'I don't care about that,' Ethan replied as he pulled over alongside a pair of Sheriff's Department cruisers parked outside the smoldering remains of a large ranch. 'I want to know what the hell we're doing out here. If our enemy is in Russia or at the very least Syria, why would Nellis send us all the way out here?'

'Beats me,' Lopez replied as she got out of the car in time to be approached by a young sheriff, handsome and with a clean jaw and gray eyes.

'Miss Lopez?' he asked, clearly already knowing the answer.

'Every bit of me,' Lopez replied with a bright smile that Ethan suspected was more than a little flirtatious. 'You must be Sergeant Robbie Dixon.'

Dixon shook their hands, Ethan judging the young trooper to be born and bred Utah, an all American boy who was somewhat out of his depth.

'What's the story?' Ethan asked.

'You haven't been briefed?'

'We have,' Lopez replied, 'but we want to hear it from your perspective, right from the beginning.'

Robbie nodded, took a breath and started talking. Ethan listened as the trooper explained the cult's history in the area, the abduction of two young girls, the connection to one of the cult members and the subsequent raid on the building.

'We came in through the front, with two teams in support at the rear and above on the mesas,' Robbie explained. 'Everything was going fine right up to the point when we got into the center of the building. There must have been an explosive device waiting to be tripped, or maybe one of the loonies in there was waiting to hit the button when we got close enough. Either way, the blast took out five men including our lieutenant.'

'How come you got clear?' Ethan asked.

'Dumb luck,' Robbie replied. 'I was at the rear when I entered one of the side rooms and cleared it. There was a female hostage and one other woman who made a play for me with a knife. I took her down, told the other woman to stay put, and was advancing down the corridor after the rest of my team when I noticed the pictures.'

'Pictures?' Lopez asked.

'Yeah,' Robbie replied. 'It's gonna be easier to show you than tell you. The fire didn't reach them so the images are mostly undamaged. Darn'est things I ever saw.'

Ethan and Lopez exchanged a glance as Robbie led them through more police cordons and into the remains of the building, and Ethan momentarily experienced the sensation that he was walking into the charred remains of hell itself. The air was thick with the stench of smoldering blackened timbers and ash, gray smoke rising in lazy coils from charred walls and collapsed roofing.

A few forensics teams were picking over the debris nearer the center of the building, much of which was also drenched in fire retardant foam, and Ethan could see where markers had been placed denoting the fallen officers whose lives had been claimed by the apocalyptic cult.

As he walked he saw a curved piece of metal half–buried in the ash to his right. Ethan moved across to it and pulled on a pair of latex gloves before he crouched down and pulled the metal from the ash.

The curved band was scorched black, but he could see melted wires dangling from it and other cables snaking away through the debris. Lopez moved to his side and looked at the device.

'Trans Cranial Stimulator,' she said as she identified it, 'just like Hellerman showed us. What the hell were they doing here?'

'Here,' Robbie said, and gestured to a nearby wall.

Ethan moved across to him and could see that a small lamp had been placed in the corridor that now illuminated the wall before them, and for a moment he felt as though he could have been standing in the pyramids or the Sphinx of ancient Egypt.

The wall was painted the color of old sandstone, and before them were emblazoned upon the wall endless lines of Egyptian hieroglyphs. Ethan was no historian but he recognized easily the stylized imagery, the shapes denoting letters and numbers, the images of Atum and other famed gods of Egyptian lore. What captured his attention were the ranks of Egyptians bowing or kneeling before the gods, arms raised toward them, and the brilliant depictions of the sun blazing above their heads.

'What the hell is this doing here?' Lopez asked Robbie. 'Was this cult based on some kind of Egyptian worship?'

'No,' Robbie replied, 'that's why this caught my attention. The cult was apocalyptic in nature and based on the Old Testament, the lunatic fringe fire–and–brimstone Christianity. There is nothing in any of our records suggesting any connection to ancient Egypt. I would have put it down to just the madness of the members, or maybe drugs or something, but what happened next really freaked me out.'

'What did happen next?' Lopez asked.

'I got to the center of the building after the blast, and although my team were already down and in the flames and I couldn't reach them I could hear somebody calling for help. I made my way over and found a girl in a cage in a revetment in the wall. She'd escaped the blast, but would have burned if I'd left her there. The thing was, she was calling me by name.'

'She knew you?' Ethan asked.

'Never saw her before in my life,' Robbie replied. 'I get her out of the cage and we make a dash for the rear entrance. The thing is, all the way she's whispering warnings to me: turn left, turn right, get down. Every time I did what she said and it saved my life.'

'How so?' Lopez asked.

'Because right after she warned me, something happened that would have killed us both,' Robbie explained.

'Wait one,' Ethan said. 'Right after she said something?'

'Yeah,' Robbie confirmed. 'It was like she knew what was going to happen before it actually happened. She did it several times, even saw my support team coming through the back door with guns blazing before it happened. If I hadn't followed her directions, we'd both have been perforated with buckshot and died on the spot.'

'She could have seen them coming maybe,' Lopez surmised, 'perhaps had a view in her cage that gave her an edge?'

'Her cage was against a solid wall,' Robbie replied, 'and besides, that wouldn't have made any difference anyway.'

'How come?' Ethan asked.

'Because when we got outside I got my first good look at her,' Robbie replied, and for the first time Ethan noticed goose bumps on the trooper's forearms despite the heat. 'Her eyes were gone, totally useless. The medical teams confirmed it a few hours later – that girl was totally blind and had been since birth.'

Lopez looked at Ethan. 'Second sight? Just like Hellerman said.'

Ethan shrugged, not willing to commit himself yet.

'Let's just keep an open mind about this for a moment,' Ethan said as he crouched down before the wall and looked more closely at the hieroglyphics. 'Has anybody come down here to decipher this?'

Robbie shook his head. 'No, we figured it was just insane ramblings or something. A lot of the folk down this way are committed Christians, so anything like this is pretty much the work of the devil to them: they'll probably destroy it.'

'Not now they won't,' Lopez snapped. 'This is evidence in an ongoing investigation. Anybody tampers with it, they'll be facing federal charges.'

'Why?' Robbie asked. 'They're just drawings.'

The reply came from Ethan. 'No, they're not.'

He turned and beckoned Lopez to kneel down beside him, and in the shadowy confines of the corridor Ethan pointed to one particular corner of the artwork.

'What do you make of that?'

He watched Lopez as she peered down at the hieroglyphics and then suddenly she saw what Ethan was pointing at and her eyes flew wide. 'No way.'

Amid the rows of servants queuing up to serve the gods was a single figure, smaller than the others, with long slender arms and short legs, a bulbous head and slanted almond eyes far too large for its skull to be human.

'It's got to be fake,' Lopez said finally. 'Maybe these cultists were on drugs, worshipping some kind of alien sky god and killed themselves. It's happened before, right? Wasn't there that cult that committed mass suicide when a comet went past the earth a while back?'

'The Heaven's Gate cult,' Robbie confirmed from nearby, 'thirty–nine of them committed suicide when the comet Hale–Bopp passed earth in 1997. They believed that it was an alien vessel that would take them to their salvation.'

Ethan pulled his cell phone from his pocket and dialed a number. Hellerman answered on the first ring.

'What's up?'

'I'm sending you an image,' Ethan replied as he set the cell to speaker and took a photograph of the images on the wall before them. 'Can you identify any of this?'

Ethan sent the image, and a few moments later they heard Hellerman's intake of breath on the cell.

'Whoa,' he muttered. 'Where did you find this?'

'It's right here in Utah,' Ethan confirmed. 'We figure it's just mad scrawlings but thought you might have some insight on how to translate it?'

'They're not mad scrawlings, Ethan.'

'Well what are they then?'

Ethan, Lopez and Robbie listened intently as Hellerman replied.

'You're looking at an incredibly precise copy of hieroglyphics found in the tomb of an Egyptian sage and philosopher known as Ptah–Hotep, which is located in Saqqara, Egypt. Ptah–Hotep served during the reign of Izezi, the eighth king of the 5th Dynasty who ruled from 2388 BCE until 2356 BCE.'

'You're saying that this thing is several thousand years old?' Lopez gasped.

'The original is,' Hellerman confirmed, 'and that strange humanoid in the corner is present on the original too.'

'You're kidding,' Ethan uttered.

'I'm not,' Hellerman confirmed. 'Those murals appear in no official Egyptian guidebooks and are never referenced anywhere in accepted archeological papers, making them extremely hard to find. Even on the Internet only a handful of images exist.'

Lopez leaned back on her haunches. 'I guess if the word got out they'd have a real problem explaining this away.'

'It's been conveniently ignored for years,' Hellerman confirmed. 'I figure the Egyptian government cannot just erase such valuable evidence so they hope that tourists just walk on by and don't notice anything out of place.'

Ethan thought for a moment before he replied. 'We've got one more thing to check out here in Utah and then we'll come back to DC. Can you do some digging into this, find out if there's any connection between this cult and these hieroglyphs?'

'You got it.'

Ethan stood up and turned to Robbie Dixon.

'The girl you rescued, where is she? We need to talk to her and any other survivors of this cult.'

***

THE GENESIS CYPHER　　　　　　　　　　　　　　Dean Crawford

X

Defense Intelligence Agency,

Joint Base Anacostia–Bolling,

Washington DC

General Nellis was given no warning of the delegation.

It had been a very long time since he had last had to deal with an unannounced visit from high ranking government officials, especially those who had turned up only minutes before and demanded an immediate meeting, but these were extraordinary times and Nellis had half–expected Homeland Security to turn up at some point.

'Clear all monitors and shield the main screens in the ARIES Watch Room,' he said to Joseph Hellerman, who had rushed to the general's office as soon as he had been called.

'You think they'll try to access the ARIES complex?' Hellerman asked, somewhat stunned.

'I don't know how much authority they carry,' Nellis replied. 'Get down there and make sure everything is shut down. They don't get in unless the President himself says that they can.'

Hellerman hurried away as Nellis closed his notes and his computer screen and sat in contemplative silence as he considered his position. The closure of the campaign against Majestic Twelve had been an earth–shattering event and one that had only narrowly been contained by the administration. Many high ranking senators and congressmen had been intimately involved with the cabal, whether they knew it or not, so far had MJ–12's tentacles reached into the political system. The president had effectively been forced into a delicate position by what should have been heralded as a great victory against the forces of corruption and greed, because widely publicizing the success of the operation would also have exposed the sheer degree to which politicians were controlled by businesses.

Most all people knew that democracy in the modern sense was merely a veil, a sheen of respectability placed upon governments that provided the population with the impression that their vote counted. In truth, it didn't matter who sat inside the White House at any one time: the campaigns of all presidential hopefuls were funded by big business, and big business didn't spend millions placing a president in power for the good of the population: they did it to ensure that political decisions reflected their own desires. Corporate funding was the disease that placed profits above people, election after election, and as a result the deeper details of the exposure of Majestic Twelve, including its name, had been kept far from the media and public eye.

The White House had cleverly steered the media away from these inconvenient truths by placing huge spin on how much tax payer's money had been recovered from the illegal activities of powerful businessmen as a result of valiant government missions: in excess of an astonishing three billion dollars.

What made Nellis more uncomfortable was that in addition to those three billion dollars, some thirty billion remained unaccounted for and the chief architect of Majestic Twelve's demise, Doug Jarvis, had unceremoniously disappeared within hours of the exposure coming to light. Homeland would only give Nellis so much time before they took over the search for a man who had once been a dedicated patriot and was now probably the most wanted individual on earth.

Nellis heard a knock at his door and before he could respond the door opened and four men in dark gray suits walked into the general's office and closed the door behind them.

'General Nellis,' the first of them announced, 'I'm sure you're familiar with us all?'

Nellis knew all four men by sight, high ranking former military figures from the Army, Air Force, Navy and Marines. All of them were in their late fifties to early sixties, ram–rod straight backs and hard jaw lines forged from decades either on the front line or on the parade grounds of military bases across the country.

Nellis shook hands with Dillinger, Marston, Green and Foxx before they sat down, the ice broken a little by the simple gesture. Whatever happened next, it was business and not personal, but that didn't prevent Nellis from feeling anxious as Dillinger spoke.

'You're probably aware of why we're here.'

'MJ–12,' Nellis replied without hesitation.

'No,' Dillinger said. 'MJ–12 are finally history, and frankly I can say good riddance. The cabal had become twisted and corrupt and deserved the ending it received in South America, but we're not here to deal with that. We're here to deal with thirty billion dollars.'

Nellis nodded, actually relieved at Dillinger's candor.

'So are we,' he replied. 'My team have been on the case since before the administration made its announcements concerning the funds recovered from MJ–12.'

'And yet you have achieved nothing,' Green said sharply.

'We were not prepared for the scale of the deception, nor the professionalism with which the funds were distributed and concealed from us.'

'You weren't prepared for a defection from within your own department either,' Foxx added as he tossed a photograph of Doug Jarvis onto the desk between them. 'You weren't prepared at all, general.'

'The administration needs to place a cap on this and start picking apart what happened,' Dillinger went on before Nellis could reply. 'If the media were somehow to figure all of this out it would blow the White House wide open and leave us all facing accusations of incompetence, not to mention the public outcry of yet more political corruption.'

Nellis spoke quietly.

'The corruption of politicians is not the fault of this agency.'

'Nor is it within the remit of Homeland Security's various agencies' investigative reach, unless the security of this country's borders could be compromised by said corruption,' Green countered. 'The apparent disappearance of Douglas Jarvis would suggest that, considering his security clearances and knowledge of our intelligence services, your security has been very much compromised.'

'And we're working on it,' Nellis assured Green. 'Jarvis is a patriot and unlikely to be willing to part with any state secrets that he may have…'

'Who said anything about a willingness to part with state secrets?' Dillinger interrupted him. 'Do you think that the Chinese or the Russians will wait for someone like Jarvis to decide to spill the beans on ARIES or any other DIA projects? They'll wire him to the mains and crank the handle until he's screaming state secrets to anybody who'll listen!'

Nellis sighed.

'There's no place for conjecture until we know where he is and why he's gone.'

'You don't think thirty billion dollars is anything to do with why he jumped ship and betrayed his country?' Foxx uttered.

'We don't know that he's betrayed anybody yet,' Nellis snapped back.

'Are you kidding?' Dillinger asked.

'Jarvis, as I've come to know him, has what you might call an unusual way of working,' Nellis replied. 'Despite all that's happened, I don't for a moment believe that he's betrayed his country or that he's suddenly become slack enough to allow himself to be captured and interrogated by rogue nations.'

'That's a level of faith that should never be placed in any single agent or operative,' Dillinger pointed out. 'We all know that.'

'Jarvis is unlikely to be working alone,' Nellis replied. 'He would have made plans for his disappearance months before doing so, and we know that in the weeks before he vanished he was working with a man named Aaron Mitchell.'

'Former Vietnam veteran,' Foxx confirmed, 'and until recently a paid assassin for Majestic Twelve. Why would Jarvis be working with somebody like that, the enemy of our country?'

'Mitchell was also a patriot, once,' Nellis reminded them. 'He worked for MJ–12 until he realized the level of corruption he was being paid to support. He betrayed MJ–12 and then actively went after them, presumably with Jarvis working alongside him.'

Foxx frowned.

'What are you getting at here? Jarvis working with an enemy of the state isn't exactly what I'd call a defense.'

'Depends on what you're defending,' Nellis smiled bleakly. 'If I know Jarvis like I think I do, he's seen enough internal corruption that he decided to take matters into his own hands.'

Dillinger frowned. 'You think he's gone rogue and set up his own little cabal?'

Nellis shrugged.

'Doug told me once that he was tired of defending his country only to see that country defrauded by the people who are paid to govern it. He's an old man now, with nothing to lose if he's caught. My guess is that he's on a warpath of his own to expose whatever other corruption he can find in our political system, and now he's got the funds to do it.'

Dillinger glanced at his companions briefly before he spoke.

'I think that you and I both know that such leaks as we've seen in the recent past are precisely the kind of media attention we're trying to avoid.'

'Why?' Nellis demanded. 'Don't you want to ensure that congress and the senate are filled with representatives devoid of criminal intent? Don't you want to see the people have respect for their leaders again?'

'Not at the expense of civil unrest or even a collapse of government,' Dillinger replied. 'We've already seen the mess that Wikileaks has made of public perception of government. Throwing another few senators to the dogs isn't going to help our mission.'

'And what is your mission, exactly?' Nellis asked.

'To ensure that our government is presented to the people in the way that it should be, when compared to the governments of other countries.'

'Like North Korea or China,' Nellis murmured wryly. 'That doesn't inspire confidence in either our government or Homeland Security.'

Foxx peered at Nellis suspiciously. 'You sound like you're on Jarvis's side.'

'I'm on the side of the American people,' Nellis snapped. 'How about you?'

'We're representing officials elected by those people,' Dillinger said smoothly. 'We need Jarvis found regardless of his intentions and we need the thirty billion dollars he somehow managed to pilfer from Majestic Twelve returned to the government. The Defense Intelligence Agency cannot be used by people like Jarvis for criminal acts, and right now we don't believe enough is being done to locate him.'

'We have other duties,' Nellis said defensively.

'The ARIES program,' Foxx said. 'This isn't the first time we've been here, general. This department of yours was subject to discontinuation orders from the CIA and the FBI in recent years under charges of lack of security. Homeland now believes that your program is again in danger of spilling national secrets all over the headlines and we cannot guarantee that Jarvis will not go the same way as Edward Snowden if he has come to believe that all government officials are somehow corrupt.'

'Jarvis is no fool, he wouldn't sell secrets to Wikileaks,' Nellis shot back. 'We're not talking about some low–level programmer here; we're talking about a senior operative with decades of experience.'

'Which is why it becomes all the more important that he is found and brought to justice,' Foxx insisted. 'If he cannot be found, then the only viable alternative is to shut down the ARIES programme.'

Nellis stared at Foxx in disbelief. 'You want to shut down one of the most successful DIA initiatives of all time?'

'We don't want to,' Dillinger replied, 'we're forced to. If you cannot keep the program watertight, then the program ends.'

'We have operatives working across the globe,' Nellis said. 'You can't just pull the plug on them overnight.'

'We can and we will,' Dillinger replied as he set a sheet of paper down on the desk between them. 'A Presidential Order, laid out as a result of both the Edward Snowden affair and the exposure of MJ–12 a few months ago. We're closing down all and any programs that operate outside Homeland jurisdiction.'

Nellis stared down at the order and he could see in an instant that it heralded a complete sea–change in the way the administration operated its intelligence services.

'The president was the man who signed ARIES into operation,' he said in reply.

'And he's serving the last few months' of his second term,' Dillinger pointed out. 'He knows as well as you and I do that ARIES and other classified operations like it have operated throughout his tenure as president. If somebody like Jarvis has gone rogue, then everything that the DIA did over those eight years could become public knowledge, and he would be considered liable for signing ARIES into operation in his first year as President. You think he wants that hanging over his legacy?'

Nellis shook his head.

'I believe that he has the integrity not to try to sweep our operations under the carpet to save his own reputation. I also know for a fact that he would not shut ARIES down at this moment.'

'Why not?' Green challenged. 'MJ–12 are gone. The program's main initiative has been completed.'

'Except, as you all have stated so clearly,' Nellis replied, 'thirty billion dollars are not accounted for. Neither you nor the president would shut ARIES down without having first recovered that money. It's the only government effort getting anywhere close to recovering those billions…'

Nellis broke off as Dillinger and the other three men stood and made to leave, and he finally understood what was really happening behind the scenes.

'We'll be in touch,' Foxx promised with a curt nod.

'Who's taking over the ARIES program?' Nellis asked him outright.

Dillinger smiled but said nothing as he left the office. Nellis sat for a long moment and then he picked up a phone on his desk and dialed Hellerman's number. The specialist answered immediately.

'How bad is it?'

'We need to find Jarvis and thirty billion dollars real fast, or we're all out of a job.'

***

XI

Green River Medical Center,

Utah

'I can't stand these places.'

Ethan walked with Lopez across the parking lot of the medical center, a low building set against the dead straight main road through the town of Green River and surrounded by the burning deserts and distant mountains that were a soft blue in the haze. Many of them appeared to float on transparent oceans of rippling heat as the sun blazed down above them.

'Nobody likes hospitals,' Ethan replied. 'Homeland and the FBI will be here soon, so let's get this done before they arrive and start asking too many questions.'

The interior of the center was cool and air conditioned against the savage heat outside as Ethan and Lopez showed their identification badges at reception and were hurried through the center to a private room. Inside, lying on the pristine white sheets and with her eyes closed, was the girl.

She looked vulnerable to Ethan to say the least, maybe thirteen years old, thin but with perfect skin and long dark hair. Her face was genuinely beautiful but tinged with sadness, and the color of her skin betrayed her foreign origins.

'She looks like she's Middle Eastern,' he said to the duty nurse. 'Do we have any ID?'

'Nothing,' the nurse replied. 'This one's a real mystery. We got a blood sample and ran DNA on it but she doesn't show up on any database. No name, no address and she doesn't want to speak to anyone.'

'Shock,' Lopez replied. 'She's trying to come to terms with everything that's happened. Do we know how long she was kept by the cult in their compound?'

'No,' the nurse replied. 'Could've been days, could've been years. She may not even know herself.'

Ethan nodded. Preventing captives from keeping track of time was one of the most common and effective means of disorientating and breaking down a prisoner's ability to resist whatever coercion was being used against them.

'We'll take it from here,' he said, and opened the door to the room.

'Maybe I should go in first,' Lopez suggested.

Ethan didn't argue and let Lopez inside ahead of him. Despite her ferocious temper Lopez had a knack of winning people over, especially children, a skill that evaded Ethan. As they walked into the room he saw the girl stir but she did not open her eyes, merely lying in silence on the bed.

Lopez eased closer to the girl and sat down on a chair beside the bed.

'Can you hear me?' she asked, her voice soft in the quiet room.

The girl did not move but Ethan could see her eyes shifting beneath her eyelids, evidence of brain activity. Either she was dreaming or she was perfectly awake and trying not to react to their presence.

'It's okay if you don't want to talk,' Lopez purred. 'We're just here to make sure you're feeling better.'

Ethan remained silent, not wanting to interfere, but he doubted that even Lopez could reach the girl in the short amount of time that they had.

'We know something of what you went through,' Lopez went on, 'inside that building. I know it must be tough to think about, but we were wondering what the hieroglyphics were about?'

The girl did not move but Ethan could see her eyes still flickering beneath the lids and so he took a chance.

'We want to know about Atum.'

The girl's eyes flew open, pale white discs that flicked to the right to look directly at Ethan. For a moment it seemed as though she was looking straight at him, and then she turned away and stared sightlessly at the ceiling.

'Atum,' she whispered.

'Do you speak English?' Lopez asked softly.

Ethan watched as Lopez gently placed one hand on the girl's. The girl recoiled slightly but then she relaxed as Lopez spoke.

'It's okay. Just take your time. If we can understand what happened to you, we can prevent it from happening again to somebody else.'

The girl's head turned toward Lopez, who spoke in a voice so gentle that Ethan could barely hear her.

'We think that there may be others,' she whispered.

The girl watched Lopez for a moment and then she nodded slightly. 'There are others.'

Her voice was heavily accented with the musical lilt of Arabic, but Ethan felt galvanized as he realized that the girl could indeed speak English. Lopez did not rush, waiting for a respectful few moments before she went on.

'What's your name?'

The girl replied softly. 'Aisha.'

'That's a great name,' Lopez enthused gently as though she had heard it for the first time. 'Where are you from, Aisha?'

'Hims,' she replied. 'Syria.'

Lopez nodded as though she'd known all along, recognizing the girl's use of Arabic for Homs. 'You speak good English, Aisha.'

'My father was an English teacher.'

Aisha's voice had changed tone, became flat and emotionless as though she were reciting from some unseen page. Ethan guessed that she was unable to properly process the horrors that she had seen and endured, the death of her father and probably the rest of her family simply too traumatic to contemplate beyond flat statements of fact.

Lopez detected the same vibe and steered gently away from the subject.

'How did you come to be in Utah, Aisha?'

A pause, long, thoughtful. 'They bought me.'

'The cult?'

'The one they call Messian.'

'He's dead now, Aisha, he can't hurt you.'

'I know.'

Lopez hesitated, thinking carefully before asking her next question.

'Why was the cult interested in Atum, Aisha? Do you know?'

Aisha sighed softly.

'They seek the knowledge of the Egyptians, the understanding of god, of Atum.'

Lopez frowned. 'How did those hieroglyphics get onto the wall of the ranch?'

'I drew them,' Aisha said, 'I drew them as they were being drawn thousands of years ago. My hand followed the hands of the artist's.'

'Trans Cranial Stimulation,' Lopez voiced silently to Ethan, who nodded in response.

'They seek the knowledge,' Aisha went on. 'They seek power.'

'What knowledge and power?'

'That of the ancients,' Aisha replied. 'They seek the power of The Watchers, of The Nine.'

Lopez glanced at Ethan and gave a vague shrug. Ethan returned the gesture and with a start of shock he realized that, somehow, Aisha detected their failure to understand.

'There is no time, no space, only our place within it and our own frame of reference,' Aisha said in a calm voice as though reciting from a sheet, or perhaps from memory. 'Those who came before can commune with us and we with them, if only we are able to open our minds.'

Lopez hesitated again, this time from uncertainty.

'I don't understand what that means,' she said finally. 'We just want to make sure that this never happens again.'

Ethan saw Aisha's expression quiver, saw a tear trickle from her eye down one flawless cheek. Lopez's concern turned to distress and she got to her feet even as Aisha rolled onto her side and threw her arms around Lopez's neck.

Ethan stood for some long minutes as Lopez held the girl's trembling body in her arms and waited until she calmed. Slowly Aisha lay back on the bed and now her features were filled with urgency, as though something in her had changed.

'You must listen to me,' she said.

'We're ready,' Lopez promised, one hand still holding Aisha's.

The girl spoke quietly and confidently, gazing directly at Lopez with those unnerving, unseeing pale eyes.

'The past, the future, all times are as one,' she said. 'Some of us can see through the veil of history, can hear the whisper of voices long gone. They call us the Oracle.'

Ethan felt a twinge of superstitious awe creep like insects beneath his skin as Aisha went on.

'Messian made us commune with The Nine.'

'Who are The Nine?' Lopez asked.

'Atum and his followers, those who came before us. You know something of them, for you know of the descent of the Black Knight.'

Ethan almost staggered off balance as he heard Aisha speak of the bizarre satellite that the DIA had discovered orbiting the earth only the previous year. Cloaked in secrecy, that the event had ever occurred was unknown to all but a handful of people on earth.

Ethan wanted to ask her how she could possibly have known about the satellite, but Lopez shook her head at him to warn him off and let Aisha continue.

'Atum will return,' Aisha said, 'may have already returned. Messian and his Russian friends want to know how to contact Atum and…'

'Russians?' Ethan asked, unable to stop himself this time. 'There are Russians involved in this here in the US?'

'There are others,' Aisha said softly, 'others like me. They are not in this country but in Syria and they are being held as I was. One of them, she is powerful, stronger than I in her mind. They are using her to find the tablets, and they must be stopped.'

Lopez squeezed Aisha's hand gently.

'Tablets? What tablets?'

Aisha looked at Lopez, her eyes wide. 'The tablets that started it all. The instructions of The Watchers that fell from the sky and were written upon the tablets.'

Ethan's mind spun as he listened to Aisha's bizarre descriptions, Lopez soothing the girl and trying to extract more information.

'Like the Ten Commandments?' Lopez asked, clearly wondering like Ethan whether Aisha's memory was warped by the suffering she had endured.

'The Ten Commandments of the Bible are a fallacy,' Aisha replied scornfully, 'there were originally forty–two and they were the principles of Ma'at, an Egyptian god, written down two thousand *ndash; *no, three and a half thousand* years before the Old Testament. The tablet I speak of is much, much older.'

Ethan eased forward. 'Do you know where these tablets are?'

Aisha stared vacantly into the middle distance as she replied softly.

'Abraham Messian said that they are in a place of secrets, stolen and hidden like so many other secrets, in Rome. I can see them, but others could do better than I. Can you find them? They suffer still.'

'We will find all of the others,' Lopez promised. 'Can you help us find the tablets, and the other girls?'

Aisha turned her head toward Lopez.

'If you let me try I can take you right to the tablets,' she replied softly and with a confidence that Ethan found somewhat unnerving. 'I can see them.'

Ethan dialed a number on his cell phone, and Hellerman answered on the first ring. 'We're going to need the DIA to take custody of Aisha,' he said.

***

THE GENESIS CYPHER   Dean Crawford

XII

Defense Intelligence Agency,

Washington DC

Hellerman was waiting for Ethan and Nicola in the ARIES watch room as they arrived after their flight from Utah, and he beckoned them quickly to follow him into his office. Ethan noted that many of the giant wall–mounted screens in the watch room were tuned in to news channels covering the civil war in Syria, images of fighting amid shattered cities and political wrangling dominating the news.

Hellerman closed his door behind them.

'Did you manage to dig anything up about those hieroglyphics?' Ethan asked as he leaned against the office wall.

'Oh hell yeah,' Hellerman replied, 'and you're not going to believe what's been going on.'

'Where?' Lopez asked.

'Not where,' Hellerman replied, 'but when.'

'I'm not following,' Ethan said.

'Okay,' Hellerman enthused. 'Your first assignment for the Defense Intelligence Agency concerned a Doctor Lucy Morgan, who had gone missing after discovering a tomb in Israel that contained the bones of a seven–thousand–year–old humanoid that wasn't human at all, right?'

'Sure,' Ethan replied, 'Lucy's been a friend ever since. What's that got to do with the hieroglyphics?'

'Nothing,' Hellerman said, 'and everything at the same time. Here, take a look at this.'

Hellerman unrolled a large print that he had made, showing the hieroglyphics on the walls of the Egyptian temple at Saqqara.

'These are the original hieroglyphics found in the tomb of the Egyptian sage Ptah–Hotep, the ones that were copied by the cult in Utah on the walls of their ranch building. They're around four and a half thousand years old, yet as you can see there is a clear image of an alien, humanoid figure among the images, identical to what those in UFOlogy would now term a "gray".'

Lopez leaned in close, able to better see the original image now before her at full–size and in full color.

'How the hell can this be there on that wall?' she asked. 'Grays and alien stuff is from the modern age, the X–Files and things like that.'

'So people would believe,' Hellerman replied, 'but as Ethan knows the phenomenon is far, far older.'

'That doesn't mean that this artefact is genuine,' Ethan replied. 'It could conceivably have been added at a later date, some kind of forgery perhaps?'

Hellerman blinked in amazement.

'I doubt it. It's in a tomb thousands of years old, which is well protected against such attempts at defacing due to the number of tourists passing through all the time, not to mention armed guards and such like. Besides, what end would such a defacing of an ancient monument achieve? Archeologists would spot the fraud in an instant, and they're all quietly ignoring this artefact rather than queuing up to condemn it as a fake.'

Ethan knew that history was littered with countless examples of ancient people recording the appearance of bright lights in the sky, from which came down powerful beings who taught the people how to manipulate the world around them. Virtually every religion on the planet had an origin story that described sky gods mingling with humans and warring with each other in the skies, ending with a great flood that sent mankind back into the Stone Age and the gods back into the heavens.

'So, the hieroglyphs are real,' Ethan said. 'Where do we go from there?'

'To this,' Hellerman said as he produced another large image and rolled it out in front of them. 'This was written on another wall in the Utah cult building, and is one of the most controversial historical documents you will ever see. It is called the Tulli Papyrus and is thousands of years old, and what it says will absolutely blow your mind.'

The image before Ethan was almost square and contained rows of hieroglyphics, beneath which were English translations. Hellerman looked at them both expectantly and Lopez smiled fondly at him.

'Jo honey, my ancient Egyptian's a little rusty, y'know?'

'Oh,' Hellerman flustered, 'right, of course. Okay, here we go: "In the year twenty–two, on the third month of winter, sixth hour of the day, among the scribes of the House of Life it was found that a strange fiery disk was coming out of the sky. It had no head. The breath of its mouth emitted a foul odor. Its body was one rod in length and one rod in width. It had no voice. It came toward His Majesty's house. Their heart became confused through it, and they fell upon their bellies. They went to the king to report it. His Majesty ordered that the scrolls in the House of Life be consulted. His Majesty meditated on all these events which were now going on."'

'Are you telling me that this is a UFO report from ancient Egypt?' Lopez asked.

'It's the earliest report known to man,' Hellerman confirmed before going on: 'After several days had passed, the lights became more numerous in the sky than ever. They shined in the sky more than the brightness of the sun, and extended to the limits of the four supports of heaven. Powerful was the position of the fiery disks. The army of the King looked on, with His Majesty in their midst. It was after the evening meal when the disks ascended even higher in the sky to the south. Fish and a variety of birds rained down from the sky: a marvel never before known since the foundation of the country. And His Majesty caused incense to be brought to appease the heart of Amun–Re, the god of the Two Lands. And it was ordered that the event be recorded for His Majesty in the annals of the House of Life to be remembered forever."'

Hellerman stood back from the manuscript and looked at them expectantly.

'Who was the Pharaoh in the manuscript?' Ethan asked.

'Thutmose III,' Hellerman replied. 'The manuscript was written by a scribe of his known as Tjaneni, famous for recording the Battle of Megiddo that occurred shortly after the sightings.'

'Veracity?' Lopez asked, somewhat stupefied.

'Unquestionable,' Hellerman replied. 'The original Egyptian papyrus, written in hieratic, was described in great detail by the Italian scholar and Egyptologist Prince Boris de Rachewiltz. The original was part of the Royal Annals of Thutmose III and was held by the Vatican, but mysteriously was lost to history after Doctor Edward Condon, the head of a U.S. Government sponsored committee to study UFO reports called Project Blue Book, pursued the papyrus via the Scientific Attache at the U.S. Embassy in Rome. The New World Encyclopedia includes the Tulli Papyrus in its list of ancient papyri.'

'So this is the real deal,' Ethan said. 'How does it connect with anything that we're looking into here?'

Hellerman sighed as he rubbed his forehead. 'It's at times like this I wish Jarvis were still working here, because I can sense a connection in all of this but I can't quite define it. Essentially, the UFO connection between ancient peoples and the modern phenomena is something that Majestic Twelve seemed inordinately interested in. Their people showed up almost every time you and Nicola were investigating these kinds of things, and that suggests that whatever they were trying to achieve involved these kinds of artefacts. It's only your hard work that prevented MJ–12 from getting hold of the Black Knight.'

Ethan nodded, recalling well the dangerous expedition to the Antarctic to obtain a thirteen–thousand–year–old satellite that had fallen from earth orbit. The mission had cost the DIA dearly in lives as they fought to prevent MJ–12 from gaining control of one of the most incredible objects mankind had ever encountered.

'You know that we found more of those Trans Cranial Stimulation devices at the ranch in Utah,' Lopez said to Hellerman, 'and that the girls they were working on were being forced to wear them.'

Hellerman nodded.

'That's what I was afraid of,' he said. 'You see, I don't think that the girls there painted those hieroglyphics on the walls of that ranch by copying a picture like this one. I think that they were being made to use the headsets in order to see the hieroglyphics as they were being written, in the past.'

Ethan blinked. 'Like remote viewing?'

Hellerman shrugged as though he had come to the only conclusion that made any sense.

'I think that the leaders of the cult were using these young girls to figure out what went on in ancient Egypt because they obviously consider events from that time period to be of great importance. Many of the hieroglyphics of the time show Pharaohs who look somewhat bizarre, with elongated heads and almond eyes, which some conspiracy theorists point to as evidence of an alien presence either in the population or through genetic manipulation.'

'Sounds far-fetched,' Lopez said, 'they could have just been really ugly or interbred.'

Hellerman inclined his head. 'True, there was much interbreeding at the time due to the belief that the Pharaohs were of royal blood, and that such blood should not be contaminated by lesser peoples. They didn't know much about genetics themselves at the time.'

'So any visiting aliens did a poor job of educating them,' Ethan smiled wryly. 'Anything else?'

'Like people seeing into the past wasn't enough?' Hellerman asked, as though disappointed. 'Whatever these people were looking for, it involved something that happened a long time ago. Did any of the other cult survivors give us anything to work with?'

Lopez shook her head.

'Most of them are ardent believers and wouldn't share a thing,' she said. 'But two of the women there were long time captives and seemed to try to help. One of them kept talking about this Tulli Manuscript of yours, and they mentioned Rome.'

'They said that the girls were looking for guidance from Rome,' Ethan said. 'Aisha also mentioned that there were tablets involved, and that they were in Rome.'

'Tablets?' Hellerman echoed.

'Yes,' Lopez confirmed, 'tablets, like the Ten Commandments.'

Hellerman's eyes glazed over in awe.

'The ancient Egyptians were the originators of the Ten Commandments,' he said in a whisper, 'and they created forty-two of them, which were written on tablets and broken before being placed in...'

Hellerman turned and grabbed a book from his shelves, leafing through it until he found what he was looking for, reading the relevant details from within the pages.

'The Tulli Manuscript was said to be in the possession of the Vatican's Secret Archives, although the Vatican denies its presence. Project Blue Book tried to access it but the Vatican claims that it never possessed the piece. My guess is that if this cult couldn't physically get a hold of the manuscript, they would instead use the girls to look back in time and see it being written. If they saw the same text on tablets in Rome, then that may mean they are talking about the original tablets themselves, from which the Tulli Papyrus recorded the story. Aisha and the others were literally being used as what were once known as Divine Oracles.'

XIII

Lopez folded her arms and confronted Hellerman with a flat gaze. 'So we're still going with the crystal ball gazing theory?'

'It's not actually as crazy as it sounds,' Hellerman replied. 'Historically, nations across the globe have used young girls as a means to divine the future or peer into the past.'

'Sure but that was all hokum,' Lopez said. 'If people were really capable of seeing the future we'd have solid evidence of it by now. I always find it suspicious that so–called psychics never win their state lotteries.'

Hellerman smiled.

'Like many, I suspect that the natural ability of young girls and even children to experience paranormal phenomena becomes stilted with age. Most people just assume that the childhood belief in magic and monsters under the bed is just natural fear of the unknown that they learn to overcome as understanding grows. But what if the open mind of a young child also allows them to see more than we do, and that it is a genuine ability that is removed when their minds are closed by our modern world?'

'I'll believe that when I see it,' Lopez said.

'You already did once, in New York,' Ethan reminded her.

'That was different,' Lopez replied, 'that was a spectre, a wraith.'

Hellerman looked as though he was going to ask about that particular investigation, and then he decided better of it and went on.

'It has often been the case the young girls of pubescent age have been at the epicentre of major paranormal events. The most famous case occurred in 1967 in Rosenheim, Germany, when scientists from none other than the Max Planck Institute visited a lawyer's office to investigate an immense surge of poltergeist activity. Drawers were opening and closing, lights swinging, printers were spilling their ink, telephone calls would be made when there was nobody actually using a phone. One set of records shows the talking clock being dialed three times per minute, that's forty–five times in fifteen minutes: far too fast for the dialing system of the phones of the time to handle. On one occasion every light bulb in the building blew up at once, on others all the bulbs were unscrewed even when people were in the office. Such events required huge amounts of energy and yet nobody was doing anything untoward. The scientists set up cameras and voice recorders to monitor events and recorded some of the only existing footage of things like pictures rotating on their hooks, far beyond the reach of the witnesses. They also noted that electrical equipment would falter and lights would flicker when a nineteen–year old employee was in the building. They eventually traced the events to her, and when she was sent on vacation the poltergeist activity ceased.'

'So?' Lopez challenged. 'Maybe she had some kind of psychokinetic ability, but that's not the same as looking forward and backwards through time is it?'

'No, but it is possible that what we have in Syria is a coordinated search for a modern day oracle.'

'A seer?' Ethan echoed. 'I wouldn't have thought that the Russians would waste time and money on a search for something so mythical?'

'No, but in classical antiquity an oracle was a person considered capable of wise and insightful counsel or prophetic predictions of the future, inspired by the gods,' Hellerman explained. 'They took these seers very seriously, truly believing them to be capable of divination, of speaking to the gods themselves. The word itself, oracle, comes from the Latin verb orare, "to speak", with the ancient Greeks referring to the divinations as khresmoi. However, seers, or manteis, divined messages through the actions of nature around them, bird signs and so on.'

Ethan shook his head, unconvinced. 'I won't believe that a world superpower would be messing around with something that is little more than divining tea leaves.'

'Don't underestimate what these people could be capable of,' Hellerman said, showing a rare sign of genuine interest in the paranormal. 'The most important oracles of Greek antiquity were Pythia, priestess to Apollo at Delphi, and the oracle of Dione and Zeus at Dodona in Epirus. The Greeks had temples of Apollo located at Didyma on the coast of Asia Minor, at Corinth and Bassae in the Peloponnese and at the islands of Delos and Aegina in the Aegean Sea. From these temples the oracles were consulted on a regular basis, the prophetesses revealing their divine revelations in frenzied states probably brought about by the use of mind–altering substances.'

'Seriously?' Lopez uttered. 'They were taking advice from pot–heads?'

'And what does this have to do with the Tulli Manuscript or those hieroglyphics?' Ethan asked.

Hellerman looked at the mysterious image of the hieroglyphics at Saqqara. 'I looked into the leader of the Utah cult. Abraham Messian was indeed a hard–core Old Testament preacher who was expecting the End of Days, but the Old Testament contains many references to a Pharaoh, as well as references to supposed alien encounters in the book of Ezekiel, with descriptions of flaming wheels descending from the sky from which emerged humanoid figures.'

'Did the Egyptians have oracles too?' Lopez asked.

'Plenty, because they existed before the more famous Greek oracles,' Hellerman confirmed. 'The "frenzied women from whose lips the god speaks" are recorded in the Near East in the second millennium BCE and in Assyria in the first millennium BCE. In Egypt the goddess Wadjet was depicted as a snake–headed woman and her oracle was in the renowned temple in Per–Wadjet. The oracle of Wadjet may have been the source for the oracular tradition which spread from Egypt to Greece. If we're assuming that any of what's happened in Utah is possible, then the most likely conduit would presumably be through the eyes of a person who lived at the time. That's to say that a modern day oracle would see past events through the eyes of a long–dead one.'

'Who was high on drugs at the time,' Lopez added.

Hellerman shrugged apologetically. 'It's not an exact science.'

'Any evidence that these supposed oracles were in any way reliable?' Ethan asked.

'The Delphic Oracle exerted considerable influence throughout Hellenic culture and was essentially the highest authority both civilly and religiously in male–dominated ancient Greece. She responded to the questions of citizens, foreigners, kings and philosophers on all issues. The semi–Hellenic countries around the Greek world, such as Lydia, Caria and even Egypt also respected her and came to Delphi as supplicants.'

'That's a sign of popularity, not accuracy,' Lopez said.

Hellerman tilted his head in acquiescence.

'Croesus, the king of Lydia in 560 BCE, tested the oracles of the world to discover which gave the most accurate prophecies. He sent out emissaries to seven sites who were all to ask the oracles on the same day what the king was doing at that very moment. Croesus proclaimed the oracle at Delphi to be the most accurate, who correctly reported that the king was making a lamb–and–tortoise stew, and so he graced her with a magnitude of precious gifts. He then more famously consulted Delphi before attacking Persia, and according to Herodotus was advised: "If you cross the river, a great empire will be destroyed". Believing the response favorable, Croesus attacked, but it was his own empire that ultimately was destroyed by the Persians.'

'Ambiguous advice at best,' Ethan countered. 'It allowed the battle to go either way and still prove the Delphi correct.'

'The Delphi also proclaimed that there was no man wiser than Socrates. As a result, Socrates dedicated his life to a search for knowledge that was one of the founding events of western philosophy. He claimed that she was "an essential guide to personal and state development."'

Ethan looked at the images of the hieroglyphics, the Tulli Manuscript and then at the Trans Cranial Stimulation device on Hellerman's desk.

'What if they're searching for evidence of UFOs in the past for some reason?' he speculated. 'Even if the method does seem crackpot, these people are insane enough to try something like that.'

Hellerman stared at Ethan for a long moment, and he could almost see the sudden rush of thoughts flashing past the scientist's eyes as he performed a rapid mental calculation and then whirled to his desk and sifted frantically through his papers.

'What is it?' Lopez asked.

Hellerman pointed a finger up in the air beside his head as he ordered his thoughts.

'If the Tulli Manuscript is in the Vatican, and that even a major figure like General Condon with the backing of the United States Government could not retrieve it, then the Vatican must consider whatever is written on the papyrus to be explosive to say the least. The best bet we have is to see if Aisha can envision what they're hiding so that we can go take a look.'

'Go take a look,' Lopez echoed. 'So we just stroll into the Secret Archives of the Vatican, take the papyrus and waltz right out of there with it? C'mon Jo, I've seen the movies, that place is locked up tighter than a nun's panti…'

'Partly true,' Hellerman interjected, 'but in fact anybody can walk into the secret archives. However, you cannot browse – you have to know where the artefact you're looking for is before you enter the archive.'

Ethan frowned.

'Okay, but Aisha is no natural oracle. She would need to be wearing that device to make it happen.'

Hellerman nodded.

'We can only ask,' he said simply, 'because without knowing where the artefact is, we won't be getting anywhere near it.'

***

XIV

'Are you sure you want to do this?'

Aisha turned her head and looked in Lopez's direction as she heard her voice.

Lopez stood in the doorway of a briefing room inside the DIA Headquarters, one of several units designed to block not just all sight from outside in the watch room but also all sound. With the glass windows fogged out and the doors sealed, briefings on extremely classified or otherwise sensitive material could be conducted without concern for being overheard by passers–by with lower security clearances.

The man called Hellerman had converted the room into a simple medical chamber, complete with reclined bed, soft lighting, a heart monitor with the volume switched off and a second set of screens attached to a Deep Trans Cranial Stimulator. Upon the bed lay Aisha, her hands crossed calmly upon her stomach and her head resting back against the pillows, her head surrounded by the DTCS's myriad wires and connectors.

'I've done it before enough times,' she replied quietly.

'Under duress,' Ethan's voice added from nearby. 'We don't want to put you through anything that you don't feel up to enduring.'

Aisha turned her head toward the man and the woman. She suspected somehow that they were both dangerous individuals. Warner sounded as though he may have served in the military and Lopez appeared kind hearted but was surrounded by an aura of contained ferocity, like a caged leopard always on the lookout for an opportunity to strike. And yet, right now, they were more concerned with her welfare than anybody she had known for years, since before her parents had…

Aisha's train of thought cut off automatically, and she sighed and nodded.

'I know, and that is why I want to do it. I know that I will be safe here.'

Warner squeezed her shoulder.

'Fine, but the moment you want out you shout, got it?'

Aisha felt a warmth in the pit of her belly and she realized that she was smiling as she nodded back at Warner. Lopez rested one hand against her cheek.

'We'll be right next door,' she promised, 'and we're not leaving until this is done and we know you're okay.'

Warner and Lopez left the room and as they closed the door behind them Aisha heard it hiss shut, sealing her in. All external noises disappeared and she knew that soon the device would begin working. From a speaker in the room, Hellerman's voice sounded gently.

'We're just getting ready,' he told her. 'Two minutes and we'll start the device, just try to relax.'

*

'Talk to us,' Lopez said to Hellerman as they joined him at a desk outside the briefing room where the scientist sat at a computer terminal.

Hellerman gestured to the screen as he worked.

'Aisha's wired up to this device so we can monitor her heart–rate and other vital signs while she's in seizure.'

'You're actually going to do that to her?' Lopez asked, clearly horrified.

'This is the only way,' Hellerman confirmed, 'at least it's the only way that the Russians had found that worked. It's not pretty but it's how Aisha described to me the procedures Abraham Messian put them through in order to provoke their ability to visualize past and even future events.'

'And this will lead us to the girls the Russians are using, and these supposed tablets?'

'That's the hope,' Hellerman said. 'The technique being used here isn't really Deep Trans Cranial Stimulation although the procedure derives from it. This process is actually known as Electroconvulsive Therapy.'

'What's the difference?' Lopez asked.

'Typically, the severity of the condition being treated. ECT is used to treat serious mental disorders, and only then if every other form of treatment has failed. It's used in the west if the patient is on the verge of suicide or catatonia, and is the last resort.'

'And we're using it on Aisha to go sight–seeing,' Ethan said dryly.

Hellerman nodded, equally uncomfortable with the procedure.

'I don't like it, but if Aisha struggles at any point I'll stop the device,' he said. 'Normally, a patient undergoing ECT is sedated with general anesthesia and given a muscle relaxant to prevent movement during the procedure. But our friends the Russians forego that safety measure in order to provoke the seizures that lead to the girl's visions. Worse, instead of passing electric currents through the brain for sixty seconds, Ivan does it for ten minutes or more.'

'We're not Ivan,' Lopez reminded Hellerman. 'Are there any side–effects?'

'Headaches and muscle aching, upset stomachs and memory loss,' Hellerman replied. 'Research has found that memory problems seem to be associated with the traditional type of ECT called bilateral ECT, in which the electrodes are placed on both sides of the head, the process the Russians were using. We're using unilateral ECT, where the electrodes are placed on just one side of the head—typically the right side because it is opposite the brain's learning and memory areas.'

'What happens to Aisha after this?' Ethan asked.

'I'll have her sent to Social Services and looked after,' Hellerman promised. 'She'll be fine.'

Lopez sighed. 'Okay, let's get it over with.'

Hellerman nodded, and then he reached out and one finger hovered over a switch on the keyboard before him as he spoke softly into a microphone.

'Okay Aisha, here we go in five, four, three…'

Aisha heard Hellerman's voice echoing gently through the room around her as she did her best to relax and focus on the subjects that the Russians had demanded her to, just like Hellerman had asked. Her eyes were closed, her breathing steady, and apart from Hellerman's voice the room was utterly silent.

'three…'

Aisha's heartbeat fluttered in her chest as she cleared her mind of thoughts.

'two…'

Her breathing slowed, and she almost felt calm. She knew that she had to be as still as possible before the machine started.

'one…'

Aisha sighed softly to herself and let a smile drift onto her face as she thought of home and of happier times. That worked sometimes, made the transition easier, less stressful. She focused on the object that Warner and Lopez required, set its image in her mind.

'Switching on, now.'

For a brief moment of time nothing happened, Aisha adrift on a dark sea of serene solitude. Then the darkness was ripped apart by blinding light that seared her retina as live current surged through her brain, giving her a vision that she had been denied her entire life. For an instant she felt as though she were in the center of her own mind, a blazing sphere as large as the entire universe rippling with brilliant but confusing whorls and jagged lines of light that zipped and raced in random directions and bored into her eyes.

Aisha felt her body shuddering and twitching on the bed, but it seemed as though she were floating above it in a quivering haze of energy at the same time, both a part of her body and beyond it. The image of the tablets lurched out at her as though hurled from the abyss of light and then it shot away from her again.

Aisha saw rows of shelves, endless rows stretching away into the distance. The spines of boxes on the shelves were inscribed with Latin and red wax seals, the light low, the air musty. She saw an elevator shaft nearby, old shutter doors upon it, saw an ageing building of sandstone. Towers. Spires. Bright blue sky. Crowds milling everywhere.

A wide open square opened up beneath her, and in its center soared a towering obelisk engraved with strange symbols that she recognized but could not quite place. The symbols drew her in deeper, and despite wanting to get away she found herself obsessed with them. They rushed closer, and she saw the huge obelisk enveloped in a roiling dust storm, the huge plaza and milling tourists vanishing to be replaced with sprawling deserts.

Aisha felt her sanity trembling, as though the universe was imploding around her beyond the vision now searing her retina. She felt great heat choking her, the desert sand scalding below, the sky burning blue above. She saw massed ranks of men laboring in the heat, saw huge constructions before her.

A temple.

Massive columns soared upward, chambers buried deep into the living rock, more strange symbols etched into them. The laborers marched in teams, the dust swirling in golden vortexes about their feet as they hauled immense stone blocks across the desert, the rocks sliding on a wooden path slick with pooled water.

A voice spoke to her, a girl's voice.

'It is his time.'

Aisha looked for the source of the voice. She turned and saw a girl shimmering like a phantom before her as behind the girl the desert was swallowed by a vast dust storm, lightning crashing across darkened skies. Strange lights hovered in the tumultuous heavens as Aisha kept her gaze on the girl. Young, pretty but sad, like a reflection of Aisha herself. The girl looked at Aisha, her expression somber.

'They are coming. You must find the tomb of Tjaneni.'

Aisha tried to speak but her lips would not move, and instead she thought the question in her mind.

'Who is Tjaneni?'

The girl smiled. 'He who spoke with the gods. Within his tomb resides the word of God, and only Amenhotep knew its location. The tablets, you must find the tablets.'

'Where are you?'

The girl looked around her. 'I am in Homs, Syria. You must hurry or we will all die here.'

Aisha felt concern for the young girl, saw the fear in her eyes as she spoke again.

'There is little time. Run, Aisha, for the American will kill us all.'

'The American?'

The girl nodded, looking around her now as though she were being pursued and she began to back away.

'I have to run!' she yelled. 'I have to run!'

'No!' Aisha cried out, reaching out for the girl through the flying sand biting into her skin.

'Warner!' the girl yelled. 'Warner will…'

The vision was suddenly shattered and plunged into darkness. Aisha cried out and felt her body jerking spasmodically around her, felt the DTCS being lifted from her head as her heart thundered in her chest. In her mind she heard the thunder echoing away into the distance as the eye–protectors were removed and the straps pinning her in place loosened.

Aisha felt Lopez wrap her arms around, her voice soft in her ear.

'It's okay, you're done. That's enough.'

Aisha trembled as Lopez held her, and sensed Warner and Hellerman standing nearby. Aisha found herself focusing on Warner the most, more aware now than ever of the aura of danger that surrounded him, a determination to get a job done no matter what the consequences.

'Are you okay?' Lopez asked her as she drew back.

Aisha nodded, wiped tears from her eyes with one arm that twitched and trembled uncontrollably. Lopez helped her as she dried her eyes.

'What did you see?' Hellerman asked. 'I know that this is tough but memory loss can be acute after such a procedure.'

'What about the girls, did you see them?' Lopez asked.

Aisha nodded slowly, recalling the same worries of the Russians that anything the oracles saw would be lost to the side–effects of the procedure itself.

'They are in Homs,' she replied. 'They do not have long left. You must hurry. The object you seek, the Tulli Tablet, is in Italy,' she said. 'It's in the Vatican, underground in a vault where everything is in Latin.'

Hellerman raised an eyebrow. 'The Secret Archives? Can you see where the object is hidden?'

'I saw enough to get you close,' Aisha promised. 'It's at the back wall of a subterranean section concealed from view, the lower levels of the archive. There is an elevator. I saw something else, too.'

'What was it?' Lopez asked.

'I saw the past, but I think also the present,' Aisha said. 'I saw Egypt and a great storm, and great danger.' She turned to Lopez. 'A girl told me that we must find the tomb of somebody called Tjaneni.'

Hellerman's jaw dropped open. 'The scribe of Thutmose III,' he gasped as he rested one hand on the DTCS. 'Man, this stuff actually works!'

'The tablets of Amehotep will lead you to the tomb,' Aisha said softly, and Lopez caught a sense of sadness in her tone.

'What is it, Aisha?'

Aisha chose her words with care.

'It wasn't what I saw,' she said softly, 'it was what I felt.'

Ethan moved closer, and Aisha spoke as the visions filled her mind's eye once more.

'There is something coming,' she said, 'something that is dangerous and…, cruel. There were storms, confusion, images in my mind of world leaders, of struggle and suffering. One word kept coming up over and over again: Megiddo.'

The room seemed to darken as Aisha spoke, an oppressive air weighing down upon them as Aisha whispered almost to herself.

'This thing that you're chasing, this event, everything that is happening right now, it leads to great sorrow. Everything leads to Megiddo, to flames and smoke.'

Lopez frowned and glanced at Hellerman, who swallowed thickly.

'You got any idea what that means?' Lopez asked.

Hellerman nodded.

'Megiddo is in Israel and was the sight of a great battle won by Thutmose III thousands of years ago,' he replied. 'Tjaneni recorded that battle. But the city is known now by a different name popularized by the Old Testament, in which the final battle between all good and evil will be fought.'

'What name is that?' Ethan asked, already knowing the answer.

Hellerman appeared ashen faced as he stared at Aisha and replied.

'The city is more popularly known as Armageddon.'

**

XV

Ilha Ferando de Noronha,

Atlantic Ocean

The deck of the yacht flared white in the brilliant sunshine as Jarvis leaned back in a recliner and let the warm sunshine wash across his body. Anchored in a harbor off the bay of an island most people on earth had never even heard of, the massive vessel dwarfed most of those around it.

One of an archipelago of twenty–one islands in the Atlantic Ocean and over two hundred miles from the Brazilian coast, Fernando de Noronha had long been one of Garrett's favorite bolt–holes. Although the island promoted tourism, it was a difficult place to reach and some three quarters of the entire island was designated as a national maritime park. Thus, the population was less than three thousand and the interferences minimal, especially when Garrett remained on the deck of his vast vessel and had local cuisine shipped aboard at his pleasure.

Beside them was stacked a mountain of papers, folders and archive boxes that littered the deck.

'This is going to take us years.'

Amber Ryan and Lucy Morgan sat on the deck near Jarvis and watched Rhys Garrett quietly as he spoke.

'Perhaps, but the point of us doing this is to begin to unravel what Majestic Twelve's purpose was. While we also have our mission to root out corruption within world government, we must also ensure that we understand where our new–found wealth originated. Doug, I know that you're better versed in these matters than I?'

Jarvis nodded, basking in how much more agreeable a briefing on the deck of a luxury yacht was compared to one in a dingy conference room at the Defense Intelligence Agency.

'The cabal known as Majestic Twelve was formed during an extraordinary meeting between military leaders and President Harry S. Truman via an Executive Order in 1947, in direct response to the recovery of an extra–terrestrial craft from Roswell, New Mexico during that year. That recovery, along with a now famous sighting of "flying discs" by pilot Kenneth Arnold in Washington State the same year, prompted a unification of government and the military industrial complex that continues to this day.' Jarvis looked at the rest of his team to see if any of them appeared bemused by his statements. None did, all of them more than aware in their own way of the incredible history of what Majestic Twelve had been investigating. 'Majestic Twelve had originally been composed of senior military figures and one or two prominent heads of industry, but had evolved over the decades to be comprised entirely of immensely powerful businessmen who had ultimately become ever more corrupted by their wealth and power. It is that cabal which we destroyed six months ago in South America.'

Garrett took over for a moment after Jarvis gestured in his direction.

'Majestic Twelve operated through a secretive annual meeting of world leaders in government, industry and banking known as the Bilderberg Group. Members of the Bilderberg, together with their sister organizations – the Trilateral Commission and the Council on Foreign Relations, are charged with the post–war take over of the democratic process. The group provides general control of the world economy through indirect political means.'

'Despite everything I've heard,' Lucy Morgan said, 'that sounds too much like conspiracy.'

'I've attended Bilderberg myself,' Garrett replied, 'and they have a website you can view for yourself. For the most part they are immensely constructive meetings which allow politicians to speak freely without fear of journalistic interference, the media not being allowed to attend the meetings. It's that more than anything that builds the conspiracies around Bilderberg, but of course there is no smoke without fire. If you're a powerful figure looking to commit crimes beyond the reach of prying eyes with other like–minded politicians and businessmen, there's no better place to plan it than Bilderberg.'

'So is that our next target, this Bilderberg Group?' Amber Ryan asked.

'No,' Jarvis replied. 'Bilderberg is merely a vehicle with which Majestic Twelve were able to move freely and recruit other figures of power to support their cause. Our mission is to expose their original cause. My department at the Defense Intelligence Agency was not the only one performing these kinds of investigations, and with the collapse of Majestic Twelve we have created a power vacuum which is already being filled by Russian agencies keen to take advantage of the opportunity. *Mat' Zemlya,* or Mother Earth, is a small but well equipped unit we suspect has been picking up the threads of our work, based on that conducted by a Russian oligarch named Yuri Volkov.'

'Volkov,' Garrett explained, 'was a billionaire who devoted much of his later life to the exposure of the falsehoods of all religions. He was hated by established religious figures for his straight–talking manner, which made all religious claims of divinity look ridiculous. The only claims he found it difficult to refute were those by amateur archeologists who claimed that what ancient peoples called "gods" were in fact visitors from other worlds whose technology was so advanced that to our ancestors would appear literally to be magic.'

'Volkov died a few years back,' Jarvis went on. 'Now, the Russians are keen to continue his work. Lillian here has been going through the reports of Majestic Twelve and has uncovered evidence of a recent televised report by a former Soviet official with impeccable credentials that may have given us the edge on these new competitors. Lieutenant general Alexey Savin, a PhD and fellow of the Academy of

Natural Sciences, reported that in the late 1980's researchers from the Expert Management Unit of General Staff appeared to make contact with another civilization.'

A wall of silence confronted Jarvis, which lasted for a long time before anybody managed to speak.

'They made first contact?' Lucy Morgan finally whispered.

Jarvis nodded, clearly as amazed as anybody by the recent findings, and gestured for Lillian to speak.

'The report was followed up by FIB Major General Vasily Yeremenko, academician of the Academy of Security, Defense and Law Enforcement,' Lillian said. 'A former KGB and Air Force officer, he was responsible for collating information on the appearance of unidentified flying objects over the Soviet Union, which had become a regular occurrence in the early 1980's. Missile units were even given a directive in case of detection of UFOs. The main task was not to create opportunities for reciprocal aggression. In 1984 at the testing grounds of the Academy of Sciences by Vladimirovka, the Ministry of Defense and the KGB organized a large scale study of paranormal phenomena. The choice of a military training site was not random, as their experts had long before come to the conclusion that UFOs inevitably appeared in places where military equipment and weapons were tested.'

Amber Ryan frowned. 'So what, they switched on all the lights and hoped for the best?'

Jarvis took a breath as he prepared for his next revelation.

'By all accounts, the Soviets learned to actually summon UFO appearances,' he said. 'They purposefully massively increased the number of military flights, movement of troops and equipment and missile tests around specific sites, often at the risk of attracting the ire of the United States, with the express purpose of attracting the attention of UFOs.'

Lucy's eyes narrowed. 'What were their conclusions?'

'Threefold: firstly, that modern science was unable to identify such phenomena,' Lillian said. 'Second, it could be some kind of exotic reconnaissance aircraft deployed by America or Japan. Third, it could be the presence of an extra–terrestrial civilization. Vasily Yeremenko pointed out that both civilian and military pilots across the globe see these things all the time, but they have a veto on the topic and do not discuss it publicly. That veto comes from their employers, and their employers are directly influenced by the governments of their respective countries who have policies in place based on the supposed desire to prevent damaging public trust in pilot's mental stability should they report sightings of UFO's. Many of the solid reports Majestic Twelve did get were made anonymously, although witnessed at the same time by many other staff and civilians not bound by the same protocols. The 2006 incident at Chicago's O'Hare International airport would be a good example.'

'What happened there?' Rhys Garrett asked.

'On November 7th, 2006, an O'Hare airport employee noticed a large, dark disc hovering above the runway,' Jarvis said. 'The employee realized that what they were looking at was not normal and should not be there. The word spread quickly of a mysterious floating object above the airport. Pilots, air traffic controllers, employees and travellers alike bore witness to the UFO. There were reports of pilots on the runway peering out of their cockpit windows at it and staff going outside for a better look at the object. In the midst of all the commotion and without warning the disc shot straight up at tremendous speed through a cloud bank above the airport, leaving a large hole punched through the clouds.'

'How does all of this connect to Russia's new investigations?' Lucy Morgan asked. 'Or what we're going to do next? I'm more interested in helping people than chasing UFO stories all around the world.'

Jarvis smiled at his granddaughter.

'I would have thought that after what happened in Israel, after what you found there and later in Peru, you would have come to learn that much of what we do involves chasing around the world after things that most people assume are the product of myth and fantasy.'

'I'm also interested in putting our new–found wealth to good use,' Amber Ryan said. 'Cut to the chase.'

'I have it on good authority that the Russians are active in Syria and that it's connected to a recent case of cult suicide in Utah,' Jarvis revealed. 'The DIA are already moving on it, so we're going to tag along and find out just what they're up to. As you know Aaron will deploy to Syria when we have enough information, so he'll also chase up the Russian connection while he's there and find out what they're really up to.'

Mitchell appeared on the deck, a cell phone in his hand. 'I've found him.'

Jarvis stood and straightened his shirt as Lillian and the others continued their search.

'I'll be leaving for Washington DC in a few hours. Amber, you'll join me and return to your life for now. Lucy, you stay on the yacht with Lillian.'

Amber stood up in protest. 'Why do I not get to stay here?'

'Because we need to keep people apart,' Garrett replied. 'If there is anybody watching us and they notice that we keep vanishing at the same times, they'll soon be onto us. You'll head back for now, and then switch with Lucy as soon as it's possible. If our movements look unconnected, we'll stay hidden for longer.'

'DC could be dangerous for you,' Lucy said to her grandfather. 'Why would you head back there now, knowing that the DIA are looking for you?'

'It's a risk worth taking, and Mitchell will be with me for support,' Jarvis replied. 'There's somebody I need to speak to, somebody who might be able to help us. Trust me, I'll be back as soon as I can.'

Jarvis and Amber left the deck as Garrett heard the helicopter on the yacht's stern begin to power up, and he called after them.

'We don't know what we're going to find once we get started, and we don't know for sure just how our government will react if they start picking up the threads of what we're attempting here. These are powerful people, and we already know just how lethal cabals like Majestic Twelve become when they believe that they're no longer accountable for their actions. Be on your guard at all times.'

***

THE GENESIS CYPHER   Dean Crawford

XVI

Rome, Italy

Ethan stepped out of a taxi cab into the hordes of crowds milling in the warm sunshine around the soaring sandstone walls of Vatican City. Lopez paid the driver before she moved alongside Ethan and stared up at the imposing building before them.

'You think you're of sufficiently pure heart to enter this place?'

'I'll probably burst into flames the moment I set foot through the door,' Ethan replied as they began walking toward the entrance of the most famous principality in the world.

'I'm sure you're not that bad,' Lopez said. 'Not quite, anyway.'

'What's the name of the man we're meeting?'

'Francesco Mercati,' Lopez replied, 'Cardinal Activist of the Vatican Secret Archives. Only reason we got a meeting is down to the DIA. Looks like the US Government still holds a little sway here.'

Ethan led the way onto St Peter's Square, and the first thing he saw was an enormous Egyptian obelisk that dominated the vast square before the Vatican itself.

'Just like Hellerman said,' Lopez observed, 'right in the center of Christendom's HQ, a giant monument to the worship of gods predating Christianity by thousands of years.'

Ethan looked up at the twenty–five meter tall obelisk, shielding his eyes against the sunlight as he did so.

'Why would the Vatican want a giant Egyptian obelisk stuck right here?'

The voice that replied did not belong to Lopez.

'To absorb the traditions and histories of those civilizations that came and went before us.'

Ethan turned and saw a Cardinal before them, flanked by several Swiss Guards, the entourage attracting the gazes of tourists.

'Cardinal Francesco Mercati,' he introduced himself in accented English. 'You must be Ethan and Nicola.'

'We stand out that much huh?' Lopez asked.

'I know much about you both already.'

'How come?' Ethan asked. 'Did the DIA send you our details?'

'Yes,' Mercati confirmed. 'But, we knew of you both long before that.'

Lopez shot Ethan a curious look as Mercati gestured for them to follow him. The Cardinal glanced at the obelisk as they walked past it toward the Basilica.

'The obelisk once stood at Heliopolis in Egypt, and was built by an unknown Pharaoh. It's hewn from red granite and may be over three thousand years old.'

'How did it end up here?' Lopez asked. 'I thought it was common practice to erase all memory of older religions when a new one comes along.'

'Often that is the case,' Mercati replied. 'However, the architecture of ancient Egypt was as mesmerizing to our Christian forbearers as it was to any other people, and so the obelisk was brought here by the engineer Domenico Fontana in 1586.'

Ethan saw that the mighty obelisk was capped with a feeble Crucifix, as though such a meagre icon placed almost as an afterthought could dominate the towering memory of Egypt's grandest civilization.

The Cardinal led them into the Basilica and through the massive marble halls that echoed with the voices of tourists, as though the ghost of centuries past still haunted the grand building. Not for the first time, Ethan reflected on how such tremendous grandeur had been achieved by the Catholic Church while much of the world labored in poverty through the Dark Ages, all the while preaching about how it was *"more blessed to give than to receive"*.

The archives were housed in a fortress–like wing of the Vatican behind St Peter's Basilica, and the avenue leading to the building was watched over by a phalanx of Swiss Guards in ceremonial uniform as well as officers from the city state's own police force, the Gendarmerie. Mercati spoke as he led them toward the archives.

'The oldest document we have here dates back to the 8th Century, while famous ones relate to the trials of the Knights Templar from 1308–1310. You'll find the contents fascinating.'

'How come they're called the Secret Archives?' Ethan asked.

'The name is a myth,' Mercati replied. 'The Latin name for the archives, secretum, simply means "private", as in to secrete something away. Our secretary to the prefecture of the archives ensure that nothing here is ever actually secret.'

'So there's no actual part of the archive that we cannot access,' Ethan pressed.

Mercati appeared somewhat annoyed as he replied.

'There is a section that is off–limits to all scholars,' he said. 'Nor do scholars have access to any papal papers from after 1939, which was the beginning of the reign of pontiff Pius XII and the start of World War Two.'

Ethan and Lopez exchanged a glance but said nothing as they walked.

'Why do you need access to the Secret Archives?' Mercati asked Ethan as they left the tourists behind and walked down a long corridor called the Porta di St Anna that led off from the Basilica toward the Secret Archives, adjacent to the Vatican Library.

'It's a long story,' Ethan explained, 'a real long story. We're here regarding the Tulli Papyrus.'

If Mercati was shocked or anxious about the request he didn't show it, merely walking along with the guards flanking them in silence.

'The papyrus,' Lopez went on, 'makes reference to sightings made by the Pharaoh Thutmose III around three and a half thousand years ago.'

Mercati nodded. 'I am familiar with the papyrus, but I'm afraid that I cannot help you. The papyrus was lost long ago and was never a part of the Vatican Archives.'

'That's not what we heard,' Lopez said. 'Several officials in the US Government came here hoping to view the papyrus, and were turned away.'

'I do not know of this,' Mercati said without looking at them. 'Documents archived after 1939 are not available to the public.'

'The Tulli Manuscript appeared in 1933,' Ethan corrected him.

'And 1939 is the year the Second World War began,' Lopez added. 'Why won't you let people view documents after that year, if the archive isn't so secret?'

Mercati didn't reply, but Ethan had heard of why the Vatican would not allow documents in its archive to be viewed from that year on.

'Hitler,' he said softly. 'The Vatican struck concords with the Nazis to prevent them taking over or bombing sites belonging to the Holy See.'

Ethan watched Mercati as he spoke, and although the cardinal did not reply immediately Ethan could see his face twist in something between regret and anger.

'Few knew at the time what Hitler would become,' he replied finally. 'The Reichskonkordat and other documented agreements between the Nazi regime are often quoted by those keen to discredit us, but the church also saved many lives during the conflict, Jews included.'

'We're not here to judge,' Lopez said amiably, 'although of course if there's nothing to hide then there's no need for the archives to be secret at all, right?'

Mercati looked at Lopez and gave a wry smile as the guards halted outside the doors to the Archives.

'As I said,' Mercati went on smoothly, apparently deciding to ignore Lopez's last statement, 'as the Tulli Papyrus was never here, I don't see how we can help you.'

'There is another artefact that we believe may be here in the Archives,' Ethan said. 'A tablet that precedes the famous Narmer Tablet, is associated with the Pharaoh Amenhotep and is inscribed with both ancient Sumerian cuneiform and Egyptian hieroglyphics.'

'I am sorry,' Mercati replied with an ingratiating smile, 'but our archives do not contain anything of that nature prior to around 1200 AD.'

'Just because something wasn't in your archive in 1200 AD doesn't mean you can't have obtained it since,' Lopez pointed out. 'The archives have a policy of publishing anything that is over seventy–five years old, correct?'

'That is our standard policy,' Mercati confirmed.

'One human lifetime,' Ethan mused, 'rather like governments. By the time something is released, any scandal or furor has been long forgotten except by historians.'

Mercati didn't respond as Lopez went on.

'We know that these archives are not actually secret at all,' she said. 'We're free to look at anything we want to, however the Vatican prohibits browsing to prevent the halls from being filled with hordes of tourists. So, if we knew precisely where the documents we want are we could locate and read them, no?'

Mercati smiled, somewhat smugly. 'That is correct, but there are no papyri or clay tablets here in the archives and it would take years to...'

'And what about the underground archives?' Ethan interrupted, 'in the basement?'

Mercati baulked a little, his eyes wobbling to look directly at Ethan. 'The archives are all as one.'

'The main archive is open to the public in principle,' Ethan pressed, 'but as you said there are sections which remain off–limits to the public. The Vatican uses its status as a country and a principality depending on what it wants to let people see, but we're here on behalf of the United States Government. I can come back here with armed soldiers and walk right in there, or we can do this the easy way? How about it, Cardinal?'

Mercati glared furiously at Ethan and Nicola, but Ethan could see that there was no way the cardinal could prevent them from entering any part of the archives they chose. The secrecy surrounding the archives was only as deep as the media allowed the people to think it was: in truth, neither the Pope nor his cardinals could truly prevent officials from entering the building.

'You have no *right!*' Mercati snapped.

Lopez took a pace closer to him. 'It's the Vatican that has no right,' she pointed out. 'Open up, or the cavalry will come down here and do it for you.'

Mercati scowled and jerked his head to one side, an irritable indication for one of the guards to access the archives. Ethan watched as the guard turned and pressed in a key code to an entry pad alongside the main doors, and with a hiss they opened and Ethan got his first glimpse of a vast hall filled with countless rows of shelves.

'You have ten minutes,' Mercati snapped. 'There is no browsing here, a rule that I can enforce and will do so.'

Lopez breezed past him with a bright smile. 'We'll be done in five.'

Ethan followed her into the archives and hurried to keep up. 'Are you kidding, we don't have a clue what we're looking for here. How the hell do you think we're going to find a five thousand year old tablet with such vague directions from Aisha?'

'Oh ye of little faith,' Lopez chimed airily as they walked. 'Follow me.'

Ethan felt a bemused smile creep onto his face as he followed Lopez down the long corridors, and then he noticed a small piece of paper she had fished from the pocket of her jeans.

'What's that?'

'GPS,' Lopez replied, 'courtesy of our friend Aisha.'

Ethan stared at the crude drawing on the piece of paper. 'You got her to draw where it was?'

'She couldn't tell precisely where it was,' Lopez replied, 'but she had a pretty good idea. All we've got to do is find it and get out of here before Mercati sends his Swiss Guards in to find us.'

*

Gregorie Petrov walked into the Basilica and turned right, following the di Porta Angelica toward the Library and the archives. Like all experienced agents he walked with a confident stride, ensuring that he looked like he knew where he was going and that he knew what he was doing. The more confident one appeared, the less one stood out.

He was almost at the archives when he saw the Cardinal walking toward him through a slowly closing security door, flanked by four Swiss Guards. It took only a moment for Gregorie to note the guards' sharp suits and concealed weapons to know that he would not be able to access the archives while they were present. Worse, there was no way for him to simply turn about and walk back the way he had come. Effectively cornered and with no possible explanation for the inevitable questions that would be asked of him, Gregorie fell back on his years' of training and reacted instinctively.

Gregorie reached beneath his jacket and whipped out a Makarov PB 9mm pistol that he fired in one smooth motion as it came to bear on the five men before him. Gregorie saw the looks of surprise on their faces, saw the guards' arms move for their own weapons even as the gunshots rang out.

The dedicated suppressor fitted to Gregorie's Makarov was not capable of totally silencing the weapon, but it effectively muzzled the worst of the report as Gregorie saw his first shot hit a Swiss guard in the chest. The guard tumbled backwards and blocked the door to the archives open. The second shot hit his companion high in the shoulder and spun him around. Gregorie fired two more shots as his aim swept from left to right, cutting the third guard down with a shot that plowed through his throat and sprayed bright arterial blood across the hall behind him.

Gregorie dropped down onto one knee as the fourth guard aimed at him and fired, an instinctive reaction to create a moving target at the last moment before the guard could draw aim. The bullet zipped over Gregorie's head with inches to spare as he fired his fourth shot, the round smacking into the guard's face and splitting his skull open with a crunch. The guard's weapon fell from his hand as he died instantly, the bullet tumbling through his brain and lodging somewhere in the back of his skull as he collapsed in a heap alongside the stunned Cardinal.

Gregorie wasted no time. He leaped forward and instantly fired three more shots at the men writhing on the ground, injured but not yet dead. Each shot buried a round deep in their brains as the Cardinal staggered backward from the carnage, folded over and vomited onto the polished marble floor.

Gregorie dropped his Makarov and picked up two of the Swiss Guards' 9mm Parabellum weapons, grabbed two spare cartridges from their belts and then turned to the Cardinal. They old man recovered from his retching and opened his mouth to scream for help.

Gregorie slammed one fist into the old man's belly and folded him up again, the cry for help reduced to a strained wheeze as the cardinal slumped to his knees, his arms wrapped around his belly. Gregorie took a pace forward and jammed the barrel of his pistol up against the old man's head.

'Where are they?'

The cardinal looked up at Gregorie with one strained eye, his body quivering from fear and pain. To Gregorie's surprise, a flare of defiance shone in the cardinal's eyes.

'Go to hell.'

Gregorie smiled. 'You first.'

The pistol's report was muffled further by the cardinal's skull as the round tore through his skull and exited the far side to bury itself in a wall. Gregorie glanced back down the corridor and figured he had perhaps a minute or two before somebody came to investigate the noises. Quickly, he grabbed each of the dead Swiss Guards' bodies by the legs and dragged them into the archives, and then finally the cardinal's corpse before he let the security door finally close behind him.

Sealed inside the archive with Warner and Lopez, Gregorie checked his pistol's ammunition and then stalked deeper into the archive in search of his prey.

***

XVII

'It's this way.'

Lopez led Ethan down a series of winding passages, each of them lined with towering shelves filled with folders, many of which were tagged with red labels or marked with Latin inscriptions in black ink.

'Damn, even if somebody did know what we were looking for we couldn't read these inscriptions,' Ethan said.

'The Vatican uses Latin to help conceal where things are,' Lopez confirmed. 'It's their way of saying that these vaults aren't secret, without actually letting anybody find anything. I've heard that the ATMs in Vatican City are also in Latin, so you can't even take cash out unless you know what you're doing.'

Ethan followed Lopez deeper into the vaults, the air cool due to the strict temperature controls and the lighting somehow dimmer back here than near the entrance. Ethan knew that the effect must somehow be psychological, for there were as many ceiling lights here as there were elsewhere in the archive, but none the less it felt somehow darker and more ancient.

Ethan recalled seeing movies where the Vatican's Archives were portrayed as a technological marvels of secrecy, with retinal scanning locks and temperature controlled rooms encased within impenetrable glass walls. The reality was somewhat less appealing.

A creaking, aged birdcage elevator connected the archive's floors, which contained countless millions of documents bound in parchment inventories. The archives had been open to carefully vetted researchers for more than a century, but with no way to identify where any one particular document was other than to ask and be led to it, there was no way to access any of the city state's darker secrets.

'There are about fifty–two miles of shelving down here,' Ethan said, noting the presence of 16th Century wooden cabinets lining the walls that contained priceless parchment letters sent by princes, potentates, heretics and heathens to the Holy See. Ethan knew that they held correspondence between the Vatican and some of the most prominent figures in history such as Erasmus, Charlemagne, Michelangelo, Queen Elizabeth I, Mozart, Voltaire and even Adolf Hitler.

'You can smell the age,' Lopez said as though reading his mind. 'Must be from the parchments and stuff.'

'Said the seasoned archeologist,' Ethan replied with a bemused smile.

Lopez rolled her eyes at him as she paused at an intersection, rows and rows of endless shelves filled with folders creating an immense maze from which Ethan could see no escape. He knew where the entrance was because by habit he kept a mental map of where they were going, but he knew that if he made a single mistake they would quickly become completely lost.

'Here's the elevator,' Lopez said as they reached it and she yanked open the creaking metal shutter doors. 'My guess is that it won't go into the basement.'

'Leave that to me,' Ethan said as they stepped inside.

Within moments they were travelling down to the archive's lowest floor. The elevator creaked to a halt, and Ethan eased to the side and peered downward. He pulled out his cell phone and illuminated the screen, using the glow to light up the lower wall of the elevator shaft. Instantly he could see that below them there was a cavity, perhaps to hold the mounts to the elevator shaft's floor, perhaps to descend another level.

Ethan got up and turned to the controls of the elevator. The fairly modern panel had been installed long after the elevator itself, updated and wired into the older system that he was sure was behind the panel. Ethan reached beneath his jacket and produced a small leather pouch that he opened to reveal a set of lock–picks and other small tools.

Lopez kept watch as Ethan opened the panel and examined the wiring behind it. Sure enough, there was a pressure pad beneath the other buttons that was not connected. Ethan yanked a wire from one of the pads used to select the archive's floors, and crudely attached it to the previously unconnected pad and gave the button a press.

With a rattle the elevator groaned into motion again and began to descend toward the basement. Ethan turned his head to look at Lopez with an expectant smile.

'Not bad,' Lopez smiled back. 'What's the chances that Mercati and his people will know what we've done via some alarm or something?'

The elevator stopped and Ethan looked out into a darker, dingier passageway that led into the distance between towering walls of shelves filled with archives.

'We'll have to hurry,' he said as they opened the elevator doors and stepped out. 'You sure you know where we're going?'

'Down here,' Lopez said as she led him off down another passage between the folder–filled cliffs. 'Should be at the end, just to the left.'

Ethan glanced at his watch. 'Five minutes. We're not going to have long to sort this and you said you'd be done by now.'

'I said that just to annoy Mercati. It was either that or shoot him in the head.'

Ethan was about to reply when he heard something in the distance that sent the hairs on the backs of his arms bristling. Four bursts, like a distant car engine misfiring. Ethan froze where he was, eyes closed as he listened for any further sound as Lopez walked off ahead of him, consumed in her search.

A silence pervaded the archive and then Ethan heard three further similar distant sounds. A few seconds later he heard an eighth and then silence.

Ethan was not by nature a paranoid kind of guy, but his time in service with the Marines in Iraq and Afghanistan followed by six years in the intelligence services had left him with a deep suspicion of anybody who wasn't paranoid in this game. Eight rounds was what he heard, and although it could just as easily have been somebody closing windows somewhere else in the archive Ethan had learned to trust his instincts above everything else. Instinct was the only thing that served only you and never failed to alert you to danger.

Ethan opened his eyes and hurried in pursuit of Lopez. 'Make it fast, I think we're already out of time.'

'Mercati's here already?' Lopez asked as she glanced behind them in confusion.

'Eight rounds, coming from the entrance area.'

Lopez didn't argue, didn't question Ethan's suspicions. After so many years of working together, whether he was right or wrong she knew that he wouldn't have said a word about the noises unless he was genuinely concerned. Lopez quickened her pace as she reached the end of the row of shelves and turned left.

The rear wall of the archive stretched away to either side of them, Lopez walking slowly to one particular row and peering at it and the drawing she held in her hand. Ethan joined her and looked at the hundreds of vertically racked folders before them.

'It's here somewhere in this row of shelves,' Lopez said.

'Great, at least there's only a few hundred to check.'

Lopez offered him a dirty look. 'Aisha did what she could and got us this far.'

Ethan shook his head and wracked his brains for some way in which they could narrow down the search, but with all of the folders marked with Latin inscriptions and literally hundreds of them to rummage through, even if he deliberately emptied their contents on the floor at his feet one after the other it would take hours to go through them all and…

Ethan's train of thought slammed to a halt as he thought for a moment.

'I know that look,' Lopez said. 'You get it once in a while when you have an idea.'

Ethan looked across the shelves.

'Hellerman said that these tablets would be made of clay, right?'

'Yeah, so what?'

'Clay is heavy,' Ethan replied. 'Most of the records in these boxes are likely parchment and paper, even papyrus like the Tulli Manuscript.'

Lopez didn't need any further prompting. Ethan hurried to one end of the shelves as Lopez dashed to the other, and one by one they began working their way back toward each other. Ethan used a finger to lift the boxes one after the other, testing the weight as he made his way slowly to the left. Lopez performed the same actions far to his left, moving quickly but methodically toward him until he heard a soft thump as Lopez tested a container.

'Here,' she whispered urgently.

Ethan marked his position by pulling one of the containers out slightly and then hurried to Lopez's side as she lifted one of the containers from the shelves and set it on the floor. Ethan watched as she opened it, lifting the lid to reveal a layer of thin paper wrapped around something.

Carefully, Lopez unwrapped the paper to reveal a clay tablet no larger than a hardback book, engraved with the tightly packed cuneiform script that they had seen in the images that Hellerman had showed them.

'We don't know what it says,' Lopez pointed out. 'This could be somebody's three–thousand–year old shopping list for all we know.'

'We don't have much choice,' Ethan said as Lopez hurried back to the shelves and kept searching. 'You check the rest and then let's get out of here.'

Lopez hurried through the rest of the pieces on the shelves as Ethan carefully photographed the front of the tablet.

Lopez reached his side and noted that there had not been a single other clay tablet on any of the shelves this far back in the archive. Although Ethan could not speak a single word of Latin, he figured that whatever was written by the Vatican's archivists on the outside of the tablets container had nothing to do with ancient Sumer.

'Done,' Lopez said. 'Let's move.'

'Wait,' Ethan said. 'I've got an idea.'

Lopez watched for a moment as Ethan grabbed another box from the shelves, and then they turned and began to walk back toward the entrance of the archives. They were half way there when they heard a distant, horrified scream that drifted down through the elevator shaft toward them.

Although Ethan could tell that it was a woman's voice and that it came from the archive entrance on the floor above them. The memory of the gunshots he had heard echoed vividly through his mind, as did the knowledge that somewhere outside the building people would be scrambling for telephones as Swiss Guards rushed to the scene.

'We're not armed,' Lopez whispered as they both froze in position deep inside the archive.

Ethan nodded but his mind was already racing. Whoever was inside the archive with them was also aware that their presence had been discovered, and they would now hunt Ethan and Nicola with extreme prejudice.

'There's no way out of here but the elevator,' Lopez added. 'They don't fit secret archives with multiple exits.'

Ethan listened in silence, waiting to hear the man he felt sure was closing in on their position give his position away. It was only a few moments before he heard soft foot falls just meters away to their right. Ethan pointed Lopez to move to one side and then he stepped out toward the entrance again.

'Don't move.'

The voice was Russian accented, quite deep and coming from Ethan's right. He froze and turned to look directly into the uncompromising gaze of a tall, bulky man in a tailored suit, a 9mm pistol pointing straight at him.

A sudden commotion of voices rang out from the archive entrance somewhere far above them, the deep voices of Swiss Guards bellowing to one another. Ethan remained still as he turned to face the man, who looked at the container tucked under Ethan's arm.

'Slide it to me,' he growled.

Ethan crouched down slightly as he lowered the container to the floor and then kicked it toward the Russian. The box slid most of the way there and came to rest alongside one of the shelves.

The Russian carefully approached the container, never taking his eyes off Ethan's as he crouched down alongside the box and lifted the lid from it. With one hand he brushed aside the wrapping paper to reveal nothing but an empty box.

The shelf beside the Russian suddenly burst outward as a dozen containers tumbled off the top shelves and plunged down onto him. The gunman staggered to one side as Lopez shoved the material down onto him and Ethan leaped out of sight.

Ethan sprinted down a corridor past the Russian and joined Lopez as she rushed into view and they fled toward the elevator. They were half way there when they heard the voices of men pouring into the archive, shouts and warnings that echoed through the miles of shelves.

'The Swiss Guard are inside,' Lopez hissed as they slid to a halt and concealed themselves behind a row of large cabinets. 'If they find us down here, we're done.'

Ethan searched for any sign of the gunman they knew to be inside the archives with them, but he could see no sign of the Russian.

'Ivan's in the same boat,' Ethan whispered.

'We could make it to the elevator, cut around behind them,' Lopez suggested.

'No,' Ethan shook his head. 'They'll have posted a guard on the elevator to prevent that. We need another way out of here.'

'There is no other way out but the elevator!'

Ethan looked at the walls of the archives and searched their aged surfaces, and then he smiled to himself and headed off down the corridor once more, away from the advancing Gendarmerie.

'Follow me.'

Ethan hurried along to the back wall of the archive with Lopez close behind, and turned to where the broad main wall of the archive spread out to the left and the right, rows of ceiling lights tracing a line to the distance.

'There's nothing but a wall, and shelves,' Lopez uttered. 'How the hell are we going to get out of here?'

'Help me with this,' Ethan said.

Lopez moved to assist him even as they heard the Gendarmerie guards calling out.

'They're here!'

'Quickly!' Ethan snapped.

***

THE GENESIS CYPHER   Dean Crawford

XVIII

Sergeant Marco Rossi of the Vatican's Gendarmerie hurried along with his pistol drawn and held before him in a double handed grip, his eyes scanning the corridors and shelves of the archives as his men spread out around him.

'A male and a female, both American,' he said into his microphone in a hushed whisper. 'They were the last people to be signed into the archive. They're armed and dangerous.'

His radio crackled as a subordinate replied from somewhere else in the archive basement. Rossi knew that his men were spreading a wide net from left to right across the basement and then advancing forward. He checked right and left and saw his men lining up. With a jerk of his head, Rossi ordered them forward and they began to advance as one, each covering an aisle of their own.

Rossi did not know how the two Americans figured out how to get into the archive basement and he didn't care. All that mattered were the prefecture dead upstairs, surrounded by the bodies of his escort. Rossi had no idea what kind of international uproar would be caused by the brutal homicides or what had driven the two Americans to commit murder on such a scale, but he had a pretty good idea of what would happen if he didn't capture them and bring them to justice real fast.

'Keep your eyes open, they could be anywhere down here,' he whispered.

The basement archive was accessible only using the elevator, upon which he had stationed no–less than three men to prevent their quarry from slipping by and escaping topside. With no other exits, Rossi knew that this would end either in two arrests or a bloodbath to match the gruesome crime scene at the archive entrance.

'South aisle clear,' came a report into his earpiece.

'Cut north,' Rossi ordered. 'Close the net down.'

His men had reached the eastern wall of the archive basement, and now they were turning north as the rest of Rossi's team swept east toward them from the elevator. The number of places the Americans could hide was diminishing swiftly, and it would be only moments now before gunfire was exchanged. Rossi did not believe in his heart of hearts that the two killers would surrender. They would fight to the death and…

'East wall is clear.'

Rossi frowned, acknowledged the call, and closed in on the north wall. He saw other members of his team moving alongside him in other aisles, closing in on his position as he advanced, and then all at once they emerged into the aisle running along the basement's north wall.

Rossi looked left and right and lowered his pistol.

'What the hell? This is impossible. Where did they go?'

One of his officers looked back toward the west wall. 'Maybe they got behind us?'

Rossi turned and looked behind them as he keyed his microphone.

'Pierre, Alan, do you see anything?'

The radio hissed in static, no answer from his companions.

Rossi broke into a run and sprinted back across the basement even as he heard the elevator's mechanical engine clatter into life and climb away. He burst out of the main aisle and saw three bodies sprawled on the floor in the aisle, eyes staring lifelessly at the ceiling, blood spilling from massive wounds in their necks in which were buried steel throwing stars.

'No!'

Rossi dashed to the elevator's doors and peered up into the darkness to see the elevator climbing sedately away from them. He keyed his radio and shouted a warning to those above.

'They're coming up! The Americans are in the elevator!'

*

The Gendarmerie soldiers poured into the archive, twenty men streaming past the detectives already examining the bodies of the dead guards and their prefect as they rushed to the elevator.

The men, all dressed in black camo fatigues and cradling assault rifles, swarmed into strategic positions across the archive, crouching behind shelves and desks as they aimed their weapons at the elevator gates and waited. The sound of weapons being cocked in readiness echoed briefly across the archives and then there was nothing but the sound of the elevator's antiquated mechanism hauling the elevator up from the basement.

The troops aimed more carefully, thin streams of red laser–light catching on dust motes swirling silently in the air as the elevator reached the entrance level and the gates rattled open.

Twenty or more men flinched as they prepared to open fire, and then one of them stared at the elevator in shock for a moment before he spoke into his microphone.

'The elevator is empty. Repeat, the elevator is empty.'

He stared for a moment longer at the empty elevator car and wondered what the hell was going on.

*

'The elevator car is empty.'

Rossi stared blankly into space, unable to believe his ears. He stared at his men, all of whom had accompanied him down the central aisle having swept the entire basement. Nobody had been seen and yet three of his men were dead and the elevator had been sent up by somebody. He tried to ignore the superstitious chill rippling up his spine.

'Why would they kill the guards and then not use the elevator?' he asked out loud.

The answer snapped to his attention even before his men could suggest a reason.

Distraction.

'They're still here somewhere,' he said finally.

'But where?' one of his men asked helplessly. 'We searched everywhere. Two people couldn't have slipped past us.'

Then from somewhere at the back of the archives Rossi heard a faint noise, a scraping sound as though a box were being dragged across the floor. The troops raised their weapons and whirled toward the noise as Rossi rushed past them in pursuit.

*

'Y'know, most times I think you're a dork but then every now and again you really impress me.'

Lopez's voice followed Ethan in the pitch darkness as they hurried up a flight of narrow stone steps, and he smiled to himself before he replied.

'The Vatican was built centuries ago,' he said. 'They didn't have much in the way of elevators back then, so I figured there had to be a stairwell somewhere that led down to the basement. I just looked for plaster work that might conceal a doorway.'

'Damned lucky we could heave that shelving out of the way and get through the door in time,' Lopez replied. 'How long do you think before they figure it out?'

'Not long,' Ethan said as he fumbled his way through the darkness in the narrow, medieval stairwell. 'Chances are this will bring us out alongside the Cortil de Belvedere, and if we're lucky we can get across the car park there and back to St Peter's Square before the Gendarmerie can follow suit. With a bit of luck they'll capture the Russian down there too.'

Ethan reached the top of the steps and a large, heavy locked door. Beside him Lopez pulled out her cell phone and flipped it open. The glowing screen illuminated a wide, old fashioned iron lock. Ethan crouched down and peered through it to see an ornate corridor, with windows overlooking a courtyard beyond.

Ethan once again pulled out the small bag of lock–picks and began working the door in front of them. He was in the process of unlocking it when they both heard the sound of something scraping the floor at the bottom of the darkened stairwell far below them.

'They're coming through,' Lopez whispered softly as she shut off the light from her cell to avoid giving away their presence. 'Any time now please, Bond.'

Ethan focused on the lock, feeling his way with his eyes closed even as he heard footsteps rushing up the stairwell toward them. The sound of a man's heavy breathing was behind it, moving fast, pursuing. Ethan felt the picks catch on the lock inside the old door and then it clicked loudly.

Ethan twisted the picks and then pushed on the door and it creaked open even as the footsteps rushed up the last few steps and he caught a glimpse in the light of the burly Russian, his cold blue eyes fixed upon them as he pointed with one hand at Ethan. Ethan yanked his picks out and barged through the doorway even as he heard the whisper of a throwing star that flashed past behind his head and smacked deep into the wall where he had been standing.

Lopez stumbled through behind him as Ethan turned and slammed the door shut, then cranked the handle and tried to lock the door once more with the picks as Lopez looked up and down the corridor and saw nobody.

'We won't have long before they close the whole place down,' she said breathlessly as the Russian tried the door handle on the other side.

Ethan tried to lock the door but he couldn't force the pins back into place. Instead he stepped back and drove the sole of his boot against the picks, ramming them into the lock and jamming them in place.

'That won't hold him for long,' Lopez said.

'Long enough,' Ethan shot back. 'Let's get out of here.'

*

Rossi dashed to where they had heard the scraping sound in the basement, but he and his men came up short as they looked up and down the east wall and saw nothing but empty aisles.

'What the hell is going on here?' he uttered out loud.

He was about to start cursing when his eyes were drawn to a semi–circular scratch on the floor nearby. His men saw it a moment later, along with the shelving that was out of place, poking further out into the corridor than the others around it.

'What's this?'

Rossi moved across to the marks on the floor and crouched down, then looked up at the shelving unit.

'Get this out of the way!' he snapped.

His men dashed forward and heaved the shelves back to reveal a wooden doorway concealed behind them. Rossi saw that the locks had been forced on the door, which must have been hundreds of years old, and that the shelves had then been pulled back into place as far as possible before the door was once again closed.

Rossi turned back to face west, where the elevator gates were.

'They're cornered here, they get past us, then kill the guards only to come back here again?'

Rossi's second in command shook his head.

'They're insane,' he uttered.

'Where does this lead?' Rossi demanded.

'We're under the archive and the Cortil de Belvedere. If they get up there they could make it back to St Peter's Square and out of the city.'

Rossi wasted no more time. He grabbed his microphone and spoke into it quickly.

'Alert all guards and local police, the Americans are out of the archives and will attempt to escape the city. Shut down all exits immediately!'

***

XIX

Ethan hurried with Lopez out of the archives and along the di Porta Angelica, heading for the Basilica. He forced himself not to look behind as they walked as fast as they could without appearing suspicious, the ceremonial Swiss Guards paying them little attention as they passed by and entered the Basilica. Two tourists, both with backpacks slung over their shoulders, mixed easily with the countless others around them.

The vast marble halls inside were filled with a venerable silence punctuated only by the soft echoing whispers of tourists and the occasional hushed voice of a translator or guide pointing out major artefacts. Ethan led the way, taking a chance and looking behind him.

Beyond the crowds he saw the Russian's powerful form loom as he entered the building a hundred yards behind, looking around briefly before he spotted them and struck out across the Basilica.

'He's out,' Ethan reported as they walked. 'Probably brute force.'

'You want to split up?'

Ethan shook his head. 'Not in a city we don't know well. We're going to have to move fast before the Gendarmerie shut the exits.'

Ethan led the way out onto St Peter's Square, the vast open plaza now filled with crowds of tourists milling in their thousands. They hurried down toward the Via Della Conciliazione where Ethan could see the traffic splitting either side of the piazza.

'He'll follow us there,' Lopez said. 'He'll assume we'll make for a vehicle.'

'I'm counting on it,' Ethan replied. 'Come on.'

'We should disguise ourselves,' Lopez argued, 'he could lose us in this crowd.'

Ethan looked back and saw Gregorie already jogging down the oval steps in front of the Basilica.

'Too late for that,' Ethan replied. 'Move, now!'

Lopez increased her pace as they crossed to the far side of the square and reached the Via Della Conciliazione, rows of low fences patrolled by armed Gendarmerie, bright blue police vehicles parked nearby.

'We could use their help,' Lopez said.

Ethan knew that if they went to the police to deny the Russian his prize, the police would question them and the evidence on their cell phones would reveal their presence in a secret section of the Vatican archives along with several dead bodies. If their Russian pursuer saw the commotion of a police presence he might choose to slip away quietly, leaving Ethan and Lopez to face the music.

'We can't chance the exposure and the Gendarmerie might not know anything about the Russian being in the archives,' Ethan replied. 'We've got to do this on our own.'

Ethan led the way to the exits and with Lopez they filed patiently through and out of the piazza. Ethan checked behind him again and saw that the Russian was now closer behind them but also obliged to join the exit queue to avoid drawing unwanted attention from the police.

Ethan turned back to the exit and filed out, the queue moving agonizingly slowly. Two policemen were standing idly beside the exit with their hands clasped before them, eyes hidden behind designer sunglasses and watching the tourists as they left the Vatican.

'They must know we're out,' Lopez said.

Ethan nodded but did not reply as he waited for the Italian Police to get the call that would shut the Vatican down. There was no way they could vault the fences surrounding the square in plain view of so many police.

The tourists ahead of them slowed, asking for selfies with the police. Ethan gritted his teeth but said nothing as a pair German holidaymakers posed with the officers, rare smiles on their faces and thumbs jabbed up at the camera as an elderly woman snapped shots of them.

Ethan slid past the German tourists and strode out of the square with Lopez alongside him, the police engrossed in their picture taking. Even as he passed by he heard the officers' radios crackle and an urgent sounding voice speaking quickly in Italian. He heard among the jabbering one word that he recognized. *Americano*.

As the police looked up in shock at the tourists filing past the exit Ethan turned to Lopez.

'Ou allons–nous aller maintenant?'

Lopez replied smoothly to his French, loudly enough to be heard by the police alongside them.

'Allons à l'restauraunt, s'il vouz plait.'

The eyes of the police passed over them and Ethan saw the officers move and stop a pair of Amercians just behind them in the queue. Ethan kept walking with Lopez, headed toward the nearest alley he could see that would take them out of the line of sight of any law enforcement or street cameras around the Vatican.

The police officers suddenly began shouting at the crowds as the metal gates to the square were hauled shut, the officers jabbering into their radios as tourists began complaining and asking questions.

Ethan led the way across the street and directly away from the Vatican. Lopez hurried alongside him and as soon as they were alongside the Libreria Ancora and out of sight of the Russian and the police Ethan ducked right into a side street. He looked over his shoulder at the last moment to see the big Russian staring at him from the queue.

The police officers began vetting the tourists leaving the Vatican, the crowd slowed but not stopped as they began looking for two Americans.

'He'll get through,' Ethan said. 'The Italians are looking for us, not Russians. Let's go!'

They broke into a run onto the Borgo Santo Spiritio and headed down it. Lopez caught him easily as they sprinted down the street, ignoring the surprised looks on the faces of tourists strolling casually in the warm air.

'Where to?' Lopez asked as they ran.

Ethan hit another junction in the cobbled streets and then he saw what he was looking for.

'Oh, not again,' Lopez uttered.

A pair of Italian scooters were parked against the sidewalk, neither of them chained or locked in any way. Ethan leaped onto one of them and quickly used a small key from his DIA pack to free the steering lock before he started the engine. Lopez mimicked his actions nearby, and both of the scooters rattled into life as Ethan turned and pulled away, heading south for the river.

He heard a commotion to his left and saw the Russian running toward them in full sprint as he pulled a pistol from beneath his jacket and aimed at Ethan as the scooters accelerated. Tourists screamed as they saw the gun, the Russian not much more than ten meters from Ethan's scooter.

Ethan had no time to think, only briefly calculating that even at a full sprint the range was close enough that the Russian would be unlikely to miss. As Lopez soared away south, Ethan turned the scooter and wound the throttle fully open as he aimed directly at the Russian's madly sprinting form.

The gunman's eyes widened visibly in surprise at Ethan's unexpected move, and running at full tilt he had little chance of avoiding the scooter now rushing toward him at full throttle. Ethan saw the gunman's aim shift slightly to try to shoot Ethan in the head or upper body and then it was too late and the scooter was upon him.

The Russian hurled himself to one side to avoid the scooter, and Ethan threw himself off the saddle and slammed into the gunman with enough force to throw the man down onto his back on the cobbles with a deep thud.

The impact stunned the gunman as Ethan crashed down on top of him, one hand reaching to push the man's weapon down against the hard stone as he saw the Russian's eyes briefly lose focus with the impact and the pistol skittered away across the stones. Ethan jerked his head back and then slammed his forehead down into the Russian's face, bone smacking against bone as the blow impacted the gunman above his right eye.

The Russian's head crashed again into the unforgiving cobblestones but he heaved one leg up and forced Ethan to roll aside as a blade flickered in the sunlight. Ethan quickened his escape as the thick steel weapon clashed against the stones alongside him and he scrambled to his feet, the Russian's clumsy blow just missing Ethan's flank.

The Russian sprang into a crouch and glared up at Ethan as he recovered from the attack. Probably ten years younger and ten pounds heavier than Ethan, he had former Spetsnaz written all over him. Ethan could see muscle barely contained by the man's suit as he prepared to launch himself into a fresh attack, and Ethan turned for the dropped pistol and hurled himself toward it.

The Russian dove for the weapon and rolled over it, beating Ethan by inches as he came up and turned, aiming the pistol directly between Ethan's eyes from scant inches away. Ethan froze, knowing that there could be no escape, and then he heard the sirens.

The Russian glanced to one side briefly as the sound of police vehicles rushed toward them, sirens wailing as concerned members of the public huddled inside cafes and doorways and pointed at them.

'The tablet,' the Russian growled in accented English.

Ethan glared at the gunman, who aimed more closely at his forehead. Ethan reluctantly shrugged his backpack from his shoulders and retrieved the densely packaged tablet and held it out. The Russian retracted his pistol slightly out of Ethan's reach before he snatched the tablet away and tucked it under his jacket, feeling this time the weight inside the box.

'And the camera,' the Russian added.

Ethan's shoulders sank and he pulled the camera from his jacket pocket and handed it over.

'Another time, Ivan,' Ethan said bitterly.

The Russian scowled and put his weapon away. 'Your time is done, Warner.'

Before Ethan could ask the Russian how he knew his name, the gunman whirled and dashed away down a side street. Ethan watched him go as a scooter rushed up to his side and Lopez waved at him to hurry.

'Get on!'

Ethan leaped onto the back seat and the scooter accelerated away, Lopez pushing hard as they exited the street onto the Ponto Vittorio Emanuele bridge across the River Tiber. Ethan checked behind them to see if the police vehicles were following, but he could see nothing and assumed that the police had stopped to question witnesses.

'They'll be onto the scooter quickly,' Ethan said above the warm wind rushing by them. 'We need to lose it.'

'We'll dump it in a side street,' Lopez promised. 'Who was that guy?'

'I don't know,' Ethan replied. 'He was Russian, but he knew my name.'

'Your infamy precedes you,' she chortled back. 'Luckily for us, my ingenuity doesn't.'

Ethan saw her tap her jacket, wherein was tucked the tablet they had stolen from Vatican City, minus the packaging. The stacks of papers and a hefty tourist guide to the Vatican that Ethan had stashed in the package he'd handed to the Russian would be sure to disappoint when he opened it up.

'They got the camera,' Ethan said.

'Nothing we can do about that,' Lopez called back as she accelerated the moped down a narrow side street. 'It looks like the unit Nellis warned us about is already on the same trail as we are.'

'Let's get back to the safe house and see if Hellerman can figure out what's on this thing,' Ethan said. 'If there are Russians here in Rome already willing to kill for it, we need to stay one step ahead of them or this is all going to be over real fast.'

***

XX

Ethan sat down at a small glass table in a hotel room in Rome, the setting sun streaming through the open balcony and glowing through the apartment. Upon the table was a laptop that he and Lopez had brought with them from Washington. Equipped with very high-technology security software and equally powerful satellite live-streaming, the laptop could connect directly to the DIA Headquarters via military communications satellites rather than the conventional Internet.

It took only moments to establish a video link with Hellerman inside the ARIES facility, the uber-geek already quivering with excitement and putting his lunch down as Ethan de-briefed him.

'You got into the Secret Archives?' Hellerman gasped, his face so close to the camera Ethan thought his head might pop through the laptop's screen. 'And into the secret bit of the Secret Archives they don't tell people about?'

'Yeah, we got in and we got out again,' Ethan replied. 'Unfortunately, we weren't the only people in there looking for the tablet.'

'Who else was there?'

'A Russian agent,' Lopez replied from behind Ethan. 'Highly trained, although he seemed to be working alone.'

'For now,' Ethan added. 'They're on our trail so he's bound to call in support, and he knew my name.'

Hellerman nodded thoughtfully. 'If the Russians are onto the same trail it could be something to do with your work of a couple of years ago in Peru. I'll have them checked out. You got a description?'

Ethan listed everything he could remember about the Russian agent, Hellerman noting it all down before updating them.

'We managed to identify an individual who we believe may be the go-between for Russian traffickers working in Syria,' he said. 'This guy is called Muhammar Hussein and he's working out of Beirut, Lebanon.'

Ethan looked at the image of a greasy, overweight man wearing garish jewellery and an expensive suit.

'He looks the part,' Lopez said in disgust. 'You think you can set up a meet?'

'Already on it,' Hellerman confirmed. 'Beirut's your next stop and I'll fill you in on the details once we've got our agents to contact Hussein's people.' Hellerman began virtually salivating again as he looked expectantly at Ethan.

'The tablet?'

Ethan shifted to one side as Lopez carefully held the tablet out for Hellerman to see, her hands protected by latex gloves. The scientist gasped, one hand over his mouth as he stared at the artefact as though he were looking into the eyes of God.

'Do you have any idea how old that is?' he asked rhetorically.

'If any of the previous investigations we've done are anything to go by, probably several thousand years,' Ethan replied. 'But right now we're not interested in how old it is. We need to know what's written on it and why the Vatican would hide it so deep in their archives?'

Hellerman used his computer to record an image of both sides of the tablet before he scrutinized them in great detail, his brow furrowed and his chin resting on his balled fists as he read the text. His lips mumbled a near–silent stream of inaudible words.

Lopez leaned in alongside Ethan's shoulder.

'In English, Jo.'

'Sorry,' Hellerman roused himself. 'This is fascinating, although the cuneiform being used on the reverse side is of an archaic form.'

'There's any other kind?' Ethan asked.

Hellerman looked as though he was about to launch into an extensive oratory on the ancient history of the Sumerian peoples when he saw the impatient look on Ethan's face.

'Russian agents are looking for us,' Lopez reminded him. 'They have guns and other nasty stuff, y'know?'

'Right, of course,' Hellerman said. 'Okay, so this tablet is at least five thousand years old and commemorates the founding of the city of Nippur in ancient Babylon, which is now Iraq. The fertile crescent, as the area is known to archeologists, was where civilization first emerged as far as we know. What's special about this tablet is that the inscriptions prove that it predates most of the others found at Nippur by almost a thousand years, and what it says is even more important.'

Hellerman lifted his finger as he read from his computer screen, tracing a line from his perspective of right to left as he spoke.

'It describes the Great Flood,' he said finally. 'It describes the judgement of the gods upon mankind, and the survival of an ark.'

Ethan blinked. 'That's from the Bible, isn't it?'

'No, actually,' Hellerman replied. 'The entirety of the Bible's legends are all taken from much older religions, of which there were many. You'll recall from previous investigations that it was Buddha who fed the five thousand with nothing more than what he held in his hands, thousands of years before Christianity was conceived. The Hindu god Vishnu was part of a triune religion with Shiva and Krishna, just like the Father, Son and Holy Ghost. Krishna was born on December 25th of a virgin in a stable and was the subject of an infanticide assassination plot by an evil king. He predicted that he would die to attone for the sins of humanity and was promptly killed and resurrected, and all of it long before Christianity.'

'And the flood myth has the same origin?' Lopez assumed.

'It's identical and shared by most ancient mythologies,' Hellerman confirmed. 'The Dravidian king Manu in the Matsya Purana and the Utnapishtim episode in the Epic of Gilgamesh both describe an ancient flood that wiped out mankind but for a chosen few. The ancient Greeks have two similar myths from a later date; The Deucalion and Zeus's flooding of the world in Book I of Ovid's Metamorphoses. The flood also shows up in Bergelmir in Norse Mythology, in the lore of the K'iche' and Maya peoples in Mesoamerica, the Lac Courte Oreilles Ojibwa tribe of Native Americans in North America, the Muisca people and the Canari Confederation in South America. Virtually every ancient society records a sort of genesis story ending in a global flood that matches the Sumerian original, so there's nothing in either of the Bible's Testaments that is true or even original. However, I've never encountered a record quite this old that may actually be the origin of the entire myth.'

'What does the tablet actually say?' Lopez asked.

Hellerman squinted at the images of the tablet and spoke slowly as he once again traced the path of the carvings in the ancient clay.

'There are some lines missing due to damage, but the text picks up as: the gods An, Enlil, Enki and Ninhursanga created the black–headed people and comfortable conditions for the animals to live and procreate. Their kingship descends from heaven and the first cities are founded: Eridu, Bad–tibira, Larak, Sippar, and Shuruppak.'

Hellerman paused as he read.

'The next bit is missing from other Sumerian tablets and some Akkadian versions: The gods decide not to save mankind from an impending flood. Zi–ud–sura, the king and *gudug* priest, learns of this. Ea, or Enki in Sumerian, the god of the waters, warns the hero, Atra–hasis, of the impending disaster and gives him instructions for the ark.'

Hellerman traced downward slowly, speaking but his gaze lost as though he had returned to distant times himself.

'A terrible storm rocks the huge boat for seven days and seven nights, then the sun god Utu appears and Zi–ud–sura creates an opening in the boat, prostrates himself, and sacrifices oxen and sheep. The flood ends, the animals disembark and Zi–ud–sura prostrates himself before the sky god An and the chief of all gods, Enlil, who give him eternal life and take him to dwell in Dilmun for preserving the animals and the seed of mankind.'

Ethan leaned back and frowned. 'So what's the big deal? There's nothing written on that tablet that's worth killing over, or for the Vatican to bury the artefact in their archives.'

'Isn't there?' Hellerman asked. 'It's just these sorts of evidences that have eroded the power of the church across the globe, year on year, decade upon decade. The Vatican itself is seen now as more out of touch with humanity than it has ever been, and sciences like archeology have long proven that the Bible is not an historical record but a work of fiction. This would be just another nail in the coffin of all religions.'

Lopez shook her head.

'There must be something else,' she said. 'I can't believe that Russia would have gone to such lengths to get hold of this just to sink the Catholic Church. And why would they also go after it now, just as we're looking for it?'

Ethan thought back to their investigation in Peru, where they had come to realize the extraordinary correlation between the worship of supposed sun gods around the world. Long thought to be an extension of ancient man's dependence and worship of the sun in the sky, an entirely new hypothesis had emerged that in fact the gods they had worshipped were in fact beings of light, or beings who emerged from conditions of brilliant light. Even the relatively recent Biblical depictions of saints with halos of light were themselves borrowed from older images of holy men with the sun encircling their heads, which in turn were evolved from images of pure sun worship.

'We were once told by an expert that the supposed fallen angel Lucifer was in fact not the bad guy in history,' Ethan said, an idea forming in his mind. 'That the Bible had again twisted the truths in an older tale or myth of some kind.'

'True,' Hellerman said cautiously. 'The word Lucifer in the original Hebrew actually means "light" or person of light. The modern appearance of the Biblical Satan, or Lucifer, is actually all borrowed from older pagan traditions and amalgamated by early Christians to demonize the older legends. Lucifer's trident actually belonged to the Roman God Neptune, and Satan's goat–like appearance was due to the Romans' worship of the goat as a sign of natural happiness, of the return of spring as goats frolicked in fields, and a source of food in its meat and milk. The Christians just took all the things the hated Romans worshipped and turned them on their heads.'

'Where are you going with this?' Lopez asked Ethan.

Ethan thought for a moment, not sure of his direction but letting his instincts do the talking.

'Beings of light,' he echoed. 'When we were last in Egypt, and remember that it's Egyptian hieroglyphics that got us into this, we were told that Akhenaten, one of the pharaohs, abolished all of the old religions during his reign and began worshipping only the sun instead.'

Hellerman nodded, warming to the theme. 'And Akhenaten was an unusual pharaoh to say the least, and not just in his thinking. His physical features were abnormal, his skull elongated considerably more than was natural.'

'How much do we know about this Sumerian god, An?' Ethan asked.

'He was supposedly a Sumerian God of all Gods, the father of all Gods, who brought creation to the earth and who wielded the ilu sebattu, the Seven Gods of destruction who were used to destroy mankind.'

Ethan considered that for a moment. 'Kind of like the Four Horsemen?'

Hellerman shrugged. 'I guess. The sebattu were considered the most notorious and dangerous of all the Sumerian gods' weapons. You think that maybe that's what's got so many people interested in recovering this tablet?'

'I doubt it,' Ethan replied. 'If there was some kind of super weapon behind all of this there would have been wars across the Middle East for it and…'

Ethan broke off mid–sentence as he looked at Lopez.

'There have been wars across the Middle East,' she pointed out. 'For thousands of years.'

'For money,' Ethan agreed, 'for power, for oil, but never something like this. What the hell might combine the flood myth with a weapon of great destruction? If there was anything in the idea scientists would have found evidence of it by now. This must be about something else and these sun gods might be at the heart of it. Is there anything else on the tablet?'

Hellerman read across the final lines of cuneiform script on the rear of the tablet as Lopez turned it over in her hands.

'Mankind is saved, blah blah blah, prosperity grows and mankind thrives, there are great wars across the Middle…'

Hellerman broke off as he read, his eyes flicking from right to left as his jaw opened and he leaned back in his seat. 'Now that's interesting.'

'What?' Lopez asked.

Hellerman read for a moment longer and then spoke softly.

'Then shall the prophecies be fulfilled, and shall the Watchers once more come.'

'The Watchers? Who are they?'

'The lords of An,' Hellerman replied. 'The Annunaki, the supposed extra–terrestrial fathers of Sumerian culture.'

***

THE GENESIS CYPHER   Dean Crawford

XXI

'Aisha mentioned somebody called the The Watchers,' Lopez said. 'Who are they?'

Ethan had no idea who The Watchers were, but Hellerman appeared more than well versed in their history.

'The Watchers appear throughout the historical mythology of just about every major civilization on earth,' he explained. 'They feature heavily in the Bible as what are referred to as fallen angels, which has often been cited by ancient astronaut theorists as our ancestors mistaking alien encounters for angels.'

'I'd never heard of them before until we met Aisha,' Lopez said, 'and I grew up in a traditional Catholic town in Mexico.'

'That's because they appear only in the original Hebrew versions of the Bible,' Hellerman explained. 'Way back in 325 CE, a gathering of powerful Christian Bishops called the Council of Nicaea in Turkey decided that the Bible needed some adjusting. Essentially, they stripped out anything that did not support the divinity of Jesus Christ or which seemed to suggest the existence of other powers in the universe greater than that of their single god, Yawheh in the Hebrew tradition. This meant that some thirty–seven books from the Bible were removed to give us the foundation of the version that became the gospel canon for Christianity.'

'Can't let facts get in the way of the party line,' Lopez said wryly.

'Indeed,' Hellerman said, 'many of the books describe Jesus as anything but divine, others that he was married, had children, conducted a life completely normal. Many scholars have come to realize that based on the fact that Jesus's entire life story appears to be based on previous legends like so much else in the Bible, it is likely that he never existed at all.'

'Seriously?' Ethan uttered. 'How would that even be possible? He's got to be the most famous person in history, even if you don't need to believe in the stories of miracles.'

'The miracles were all attributed to other supposedly divine leaders thousands of years before Christianity,' Hellerman explained. 'The problem is that the figure we know as Jesus Christ appears nowhere in history. He only appears in the Bible, which is a bit like saying Hercules was a real figure although he only appears in Greek artwork. The truth is that despite supposedly living in first Century Palestine, the best recorded century of ancient history, and supposedly being famous across entire regions and known to kings, we have no evidence of him being alive, ever, anywhere.'

'So, if that's true, where the hell did the story of his life come from?' Lopez asked.

'Sun worship,' Hellerman replied with a shrug. 'He cometh on clouds, he is the light of the world, and so on. Christianity was preceded by Mithraism, a similar cult that worshipped the sun as a giver of life and warmth. Followers of Mithras worshipped the fact that the sun descended into the underworld for three days before being reborn on December 25th. Mithras was born of a virgin, was mankind's salvation, water was a strong symbol associated with him and he would sign with water the foreheads of his followers in the manner of modern baptisms. The cult was eradicated by the Christians, who used the popular convention of absorbing existing religions into their own over time and adopting their customs as their own, complete with false histories. It's why the New Testament contains no eye–witness records of the life of Jesus – the authors write as though they were there, but in fact the first of the gospels was written at least a century after the supposed Crucifixion.'

Hellerman gestured to the images of the tablet.

'It's why the Vatican likes to bury as many artefacts as this as they can, to further muddy the waters of history and erase any evidence of mankind's past before Christianity, including the early books of their own Bible.'

'The Book of Enoch was one of them,' Ethan said as he remembered previous conversations about the very same subject. 'It describes angels descending from the heavens on flaming wheels within wheels, that they had the likeness of a man and so on.'

'Which again is interpreted by some as evidence of alien encounters in mankind's ancient history,' Hellerman confirmed. 'All of these encounters are of course unsupported by evidence, but it's the sheer number of them that stagger researchers looking into the phenomena, and the way in which the same legends manifest themselves across different regions, even different continents.'

'And these Annunaki are the earliest we know of?' Lopez asked.

Hellerman nodded.

'According to Sumerian creation myth, they were the founders of their culture. An was the chief God of Sun and Sky, and his name means The Shining One. Anunnaki were, according to this, the Sons of Light, just as Lucifer's original name meant a being of light. The Anunnaki were culturally and technically advanced people who lived in the Middle East around 8200 BCE, which precedes our own technologically advanced civilizations by several thousand years. Their primary goal was to establish an agricultural center for learning and training of the local population. Early Sumerians described themselves as being always nurtured by the Annunaki. The important thing here is that the associations made then remained with later civilizations. The Annunaki's character and functions formed the base for the Egyptian, Greek and Roman pantheon of Gods. Ancient God Ninlil was the God of War, just like the Biblical Nimrod, which just like Osiris became linked with constellation of Orion, and Orion features heavily in Egyptian lore and their megastructures.'

'How so?' Ethan asked.

'The pyramids,' Hellerman explained. 'They're not just massive monoliths to power. They're a map.'

'Of what?' Lopez asked.

'The constellation of Orion,' Hellerman replied. 'If viewed from above, the three pyramids perfectly align in the same way as the three major stars of Orion's belt. Travel further out into the deserts, and you find pyramids erected at the four points of the Orion constellation, just as there are four giant stars marking the corner of the constellation in our skies.'

Ethan stared at Hellerman for a long moment.

'The entire Egyptian monument building campaign was designed to construct a giant map of the constellation Orion?'

'Well, not the whole thing, but the major monuments all fit with that plan and they were all built at around the same time. The thing is, we still don't know who built them.'

'I thought that they'd found the tombs of the pyramid builders?' Lopez said, briefly recalling things that she'd seen on the news. 'I thought that chapter was closed.'

'The tombs of builders were found on the Giza plateau,' Hellerman confirmed. 'Their remains bore testimony to huge physical labor. But that didn't mean that they built the pyramids, and none of the artefacts or imagery found with them bore any reference to the pyramids themselves. Only the media made the connection, not really the scientists themselves.'

'That's not what I heard,' Ethan said. 'I heard that it was worked out that the pyramids could have been built by humans, using the technology available at the time, using four or five thousand men over twenty years.'

Hellermen appeared somewhat annoyed at Ethan as he replied.

'Nobody is saying that human hands didn't build the pyramids, okay? Researchers have found graffiti that was never supposed to be seen, on the inside of foundations inside the pyramids. The images and texts reveal that the workers were divided into crews, and then again into what were called phyles, a Greek word meaning tribe. Those phyles were again subdivided into teams with hieroglyphic names that meant things like strength, endurance, perfection and so on. One of the teams called itself the Friends of Khufu Gang.' Hellerman sighed. 'People built the pyramids, that much is not in question. What is important is why they should build such extraordinary structures in the first place, and why they would erect them in such a way as to mimic a constellation in the sky thousands of light years away.'

Ethan nodded, understanding the point. The pyramids were not just amazing creations in and of themselves: the Great Pyramid had been the largest man–made thing on earth until the 20th Century.

'And you think that these Watchers are the reason why ancient cultures built massive structures?' he asked Hellerman.

'It's not what I think,' Hellerman argued, 'it's written all over everything they ever did. Every major civilization in history built as big as they could, and yet many of the structures they built had no defensive purpose at all. They could have built gigantic walls, immense fortifications, but no – they chose instead to build giant pyramids across continents separated by thousands of miles of ocean.'

Hellerman counted civilizations off on his fingers as he spoke.

'The Sumerians lived in the land of Sumer, which literally meant the Land of the Watchers, and described intelligent beings who came from the water and taught them the skills of civilization. The Egyptians describe Ta Neter, the Land of the Watchers, as the lands from which the gods had come to Egypt, and in the Old Testament the Elohim or Shining Ones had also come from the same place of origin. They took their name from the Sumerian El, which means bright or shining. The Baylonian Ellu also means bright or to shine. The Old Cornish El means the same, and is where the word Elf originates, describing a mysterious shining and magical being. The Incas in South America referred to bright, shining figures who came from the sea as Illa, which meant "to shine", who helped found their Empire. Ta Neter is also the Egyptian name for the Red Sea straits, which connected Mesopotamia to Egypt and is known as the place of the gods.'

Lopez folded her arms.

'Okay, so these Watchers connect some ancient societies and maybe mean there's something in the legends, but again, so what? It's not that ground breaking.'

Hellerman slapped his head in exasperation.

'Do I have to spell it out to you both? The Egyptians say in their Book of the Dead that the Watchers had come from Ta–Ur, which meant far or foreign land across the sea. Mesopotamian records and Biblical references name this land as Ur, the place where the father of the world's great religions resided, Abraham. Likewise the legend of Votan in Mesoamerica and the Nordic Wotan both describe an aquatic origin of The Watchers, who then came and instructed mankind in technological matters before a great flood wiped men from the face of the earth.'

Ethan finally got it.

'The division between religions.'

Hellerman clapped as he rolled his eyes. 'Finally! The division between the world's religions is false, and is provoked by the heirachy of some religions in an attempt to disguise the understanding that they're actually all one and the same. The whole concept of having more than one faith is redundant and always has been.'

Hellerman pointed at the tablet's inscription.

'The reason the Catholic Church or any other religion would like to see evidence like this buried for all time is that it proves that before any of them existed, the true foundation of all civilization's great legends and religions existed for real. It wasn't a myth, a story, a fable – it really happened and everything that's stood since, all the world's religions, are simply twisted and falsified memories of that one great event.'

Ethan shook his head as he recalled the famous words of the late, great Arthur C. Clarke.

'Any sufficiently advanced technology would be indistinguishable from magic.'

Hellerman nodded as he slumped back in his chair.

'They're hiding the origin of faith,' he said finally. 'This is the path that leads to an understanding of the origin of all the world's deities. Majestic Twelve and all the others weren't looking for aliens, per se. They truly believed that they were looking for god.'

Lopez looked down at the inscriptions on the tablet.

'And now, so are we,' she said. 'But what the hell are the Russians looking for?'

***

XXII

Megiddo, Canaan

1457 BCE

A hot wind moaned across the deserts, rumbling through the long shawl that protected Tjaneni from the savage heat now blazing down upon them as they rode. The hills were not far from the Pharaoh's camp site, but even a few miles across these arid plains represented a dangerous ride to all but the most experienced of tribesmen, and Tjaneni was no soldier.

He followed Ahmen, the old man's robes flowing like banners in the wind and his gaze set toward the east, where now the line of low hills was clear against the horizon. They appeared as barren and deserted as they always had, devoid of life. The old man showed no signs of breaking his pace as he rode to the very edge of the slopes and guided his horse into the cooler shadows of a deep gulley.

Ahmen dismounted and tied his horse to an outcrop of rock nearby, Tjaneni following suit and trying to quell the anxiety coursing through his veins. It was as if the hills were warning him to proceed no further, to go back from whence he had come and not risk incurring the wrath of the gods themselves.

'We should not be here,' he whispered to Ahmen as he tied his horse.

Ahmen raised an eyebrow. 'How do you know?'

Tjaneni made to reply but then realized that he had no answer for the old man's impenetrable logic. Misha walked up to them, his countenance even more nervous than Tjaneni's.

'You can stay here and watch the horses if you wish,' Tjaneni said to him.

Misha looked at the lonely gulley and the empty deserts beyond and then he shook his head, clearly more afraid of being left alone than of facing whatever awaited them on the far side of the hill.

'No, I will come.'

Tjaneni turned to see Ahmen already making his way up and over the slopes of the hills before them, surprisingly agile for a man of his age. Tjaneni hurried to catch him as they climbed over the top of the hill, ready to descend the other side and into the deeper ravines there.

'We don't know what's in there,' Tjaneni persisted. 'We should have brought an escort.'

Ahmen humphed in disapproval.

'The King's men would attack anything that provoked them even if they were unprovoked. This is an opportunity that must not be entrusted to a mob of angry young men. We saw that light descend here and it has not emerged since. Whatever great fiery bird landed must still be here.'

Tjaneni nodded, wishing all the while that it were not so, but he knew that Ahmen was right.

'You are not afraid?' he asked Ahmen.

The old man smiled as he labored ever upward. 'Of course I am afraid! But what courage is there in an absence of fear? We must see for ourselves what awaits, and then judge whether our fear is misplaced.'

Tjaneni followed Ahmen over the ridge and down into a deep gulley that bisected the hills, where once had a river flowed between the rocky peaks and burrowed deep cave systems through the ancient sandstone. Tjaneni could see the stepped cliffs either side of him, denoting the different levels of the water in some long bygone age when this parched wasteland had been rich with rivers and life.

'There,' Ahmen said, his voice pinched with excitement.

Tjaneni looked up and saw before them a large cave at the end of the gulley, its gaping black maw ominous and foreboding. He slowed as they approached the cave, like a giant gaping mouth leading deep into the bowels of the earth.

As they walked he heard the sand beneath his feet crunch loudly and he looked down in surprise. Beneath them the sand was solidified and reflective, some of it scorched black and sitting in sheets as though rivers of oil had streamed down the gulley.

Ahmen crouched down and gently pressed one hand against the black material, then lifted it away as he looked up at the cave.

'It's still warm,' he said quietly. 'I have seen this before.'

Tjaneni had seen it too, once before, in the aftermath of a terrific battle when the enemy had poured what looked like pieces of the sun onto the battlefield. The molten metal had rained down on Egyptian troops and burned them alive, scorching the sand into this hard, glossy substance that sometimes appeared almost transparent.

'They are inside,' Misha said nervously. 'The lights, they will burn us too.'

Tjaneni looked at Ahmen, who leaned on his cane and took a deep breath.

'Had they wished it so, it would have happened by now. They know that we're here.'

Tjaneni's legs trembled as they began walking once again, and with each pace the shadowy entrance of the cave swallowed them until the warmth of the sun was gone and only darkness prevailed.

The air smelled dry, and Tjaneni paused for a moment as he allowed his eyes to adjust to the darkness. The cave extended away from them, descending as it went, and the further they travelled the cooler the air became.

A new scent drifted on the still air, a strange chemical taint that Tjaneni recognized as metal, as though fresh swords had been forged somewhere nearby.

The acrid taint of smoke wafted around them, Tjaneni's eyes stinging as it drifted by.

'Stay close,' Ahmen whispered to them. 'We have not far to go.'

Tjaneni's dread grew with each and every step, as though he were daring the Underworld to attack, taunting Seth with his audacity to tread here, a mere mortal before the wrath of the…

From the darkness burst forth an intense light that forced Tjaneni to throw his arms up over his eyes and turn away from the fearsome glare. He heard himself cry out and felt his legs weaken as he dropped to his knees and then fell flat on his face, as much from fear as from the instinct to prostrate himself before a higher power.

Ahmen and Misha collapsed alongside him, equally blinded by the ferocity of the light blazing like a new–born star before them. Tjaneni lowered his arm slightly, squinting as he peered over his forearm and was shocked to see faint tendrils of smoke coiling upward from his skin and the fine hairs above it.

He heard Misha scream and suddenly leap upright in an attempt to flee the dreadful assault, and then the boy's hair was aflame as streams of burning embers spiralled from his clothes and his skin.

Tjaneni felt a terrible heat wash over him and he tried to crawl away from the ferocious glare, cried out again in fear as he realized that he could only be staring directly into the All Seeing Eye of Horus himself.

'Forgive us!' Ahmen yelled at the light as he knelt alongside Tjaneni, rivers of bright embers flying from his smoldering shawl, 'for we are but mortal men!'

The fearsome light seared their eyes with a force so powerful that Tjaneni could see the red glow of the blood flowing through his eyelids even though he was shielding his eyes with his arm and squeezing them tightly shut. He felt another wave of terrible heat wash over the three of them, cried out in pain and terrible fear as he collapsed onto his face in the dust and covered his head with his hands as he smelled his hair burning.

A tremendous screaming gale soared through the cave as though a storm had rushed from the hot bowels of the earth to scorch the very air, its stench metallic and fierce. Tjaneni cried in pain as he felt his skin burning on his back, prayed that the earth would swallow him whole to save him from the agony he was enduring, and his ears ached with the sheer volume of the diabolical roar thundering through the caves.

Suddenly the heat faded away and Tjaneni realized that the screaming wind that had been howling through the caves throughout their ordeal was now gusting out. The banshee wail faded away like a horrific nightmare and the air cooled around him as though the fiery source of the storm were ascending away from them. Tjaneni lay face down in the dust, his body trembling and the smell of scalded skin and hair lingering as he turned to one side and looked at Ahmen.

The old man was lying on the ground alongside Tjaneni with his face turned toward him, but his features were slack and his eyes empty, their rheumy lenses pale white and devoid of life. Tjaneni felt fresh panic rise up inside of him as he turned his head to search for Misha. There, before him, was a sight so terrible that he felt physically sick.

Misha was kneeling as though in silent prayer, his eyes empty black sockets and his mouth wide open in a silent scream for mercy that had gone unanswered. His form was as that of rich, black soil, his skin charred beyond recognition as though he had been scorched to cinders like a pillar of burned salt. Tjaneni fought back tears of horror and superstitious awe as his eyes slowly adjusted once again to the darkness and he looked up fearfully at where the infernal light had blazed so fiercely only moments before.

There in the shadowy darkness he could see a faint afterglow, a nearly perfect rectangle of light as though a fire had been extinguished and the embers still retained some heat and light. Tjaneni was about to try to stand when he saw movement in the depths of the cave.

He froze, catatonic with terror as he saw figures moving silently in the darkness. They were tall, pale, on two legs as all men were but somehow different. Tjaneni feared that they would detect him and the light would return, and he dared not breathe for fear of giving himself away. The figures moved silently around something in the darkness before Tjaneni, and then one of them emerged slightly from the darkness and stared directly at him.

Tjaneni's entire body began to quiver with terror as he looked into a pair of slanted, black eyes that seemed to him to hold no sense of a soul, no heart that breathed life into all beings. There was no expression, no communication, nothing.

The strange human watched Tjaneni for several long seconds, and then in silence he turned away and walked into the darkness. The other figures joined their companion and Tjaneni heard the soft shuffling of feet in the sand that faded away into the depths of the earth, back into the hellish underworld from whence they had come.

Tjaneni, trembling with terror and fatigued beyond all measure, crawled to his knees. His limbs felt weak, his heart fluttering in his chest and his breathing coming in short, sharp gasps that seemed to snatch the life from his body with every convulsive breath. Pain soared across his skin, which had blistered in the terrible heat. He knelt there for how long he knew not, until he heard shouts coming from behind him near the entrance to the cave.

Tjaneni did not turn as he heard the men approaching, even though some dim recess of his awareness reminded him that they could be the Caananites approaching to slaughter him. Dim light flickered into life around him, the crackling of flaming torches, and with a vague sense of relief he recognized the sound of Coptic Egyptian voices.

'Tjaneni?'

The soldiers hurried to his side, and then recoiled in horror as they saw the two corpses either side of Tjaneni. Then their torches illuminated what was before him in and their gasps of awe filled the cave, fearful whispers fluttering like dark thoughts around Tjaneni.

'Tjaneni?' one of the men called him again. 'What happened here? The King is asking for you, for the battle will soon begin.'

Tjaneni stared silently at the tremendous sight before him, his mind empty and unfocused, his body weak and yet charged with something he had never felt before and did not understand. When he spoke, it was in a ghostly whisper.

'The stars have fallen from the sky,' he replied to them, 'and we witnessed Horus himself bring one of them here to this cave.'

The soldiers all began backing away from the sight before them as Tjaneni spoke again.

'Bring the King here and do not approach but upon your knees, or you will all suffer the same fate as Misha.'

The soldiers looked at the blackened pillar that was all that remained of Tjaneni's man servant, and as one they collapsed onto their knees before the spectacle.

'Go,' one of the chiefs ordered his men. 'Go and tell the King that the prophecy has truly been fulfilled!'

Tjaneni heard several soldiers crawling backwards out of the cave on their hands and knees, but he did not take his eyes from the object before him that now reflected the lights of the flaming torches as though it too were alive and watching them.

It was rectangular, no more than three cubits long by two high and two wide, and it was cast in solid gold so perfectly polished that Tjaneni could see his own face upon it. Like a large box, the device was still glowing with escaping heat and light, as though unstable and always on the verge of an explosive reaction.

Tjaneni called to the men behind him.

'Leave,' he said. 'I do not know what this is, but it is a danger to us all and must be housed safely. I have seen its power, and there is nothing like it anywhere in this Kingdom or any other.'

As the soldiers began backing away, Tjaneni made a solemn promise to himself.

'We must guard this object for all time,' he whispered, 'for this Ark is born of the gods themselves.'

***

XXIII

Washington DC

Joseph Hellerman gripped the controls with all of his might, his palms sweaty and his eyes fixed ahead as the interior lights of an immense complex raced past at lightning speed. Glossy floors reflected the flashing lights as he yanked the controls to one side and banked his craft steeply, flashing around a tight corner as he heard the engines of another craft hot on his heels.

Hellerman focused intently as the craft soared down a long tunnel filled with more lights racing past him, images of X–Wing fighters thundering through the Death Star's interior flashing through his mind as a smile creased his thin beard.

'Use the Force, Luke…'

He heard the drone of another engine alongside him and risked a quick glance to his left. Another craft seemed to hover alongside his own as the walls and lights flashed past at terrific speed, its engines humming. Hellerman stared ahead again and saw a narrow gap rushing upon him. He frantically jerked the controls to one side and the drone banked up steeply onto its side and soared through the gap as he heard a sudden clattering noise and looked up from his display screen.

Before him a tiny model drone shot out of an open doorway and into the open air as behind it a cloud of debris sparkled in the sunshine as the second drone was shattered against the school corridor's walls. Beside him Hellerman heard somebody growl in fury and hurl their control transmitter away across the asphalt.

Four more drones burst from the interior of the school and soared across the yard in pursuit of Hellerman's machine, but he already knew that they couldn't catch him now as he flew the remote controlled drone around the periphery of the yard and aimed for the finish line.

'All hail the Hellerman!' he hooted as his drone whizzed past the finish line, four more following it a few seconds later.

Hellerman brought his drone around in a wide, slow arc and touched down in front of the pilots where they sat in a row on plastic chairs, their laptops erected in front of them. He took off his Infra–Red motion detecting headset, which was connected to a rotating camera mounted on the drone that allowed him to look around in real time as though he was sitting on top of the drone itself.

'Man, school never used to be this much fun.'

The high school was closed on a Sunday, allowing them to use the empty halls as drone–racing courses. Initially the school cleaners had complained of having to duck with moments to spare as the drones flashed past at thirty miles per hour through the narrow corridors, but having worked out a compromise of races taking place during staff lunch–times, an uneasy peace had been achieved.

Hellerman stood up and walked to a pedestal, upon which stood a golden trophy of a striking eagle clasping a lightsabre in its talons.

'Same time next week, my young Padawans?' Hellerman asked his companions.

Before him sat five DIA employees, variously cryptographers and programmers who worked for the agency and had a combined IQ of more than seven hundred fifty. They still don't understand the importance of a good racing line though, Hellerman reminded himself.

'I say your drone is rigged,' said the man who had trashed his drone into a wall at the last hurdle.

'I say your faith is lacking,' Hellerman replied. 'We could have run the race again with each other's drones, but you broke yours.'

The older man turned and Hellerman's cocky bravado withered as he saw the threat of violence flicker like a distant storm across his opponent's face. He was suddenly aware that his opponent was thirty pounds heavier and four inches taller, his fists clenched as he turned toward Hellerman with his shoulders bunched up around his neck.

'How about I break something else, Hellerman?' he growled.

'How about we all take a break,' Hellerman suggested as he raised a hand and backed up. 'It's just a game, y'know?'

Hellerman was about to turn and run when his opponent suddenly came up short, his rage vanishing as a look of vague panic flickered across his features and he turned away. Hellerman blinked in amazement and shrugged.

'I'll let you go just this once man, don't do it again or I'll…'

'Hellerman.'

Hellerman's heart almost stopped beating as he heard the deep, melodious voice rumble his name. He felt the fine hairs on the back of his neck stand on end and his shoulders tense. He turned slowly and saw Mitchell's immense, towering form looming before him.

'With me,' Mitchell growled, then turned and stalked toward the school exit.

It wasn't a request, or even a command – a simple statement laden with the threat of what would happen if Hellerman didn't comply immediately. He picked up his drone and transmitter, then reluctantly followed the big man out of the school yard to a long, black limousine that pulled up smoothly near the sidewalk. Mitchell opened a door and stood beside it, giving Hellerman no choice but to climb in. The door shut behind him and Mitchell got into the driver's seat. The limousine moved off as Hellerman's eyes adjusted to the darkness inside and then widened in amazement.

'Doug?!'

Jarvis inclined his head, smiling softly as Hellerman's prodigious intellect conducted a series of rapid but predictable mental calculations.

'But you're… and we're… and I'll be arrested… and people are…'

'Looking for me,' Jarvis cut him off. 'I know, so this has to be brief.'

'Brief?' Hellerman uttered. 'If I'm seen with you I'll be arrested. You abandoned us and stole the money from Majestic Twelve that we were supposed to…'

'To give to the government so that they could squirrel it away in the Black Budget or share it out among some other cabal of powerful industrialists?' Jarvis snapped. 'Joseph, you know as well as I do that all of the money MJ–12 accrued from its deals was out of the public eye and would have stayed so had we let it go.'

'Let it go,' Hellerman echoed. 'You make it sound like it belonged to you in the first place.'

'It belongs to millions of people, variously murdered or robbed by MJ–12 over the decades. It's my job to ensure that the money starts working for them instead of against them.'

'By betraying your colleagues and abandoning them?'

'By taking the heat from them and putting it on me,' Jarvis countered. 'I take it that in the rush to find the missing billions you, Ethan, Nicola and General Nellis have escaped any serious scrutiny from Homeland Security?'

Hellerman's outrage faltered. 'We had only basic reports filed, ensuring that all loose ends were tied up.'

'And now Homeland is working with the agency to hunt me down?' Jarvis asked rhetorically. 'They have partnered with Nellis to locate us and recover the money?'

Hellerman nodded. 'You're considered a criminal.'

'Strange then, that my picture isn't all over the news, don't you think?'

'Security is tight around ARIES,' Hellerman said, 'they won't want to draw attention to…'

'Bull crap!' Jarvis snapped. 'They don't want to admit they lost thirty billion dollars and they don't want to have to let local law enforcement here or in other countries get in on the act. They want it back for themselves, and they'll do anything to get their hands on it. This is about money Hellerman, not justice.'

'And where is that money?' Hellerman asked.

'Safe,' Jarvis replied, 'and split into so many accounts it would take half the age of the universe to track them all down.'

'Too many accounts for one man to keep track of,' Hellerman replied.

Jarvis smiled. 'This is why I miss you Hellerman.'

'What do you want from me?'

Jarvis stared at Hellerman for a long moment before he replied. 'I want you to come and work for us.'

Hellerman stared back, suddenly cold inside the limo. 'Us?'

Jarvis leaned forward in his seat. 'Lillian Cruz, Rhys Garrett, Aaron Mitchell, Amber Ryan and Lucy Morgan.'

Hellerman's eyes flew wide as he heard the names. 'They're all people who…'

'Suffered in one way or another at the hands of Majestic Twelve and who have a vested interest in ensuring that the ill–gotten gains of that cabal are used to promote justice and fight the corruption that festers inside the hearts of all governments.'

Hellerman turned his head away and looked out of the tinted windows at the Washington skyline passing slowly by outside. He had lived in the district all of his life, and his prowess in computational science had meant that as soon as he had completed high school he had been picked up by the government for employment. Not the MIT route for Hellerman – he'd been selected and trained for the purpose of government policy.

Although he had not always agreed with those policies and the politicians who wielded them, Hellerman had been part of a secure agency for his entire adult life, fighting the good fight. Despite its flaws, he had no doubts whatsoever that the United States were the good guys in a war against forces of chaos and dictatorship in lands he had never seen. With a start of realization he noted that he had not ever set foot outside the United States of America, and he recalled that the vast majority of Americans also had never ventured beyond their own shores.

'I know what you're thinking,' Jarvis said. 'It's a big leap to make. Leaving the DIA would be breaking new ground for you.'

Hellerman shook his head. 'That's not what I was thinking.'

'What then?'

'I was just wondering, who the good guys and the bad guys really are.'

Jarvis frowned. 'You know who we are. You've worked for us all your life.'

'I've worked for America,' Hellerman said. 'I don't know what you're doing but it sounds to me like Majestic Twelve all over again. As far as the DIA is concerned, I'd be working for the enemy.'

'The enemy of my enemy is my friend,' Jarvis replied.

'And that's my point, right there,' Hellerman said. 'You have a talent for confusing issues, drawing veils over the truth, concealing and misdirecting. General Nellis doesn't do that, I know where I am with him.'

'But does he know where he is?' Jarvis challenged. 'Nellis is a good man but he's another cog turning the wheels of a machine that he doesn't understand. Like you he wants to believe that he's on the right side, but we all know that the country works for the politicians and the politicians work for themselves. This isn't about good or bad Hellerman, it's about breaking free of the system that prevents us from tackling the problems at the root of all governed societies. We need free reign to bring an end to corruption, to expose criminality at the political level.'

'Free reign,' Hellerman said, 'sounds like absolute power is what you want, and absolute power corrupts, absolutely.'

Jarvis leaned forward, smiling.

'When placed in the hands of a single person,' he agreed. 'But what if you place that absolute power into the hands of the people themselves?'

Hellerman's breath caught in his throat and he thought hard for a moment before he replied.

'Isocracy?'

'The rule of the people,' Jarvis nodded. 'Democracy is a lousy system but it's the best we've got right now, or at least it was until capitalism ran amok and governments were taken over by corporations. We all live in dictatorships now, Hellerman. The rules are no longer made by our leaders but by the companies that fund their campaigns. We're ruled by commerce and trade, profit and loss. That's not democracy. The only way to break those chains is to hand the power, all of the power, back to the people.'

Hellerman glanced at the city skyline in the distance, the dome of the Capitol visible against the hard blue sky.

'And that's your end game?'

'It's the only end game,' Jarvis replied. 'I'm a wanted fugitive, with enough knowledge of the inside of America's intelligence community to bring down the government overnight. They're not going to want me on trial, not even before Congress. They find me and I'll conveniently disappear.'

Hellerman struggled with the uncomfortable truth that Jarvis would indeed be unlikely to survive capture, and though he reminded himself that the ever resourceful Jarvis might be deliberately pulling on his heart strings to get what he wanted, it was a fact that for many years Jarvis had faithfully served his country. Now he was out on his own, and in the company of people whose motives were unquestionable.

The problem was, whether they were likewise being manipulated?

'If I get caught,' Hellerman said finally, 'I'll be imprisoned for the rest of my life, and I doubt that you'd come get me.'

From the front of the vehicle, Mitchell rumbled a reply.

'If he didn't, I would.'

Hellerman felt a strange sense of gratitude toward the towering assassin, and then wondered what could have transformed him so completely. Hellerman looked at Jarvis.

'And if I say no?'

'Then we drop you off wherever you want and we'll disappear,' Jarvis replied. 'We're not Majestic Twelve, Hellerman, you're not in danger here.'

Hellerman rubbed his temples with one hand and shook his head. 'I don't know what to do.'

'I know,' Jarvis said. 'How about I make this a little easier for you. Why not ask Ethan what he would do?'

'You're asking me to tell him about this?'

'Why not? It'll save me the job.'

Hellerman sighed. 'I would do, but he's not here right now.'

'Where is he?'

Hellerman opened his mouth to reply, the act so natural to him that he was barely able to catch himself. Jarvis saw the hesitation and grinned.

'If it's classified, don't worry.'

Hellerman shook his head.

'It's more than that,' he said. 'We've got a real weird investigation ongoing right now. Ethan and Nicola are looking into a cult in Utah. The local sheriffs busted in there and found Egyptian hieroglyphics everywhere.'

Jarvis's eyes lit up and he leaned closer. 'Go on.'

'So one of the troopers finds a blind girl trapped inside the cult's burning ranch, and yet this girl guides him out. She predicted the future, right there. I did some digging into the hieroglyphics, and on the basis of that and other intelligence we figured the Russians were up to something in Syria.' Hellerman sighed. 'Ethan and Nicola were in Rome, looking for something called the Tulli Papyrus and the tablets associated with it. Right now, they're heading for Lebanon to intercept Russian traffickers abducting young girls believed to be oracles. They're using them to search for something that the Russians clearly consider important.'

Jarvis turned to Mitchell. 'The oracles. You need to get out there and locate them, as quickly as you can.'

***

XXIV

Kafr Aya,

Syria

The halls of the compound were bare, paint flaking from them to litter the corridor and the air damp and cold. The stale scent of mold permeated the building and clung to her skin like a cold, dead cloak as she shivered in the darkness.

Elena Viskin sat on the bare concrete floor with her knees tucked up against her chest, her head resting on them and her arms wrapped around her legs. She did not know for how long she had been there, for she had long ago lost the ability to keep track of time. Only the endless thumping of distant artillery fire and landing shells accompanied her in the darkness, the hymn of war echoing through the lonely vaults of her mind.

Elena had lived in the Russian Southern Federal District of Elista all of her life, the town just north of the borders with Chechnya and Georgia. Turkey and Syria had always lain somewhere far beyond, their lands adrift with turmoil and change of which she had heard much growing up. Elena heard everything with particular acuteness, for she had been blind since birth. It had only been at the age of seven when she had been able to tell her parents that although she could see nothing while awake, in her dreams her eyesight was perfectly normal.

Nobody had seemed able to understand why Elena should be able to see in her dreams, mostly because her brain should never have been able to interpret anything from her eyes into a meaningful image because it had no frame of reference. As a doctor had once told her parents: how does one describe a horse if one has never seen a horse? And yet Elena had given a detailed description of a horse, enough so that she had been able to draw a crude image of one with her dear father's help.

Elena's affliction and remarkable ability had been nothing more than a novelty for two or three years, but then had come the men from the Kremlin. They had asked many questions and then had made Elena the offer of a lifetime: four years work for the Kremlin, ending upon her seventeenth birthday, in return for her parents receiving a sum of money that was more than her father could have earned in a lifetime. Despite the excitement and hope of a future devoid of poverty, her parents had ensured Elena that she should only take the offer up if she was sure she could cope, that money was nothing without the bonds of family. Elena had not hesitated, and three days later she was picked up in a small bus bound for Moscow.

Or so she had thought.

Instead she had been driven south, far south, into the deserts of Syria and she had been here ever since. The only thing that she knew for sure was that she had been captive among other girls of a similar age, and that she had heard their drunken guards twice sing old Soviet songs about Christmas when the cells were especially cold and the nights long and dark.

Two years.

Elena had been taken out of her cell over that period twice per day and guided to a room that was warm and comfortable. There, relieved to be free of the cold and the darkness that she could not see but somehow knew surrounded her, Elena had been forced to wear some kind of garment on her head that had caused her to experience some of the most frightening and disturbing visions she could have imagined, and many that would never have entered her head until they were forced there by whatever contraption it was that they placed upon her.

The early experiments were gentle but none the less strange: she had felt as though there were people in the room with her despite knowing that she was alone, the guards and the scientists all leaving before the experiments started. A voice would ask her questions through a speaker in the wall: How did she feel? Could she see anything? Did she feel as though she could sense another time or place?

Gradually, with each successive session the intensity of the sensation that she was not alone in the room would increase and she sensed halos of light flashing and flickering on the periphery of what she assumed was the same vision she enjoyed in her dreams. The flashes of light became images, flaring with vivid brilliance only to vanish again like a word on the tip of her tongue.

Then, between the sessions, the headaches started.

One of the things least known about blind people was their acute sense of smell. Elena could detect scents with astonishing accuracy, but some were more easily recognized than others and when Elena was in the company of others girls in the facility she smelled the blood instantly. It was only after a few days that she realized the blood was the result of nosebleeds, the same ones that she began to have and that accompanied the blinding headaches. Elena knew that the strange device placed upon her head each day was to blame, and she figured that it was also to blame for the disappearances of the girls. Like her sense of smell, Elena's hearing and even rudimentary echo–location were abnormally well formed, nature giving back in recompense what it had taken away. The girls' voices and their own personal scents vanished from the corridors one by one as time went by, never to be heard or sensed again.

The visions followed the nosebleeds while wearing the device and eventually, shockingly, without it, often occurring in bright flashes amid the terrible pangs of pain that seared Elena's skull. She saw things, real things, events happening that she could not understand but was required to relay to her captors with unerring accuracy. Elena knew well the consequences of attempting to deceive them as retribution for her captivity, the memory of the wicked lashes on her bare skin as bright and painful now as the day she had first felt them.

They would come soon, Elena knew, for she could sense them already. The puddles in her miserable cell shifted almost imperceptibly with tremors from the thuds of their heavy boots as they marched toward the cells. The air moved as they opened nearby doors, the pressure changing slightly in the cell around her and causing individual hairs on her cheeks to drift with the changing flow. A voice, distant but recognizable caused the hairs on the backs of her arms to rise up as fear drained slick and cold into her belly. Her only consolation was that she knew they could not violate her; such an act apparently rendered the girl's visions useless.

Elena huddled on the floor and thought of her dear mother and father, so proud of her as she left them behind, and she fought back tears as she heard the cell door open and rough hands hauled her to her feet and dragged her out into the corridor.

Elena walked the sixty–seven paces to the metal gates, the scent of cheap tobacco and unwashed uniforms swirling around her. Through the gates they went, a bubble of warm air from a heater in the guardroom wafting across her along with the smell of sandwiches and coffee. Then the quieter part of the building, the sterilized scents of a further corridor for twenty–nine paces and the hiss of automatic doors as she was guided through into an open laboratory.

Other people were inside, six of them moving about as Elena was guided to the door she always went through. Inside, the smell of soft leather and warm air, food on a table nearby. The guards released her and she stumbled to the food, shoveling it in her mouth and guzzling clean water from a glass, always on the right side of the plate of food.

The voice once again, the same as always, Moscovian and harsh.

'Hurry, we are waiting.'

Elena felt hands grab her shoulders and she reached for the last of the food as she was dragged backwards and lifted bodily onto a reclining chair, thick straps pinning her down. She knew better than to struggle, to kick and punch and scratch, for it only made it worse. The heavy, metallic device was clamped down onto her head and fixed in place, and then the other people left the room and she heard the door close.

Although she could see nothing, somehow she sensed the lights in the room dim and she closed her eyes and prayed silently that the pain would not be so bad this time.

Through the speakers, she heard the voice again.

'Just like last time, Elena. You must see Edfu. You must see the temple, the tomb.'

The air around her head suddenly became charged somehow and she felt her long hair rise up with static as a flow of electrons surged through her brain. Flashes of light darted across her eyes and she felt something like a hot poker lance behind her eyeballs from right to left. Elena gritted her teeth against the pain that flashed through her skull and suddenly subsided again, and then light flared before her despite her closed eyes and she saw a massive temple of some kind.

Immense stone pillars the color of sand towered before her, carved by human hands that seemed incapable of such incredible achievements. The sky above was hard blue, not a cloud to be seen, and she was surrounded by deserts that stretched away into a horizon that trembled with heat. Her lungs felt heavy with the hot air, the sunshine burning her skin. Voices called out in a language that she did not recognize, men marching in groups and wearing white tunics, some of them with bizarre head dresses that she recognized from school but could not place.

Then she saw the statue.

Fifty feet high and one of a pair, it had the body of a man but the head of an animal, some kind of dog or wolf. As she squinted up at the incredible monuments, a word leaped into her mind and she whispered it out loud, her voice trembling as the seizures took hold.

'Anubis.'

A voice replied to her as though from far away. 'What do you see?'

Elena knew what was expected of her, and she complied.

'They're building a temple to Anubis,' she said. 'It's larger now than when I last saw it.'

The view of the temple changed as though the world had spun around her, making her feel queasy and reminding her that she was not looking upon this world with her own eyes: she was seeing the past through the eyes of another.

'I'm moving.'

Elena was walking across the burning sand, moving past teams of laborers hauling enormous blocks of stone across paths of wet sand, other teams of men tossing sparkling green water from the nearby river in front of a sled on which the stone blocks sat.

The air was filled with swirling dust as hundreds labored all around Elena, and she realized that she too was one of the workers, that she was seeing a day in the life of a man who had lived thousands of years before her.

'What else do you see?'

The images of the desert seemed to blur before her, and suddenly she saw a man rushing out of a swirling dust storm, dark clouds above and the roar of thunder. The air turned deathly cold and Elena saw a helicopter's blades thumping the air, saw men in vehicles, guns flashing with fire and death as they charged through the deserts.

She saw a crescent shaped canyon, almost perfect in its symmetry, the storm rushing in upon it and other people fleeing. Men, women, a young girl who stared ahead with eyes as blind as Elena's. Elena gasped as she realized that she could see another like her, an oracle, a seer, running away from the armed men that she somehow knew were Russians. Leading them was a tall man with light brown hair rippling in the storm, his eyes cold and gray, a large pistol gripped in one hand that he pointed directly at her.

The storm roared in and covered the canyon, and suddenly Elena could see a tomb with Egyptian hieroglyphs across the walls and thick pillars supporting an ancient ceiling. In the tomb was a vivid golden box, like a sarcophagus but smaller, and she saw the people who had fled the Russians lifting the ornate lid of the box from its mounts.

The vision swirled in clouds of dust before Elena and from the miasma a blaze of ferocious white light seared her vision. Terrible heat scorched her skin and she saw men burning, their bodies blackened to the color of soot and blasted away by tremendous winds that melted metal and turned bones to dust. A shrieking gale blasted the remains away, scorching the earth of life.

From the diabolical firmament she heard a woman's voice scream a name and then the vision disappeared and Elena jerked awake, her chest heaving and her heart thundering in her chest. The seizure subsided, her limbs twitching and her body shaking

'What did you see?' the voice asked her.

Elena stared at the ceiling above her, but all she could see was the man charging toward her out of the storm, blood on his hands, the flashing blade and the cold determination in his eyes.

'What did you see?'

Elena got her breathing under control.

'A storm, people fighting,' she whispered. 'People dying in flames, it was horrible.'

'Did you see the tomb, Elena? Did you see anything inside it?'

Elena hesitated, wanting to lie, but she knew that the strange devices would pick up her brain waves and that the Russians would know. She sighed.

'There is a canyon,' she whispered, 'shaped like a crescent moon. The tomb is there.'

'Where, Elena?' the voice demanded. 'Where is the canyon?'

Elena's head sank until her chin touched her chest, blood trickling from her nose as her headache intensified.

'Egypt,' she said softly, 'it is somewhere in Egypt but I couldn't see where.'

There was a long pause, and then the door to the room opened and Elena knew that the session was over. She was lifted from the bed and out of the warm room into the cold corridor outside, the cosseting warmth leaving her just as it had in the storm in her vision, and as she was led down the corridor so the woman's anguished voice she had heard pursued her like a demon from a nightmare along with the gunman staring down at her, all the way to her cell.

'Ethan, no!'

***

XXV

Homs, Syria

The facility was as battered as the rest of the city as Colonel Mishkin was driven toward it, only the ranks of Russian and Syrian soldiers guarding it providing any clue to the importance of what was hidden inside. The small village of Kafr Aya, on the south western edge of the crippled city, was anonymous enough that the Russian contingent could continue their work without attracting unwanted attention from Damascus.

'The enemy are close,' his companion said, a Syrian doctor and scientist named Akhmed as he gestured out to the south east. 'We have pushed them back again with the help from your bombers, but once they melt into the desert they become hard to track and locate. We know they're out there, waiting.'

Mishkin knew that fighter pilots of the Russian Air Force had pummelled enemy positions to the south east of the city, and he knew also that the civilian casualties had been high. In densely populated areas it was almost impossible to direct effective fire against the fast moving rebel forces without collateral damage. Such was the fog of war, but as far as Mishkin was concerned the people had asked for it: it was they who had risen against their own government and who now decried the attacks on unarmed civilians.

'Let the rebels wait,' Mishkin replied without interest. 'Let them bake in their own sweat in the deserts.'

Akhmed smiled brightly, enthused by Mishkin's grim tone as the vehicle drove to a checkpoint and pulled up at a set of metal gates between twelve–foot–high concrete barriers that surrounded the facility. Akhmed cleared them through with his identification and moments later the vehicle eased into a small courtyard and turned fully about, the driver facing the vehicle toward the entrance in case they needed to escape in a hurry. Mishkin could see numerous shell holes peppering the interior walls of the compound where rebel forces had attacked the site.

'We are safe for now,' Akhmed said as he noted the direction of the colonel's gaze. 'This compound has not been hit for two weeks.'

Mishkin got out of the vehicle and directed a withering gaze at the aide. 'More's the pity.'

Akhmed smiled again, but this time a shadow of concern flickered behind his eyes as he led Mishkin to a steel door, again guarded by two armed soldiers. One of them rapped on the door with his knuckles and the door obligingly opened to allow the two men inside.

THE GENESIS CYPHER   Dean Crawford

The interior was dark and laden with the scent of sand and cool stone. Akhmed led the way into the interior, where heavy doors lined the corridors with unsmiling guards outside each one.

'These are the storage rooms, where we keep the subjects,' Akhmed reported proudly. 'Escape is impossible. The walls inside are reinforced concrete and the doors are four–inch thick steel.'

Mishkin raised an eyebrow. 'Why would you need so much security for such weak captives?'

'Because they are weak only in body,' Akhmed replied, 'not in mind.'

Mishkin frowned as they walked. 'What are you doing to them here?'

Akhmed waved the colonel forward, not replying but clearly eager to show him something as they reached a small room that was equipped with a two–way mirror. Akhmed showed the colonel into the room and closed the door behind them, and Mishkin got his first glimpse of what the general had hinted about in Moscow.

Inside an adjoining room was a gently inclined bed, upon which lay a young girl of no more than thirteen. Mishkin instantly saw the restraints pinning her in place on her back, and the blocky contraption that was wrapped around her skull. Electrodes were secured against her forehead and temples, bundles of wires snaking down to a series of parallel–linked computer processors, their lights blinking and flashing as Mishkin watched. Although he could not hear her, he could see her lips moving as though she were talking softly to herself.

'What are you doing to her? Recording her brain waves?'

Akhmed shook his head, his body almost trembling with excitement.

'No, we are recording the future.'

He reached out and flipped a switch on a control panel before him, and suddenly Mishkin could hear the girl's words as clearly as if he were standing right next to her.

'… they are closer now, watching.'

Mishkin found himself rooted to the spot as he listened to the girl's soft voice, speaking in the lilting, colorful inflection of Arabic with a Russian translator repeating her sentences so that Mishkin could understand them.

'Can you tell me who they are and where they've come from?' asked the voice of another scientist somewhere else in the building.

The girl remained silent only for a moment.

'They are two, one from here, the other who has travelled far.'

'Tell me about the one who has travelled.'

'He is tall, a soldier from Moscow,' the girl whispered softly. 'He is standing in the room nearby and he is watching me.'

Mishkin felt the hairs on his neck stand on end and his jaw slacken as he stared at the girl, who was lying with her eyes closed and had not moved an inch.

'Why is he here?'

'He comes seeking The Watchers.'

Mishkin turned to Akhmed. 'What is this?! She must have been told about me?'

Akhmed shook his head earnestly. 'The girls are kept in seclusion to avoid contaminating the data in such a way.' He reached out and pressed a button on the control panel.

'Tell me everything you can about him,' he ordered the young girl.

The girl hesitated for a few moments, screwed up her brow as though in concentration.

'He comes from the farms of Saransk,' she whispered. 'His parents died while he was away as a soldier. He hates the country for what it has become and yearns for a return to the glory days, for the chance to avenge all that his family lost. There is no greater enemy than the United States.'

She hesitated again, and Mishkin found himself waiting in horrified fascination until he heard her speak again.

'He fears the future just as his father did before him,' she whispered, and then she appeared to quote somebody. 'Trust nobody my son, for when everything we know and believe in falls apart so does the honor of those who claim to lead us.'

'Shut it off,' Mishkin uttered, his throat dry.

'She isn't finished yet and…'

'Shut it off now!' Mishkin roared as he whirled and loomed over Akhmed.

Akhmed cowered beneath the towering colonel as he hastily shut off the feed from the adjoining room and collapsed backwards into a chair. Mishkin stood with his fists clenched, visions of Akhmed's body jerking in anguished spasms beneath the Colonel's boots. With an effort he controlled his rage.

'How is this possible?' he growled.

Akhmed spoke quickly, cowering away from the bigger man.

'The program is part of the Expert Management Unit of the General Staff, whose task it is to examine unusual phenomena outside the experience of other departments. The main project of the unit is a state program on the discovery of intellectual human resources. The goal of the program is to identify ways to make the human brain work in a special regime. The Scientific Council of the program was led by the academician and neurophysiologist Natalya Bekhtereva, who until her death served as a scientific director of the Institute of Human Brain of RAS.'

Mishkin peered at Akhmed curiously. 'What the hell are you doing to these girls?'

'The work is an extension of projects carried out in the 1980s,' Akhmed replied anxiously. 'Hundreds of Soviet scientists worked on programs which concluded that a human being was in some respects an energy and information system that receives information from the outside, rather in the same way that a television aerial receives signals from a satellite. If you tune a human brain correctly, it acts just like an antenna and receives information in a way that most people would consider paranormal.'

Mishkin turned and looked again at the girl in the room nearby, still whispering to her captors about whatever she had seen, perhaps Mishkin threatening Akhmed. Suddenly self-conscious of his actions, Mishkin backed away from the scientist and forced himself to relax. His father's words, uttered long ago, echoed through his mind: When everything we know and believe in falls apart, so does the honor of those who claim to lead us.

Mishkin took a deep breath, and then spoke quietly.

'How many of these girls are there?'

'We have seven with confirmed telepathic abilities,' Akhmed replied.

'Out of how many potential subjects?'

Akhmed swallowed. 'We've captured around ten thousand girls over five years, ever since the country's civil war began. Most of the girls showed no innate abilities whatsoever and were released, but those who were blind showed amazing telepathic skills…, for a while.'

'Go on,' Mishkin snapped, sensing more.

'Some girls demonstrated these considerable abilities, but then lost them.'

'Lost them?' Mishkin echoed.

Akhmed nodded, his eyes wobbling in their sockets with fear. 'When the girls lose their virginity, they lose their skills. They can no longer see.'

Mishkin felt the rage return. 'And how did they lose their virginity inside a secure Russian facility?'

Akhmed swallowed thickly. 'The guards, they traded the girls. I didn't know anything about it and…'

Mishkin stepped toward Akhmed again and pressed one boot down on the scientist's chest as he reached out and flipped a switch on the console, reactivating the radio connection to the room in which the girl lay.

'Ask her who violated the other girls,' he rumbled.

Akhmed's face collapsed in fear and he shook his head feverishly. 'They cannot always be trusted. We have to be sure of what they're actually saying and…'

'Doctor Akhmed sold the girls to the guards or used them himself,' the girl said softly, her voice overpowering Akhmed's through the speakers in the room. 'When the raped girls lost their powers, they were thrown out into the streets or shot.'

Akhmed shrieked in horror as Mishkin lifted him physically out of his seat by his shirt and hurled him across the room. He pulled his pistol from its holster and slammed the butt down across Akhmed's skull, the loud cracks amplified by the room's close walls and Akmed's screams of terror and pain soaring until he fell silent, blood streaming from his battered skull.

Mishkin stood upright again, his chest heaving as he holstered his pistol. Behind him the door to the room flew open and two soldiers burst in. They took one look at the colonel and the motionless, bleeding body at his feet and immediately froze in position.

Mishkin turned to them, his grim expression and physical size brooking no opposition.

'Have the girls rounded up ready for extraction,' he snapped, and then pointed at the girl in the next room. 'Does over–use of those devices cause any kind of brain damage?'

One of the guards nodded.

'Too many hours inside it and the girls' seizures become uncontrollable. If they don't stop, they die.'

Mishkin's jaw ached as he held his fury inside.

'Put Akhmed in the trucks with the girls. We will keep the most capable and sell the rest to traffickers. The rest of the machines are to be packaged ready for transport out of Syria, understood?!'

'Yes colonel!'

The two guards scrambled over each other to lift Akhmed's unconscious body and escape the room as quickly as they could. Mishkin turned and looked once more at the young girl strapped to the bed in the adjoining room, and once again the fine hairs on his neck bristled with a superstitious awe. He could not explain how she had known about the words his father had spoken to him so many years before, words that resonated with him even now, but he knew without a shadow of a doubt that all of the girls needed to be smuggled out of Syria as soon as possible for they were now more valuable than the most powerful weapons in any country's nuclear arsenal.

Mishkin shook himself out of his torpor and made for the exit as he reached for his cell phone and dialed a number. He knew that they could not travel east due to the fighting outside the city, therefore the best option was to head west into Lebanon and from there to the Mediterranean where a Russian ship could take them north across the Black Sea to the Russian coast and safety.'

'Yes, Colonel?'

Gregorie's voice sounded even more monotone than usual down the line.

'You have the tablets?'

'I have images of them which we can decipher, and I have just landed in Homs.'

'Get the convoy ready,' Mishkin ordered. 'Bring the gunship and our troops also. We leave in an hour.'

***

XXVI

Beirut, Lebanon

The Le Royal Hotels & Resorts, Dbayeh in the west of the city looked as though it would have been equally at home in Las Vegas as Ethan and Nicola walked toward it alongside the coast. The sun was setting to the west on their right, the Mediterranean glittering like a stream of molten gold and the sky above turning a deep blue.

'It's almost romantic,' Lopez said as she slipped an arm through Ethan's. 'Best we look the part, right?'

Ethan smiled as they walked. 'You're not making a move on me are you?'

'We're off to see a man about smuggling children for sale in Europe,' Lopez cautioned him. 'That doesn't exactly inspire the romantic in me.'

'Me either,' Ethan agreed, 'but you're right, it's best to blend in.'

The city was filled with tourists, many of them Europeans but also a few Americans and even Russians milling about. Not for the first time it crossed Ethan's mind that despite the conflicts and political disputes that raged every day across the globe, the ordinary people of all nations happily got along without any issues whatsoever and even without the same languages. Russians waited for Americans to pass by on busy pathways, the Americans smiling in gratitude as they passed. Muslims bowed respectfully to Christians and Jews, their manners rewarded with equal gestures of friendship.

'Seems crazy, doesn't it,' Lopez said.

'What's that?'

'People,' she replied, seeming to read his mind. 'We get along just fine without politicians and governments. If only they knew, then we wouldn't have wars and people like you and me would be out of a job.'

Ethan nodded but said nothing as they turned into the immense tiered hotel, which was built it seemed into the cliffs themselves and overlooked gardens of palm trees and immaculate lawns. They walked together through a foyer bustling with tourists heading out for dinner or into the hotel's restaurant, and Ethan searched for the man they had come to meet.

From the crowds emerged a portly, dark skinned man with thick black hair and a gold chain about his neck that looked almost like a dog's collar. He wore a dark gray suit and a white shirt unbuttoned far enough to reveal a dense bush of curly black hair on his chest, and Ethan spotted rings on his fat fingers that were almost certainly solid gold.

'Mister Warner,' he breathed, the scent of alcohol and cigars brushing Ethan's face as he shook the man's hand, damp and limp. 'Welcome to Beirut, I am Muhammar Hussein.'

'This is Nicola Lopez,' Ethan introduced Lopez.

Hussein's black eyes settled on her and Ethan thought that he heard a moist sigh rattle from somewhere deep in the man's chest as he bowed and kissed the back of Lopez's hand. She did not withdraw the hand, but Ethan felt her grip on his arm tighten slightly.

Lopez smiled and looked at Ethan as she feigned delight. 'Isn't he a cutie?'

'This way my friends,' Hussein gestured for them to follow him.

The hotel's sprawling complex offered many locations for people to enjoy their evening undisturbed, and Hussein led them to the elevators. They travelled in silence up to the top floor of the hotel, Ethan instinctively understanding that no business would be discussed until they were in the safety of Hussein's apartment.

Hussein led them to a room and opened the door, gestured for them to enter. Ethan walked in and immediately caught sight of the four armed guards inside, all of them wearing suits that barely concealed the side arms in shoulder holsters. Hussein closed the door behind them and made a show of locking it before he strolled in and gestured to the expansive leather sofas.

'Please, be seated so that we can talk. We have much to discuss.'

Hussein poured two tumblers of dark liqor that he handed to them before he sat down opposite. Ethan had a few moments to survey the apartment, which was one of the hotel's penthouse suites. A broad balcony overlooked the glittering Mediterranean and the sunset beyond, and Ethan knew that each of the rooms below had similar balconies.

Muhammar's bodyguards were all muscle men with shaved or short hair, standing silently, their shirts white and immaculately pressed. Typically, trained bodyguards in the Middle East were not a patch compared to their western counterparts, but that did not make Ethan four times better than they were. If the meeting went south both he and Lopez would have to work hard to get out of the suite alive.

'Don't mind my companions,' Hussein said as he sat down. 'In this part of the world, hired guards are a necessity. You never know when the next revolution will begin.'

Ethan let a small grin spread on his face. 'The more confusion there is, the better business will be.'

Hussein chuckled heartily. 'You are a man of my cut, Mister Warner. Now, what is your business here? I was told that you have purchases you would like to make?'

Ethan leaned forward, his untouched drink on the table between them.

'We have clients across the globe, who would like to take advantage of the instability in Syria to obtain, how can I put it? Personal assistants.'

Hussein's dark eyes glittered. 'How personal?'

'As personal as it gets,' Ethan replied, 'and we're not looking for any bodies over twenty–five years of age.'

Ethan used the term "bodies" deliberately, trying to convey some sense of a man who cared little for the lives of those whom he was intending to sell. If Hussein noticed, he didn't show it.

'Boys or girls?' Hussein asked.

'Girls,' Ethan replied, 'young, orphans and unblemished, if you know what I mean?'

Hussein's cruel smile grew broader. 'I do, but what you are asking is difficult. It will cost more than other human traffic.'

'We have resources,' Ethan said. 'Our clients wish only to ensure a speedy delivery and absolute discretion, which is why we act for them.'

Hussein peered at Lopez. 'And what is your role in this, my lovely?'

Lopez's smile didn't flicker as she replied. 'Humanitarian.'

Hussein raised an eyebrow. 'How so?'

'Sleeping with a fat rich idiot for a few years is far better than being bombed, gang–raped and tortured, which is what most of these girls will face if they're left where they are in Syria. We're doing them a favor and we earn money from it as a result. Everybody wins.'

Hussein's eyes flicked back to Ethan. 'Why orphans?'

'Less people likely to be looking for them,' Ethan replied without hesitation. 'We did a good trade for years in China with young girls until the Chinese government relaxed their one–child policy. The policy had meant that families favored sons over daughters, who were rejected, sold or even murdered at birth by their own families. We saved hundreds of them, paid virtually nothing to the families to take the girls off their hands, and then took tens of thousands of dollars per baby from sterile parents in Singapore, Malaysia, America, you name it. Nobody ever came looking for them.'

Hussein raised an eyebrow and inclined his head. 'So you have done well from this business.'

'Well enough,' Lopez replied, 'until the trade slowed. Now, we're looking at war zones like Syria for fresh product. Orphans, or at worst children who have been lost by their families, represent the safest product. We can get them across borders quickly and without attracting attention, provided you can get them out of Syria.'

Ethan gestured to Hussein's gold necklace chain and rings. 'A trade that's seen you profit well too, I notice.'

Hussein set his glass down. 'There is money to be made in people, if you know where to go and who to ask.' His expression hardened. 'Fifty per cent in advance, fifty on delivery. Where should the girls be delivered?'

'Arkhoum,' Ethan replied, 'just across the border. We will transport them from there to Beirut where they will be despatched on private aircraft to their new owners. How will you get the girls?'

Hussein shrugged his shoulders. 'Most are in refugee camps across Syria, fleeing either the civil war there or internal conflict in Iraq. We get about ten to twenty viable bodies a day. Demand is high, especially for eleven to thirteen year olds.' Hussein smiled. 'Like your clients, mine prefer them young.'

Ethan smiled tightly. 'We want them fresh, not battered or sullied by other users. What guarantees do we have that these girls will be in prime condition?'

Hussein's affable demeanor vanished like a desert wind and he leaned forward and glared at Ethan.

'My reputation is built on quality,' he growled. 'That's how you found me. In contrast I know nothing about you, you haven't said how many bodies you want and I have only your word that you will pay if I supply them. In my experience, words are cheap. The money now, or this conversation is over.'

Ethan glanced at Lopez and grinned.

'You're right, I like him too.'

Ethan reached slowly into his jacket pocket, watching the guards and keeping his other hand in sight for them as he retrieved a small velvet pouch. He opened it and let the contents spill out onto the table between them.

'Still the best and most untraceable currency there is,' he said as the cluster of pristine diamonds glittered in the light from the sunset streaming through the apartment. 'These stones are valued at a quarter million US dollars, sufficient for at least a hundred bodies.'

Hussein rubbed his thick stubble as he looked at the stones. 'I'll have to get them checked out.'

'Feel free,' Lopez said as she placed a business card on the table alongside the diamonds, 'but you'll find them to be perfect stones. Once you're satisfied, you can reach us at this number. We'll be ready to do the exchange as soon as you are.'

Ethan stood with Lopez and shook Hussein's hand.

'I will be in touch,' he said, his eyes still drawn to the sparkling jewels.

Ethan turned with Lopez and they walked together to the door. A guard let them out and they walked slowly down the corridor outside, Ethan aware that the apartment door behind them had not yet closed.

'As soon as the merchandise is ready and Hussein calls, I'll contact our clients in South Africa,' Ethan said. 'You handle Brazil.'

'Will do,' Lopez replied softly. 'This could work out really well – Syria is like a gift that keeps on giving.'

The door behind them closed, but Ethan and Lopez did not speak again until they were out of the hotel and on the hot, busy streets.

'You think he'll go for it?' she asked.

'No telling,' Ethan replied, 'but most likely he'll agree to the sale, set up a meeting, then try to kill us and keep the girls and the money.'

'Sounds about right,' Lopez nodded. 'I almost puked when he touched me.'

'He'll get what's coming to him,' Ethan replied as he pulled out his cell phone and dialed a number.

'Did you do it?' Hellerman asked as soon as he picked up the line.

'Hussein's apartment is bugged,' Ethan confirmed, 'one under the table in the hotel apartment, another tucked into the sofa. Let us know what you find out.'

'Will do,' Hellerman replied and the line went dead.

*

Gregorie stood near a row of palm trees and listened to the hum of the traffic and the buzz of conversations in a dozen tongues as he watched the hotel and the couple who had just walked out of it, the Latino woman with her arm slipped through that of the tall American. Just another pair of tourists enjoying the heady atmosphere and aroma of a Cairo evening.

Gregorie looked down at his cell phone and dialed a number.

As soon as the line picked up, he spoke a simple sentence.

'I have found Warner and Lopez, they are in Beirut.'

Gregorie shut off the line and stepped out into the street, following a discreet distance behind his targets and already inventing new and unusual ways to dispose of them.

***

XXVII

Washington DC

General Nellis stepped into the interior of the White House as soon as he had been scanned and checked by the Secret Service detail manning the main entrance on the north side of the West Wing.

The Secret Service detail assigned two men to the general and led him through the building. The West Wing housed the President's Oval Office and those of his senior staff, along with the Cabinet Room and the Situation Room, much of which was contained underground in sealed bunkers where the President and his staff could shelter in the event of a global nuclear exchange or similar catastrophe.

Nellis followed the agents to the door of the Oval Office and waited patiently as one of them knocked discreetly on the door and then entered the room. Nellis heard a few muffled words exchanged between the agent and his superior, and then the door was opened fully and Nellis was allowed into probably the most famous office on earth.

The president was waiting for him, and a quickly extended hand and a genuine smile put Nellis somewhat at ease as the door closed behind him, the two agents standing in silence on the other side of the door and ready to enter at a moment's notice.

'Thank you for agreeing to see me at such short notice, general.'

'No problem Mister President,' Nellis replied as he sat down. 'What can I do for you?'

Nellis knew how busy all Presidents were, how quickly they aged in their tenures, so he wasn't surprised when the president dispensed with any preamble and got straight to the point.

'ARIES,' he said simply. 'We're shutting you down.'

Nellis stared in silence at his Commander in Chief for a long moment before he replied carefully.

'Why would you shut us down, sir?'

The President sighed.

'I'm not shutting you down, general,' he said. 'Circumstances have resulted in the program becoming a liability for us, for national security. I can't have your people wandering off into the sunset with sensitive data and considerable sums of money.'

'We're on the case, Mister President. Jarvis won't get far.'

'You sound far more confident than my Chiefs of Staff,' the President noted. 'Something I should know?'

Nellis kept his bearing upright and his chin high as he replied.

'I know the individual concerned well. I don't think that betraying his country is what he has in mind.'

'He's already betrayed his country.'

'He's acting on what has gone before, Mister President. Jarvis believes that if he simply hands over the funds and data obtained from Majestic Twelve they'll be used for further corrupt acts by other men of power.'

'That's not his call to make and you know it.'

'I agree,' Nellis conceded, 'but I don't want to see the rest of the program suffer due to the ill–conceived act of one individual. ARIES is far too valuable and the team I have far too involved to just walk away from it all…' The president smiled broadly as he listened to Nellis. 'What, Mister President?'

'You want to retain control of the program.'

'Yes sir,' Nellis replied without hesitation. 'We have agents in the field who could be compromised if ARIES is shut down or handed over to Homeland.'

'Homeland won't be controlling the program, general.'

Nellis hesitated, now unsure of himself. 'Who, then?'

The President sat back in his seat and folded his hands before him. 'General, there are some things that I simply cannot share with you.'

Nellis tried not to baulk at the statement but forty years in the military got the better of him as his allergy to bullcrap shone through.

'Mister President, I thought that we were talking about national security here.'

'We are, general. That's the whole point.'

'You think that the DIA is not secure enough?' Nellis asked, genuinely surprised.

The President leaned forward and spoke softly.

'General, I don't believe that *any* agency is secure enough.' Nellis frowned, and the president finally seemed to relent a little and opened his hands as he spoke. 'You've heard of the Book of Secrets, I take it?'

'The President's Book of Secrets?' Nellis asked, and was rewarded with a nod. 'Sure. It's a book handed down through the line of all US Presidents, detailing all of the highest security data and an annotated history of events experienced by all previous presidents during their tenures.'

'Precisely,' the president confirmed, 'all the way back to George Washington and our founding fathers. The book is a hand–written account of each president covering all of the major events they experienced so that the incoming president can get into the job with immediate effect.'

Nellis sat for a moment in deep thought.

'There's something in the book, isn't there.'

The president nodded slowly. 'Something that cannot be shared, that cannot even really be understood yet. It is as old as humanity and it is something that I simply cannot allow to be exposed. It's why the President's Book of Secrets remains hand–written and available only to elected occupants of the White House. Nobody else can access it. It cannot be hacked, stolen or copied.'

Nellis smiled wryly. 'Then it is only as secure as the integrity of the next president, just as an agency like the DIA is only as secure as its employees.'

Now, the President shook his head.

'Not quite, general. If you had read what's in that book, you would know that no human being would ever expose it, would ever even speak of it except in the guarded words that I'm using now.'

Something popped into Nellis's head as he recalled a talk show from some years' before.

'I remember you talking about it in 2009 in a radio interview with talk show host Michael Smerconish.'

The President inclined his head. 'I told him I'd seen the Book of Secrets, and I told him nothing about what was in it. It's actually no real secret that the thing exists, but its contents remain classified at the utmost level and for good reason.'

Nellis's brain flipped as he finally understood.

'We're not being shut down because our security isn't tight enough,' he said finally. 'We're being shut down because we're closing in on something.'

The president neither agreed nor disagreed, speaking softly.

'Most all presidents have been aware of factors in our species' history that have influenced us over many millennia. Turns out that we weren't the first to figure that out, and as a result almost everything we do behind the scenes politically is geared toward trying to understand things that happened in the distant past. You're aware also of our great capital city's architectural peculiarities, of the influence of the ancient world right here in America?'

General Nellis knew well enough of the history of Washington DC, and he knew too that most of the Founding Fathers were known to have been Freemasons. However, he also knew that most of the occultist trash regurgitated by many authors over the years regarding the city's supposedly Satanic layout was the result of religious mania rather than any true conspiracy.

'I know that our country and this city was built by men who worshipped no god in the Christian sense,' Nellis replied, 'but what does that have to do with the DIA's mission?'

The President searched the air above him for the right words before he replied.

'There is a reason, general, why the National monument in Washington DC is an obelisk, identical to those found in ancient Egypt. Likewise, at the Capitol and here at the White House, fluted columns are heavily featured that are identical to those found in ancient Greece and Rome. The senate itself is based on the Roman idea of proportional representation of the people, and the streets of our city do mark out on a gigantic scale the icons of Freemasony, the square and compasses that denote the inevitable and welcome triumph of science over blind faith.'

Nellis rubbed his temples. 'I get the Masonic connection, but what does that have to do with ancient Egypt or Rome?'

'The science of construction and architecture is what made our civilizations great,' the President said simply. 'I could never say this in an election campaign or out on the White House lawn, but when you have science and education at the head of government policy, countries prosper generation by generation. When you have religion at the head of government policy, the opposite occurs. The Freemasons understand this, and the only reason they became so secretive was because for much of their existence they were persecuted by those who insisted that blind faith was the only way to think. Being burned at the stake was a popular punishment in Europe for centuries for those who dared to commit blasphemy and place learning above belief.'

The president reached into a drawer by his side and produced a small wooden box with a glass top. Nellis saw that inside was sealed a dollar bill, and the President began pointing out features on the bill to Nellis.

'The Great Seal on our dollar bill, the design of which was approved by Congress in 1782, beneath which is an ancient Egyptian pyramid with a glowing eye, signifying the All Seeing Eye of ancient mythology. The sacred number thirteen is encoded throughout the design in thirteen arrows, thirteen stripes on the shield and thirteen stars of David which can be joined to form a star above the eagle's head. Beneath the pyramid is the motto "Novus Ordo Seclorum", which is Latin for the New Order of the Ages.'

Nellis stared at the bill for a moment and looked up at the President.

'Why are you telling me all of this, Mister President, instead of ensuring that ARIES continues its work? You're only giving me reasons to keep going.'

The President put the dollar bill back in the drawer and spoke quietly, as though even here in this most secure of offices he feared that there might be those who were listening.

'General, though it may pain you to learn it, there is little true power in this office or in the halls of this building. The organized government of today is a cypher, an illusion. I only hold power because massive corporations allow me to, in return for me ensuring that as much as possible is done at the executive level to bolster their growth and profits. Many believe this to be a corrupt and unjust arrangement, but it is the way that our society has grown for decades. However, there are those who know that in reality, in the long term, government is really holding the fort until...'

The President broke off for a moment, hesitating, and Nellis realized that he was leaning forward in his seat.

'What, Mister President?'

The President gathered himself again, as though speaking for the first time of something so classified that he could barely bring himself to say it.

'Until the New World Order begins,' he said finally.

Nellis stared at the President for a long moment before he could bring himself to speak.

'But isn't that what's written on the dollar bill, that this is a new order of the ages that we're creating?'

'No, general,' the President said. 'That's where all the conspiracy theorists and all the sceptics alike get it wrong. The ancient civilizations of earth built their empires and their immense structures to signal the skies that they were ready.

When Washington DC was built, the great architects and Freemasons did the exact same thing.'

Nellis felt his breath catch in his throat as he realized what the President as saying.

'They weren't starting a new world order.'

'No,' the President agreed, 'they were preparing for it to begin. We still are.'

Nellis chose his next words carefully. 'And who will govern us when this new world order begins?'

The President smiled bleakly.

'The answer to that is in the Book of Secrets, general,' he replied. 'I can never tell you, for it is up to them to announce their presence.'

The air in the Oval Office seemed suddenly cold as Nellis shifted uncomfortably in his seat. 'Them?'

The President said nothing.

'I don't like not knowing.' Nellis added.

'Nor do I,' the President replied. 'ARIES must be closed down, we have no choice. I have absolutely no control over what happens next.'

Nellis felt a sudden anxiety twist his stomach. 'I need to warn my people.'

The President sighed. 'I'm afraid it's too late for that, General. By this time, ARIES will be being shut down by Homeland.'

Nellis almost stood up out of his chair. 'You can't do that!'

'I know I can't,' the President said, 'but some people can. It's over, General. You will be reassigned and any public announcement about any of this will be considered a treasonable offence, liable to Court Martial.'

Nellis seethed in silence. 'You called me here to get me out of the DIAC building.'

The President stood, his features apologetic as he went on.

'I'm sorry, really I am, but in this case the needs of the many very much outweigh the needs of the few.'

Nellis stared at the President, almost speechless for the first time in his career.

'I have people in the field Mister President, good people, civilian contractors.'

The President nodded, gravely.

'There's nothing that I can do for them. They're on their own.'

***

XXVIII

Hellerman dashed through the ARIES Watch Room with a sheet of paper in one hand as he hurried to the main conference room and shut the door. He quickly reached out to a wall panel and pressed a series of buttons, the windows of the room that looked out over the rest of the department turning opaque in an instant.

Hellerman activated a viewing screen and placed a call to the communications specialists, who routed the agency's satellite signals toward a location in Beirut. It took only a couple of minutes for Ethan and Nicola to pick up the signal alert and activate their laptop.

'We're here,' Ethan said as his image, along with that of Lopez, appeared on the split screen before Hellerman. 'Where's the fire?'

Hellerman placed the sheet of paper before him as he spoke softly.

'We've got a target location from the bugs you placed in Muhammar Hussein's apartment,' he said, 'Al Kibur in north west Lebanon. It's a small settlement near the Syrian border where Muhammar meets up with incoming convoys of Syrians headed for the coast. Human traffic exchanges hands and crossed the border into Lebanon from the main road passing the settlement.'

'Has Hussein got a date set for the exchange?' Lopez asked.

'No,' Hellerman replied. 'He called his contact and was told that the goods, as they refer to them, were for sale. You should know that the person who answered the call was Russian and that Hussein did not appear to know him, but I was able to trace the call and identify him as a GRU Colonel by the name of Mishkin. We have already confirmed that he has been assigned to the Russian unit *Mother Earth*.'

Ethan frowned. 'You mentioned something about a Russian colonel entering the picture in Homs before.'

'Well recalled,' Hellerman confirmed. 'My take is that Russia's moved in and is clearing the site. They'll run west for the coast most likely but will not enter Lebanon.'

'Any ideas on when they're leaving?' Ethan asked.

Hellerman nodded. 'Radio traffic suggests the next few hours, right out of Homs.'

On the screen, Ethan looked at Lopez.

'If we move now we could make it to the border and intercept them.'

'Yeah,' Lopez agreed, 'and if we had a battalion of soldiers with us we might not die when we get there.'

Hellerman cut in.

'I can call in support for you,' he said. 'I can have attack helicopters in position ready to move in once you hit the convoy. Make lots of noise and smoke for them and they'll come right in.'

Ethan nodded. 'Make it happen. Have DIA agents arrest Muhammar Hussein and recover the diamonds we used as payment, while we get to the border. I don't want to be late for the Russians when they get there.'

'What about the tablets?' Lopez asked. 'Did you complete the translation?'

Hellerman grinned in delight. 'Some of it. It turns out that the cuneiform there is of a more ancient origin that I'd previously believed so it will need an expert to decipher it accurately. There were many glyphs which were pronounced the same but represented different words. Later a system of determinatives, which gave you a hint at the category a word belonged to, and of phonetic components, which indicated how to pronounce a word, developed and helped disambiguate the meanings of glyphs. Trouble is, that's all way above my skill set. We'll need a specialist in the field to finish the translation.'

'How old is it?' Lopez asked him.

'The earliest publicly recognized texts come from the cities of Uruk and Jamdat Nasr and date back to 3,300 BCE. But this tablet is inscribed with text dating back at least ten thousand years.'

Ethan blinked. 'Ten thousand? That's older than any recognized civilization.'

'Far older,' Hellerman confirmed. 'This tablet wasn't created at the time the front engravings were made but when those on what we perceived to be the back were performed. This is by far the most ancient piece of human literature ever discovered and if it was publicly recognized it would probably be worth tens of millions of dollars.'

'Tens of millions?' Lopez echoed with a smile.

'Stay focused,' Ethan peered at her before he continued. 'What does it say?'

Hellerman raised an eyebrow as he glanced down at the tablet.

'That's the big deal,' he replied, 'because this isn't a record of a transaction between two countries or some record of an ancient battle. This is a prophecy, a prediction of the future.'

Ethan leaned closer to the screen. 'Read it out, Hellerman.'

Hellerman cleared his throat and began to read.

'When the stars traverse the sky at night; when a second sun shines over the north; when the great vault is split asunder and the riches of the earth are worth no more; when the lands of ice run free and blood falls from the sky upon the land of the tiger; when giant tortoises guard the walls of Canaan; when the earth rises and swallows the sky; then, and only then, will the great union prevail and The Watchers shall return, their words heard from human skin.'

A silence followed Hellerman's reading as he watched Ethan and Lopez for their reaction.

'Could just be more drug–addled ravings,' Lopez said, dismissive as ever. 'There's a whole industry that's been built up over the predictions of people like

Nostradamus or whatever, but nothing they've ever written has been proven to be a true prophecy.'

'I agree,' Hellerman replied, 'but this tablet was written thousands of years ago and contains nothing that suggests the author stood to gain anything. I did a little checking of things, and came up with this.'

Hellerman held out the piece of paper he had been carrying with him.

'The stars traversing the sky at night could refer to modern satellites in orbit, catching the light of the sun after it's already set. A second sun shines over the north could refer to the recent meteor that came down over Russia: it was supersonic debris and the shockwave shattered windows for hundreds of miles. The great vault I believe is a reference to the diamond mines of southern Africa – so many diamonds have now been mined that they sit in warehouses piled roof-high and are technically worthless. Companies like DeBeers keep them secret to artificially inflate the price of diamonds on the market.'

'Pity Muhammar doesn't know about that,' Lopez said to Ethan with a nudge.

'What about the rest?' Ethan asked Hellerman. 'Blood falling from the sky? How is that possible?'

Hellerman grabbed a newspaper article and showed it to Ethan and Lopez.

'The land of the ice running free is a reference to the Arctic, which due to climate change is now ice free in the northern hemisphere's summer and allows for the passage of ships. As for the blood falling from the sky, this article is from Kerala in India: blood red rain fell there in 2001, confounding experts who claim to have found alien DNA inside the rain that even looks like blood cells.'

Hellerman gestured to another article.

'Giant tortoises guarding the walls of Canaan: Canaan is what is now known as Palestine, and here we have images of tanks outside the wall that Israel is building to block the Palestinians inside, apartheid all over again.'

Even Lopez was now paying close attention as Hellerman went on.

'The only thing I can't figure out is the line about the earth rising to swallow the sky, which may possibly refer to a volcano or similar, and words from human skin. However, I don't have to elaborate on what the great union might mean.'

'The Soviet Union,' Ethan said. 'It might be a prophecy of the return to Communism for Russia, of Putin's rise to power.'

Hellerman nodded.

'The most important thing to remember here is that although the Russians were able to steal the photographs of the tablet, they only got images of one side.'

Ethan grinned. 'Then they've only got half of the information.'

'That still might be enough for the Russian president or those working for him to get close to what they're searching for,' Hellerman warned.

'And if he's sending people out based on similar prophecies, perhaps by the girls they've abducted, then he will merely be seeing himself as fulfilling his destiny regardless of what wars may come between Russia and victory.'

Ethan leaned close to the screen.

'We're moving, now. Do we have a contact here we can trust?'

'I've already deployed him,' Hellerman said. 'His name is Talal and he will meet you at Akroum near the border. Hurry, I don't know what's going on here but General Nellis hasn't returned from a meeting with the President and I know that Homeland are breathing down his back. Watch yourselves.'

***

XXIX

Akroum, Lebanon

'This is as close as I can take you without us being monitored by the border patrols.'

The battered old truck clattered to a halt by the roadside in a cloud of dust as Ethan climbed out of the cab. He paid the driver, a farmer who had agreed to drive them out to the north, while Lopez and Talal hauled their kit from the rear of the vehicle. Ethan stood back and watched as the truck turned about and drove away into the distance, abandoning them on the lonely hillside.

'Great,' Lopez said. 'Now what?'

'We walk,' Talal replied, a rather skinny Lebanese DIA agent who Ethan figured had been hired for his local knowledge rather than his field skills. 'The Syrian border is only ten kilometres to the north.'

'Only ten,' Lopez echoed as she shielded her hands to look up into the burning blue sky. 'That's a relief, 'cause I thought it might be a long way and all. Like five kilometres.'

'Stop complaining,' Ethan smiled as they set off. 'You said you could do with the exercise.'

'Yeah but there's nothing and nobody out here if the exercise gets too much,' Lopez pointed out.

Ethan knew that they were in a remote and poor area of Lebanon. Some forty miles north of Beirut, they had travelled out through Qubayyat and Aandaqet to this barren region named after one of its highest mountains. Talal gestured with animated enthusiasm as they trekked along a dusty old road heading north.

'This mountainous region is abundant with archeological sites and remnants from Phoenician, Greek, Roman, Byzantine, and Islamic civilizations,' he explained. 'There are rock necropolises and ancient tombs made of stone slabs and carved into cliffs. Down there in Akroum itself you will find a Roman temple and a large Byzantine church dedicated to Mar Shamshoum al–Jabbar.'

'That's fascinating,' Lopez grumbled as they walked. 'I didn't know you were a professor as well as a DIA agent. Where do the traffickers hide their cargo before trying to get out into the Mediterranean?'

'We don't know yet,' Talal admitted, 'but we're sure they come through here with stock bound for Europe, mostly the sex trade but some general slaves too.'

Ethan winced at Talal's casual reference to the horrendous suffering that the girls being smuggled out of Syria went through, but as it had seemed when he had been in Iraq, the scale and frequency of the suffering became so great that people became almost desensitized to it, as though it were a normal part of their lives. Sure, they detested it, but nobody was shocked any more.

'Ah, here, look at this,' Talal said.

Ethan saw a well preserved temple before them, the cella of which was divided by a gigantic arch. Nearby were the ruins of a larger temple, reduced to what looked like foundations in the desert.

'Wadi es–Sebaa,' Talal announced grandly, 'the Valley of the Lion. These are monuments that date back to the Babylonians!'

Ethan could see two massive obelisks standing on the hillside, one representing a figure wearing a tiara and confronting a lion that was standing on its hind legs. Ninety feet or so further up the hill was a conical stele that looked oddly out of place.

'What's that?' he asked Talal.

'Shir as–Sanam,' Talal replied, 'or the Cliff of the Statue. Nobody knows who built it, but presumably the Babylonians were busy here.'

Lopez stopped near something lying in the rocks, and she leaned down and picked up what looked like a rusted shell casing that she showed to Ethan.

'Looks like the Babylonians weren't the only ones busy out here,' she said.

Talal looked at the shell and nodded. 'The Lebanese Shia group Hezbollah sent its fighters on an offensive along Lebanon's eastern border with Syria, fighting alongside government forces to dislodge opposition forces from strongholds in the mountains near Qalamoun.'

Ethan looked up sharply at the surrounding hills. 'Qalamoun is a fair way south of here.'

'The area is important for the Syrians for securing a key road which connects the capital Damascus to Homs, and then on to President Bashar al–Assad's stronghold of Latakia on the western coast,' Talal said. 'The rebel forces are guerrillas, using this region as their hideout.'

Lopez was also keenly searching the hillside for signs of enemy combatants who would not hesitate to abduct a westerner for the leverage it might give them in the conflict.

'If Hezbollah is operating out here, we can't predict how they'll react to us if we're spotted,' she said.

'The US Government is providing funds to Hezbollah fighters,' Talal said, 'to help prevent Syria's war from spilling over into Lebanon, but we all know what Daesh want, and that's as many people and countries at war with each other as possible. We must tread carefully.'

Even as he spoke, Talal's cell phone rang in his pocket and he answered it. Ethan listened to the lively discussion in Arabic as Talal gesticulated and asked questions, then he shut the phone off.

'We've got radio traffic from out of Homs,' he reported. 'Some big shot Russian colonel there has just led a convoy out of the city with military escort.'

'That must be our guy Mishkin,' Lopez said.

Talal nodded. 'The frequency is heavily shielded but your National Security Agency is passing all Signals Intelligence from this region to the Lebanese government and they decrypted it. The report mentioned Operation Orakul.'

'The same one in the reports we saw,' Lopez said'.

Ethan nodded.

We're going to need some support of our own,' he said as he reached for the satellite phone. 'Hellerman's got Apache helicopters on stand–by waiting for our call.'

'Your call could be traced,' Talal warned. 'The Russians are probably assisting the Syrian forces in the same way the Americans are helping us.'

'That's a chance we're going to have to take,' Ethan said as he dialed a number. 'We can't just stroll to the border and snatch these girls out from under an armed escort without support.'

Lopez narrowed her eyes at him. 'What did you have in mind?'

Ethan raised a hand to forestall her as the line connected.

'Warner, operations, three–five–zero–nine–four: request immediate close air support.'

*

Defense Intelligence Agency,

Washington DC

'Warner, operations, three–five–zero–nine–four: request immediate close air support.'

The DIA's ARIES Watch Station picked up the signal immediately, the call being broadcast live over the tanoys inside the watch room. Hellerman leaped out of his seat and dashed across to the terminal pool as he checked his watch.

'Seventeen hundred twelve eastern seaboard time,' one of the pool operators replied to Ethan's call, 'fourteen hundred twelve local. State resources.'

Ethan's voice replied, his tones easily recognizable as though he was in the same room.

'Infantry plus attack helicopters, as fast as you can. Local intelligence suggests movement of civilians under duress by Russian forces to the south west of Homs.'

Hellerman grabbed the microphone as he replied.

'Engaging Russian forces could result in an international incident.'

'Being caught red handed abducting children out of Syria against their wishes is the justification,' Ethan replied briskly. 'The Russians won't sing about it as long as we have evidence of what they've been doing. Target our satellite signal and get on it, because by now the Russians will know we're here!'

Ethan shut the line off in customary style, leaving Hellerman no choice but to go along with the plan.

'Do it,' Hellerman said to the operator. 'Any assets within range, low profile essential.'

***

XXX

Syria

Aaron Mitchell lay prone against a low ridge as he peered through a pair of collapsible binoculars down into a shallow valley. The city of Homs was visible to the east, a gray smear in the haze that sparkled as distant windows reflected the searing sunlight.

A single arterial road travelled out from the distant city and snaked its way through the empty deserts past the settlement of Khurbat Gazi and on toward the coast at Al–Hamidiyah. At a point just a mile west of where Mitchell lay the road passed within a mile of the Lebanon border, demarked by the Al–Kabur river. Like so many of the world's borders it was guarded, but sufficiently vast that it was easy for small groups to slip through as they fled the savage civil war raging throughout Syria.

Mitchell watched as he waited, and behind him he heard the soft noises being made by a number of highly trained operatives who had been hired by Garrett and Jarvis to assist him. Aaron was still a fine field operative, but he was getting too old now for the rough and tumble of direct confrontation with armed soldiers, especially when they were likely to be as numerous as the Russian contingent due to pass this way.

'They'll be using civilian vehicles or Syrian military trucks,' he briefed the ten men behind him. 'The Russians have a legal presence in Syria but they won't want to alert the media or the UN to anything else they're up so it will have to be a small convoy, nothing that attracts too much attention.'

'If they're stealing children out of Homs for Russia,' one of the soldiers asked, 'why would they transport them west? Wouldn't they head north toward Chechnya or Georgia?'

'They're heading for Bassel Al–Assad International Airport,' Mitchell explained. 'It's held by the Russians, who will take the abductees they wish to keep with them to Russia and sell the rest to dealers who will transport them into Europe. They won't risk going too far north first because of the threat from rebel forces both here and in Chechnya, so they'll head west to the coast first and then north. This location is the best position to sell off any unwanted baggage to smugglers inside Lebanon before they move on.'

Mitchell turned to look at the men behind him.

'We won't have long before the Lebanese authorities are alerted to any firefight here on the border. They're already nervous of any advance made by the Islamic militants of Daesh toward the Mediterranean and will likely react with extreme aggression if they locate us. Our purpose is to hit the Russians hard, grab the girls and get the hell out as quickly and quietly as we can.'

To that end, Mitchell had positioned his team to the north of the main road, Syrian traffic being driven on the right and thus passing them by at close range. Banks of trees close to the river provided cover, and the river itself a simple escape route. Four compact Futura Commando assault inflatables waited by the river bank, selected for their ability to provide a quick getaway into Lebanese territory where the team could call in an extraction via road using Garrett's virtually limitless financial power.

Mitchell checked the road again, only sparse traffic heading east but a somewhat busier flow passing them by headed west, away from Syria. He settled in again and waited patiently in the stifling heat, grateful for the limited shade afforded them by the trees. As long as they spotted their target far enough in advance and no local hero was stupid enough to get in their way, Mitchell and his men would be mission–complete and out of the area long before the Russians could mount an effective defense.

*

'See anything yet?' Lopez asked.

Ethan shook his head as he crouched in the bushes on the south side of the main road, watching the flow of traffic heading past them.

'They're gonna be in unmarked vehicles to avoid attracting attention. If they're smart they'll have a couple of cars out front and in vanguard to give covering fire if the main convoy is attacked, so we need to pick those off first.'

Talal and Lopez watched as Ethan pulled a pair of hand grenades from their kit.

'Subtle as ever,' she observed. 'And once we've presumably heroically brought an armed Russian convoy to a halt with just a couple of rifles and some grenades, then what?'

Ethan gestured to the road before them.

'As long as no idiot gets in our way, we can use smoke grenades to block the view of their support guards and hit the main convoy hard and fast. We cross under the highway on the riverbank and get to the truck. The sooner we alert the Lebanese to our presence the better, as they'll be under orders to repel any armed troops they see near the border.'

'And our own support?' Lopez asked.

'The Russian and Lebanese both know what an Apache attack helicopter looks like and they know to run when they see one,' Ethan assured her. 'We make as much noise and smoke as we can, use the Lebanese to cover our escape with the girls and then the Apaches to extract us and get into RAF Akrotiri in Cyprus.'

Talal frowned.

'So we're using the Lebanese to fight the Russians, and then hoping they'll both run away when the Americans arrive?'

'Clever, no?' Ethan grinned at him.

Lopez rolled her eyes, and then her gaze fixed on something further up the road.

'Incoming.'

Ethan turned and saw a pair of four-ton trucks still some way off in the distance. The only thing that marked them out as unusual was the fact that they were more or less identical in size, color and markings. Although that could have been the result of perhaps the transport of goods or livestock out of Homs, it was a fact that Syria's civil war meant that it was hardly a haven for exports of anything other than frightened refugees.

Ethan peered into the distance and spotted a pair of cars moving ahead of the trucks, close together.

'That's the one,' he said confidently. 'Be ready.'

Talal looked nervously at Lopez. 'They'll be armed.'

'They always are,' she replied wearily as she pulled an AR–16 assault rifle from their kit bag and checked the weapon over before slamming a fresh clip in and cocking the weapon. 'Best you get your head down and make for the truck. Get the engine running and be ready to meet up with us facing in the direction of away from here, got it?'

Talal nodded and ran away to the south in a low crouch as Lopez turned to Ethan.

'Okay, what's the plan?'

Ethan looked at the two advance vehicles as they closed in on their position, and judged the distance between them and the following trucks as he readied his own weapon, an AR–16 identical to Lopez's.

'You keep the front escort pinned down once we've got smoke cover, I'll head for the trucks.'

'And the vanguard?'

'They're the unlucky ones,' Ethan said. 'They get the frag' grenades.'

Ethan pulled two smoke grenades out and watched as the cars closed in, and when they were almost upon them he hurled the grenades out over the wide road. Both of them arced across the asphalt and tumbled along as the cars passed by, spewing thick clouds of dense gray smoke.

'Go, now!'

Ethan leaped out from his hiding place as he heard the advance vehicle's tyres screech as the driver saw the smoke and emergency braked, thick veils of smoke spilling on the hot wind as Ethan glimpsed armed men hurl themselves out of the vehicle.

***

XXXI

'What the hell?!'

Mitchell lined up his rifle on the driver of the lead vehicle and was about to take his shot when he glimpsed clouds of smoke suddenly burst from the opposite side of the road. He dropped the rifle's sights from his eye to see two figures burst from concealment beneath the bank on the far side of the road, concealed from the drivers by the billowing clouds of smoke.

'We've got incoming!'

Mitchell heard the warning even as he saw one of the figures open fire on the armed soldiers pouring from the advance vehicles as they screeched to a halt, the guards leaping for cover behind the cars. Another figure dashed out of view behind the smoke screen toward the convoy that was now also screeching to a halt.

Mitchell barely got a glimpse of the fast moving figure, but he saw enough of the rangy man sprinting across the road to recognize him.

'Warner.'

The clattering of gunfire intensified from the advance guard vehicles as Mitchell spotted a tiny speck of jet–black hair amid the dense bushes fifty meters down the road on the opposite bank. A withering hail of fire from the Russian guards smashed down the bank toward Lopez as they recovered from the surprise attack and began mounting a spirited retaliation.

'Direct your fire on the lead vehicles!' Mitchell ordered.

The team behind him leaped into positon and moments later their M–16 assault rifles opened up with a savage barrage of fire. Mitchell watched as the Russian troops, completely focused on the attack from the front, were hammered with gunfire from directly behind.

The Russian's defense collapsed into disarray as the lethally accurate fire from Mitchell's team, most of whom were former US Special Forces, cut them down in a frenzy of bullets.

'Finish them and then head for the main convoy!' he snapped.

*

Ethan hit the asphalt hard and sprinted toward the two trucks as they skidded to a halt on the hot road. He could see the drivers already opening their doors, rifles in their hands as they made to return fire on their attackers.

Ethan dropped to one knee and aimed carefully before he fired. The first shot hit the nearest driver square in the chest as his boots landed on the asphalt. The driver spun sideways as he dropped his weapon and collapsed onto the asphalt, slumping awkwardly against the vehicle's tire. Ethan switched aim to the second driver, fired once and hit the man low in the belly even as he saw more troops spilling from the vehicles.

Ethan grabbed the two fragmentation grenades and hurled them both at the rear guard vehicles as they screeched to a halt behind the main convoy and armed soldiers leaped out. Ethan dashed for cover behind the first truck as he saw the troops emerging from the vehicles hit by a double blast as both grenades detonated in a bright flash. A swathe of tiny metal projectiles hammered the two cars and sliced into the soldiers' bodies as they were cut down, one of the vehicle's engine suddenly spewing a cloud of black smoke and collapsing on one side as a tire was blown out by the shrapnel.

Ethan crouched down at the front of the truck and as the troops rushed out from the rear he fired, controlled double–taps at each man, cutting two down before the rest scrambled out of sight. Ethan backed up a little, denying them the chance to creep up on him from either side, and got down prone on the hot asphalt as he aimed beneath the truck.

Four pairs of boots huddled on either side of the vehicle, and Ethan took a single breath before he squeezed the trigger. Bullets smashed into the ankles of the troops hiding behind the truck and two of them collapsed in agony, their screams competing with the gunfire clattering across the road as Ethan leaped to his feet and stormed down one side of the truck.

The Russian's were panicked and Ethan saw it in their eyes as he burst into view and fired twice at close range, his rifle set now to semi–automatic and firing three rounds in quick succession with each squeeze of the trigger. The first Russian dropped as Ethan's rounds found their mark and shredded his throat and then the side of his skull in a vivid spray of bright red blood that splattered the side of the truck. The second screamed in terror and tried to aim but all three rounds pummelled his belly and chest and he shuddered as he collapsed onto the ground, his face ashen with the fear of imminent death as the AK–47 he held in one hand clattered down uselessly alongside of him.

'Ubey yego! Kill him!'

Ethan saw the troops from the second truck emerge into view, four weapons trained upon him and more coming up from behind. There was no time to turn his rifle, no time to react. He was about to try dropping to his knees and turning all at once in the hope that he could get some rounds off and escape when suddenly a hail of bullets smashed into the second truck.

The Russian soldiers cried out as they tried to fall back into the cover of their truck, two of them collapsing instantly as double–tapped rounds smashed into them. Ethan leaped out of sight of the fresh attack and clambered up into the rear of the truck to see four young, dark and very afraid faces peering out at him from the gloomy interior. Girls, all aged perhaps twelve or thirteen, shaking with fear.

Ethan reached out his hand.

'American,' he said, hoping that would not be a word that would send the girls sprinting for the hills. 'United Nations!'

One of the girls reached out for his hand, and as one moved so they all moved. Ethan jumped down off the rear of the truck as he saw the rest of the Russian convoy being hammered by bullets. Relieved that support had come early, Ethan hauled the girls down from the convoy and led them across the road as he saw Lopez sprint through the smoke alongside him.

'Good shooting!' he said as he saw the neutralized advance guard vehicles nearby, riddled with bullet holes and eight bodies surrounding the stricken cars.

'Wasn't me!' Lopez shouted. 'We've got competition!'

Ethan hit the bank with the girls and looked back as they scrambled down the slope toward the truck now motoring toward them, Talal at the wheel.

Ethan turned and looked at the girls and saw that every one of them was blind, each holding the hand of another in absolute trust. Suddenly Ethan realized that the oldest among them was hanging on to his hand as though it were the only thing keeping her alive, and he realized just how terribly vulnerable children were when trapped in a state of civil war.

The Russians were returning heavy fire now toward a copse of trees on the north side of the highway. Ethan sprinted to the truck as Talal pulled up alongside them and yanked open the doors as Lopez dashed around the hood to get in the other side.

'Get us out of here!' Ethan snapped as he helped the girls into the rear of the cab.

Talal crunched the truck into gear and as soon as Ethan was aboard he slammed the accelerator down and the battered old truck lurched forward in a cloud of diesel fumes and clattered along in a wide circle before turning south.

'Follow the bank until you reach the Al Kabir river!' Ethan yelled to Talal as the truck rattled along. 'Cross the river wherever you can and we'll be in Lebanon! The Apaches will be here any minute!'

Talal nodded, sweating profusely as he gripped the large steering wheel. 'Where are the Russians?'

'They're occupied back there!' Ethan said as he jabbed a thumb over his shoulder and then looked at Lopez. 'Did you see the shooters? Were they ours?'

'I couldn't see anybody,' Lopez shouted in reply. 'They just started tearing up the advance guard and I pulled out and headed toward you.'

Ethan frowned uncertainly and then Talal looked in the truck's grubby mirrors and shouted jubilantly.

'The American helicopter is here!'

Ethan jerked his head around and saw the heavy, bulky shape of an attack helicopter looming toward them from the north. It took him only a moment to recognize the shape of the helicopter, and he saw Lopez's expression turn dark as she too identified it.

'That's not an Apache,' she uttered as she gripped her rifle more tightly.

The huge helicopter swept over the main road, churning great clouds of dust in swirling vortexes around its enormous rotor blades as it hugged the ground. The

Russian Mil–Mi–28 Hind gunship descended to just a few feet above the earth, its massive cannons and rocket pods pointing directly at Ethan.

'Jink, now!'

Talal looked confused. 'I too am thirsty but I don't think that we can...'

'Jink!'

Ethan grabbed the wheel and hauled it to one side, and the truck lurched to the left even as a roar of gunfire blasted past the windows and bullets churned the earth around them. Talal cried out in fear as the bullets shattered an old brick wall just ahead of them, the 20mm shells smashing their way through everything before them.

The truck pitched steeply onto two wheels and the huge gunship overshot and thundered overhead. Ethan heard the girls in the back crying out in fear as it roared by in a crescendo of rotors hammering the hot air.

'The border is over a mile away!' Talal cried. 'We'll never make it!'

Ethan grabbed the satellite phone and dialed in, knowing that without immediate air support the Hind gunship would annihilate them. The line rang as Talal drove the truck at a frenzied pace alongside the narrow stream to their right. Suddenly the line was answered as Ethan held on grimly to the truck door.

'Warner, operations, three–five–zero–nine–four: request immediate close air support! We are severely compromised!'

***

XXXII

Defense Intelligence Agency,

Washington DC

Hellerman hurried across the watch room as he waited to hear from Warner and Lopez. He was about to call them when his cell phone buzzed in his pocket. He saw the number as coming from General Nellis and answered it immediately.

'Sir, Warner and Lopez have checked in and…'

'Hellerman,' General Nellis cut him off, 'listen to me. ARIES is being shut down.'

Hellerman froze. 'It's what?'

'It's being shut down. Get out, now! Grab whatever you can and leave. Homeland are already on their way and you'll be questioned by them.'

Hellerman stared at the watch room for a moment as his brain tried to comprehend what he was being told.

'But we can't empty the archive just like that! And how can I get anything out of the building? It's the most secure…'

'I don't know,' Nellis cut him off. 'I've been reassigned, effective immediately. I no longer have access to the agency. Just get everything you can out of there, and when the questioning is over find Jarvis. It's the only way to keep this all going.'

Hellerman felt suddenly helpless and afraid, his recent meeting with Jarvis at the forefront of his thoughts. 'Why are they doing this now? We're starting to figure out the greatest mystery in human history!'

Nellis's voice appeared almost sad as he replied.

'Somebody, somewhere doesn't want us to figure it out. You've got literally a few minutes, Joseph. Do what you can, and good luck.'

The line went dead in Hellerman's hand and he slid the cell into his pocket as he turned to look at his office, filled as it was with endless gadgets and gizmos, inventions and computers, all of which belonged not to him but to the DIA. Despite the melancholia he felt at leaving it all behind, he knew that there was only one true artefact that he needed to take with him.

Hellerman dashed for the storage facility, taking an elevator down and passing through the old, dusty steel door in the back of the basement that led to the secret laboratory where he had done so much of his work. Inside, suspended in a small magnetic chamber, was a metallic sphere hovering in mid–air. Taken from inside the Black Knight satellite, its surface was like oil suspended in a puddle, a swirling miasma of color and motion that had captivated him for months.

Hellerman's cell rang again and he answered it, the DIA's internal system allowing a signal down into the basement. The anxious voice of an operator called Helen from the watch room assaulted his ear.

'Hellerman, we just got a call saying that Homeland are here and that we're to cease operations. What the hell's going on?'

He took a deep breath and replied as calmly as he could.

'Just do as they say. Your jobs are safe and you'll be reassigned. Contact Social Services and find Aisha as fast as you can, and hold Homeland up for me a bit though, if you can.'

'Will do,' Helen replied nervously, and the line cut off.

Hellerman grabbed the chamber, which was the size of a shoe box, and wrapped it inside his jacket as he hurried out of the laboratory. He travelled back up to the ARIES watch room and hurried across to his office as he saw operators and technicians leaving their posts and making for the stairwell.

Hellerman looked desperately through his equipment for some way to get the sphere out of the building. The batteries inside the chamber would maintain the magnetic field that suspended the sphere for only a few hours, and as such it was imperative that he got the chamber plugged back in as soon as possible. Hellerman's eyes fell upon the one thing that he knew could save the day and he hurried out of the office to the elevators and opened the nearest door.

'Hellerman!'

He whirled as Helen rushed to his side, her green eyes wide with concern.

'Warner and Lopez are under fire! Do we have authority to assist them? They're inside Syrian airspace.'

Hellerman hesitated and then realized that he no longer had anything to lose.

'Get them out,' he ordered. 'General Nellis authorized all and any means necessary to extract them both. Send in all three of the Apaches, weapons hot!'

Helen hurried away as Hellerman dashed back to his office. He attached the magnetic chamber to a small device on his desk and then sat down at a computer and plugged in a computer game–pad controller he grabbed from his desk.

Hellerman checked everything, and then he hit a switch on the device. A high–pitched humming sound was emitted from it and the drone lifted off. Hellerman kept his eyes on the monitor before him, which projected an image from a camera on the front of the drone as it flew past him and out his office door.

Hellerman guided it to the elevator doors and inside as with his free hand he rattled keys on a second computer monitor and directed the elevator down, giving it absolute priority over all other calls. He glanced over his shoulder and saw the elevator doors close as he directed the controller's signal through the same DIA internal network that his cell phone had connected to.

The elevator began travelling downward as Hellerman looked at a monitor and saw the view from the drone's camera inside the elevator. Quickly, he landed the craft to save power as he transferred the view from the monitor to a HoloLens device on his desk.

Essentially an advanced version of the publicly available device by Microsoft, Hellerman's lens was contained within what looked like a set of ordinary glasses. Hellerman grabbed them and put them on, instantly able to see in his right eye a small window showing the drone's camera view, then with the controller in his hand he stood up as he heard voices outside the office.

Another elevator's doors opened and ten men in suits with DIA visitor tags strode into the ARIES Watch Room and began shouting.

'All personnel out of the building, now!'

'Shut down all stations, cease and desist all activity!'

'This operation is being terminated with immediate effect. Surrender all security clearances immediately!'

Hellerman willed the elevator to hurry as he listened to the shouts and the resistance from the ARIES staff in the watch room. In his eyepiece he saw the elevator reach the lower floors of the DIA building, and then the doors opened onto the basement. Hellerman flew the drone off the floor and out into a corridor.

As per the agency's policies, the DIA's South Wing building had been specifically constructed to ensure that there were no windows that could be opened by staff. All of the building's extensive cooling was internal and computer controlled. Vents throughout the building carried air that was circulated and vented through a bank of three huge fans atop the building's roof. The entire system was connected through the basement, where cooler air was drawn in to the system through a massive network of vents and conduits.

Hellerman knew enough of the construction to be able to guide the small drone and its cargo through the building's basement and to the simple aluminium ducting that carried the airflow. Attached to the basement ceiling, most of the ducting was impenetrable except for the thin foil tubes that drew external air through tamper-proof internal filtering systems and then joined it to the building's internal ducting.

Hellerman hovered the drone alongside the thermal lining of the foil tubes and then let the craft's rotors brush against the surface. The drone quivered, but the fast moving blades sliced easily through the thermal material and opened up the tube. Hellerman guided the drone in and began flying it forward through the aluminium ducts. He settled the drone down to save power once it was safely inside the duct.

'Everybody move away from your workstations and offices immediately!'

Hellerman slipped the controller into his pocket and then hurried out of his office and confronted the men, feigning surprise.

'What's going on?' he demanded. 'Where is General Nellis?'

'You're relieved of duty,' the leader of the Homeland team snapped without interest. 'Surrender all security clearances, equipment and material immediately and egress the building under escort.'

Eight of the ten men had formed a human corridor toward the elevators and stairwell, while the other two were shepherding staff away from their workstations and toward the elevators. As Hellerman looked over his shoulder he saw one of the giant screens showing an Apache attack helicopter racing over open field and desert scrub.

'We have operatives in the field,' Hellerman snapped. 'They're under fire and need support.'

The Homeland agent looked down at Hellerman, his features without emotion as he replied.

'All operations from this site are to cease immediately. Desist from all further communications. Any attempt at further operations will result in your arrest for treason.'

Hellerman took a pace closer to the agent. In his lens he could see the drone inside the ducting vent, awaiting its next command.

'What's the charge for deliberate abandonment of a fellow officer, dereliction of duty and the cold blooded murder of your own countrymen?'

The Homeland agent stared down at Hellerman and he could see now the conflict in the agent's eyes, torn between explicit orders and his own humanity.

'They're under fire,' Hellerman pressed. 'They're going to die or be captured. You want that on your conscience?'

The Homeland narrowed his eyes.

'Is Douglas Jarvis with them?'

Hellerman did a swift mental calculation. Jarvis was still in the wind, but if Homeland were after him it may make them more wiling to extract Warner and Lopez.

'Yes,' he lied. 'Jarvis is with them right now!'

The Homeland agent hesitated and then made his decision.

'You're relieved of duty. You will report to Homeland for debrief immediately. Any attempt at further operations will result in your arrest for treason.'

Hellerman scowled at the agent and shoved his hands angrily into his jacket pockets, finally convinced that Homeland was not looking to save lives but to remove them from play.

'Their blood's on your hands,' he shot back as he stormed past into the elevator.

The doors hissed shut and Hellerman said nothing as he watched the drone now flying under his control through the aluminium ducting. He managed to stifle a wince as he guided it with one hand around a tight ninety degree turn and clanged the drone against the wall of the duct, hoping that nobody in the offices below would notice as he guided the craft ever upward toward the main vents.

The elevator in which he stood opened and Hellerman walked out onto the main foyer of the Defense Intelligence Agency's South Wing building. He aimed for the security controlled exits and joined the queue, standing alongside Helen as she shot him a concerned and confused look.

In his eyepiece Hellerman saw the drone reach the main vents at the roof, the shadows of the lazily turning blades of immense fans visible as the sun shone past them into a vertical shaft. Hellerman eased the drone up, controlling it with his hand still concealed inside his jacket and waited for a long moment as he watched the shadows of the turning blade.

The blade passed by and Hellerman climbed the drone at full power. The craft shot upward and he saw a bright blue sky leap into view. He guided the drone out across the south building's lawns and across Brookely Avenue, climbing high above the trees and the Capitol Beltway before he descended the craft into a copse of trees alongside the beltway's off ramp on the eastern side. The drone thumped down onto the grass amid some bushes as the power signal faded out.

'Stop there!'

Hellerman turned and saw the Homeland agents rush toward him.

'Hands in the air!'

Hellerman put his hands up and stared in shock at the guards as they surrounded him.

'Empty your pockets!'

Hellerman complied, aware of dozens of staff watching him. The Homeland agents advanced toward him and searched him thoroughly. Their commander eyed him angrily as the search came up empty.

'You got anything you want to tell me about, now would be a good time.'

Hellerman shouted loudly enough for everybody in the entire foyer to hear him.

'That I'm disgusted that despite my repeated warnings and requests Homeland just shut down an operation that has cost the lives of two of the DIA's most respected agents?! Yeah, let's talk about that, right here and right now in front of everybody!'

The foyer fell silent, all eyes now on the Homeland agents. Hellerman saw their sudden expressions of shame as he pushed his advantage.

'Why don't we get the media down here too and tell them all about how you refused to save the lives of those two agents, even though you could see them under fire in Syria on live camera with helicopters close enough to reach them?!'

The Homeland agents backed away as their leader put his weapon into its holster.

'You're free to go,' he muttered.

'Yeah,' Hellerman said bitterly, 'lucky me.'

He turned his back to the agents in disgust and saw Helen standing nearby, her handbag over her shoulder, the controller tucked just inside it. He did not need to signal her his gratitude for she would be more than aware of it, and he could see in her eyes that she felt the same about the Homeland takeover as he did. Now his only thought was to retrieve the drone and its incalculably valuable cargo, bring Aisha to safety before Homeland understood what she represented, and then find Jarvis.

***

XXXIII

Al Kabir, Syria

'Keep driving!'

Ethan pointed to the south as Talal struggled to keep the truck under control, the sandy riverbank too loose for the chunky tires and aged engine to maintain purchase.

'They're coming around!' Lopez warned.

Ethan looked out of his open window behind them and saw the huge Hind gunship swing upward in a tight arc, its immense rotors beating the air like endless thunderclaps as it lined up for another pass.

Ethan could see the wicked 20mm cannon protruding from beneath the gunship's bulbous nose, the tandem twin–seat cockpit with bubble canopies and the arms extending each side of the fuselage, laden with rocket pods.

'We're no match against that kind of firepower,' Ethan shouted above the wind as he ducked back into the cab and searched desperately for any inspiration as to how the hell they could survive long enough for the Apaches to arrive.

'We should surrender,' Talal advised. 'They'll kill us all!'

'No,' Ethan said, 'they want their precious cargo back. They won't risk shooting them too, especially if they're who I think that they are.'

Ethan glanced over his shoulder to look at the girls huddling with Lopez in the rear of the cab. He looked back out of the cab and saw ahead a low concrete bridge spanning the width of the river alongside them. Although the river was not large, probably no wider than about twenty meters, it was sufficiently deep to require regular bridges that would clear the flow in times of rare floods.

Ethan looked at the bridge and then craned his neck back to see the huge helicopter descending out of its steep turn to pursue them once more.

'Slow down,' he said to Talal.

'You want me to do what?!'

'Slow down,' Ethan insisted. 'I don't want us to get to that bridge too fast.'

Talal stared at Ethan as though he had gone insane but he obeyed and the truck slowed.

'I don't want to know what you've got in mind,' Lopez called from the back of the truck.

'Be ready,' Ethan snapped as he checked his ammunition and watched as the bridge loomed closer. 'This will have to be fast!'

*

'There they are!'

Gregorie pointed ahead as he hung from the side of the Mil–Mi 24 Hind gunship and saw the truck swerving awkwardly across the sandy shore of the river. The trees either side of the river made aiming difficult, and Gregorie was reduced to a frustrated passenger as he watched the pilots line up for another pass.

'Warning shots across their hood!' Gregorie shouted to the pilots through the microphone he wore. 'But if they come within a hundred yards of the border, destroy them!'

The pilots affirmed his request and Gregorie watched hungrily as they bore down on the battered old truck, the Hind one of the fastest and most powerful gunships ever built. It had taken only moments to slap temporary Syrian markings over the gunship's native Soviet iconography, swiftly averting any danger of an international incident as Gregorie had commandeered the gunship an hour before. Fully armed and fuelled, there was no escaping this amount of firepower: Warner would either be captured or killed, and Gregorie had a glorious front–row seat to witness it.

The Hind thundered down as the truck changed direction slightly and rushed toward a low concrete bridge spanning the narrow river beneath them.

'They're heading for the cover of the bridge!' Gregorie snapped. 'Cut them off if they try to hide under there!'

The Hind descended, and suddenly gray smoke billowed past Gregorie and the side hatch as the huge 20mm cannon opened fire with a loud *brrrrr* crescendo that caused the entire fuselage to reverberate around him. Gregorie held on tight and looked ahead, the wind buffeting his head and body as he saw the massive rounds smash into the ground and the bridge ahead of the truck, clouds of shattered masonry blasting across the water.

The truck swerved right to clear the worst of the gunfire, and then Gregorie saw it vanish beneath the bridge as the Hind soared overhead and climbed away. Gregorie ducked inside the helicopter and gestured to his men.

'We're going to have to cut them off and fight it out,' he snapped. 'Kill all of the adults but do not harm the children, understood? They're needed!'

The dozen Spetsnaz soldiers inside the Hind nodded grimly as the helicopter soared upward in a steep climb and Gregorie spoke once again to the pilots.

'Cut them off any way you can!'

The helicopter swung around and as the nose fell below the horizon once again Gregorie saw the truck racing alongside the river once more. The American had guts, Gregorie realized with a reluctant sense of admiration. They couldn't possibly hope to outgun the Hind and they must know that he would never let them cross the border into Lebanon. It had taken only a few bribes by Colonel Mishkin to ensure the compliance of the handful of Lebanese military outposts nearby, and the Syrians were all fully engaged against the radical militants far to the north in Homs and Aleppo. The Yanks were on their own and there was nowhere else to run.

'Sir, we have something on radar!'

Gregorie pressed his earpiece closer in. 'What?'

'Three contacts, ten miles to the south, low–level, no identification. They're coming right at us.'

Gregorie hissed a curse beneath his breath. 'Can you identify them?'

There was a brief pause as the pilots used the Hind's on–board camera to pin-point the location of the incoming signals.

'They're helicopters, Apache gunships!'

Gregorie slammed a balled fist against the wall of the helicopter as he yelled his response.

'That's it! Cut them off and grab them, right now!'

The Hind dove downward as the pilots completed their turn and began heading back toward the truck racing alongside the river. Gregorie watched as they expertly lined the truck up in their sights and then the cannons blazed again and deadly rounds rocketed toward the tiny vehicle.

Gregorie saw the terrain directly in front of the truck become churned into a gigantic cloud of dust and debris as the huge cannon ripped into sand and soil. The truck swerved to avoid it but in the thick sand and rough terrain the vehicle lost a lot of speed.

'Now, go now!'

The pilot hauled the Hind's nose up and the gunship slowed dramatically, the rotors thundering as they hammered the air with relentless blows. Gregorie held on tight as the massive gunship swung around, descending over the trees and flying sideways as the truck emerged ahead from the cloud of dusty debris.

The Hind descended until it was just a few feet above the river, clouds of dust and sparkling water sweeping into the air in a spiralling vortex around it as the pilots aimed once again.

'Fire!' Gregorie yelled.

The cannon fired a brief clattering burst and Gregorie hooted with joy as he saw the huge rounds smash into the jeep's chassis and two of the big tires were shredded by the shrapnel. The truck swerved to one side and then shuddered to a halt on the river bank, smoke spilling from beneath its hood.

'Deploy, now!' Gregorie roared as he leaped from the hovering gunship and crashed down into the shallow water at the shore, unslinging his rifle from his shoulder as he charged toward the stricken vehicle.

*

Ethan yanked the wheel to one side as the massive bullets crashed into the truck's underside and he felt the grip go from the tires as they were torn apart beneath him. He held the wheel to one side, turning the truck to the left so that he was protected from any incoming fire from the troops now spilling from inside the hovering gunship, and then he opened the cab door and leaped out.

Ethan dashed into the cover of the vehicle, pulled his last two remaining fragmentation grenades and peered past the rear of the cab at the soldiers charging the truck. He saw Gregorie among them, and without hesitation he pulled the pins on both grenades and hurled them overarm, the weapons sailing over the truck in a high arc and plummeting down among the troops.

He heard a shouted warning in Russian and then a double blast that thumped the air even above the roar of the Hind's rotor blades. The grenades spread their lethal shrapnel in a supersonic starburst across the river bank as Ethan ducked out from behind the cab.

Four of the Russians were down and screaming, but six more were up on their feet as Ethan opened fire with single shots, carefully aimed. He dropped two men before they scattered or went prone on the shore, a withering fire smashing into the cab as Ethan ducked back out of sight, bullets zipping past him and shattering the windows of the truck.

Glass sprinkled down onto him as he rushed to the far side of the vehicle, using the big rear tires as cover. He leaned out again and saw the troops maintaining position, aiming at him. For a brief moment he wasn't sure what they intended to do, and then he saw the huge Hind gunship rise up once more and begin to move to one side out over the river in a simple flanking manoeuver.

'Damn.'

Ethan was out of options and he whirled to sprint for the cover of the trees nearby when he heard another noise ahead of him. Even as he looked up he saw the unmistakeable form of three Apache helicopters rushing toward him, their cruel weapons gleaming in the sunlight.

Ethan let out a whoop of joy, a broad smile breaking on his features as he turned and saw the Hind suddenly begin to retreat back toward the beach, the Spetsnaz soldiers leaping to their feet and sprinting for the cover of their only escape as their gunship landed.

Ethan kept in the cover of the truck as he stepped forward and raised his hands, tossed the rifle to one side and waved at the incoming attack gunships. They were only a mile away, in close formation and at low altitude, coming in under the local Lebanese radar cover.

Ethan waved harder and then suddenly he felt a cold dread in the pit of his belly as suddenly all three Apaches pulled up sharply and their rotors battered the air as they turned in unison. Ethan stared in dismay as the three helicopters performed a wide left turn and began heading back the way they came.

Ethan grabbed the satellite phone and dialed desperately, listening for the ring tone in his ear. To his horror he heard nothing but static. Ethan dropped the phone and watched as the Apaches flew away into the haze, the noise of their rotors fading as those of the Hind grew louder.

Ethan heard voices behind him and turned to see the Spetsnaz troops and Gregorie rush up on either side of the truck and aim their rifles at him. Gregorie advanced with a cruel smile on his face as he stared at Ethan down the barrel of his rifle and placed one boot over Ethan's fallen M–16.

'We meet again,' Gregorie sneered.

'Too soon,' Ethan replied.

Gregorie stepped forward, turned the rifle over in his grasp in one smooth motion and rammed the butt deep into Ethan's guts. Ethan folded over at the waist and collapsed to his knees as his vision blurred.

'Get the girls out of the truck and into the gunship!' Gregorie snapped to his men.

The troops behind Gregorie yanked the cab doors open, and then shouted to him in reply.

'The truck's empty!'

Ethan managed to get control of his breathing as a grim smile spread on his face and he looked up at Gregorie.

'Oops.'

Gregorie snarled down at him as he swung the rifle once again and the weapon smashed into Ethan's skull and knocked him sideways onto the warm sand. Despite the aching in his belly and the pain throbbing through his skull, the shore felt almost comfortable and he realized suddenly how tired he was.

'Search the river, they can't have gone far!'

The troops dispersed as Gregorie looked down at Ethan, smiled, and then slammed one heavy boot into his face and Ethan's world vanished into blackness.

***

XXXIV

'Damn it.'

Lopez uttered the words under her breath as she crouched in the bushes two hundred meters away from where the Hind gunship had landed beside the river. She could see on the shore the tall Russian they'd last seen in Rome shouting orders and his men fanning out toward them.

'They will find us,' Talal said. 'We have nowhere to run but back into Syria.'

Lopez said nothing as she watched the elite troops methodically begin combing the terrain for them. Ethan's idea of drawing the helicopter away from the girls until the Apaches could arrive had been a good one, but now that they had effectively been abandoned to their fate they were stranded on the wrong side of the border.

Lopez didn't know why the Apaches had turned back at the last moment and she couldn't think of a good reason why they would. Having crossed Lebanese airspace on a covert mission to rendezvous with Ethan and the team, to pull back a quarter of a mile from their destination was crazy in the extreme. They could have completed the extraction within minutes and everybody would have headed home happy for drinks and medals. Now, Ethan was in the hands of the Russians and Lopez was facing the tricky task of figuring out a way to smuggle the girls out of the area and then across a highly dangerous border without being spotted.

'We've got to go,' Talal urged her. 'They will find us.'

'I can't leave Ethan behind,' Lopez snapped in a harsh whisper. 'They'll kill him.'

'They'll kill us all,' Talal pointed out reasonably, 'and I can't get these girls out of here safely on my own.'

Lopez looked at the four girls, huddled in the shadow of the trees and hugging each other. Their fearful white eyes stared about them, listening to their voices as she and Talal argued about what to do.

'The Russians can't stay out here for much longer,' Lopez reasoned. 'They'll be forced to head back to Homs eventually, because the only reason that helicopter can be flying this close to the border unchallenged is if the Russians paid off the Lebanese border guards. If we can lay low for long enough and avoid being captured, we can walk to the border – it's only a half mile away.'

'And then what?' Talal pleaded. 'You think that they'll welcome us with open arms and wave us through a checkpoint? The DIA has abandoned you, both of you. Any credentials you may have had before are worthless now and you're as likely to be arrested and sold into slavery yourself!'

Lopez felt her shoulders slump as she realized that Talal was correct. Human trafficking in Beirut had reached record levels since the Syrian civil war, the

International Security Force's Vice Squad completely overwhelmed with cases of abductions and enforced prostitution. The plight of Syrian girls was well known, but the sheer scale and volume of corruption meant that few of them were ever rescued from their grim fate. Lopez looked at the girls and her heart plunged.

'We can't let them be abducted again, they won't survive,' she whispered.

'Then let us leave,' Talal urged her, 'now, while we still can!'

Lopez reluctantly crawled into the shade of the trees and took the hand of the oldest girl. The girl looked it seemed directly into Lopez's eyes and willingly took her hand, as though she recognized that Lopez was an ally. The girl then took the hand of her closest friend, and the remaining two likewise linked their hands.

Lopez knew that they couldn't understand her, but she spoke as softly as she could in the hopes that they would know she was trying to help them.

'We're going to try to keep you safe,' she said. 'I don't know if we can, but we will try.'

Lopez squeezed the hand of the oldest girl, and to her surprise she saw a faint smile touch the child's sculptured lips as she replied.

'We know, saydati.'

Lopez's eyes flew wide in surprise. 'You speak English.'

'I do, but only I,' the girl replied. 'We must hurry.'

Before Lopez could respond, the girl stood and practically dragged Lopez with her through the trees. Lopez allowed herself to be led as the girl travelled north, away from the Russians through the dense foliage clogging the banks of the river. Although Lopez had absolutely no idea where they were going, the incredible confidence with which the girl led her was such that she complied without resistance.

'What is your name?' she asked her as they moved.

'I am Sofia.'

'I'm Nicola.'

Sofia smiled. 'I know.'

Lopez began to feel like she was the younger and more vulnerable of the two as she was led through the copses of trees. She could hear the Russians behind them, making no effort to conceal their presence. She figured that they were probably hoping to flush the girls out quickly and carry them away.

'Where are we going?' Lopez asked her.

'To safety,' Sofia replied.

'But we're heading back into Syria.'

'Yes,' Sofia replied, 'but not for long.'

Lopez and Talal exchanged a glance but said nothing as they were led ever closer to the main highway where they had first ambushed the Russian convoy. She could see smoke rising from damaged vehicles, and the flashing lights of emergency vehicles as the victims left at the scene of the crash were treated or loaded into body bags.

'We can't get too close to the road,' Lopez warned Sofia. 'There may be other people looking for us and for you.'

'There are other people looking for you,' Elena confirmed, 'and they are very dangerous.'

Lopez was about to question the sense in approaching such dangerous people when Sofia raised one hand and slowed. Lopez moved into a low crouch alongside her, Talal and the other girls following suit as they moved slowly through the brush to where the river flowed quietly alongside the bank.

Lopez caught sight of four black inflatable vessels just as she heard the sound of a rifle mechanism somewhere ahead of them in the bushes. She froze, as did Sofia and the rest of the little group, and then a familiar voice growled at them from the bushes.

'Lopez.'

Lopez almost collapsed in relief as she heard the voice. 'Mitchell?'

From the bushes emerged the big assassin, dressed entirely in black fatigues and with his M–16 rifle cradled in his grasp. He moved toward her, staying low as he saw the girls with her.

'Thanks for screwing up our ambush,' Mitchell growled. 'We had everything under control until you and Warner showed up.'

Lopez shot him a dirty look. 'That's what you get for going AWOL with Jarvis instead of staying with Ethan and I.'

'Fair enough,' Mitchell conceded as he looked around. 'Where is the great white hunter anyway?'

'He got caught,' Lopez said, 'gave us the chance to get away and now the Russians have him.'

Mitchell frowned. 'What happened to your support? We thought that the Apaches picked you up?'

'They turned back before they reached us,' Lopez admitted. 'Something's gone down in DC and we've been burned.'

Mitchell looked at the four girls and then nodded as though he'd expected something like that all along.

'Trust is not something to be expected from the government,' he replied simply. 'We have room for you all but we can't move until the Russians have pulled out.'

Lopez eyed the team behind Mitchell. 'You could take them down, you've got superior numbers.'

'But we don't have a ride out of here like you did,' Mitchell reminded her. 'Our mission is to extract them through Lebanon to the coast and leave from there, quietly.'

'Your mission?' Lopez asked. 'And what the hell are you doing out here anyway?'

Mitchell smiled.

'Fighting the good fight,' he replied. 'Jarvis says hi.'

'The hell with that traitor.'

'You don't know what you're saying or what we're doing,' Mitchell cautioned her. 'I'd wait until we can show you before you swallow the DIA's lines.'

'Well excuse me,' Lopez replied tartly, 'I didn't realize that pinching thirty billion dollars was an act of charity.'

The sound of Russian voices rose up behind them.

'You can sound off about this later,' Mitchell snapped in a whisper. 'Right now, we have to disappear.'

'Take the girls,' Lopez said, 'and Talal here. I'm going back for Ethan.'

Mitchell rolled his eyes, white sockets vivid against his dark skin. 'We don't have time, you can't take on an entire troop of soldiers alone and the Russians will be here any moment. Leave this to us.'

'You're going to leave him behind,' Lopez accused before Mitchell had even begun to move.

The big man glared at her.

'Things have changed. You said the DIA burned you? Well, now you don't have anywhere to go. The best thing that could happen to you both now is that you die out here.'

'How the hell do you figure that?' Lopez uttered.

'Because somebody, somewhere in the government wants that to happen. If you survive this attack, they'll try again.'

Beside Lopez, Sofia spoke softly. 'There is another girl still with the Russians.'

Lopez stared at her. 'There's another one?'

'Yes,' Sofia nodded, 'Elena. She is the best of the seers. We cannot leave her.'

Lopez shot Mitchell an expectant look, and the big assassin sighed and rolled his eyes.

***

XXXV

Ethan knelt on the sand, his hands tied behind his back and a blindfold wrapped tightly over his eyes. He could hear the sound of the Russians clattering their way through nearby trees, trying to scare the girls out of hiding. Ethan maintained the hope that they had fled north back into Syria at the first opportunity and put as much distance between themselves and the Russians as possible.

A dull pain throbbed through his skull from where the Russian oaf had slammed his boot into Ethan's face, and he could taste blood in his mouth. Ethan sighed softly as he reflected on the fact that he was getting a bit long in the tooth to be taking this kind of beating on every other deployment, not that there would be any more. The DIA had deliberately abandoned them despite being literally within a few hundred meters of their position. Ethan had no doubt that somebody, somewhere had chosen to deny them the rescue that they could so easily have provided, and that provoked a fierce rage that threatened to burst from within him in a cry of anguish. There could never be any justification for what the DIA had done and Ethan promised himself that this would be the last time he would work for them. Damn it, even in his worst moments Jarvis had never willingly abandoned them to death, always managing to figure out a way to give them a fighting chance for survival no matter how harsh the odds.

Ethan heard foot falls nearby and the sound of a truck approaching on the road somewhere behind him and to his left. The vehicle's brakes squealed as it came to a halt and he listened as a door opened and closed. The sound of Gregorie's voice was just audible, and then he heard both men approaching him where he knelt.

The cruel barrel of a gun pressed hard into the back of his neck as a heavily accented voice whispered harshly in his ear.

'You so much as sniff in a way I don't like, I'll blow your brains out all over your face.'

The blindfold was loosened and pulled away, blinding desert light blazing into Ethan's eyes as he squinted and struggled to focus on his surroundings. He became aware of a circle of troops surrounding him, their weapons held at port arms as they watched him with uncaring expressions.

The gun was removed from his neck as Gregorie tossed the blindfold to one side and moved away, a pistol held in his grip and pointed at Ethan. From the other side appeared a new face that Ethan recognized, somebody high up in the GRU called Mishkin.

'Ethan Warner,' Mishkin uttered as though spitting something unpleasant from his mouth. 'I have heard much about you and I must say it's a pleasure to meet you, especially in these circumstances.'

Ethan's eyes adjusted once more to the light and he offered a grim smile to the Russian.

'Can't say the same.'

'I don't blame you!' Mishkin chortled as he gestured to the Spetsnaz soldiers surrounding them. 'You've killed several of their friends during your little escapade out here, and I honestly cannot imagine what they're going to do to you, alone and without any of your American friends to support you.'

Ethan shrugged.

'Mission's accomplished,' he said simply and then threw in a lie on impulse. 'The girls got away. They're long gone now.'

Mishkin peered at him and then smiled again.

'You're a clever man, Mister Warner, always thinking fast. But I don't believe for a moment that those girls are more than a half mile away and we will find them. As soon as that sun sinks far enough, our gunship's Infra–Red cameras will find them easily enough in the cooling deserts. They'll probably welcome us with open arms because they'll be freezing half to death within a few hours, but of course we don't really want to wait that long do we?'

Mishkin moved closer to Ethan, put his hands on his knees and bent down to look him in the eye.

'Sadly, the Geneva Convention does not apply out here in the deserts of Syria. In fact, not many rules apply at all. So I'll ask you just the once Mister Warner: where are the girls you stole from us?'

Ethan smiled up at Mishkin.

'Bite me.'

The Russian sighed and stood back as he turned to Gregorie. 'Let your men find out which one of his testicles he'd like to hang on to. With luck, his screams will bring his little friends running to help him.'

Ethan heard a rumble of anticipation among the Spetsnaz soldiers as Gregorie's wide jaw split in a cruel grin and he reached behind his back. From a sheath that ran down the length of his spine beneath his shirt he drew a huge, twelve–inch long combat knife that shone in the sunlight. Its steel blade flashed as Gregorie examined it with delight and then turned to his men.

'Flatten him out!'

The soldiers rushed in and one of them side–kicked Ethan in the chest. The blow sent him sprawling onto his back on the dust as his lungs convulsed inside him, pinning his arms beneath his back as the other soldiers grabbed his shoulders and ankles.

Ethan saw Mishkin gesture to the truck they'd arrived in, and from the back of it he saw two more soldiers appear. Between them was another young girl, her hands tied behind her back and her eyes blind and unseeing.

'You didn't think we'd, how do you say, put all our eggs in one basket did you?' Mishkin asked.

Ethan watched as the girl was marched down to join them, and Mishkin spoke in accented English to her.

'Elena, your friends have disappeared and this man knows where they are,' he said to her. 'I suspect that you have forseen what will happen here, but just in case you're not sure I will explain. If you do not tell us where the other girls are hiding, this man will be eviscerated one painful step at a time.'

Ethan saw the girl's expression crumple in disgust and horror as Mishkin went on.

'Tell us, now.'

Ethan strained against his captors as he spoke to the girl. 'Don't tell them a thing, you don't owe me anything and…'

Gregorie's thick hand clamped across Ethan's mouth and slammed his head back down against the sand. Ethan squirmed against them and tried to warn the girl not to speak but he could see the tears welling in her sightless eyes.

'Where are they?!' Mishkin screamed at her.

The girl flinched but she said nothing, distress twisting her dark features. Mishkin glared at Gregorie and nodded.

Gregorie crouched down and pressed his thick knife against Ethan's crotch, still smiling.

'Left, or right?' he asked as he removed his hand from Ethan's mouth.

'You do anything to me, you'll never see those girls again.'

Gregorie shrugged. 'Left it is then.'

The big Russian leaned in and Ethan felt the blade press painfully against him and then two gunshots ripped the air it seemed right above his head. Two of the watching Russian soldier's heads exploded as the bullets smashed through flesh and bone and a scream went up in Russian as Gregorie hurled himself away from Ethan and bursts of clattering gunfire ripped into the Russian soldiers with terrific accuracy.

Ethan rolled away from them as best he could, thumping awkwardly over and over across the shore as he tried to get clear of the gunfire. Bullets raked the shore around him and he looked to the north to see swiftly moving figures dressed in black advancing up the river bank through the trees.

Mishkin and two of his men dashed for the cover of his truck with the girl pinned between them and leaped inside, Gregorie joining them as the truck turned in a cloud of diesel smoke and accelerated away from the firefight. Ethan looked to the Hind helicopter and saw the massive blades beginning to turn as the pilots hurriedly began starting the engines, a deafening turbine roar blasting from the exhausts.

Four figures rushed past Ethan, putting more rounds into the fallen Russian soldiers as they passed. Two of them dashed to the side of the Hind and tossed black objects high up onto the fuselage, the objects sticking to the metal. The soldiers sprinted away toward Ethan, and on instinct Ethan turned away and tried to bury himself in the sand as the huge helicopter lifted off in a roiling cloud of dust blasted at him by the downwash from the immense rotor blades.

Ethan saw the black–suited soldiers hurl themselves down into the sand around him, and then he heard two dull thumps from the direction of the gunship. A cloud of gray smoke and debris burst from the massive engines and then suddenly he heard a shrieking cacophony of metal grinding upon metal. He looked up and saw the gunship's engines literally tear themselves apart, the huge rotors breaking up and spinning away through the air as debris and shattered engine components blasted away from the helicopter in all directions.

The Hind whined as though in its death throes and spun out of control as it plummeted out of the hard blue sky two hundred meters away and smashed into the desert. Ethan saw a huge fireball billow from the impact point as a deafening explosion ripped across the river and a vast expanding ball of oily black smoke smeared itself across the blue sky.

Ethan lay for a moment and wondered what the hell had just happened as the soldiers around him got to their feet. Ethan found himself being lifted upright and a knife appeared in one of the soldier's hands and sliced through the bonds around his wrists.

He turned as one of them approached him, taller than the rest and a face that he recognized, although he couldn't believe it.

'Mitchell?'

Aaron nodded. 'Oracles or not, I bet you didn't see this coming,' he said as he gestured to the carnage around them. 'Although I was tempted to let the Russians finish their work and save humanity the chance of you breeding another chaos-causing Warner Junior.'

Ethan rubbed his wrists. 'The girls?'

'Are safe,' Mitchell replied, 'which is more than I can say for you.'

Ethan nodded. 'Looks like this time we're working for the bad guys. How are you getting out of here?'

Mitchell gestured behind him.

'We have boats and I'm going to call for an extraction before Ivan gets his act together and comes back for more.'

'Good,' Ethan said, 'they're not going to give up easily.'

Ethan joined the soldiers as they hurried back toward the river bank.

'Whatever happened in DC means that you're a liability that the government would like to disappear,' Mitchell said. 'Lopez agrees that you've got no plays left.'

'Thanks for the vote of confidence,' Ethan said as he saw Lopez with the girls, sitting together in a military style inflatable assault craft. 'You want to drop us off in Cyprus and we'll disappear?'

Mitchell grinned to himself.

'I would love to, but I suspect somebody else would like to speak to you first.'

'Jarvis.'

'The same,' Mitchell confirmed.

Lopez waved at Ethan as he stepped into the inflatable. 'Still got a full set or are you half the man you used to be?'

'The jewels are secure,' Ethan replied, then turned to Mitchell. 'They've still got one of the girls, she's called Elena.'

Mitchell nodded. 'So we saw. We're going to have to work fast to beat them to Tjaneni's tomb.'

'The scribe?' Ethan asked. 'What does his tomb have to do with anything?'

'You'll find out when we get back to the yacht,' Mitchell said. 'For now, let's just get the hell out of Syria.'

Ethan slumped back in the inflatable as the soldiers started the engines and the craft began chugging down the river in near silence, shielded by the overhanging trees. To his surprise, two of the girls shuffled across to his side and rested their heads against his chest.

Ethan looked up at Lopez, who offered him a motherly look and silently mouthed *"aww, get you"* in his direction. Ethan was too exhausted to respond and closed his eyes as the sunshine beat down on his face. He was asleep within moments.

***

XXXVI

Mediterranean Sea

Ethan stepped off the small fishing boat and climbed the rope ladder onto the enormous white yacht's stern, the warm Mediterranean sun glistening off crystalline blue waters all around.

Rhys Garrett's yacht was anchored ten miles off the south west coast of Cyprus. Ethan, Lopez, Mitchell and his team and the girls had travelled via a private vehicle across Lebanon, staying well clear of the major ports and cities to ensure that no links at all could be made between them and Garrett should the DIA spot them on their travels.

They had then boarded a privately hired, anonymous little fishing vessel, the captain of which being paid handsomely to transport them across to Garrett's yacht.

Ethan climbed onto the stern ramp, as wide as a barn and filled with jet–skis and a powerboat all lashed to the decks. Above his head he could see the tail rotors of a helicopter perched on the upper decks against the bright morning sky. He turned, and with Lopez helped the girls onto the deck as from inside the yacht he saw familiar faces approaching them.

'Damn, this feels kinda weird,' Lopez said.

Lillian Cruz hadn't aged in the years since Ethan had last seen her, but then that was kind of the point of why Majestic Twelve had sought her so eagerly and why Jeb Oppenheimer had paid with his life in his search for the elixir, the fountain of youth. Behind Lillian was Amber Ryan, youthful and full of spirit still, and with them both Aisha, Hellerman and Doug Jarvis. A tall man in smart casual attire that Ethan recognized as Rhys Garrett followed them, his hands in his pockets but a slightly guarded expression on his features. Finally, behind them all was Doctor Lucy Morgan, a smile on her face as she spotted Ethan with two of the blind girls clinging to his hands.

'My, you've changed,' she observed.

Aisha dashed past them all and threw her arms around the girls with him as though she had known them a lifetime. Hellerman almost stumbled toward Lopez and embraced her, Nicola's scowling contempt for Jarvis briefly melting.

'I thought you guys were dead,' he said, looking at Ethan.

'Nearly were,' Ethan replied as Jarvis approached and shook them all by the hand while the oracles collapsed into a mutual embrace, whispering to each other in Arabic.

'Good to see you all again,' Jarvis enthused, 'and in better circumstances now than ever.'

Lopez folded her arms.

'Seemed the same to us when we were under fire and abandoned in Syria,' she said as she surveyed the yacht around them. 'Looks like you've been busy with that thirty billion of yours. Pity we had to walk away from a few hundred million of our own to keep your location quiet.'

Jarvis frowned and looked at Ethan.

'The DIA offered us a cut of the Majestic Twelve pie if we found you and turned you in' Ethan explained.

Rhys Garrett moved forward and replied for Jarvis.

'The yacht's mine,' he said, 'and that thirty billion is tucked away safely in over a thousand accounts around the world and earning more interest per day than even I know what to do with. We're making plans, Nicola, and right now we need to find out what we've got here from your expedition in Syria.'

'You've got a few unemployed DIA agents,' Ethan said as he looked at Hellerman. 'What the hell happened?'

'Homeland,' Hellerman replied apologetically, 'at least that's what they called themselves. They shut us down even as I was watching the Apaches approach your position. They knew what they were doing and they knew it was wrong, but it was like they couldn't wait even the couple of minutes it would have taken to get you out of there. Somebody wanted you guys buried out in those deserts.'

Mitchell hefted bags of M–16 rifles onto the deck as he replied.

'Right now that's what they probably think happened, which will give us some breathing space until the Russians catch up with us again.'

'We need to consolidate what we've achieved here,' Garrett said, 'and find a way forward.'

'The Russians might have the edge on us there,' Lopez pointed out. 'They still have one of the oracles, the one who is supposedly the best, a girl named Elena.'

At the mention of that name the other girls looked up and Aisha spoke softly.

'Elena sees more clearly than the rest of us,' she said. 'She will lead them to their prize, and there is nothing that we can do to stop them.' She stood up. 'Unless you let me use the headset again.'

'No way,' Lopez said. 'We'll find them soon enough, you can be sure of that, without you having to wear that awful thing again.'

'It might save time if she…,' Jarvis began, but then fell silent as Lopez directed a violent glare in his direction.

'Do we know where they're headed?' Ethan asked.

Jarvis nodded as he gestured toward the yacht's interior. 'We've got an idea, but there's a lot to fill you in on. Lillian's been getting to the bottom of it all.'

Jarvis led them through the vessel to the bathrooms, allowing them some time to get cleaned up as the yacht raised its anchor and began sailing south. An hour after arriving, Ethan walked up onto the yacht's upper deck with a belly full of food and feeling revived after his labors in Syria. The rest of the team were all sitting around a large table near the bow, where a small pool glistened in the sunlight as the ship forged its way across the ocean

'We're headed south,' Ethan said as he took a seat opposite Garrett. 'What's the destination?'

'Egypt,' Garrett replied. 'There's a lot for you all to catch up on, so I'll let Lillian and Lucy fill you in as they've been working together on unraveling what Majestic Twelve were up to all those decades before they were finally destroyed.'

Lucy produced a series of photographs and laid them out on the table as Lillian spoke.

'There's so much material here in Majestic Twelve's files that it's hard to know where to start, but one thing does keep coming up. A phrase, repeated often in the communications between the members of Majestic Twelve over many years on secure networks. They keep talking about The Watchers.'

Ethan sat very still for a long moment as he digested this new information and looked at Mitchell. 'You ever hear of them when you were working for the cabal?'

Mitchell inclined his head slightly.

'They were mentioned from time to time,' he replied. 'Never to me, but I occasionally overheard conversations about them.'

'What are they?' Lopez asked.

'The Watchers are a supposedly mythical being recorded since the very earliest days of human civilization,' Lucy Morgan said. 'They first appear in Sumerian culture, the first true human civilization that we're aware of, and Sumer itself means "Land of the Watchers". The Sumer civilization emerged around southern Mesopotamia over five thousand years ago.'

Amber Ryan raised an eyebrow. 'What do we know about them, and why would Majestic Twelve be interested in an ancient culture's myths?'

'That I can explain,' Lucy Morgan replied. 'We have hard evidence, covered up by governments for decades, that ancient cultures show hints of interference by advanced technologies. The Sumerians record the presence of a figure they named Oannes, an aquatic being who taught them the arts, metallurgy, cosmology and other skills at the dawn of their civilization.'

Lillian reached out for a laptop and scrolled back through a few pages.

'There was something else here, a bit like that,' she said. 'I didn't think anything of it at the time other than the fact it was an odd thing for MJ–12 to record and…. Here it is: …evidence of the Watchers Ir, neter and Oannes.'

Hellerman exuded a pulse of excitement as he heard the names.

'Ir was a name given by the Chaldean civilization to their originator god, a Watcher named Ir. In Egyptian, Neter means "Watcher" and described the beings who guarded the gates of heaven and hell to the Egyptian afterlife. They were described as small, gray beings the size of children, with a humanoid form.'

'Aliens?' Lopez uttered, as though appalled.

'And the Bible also describes such figures within it,' Garrett said, showing a surprising knowledge of the legends himself. 'The Watchers are often considered one and the same, fallen angels who came to earth and bred with humans. Their offspring were known as the Nephilim and were described as giants, not physically but in intellect and knowledge, and they often had six fingers and toes which may hint at genetic defects.'

Ethan felt a theme developing and a new thread to the mysterious nature of Majestic Twelve's ultimate goal.

'They were researching ancient historical references to what would now be termed the "ancient alien" hypothesis,' he said. 'But I never knew that they'd taken things so far back in time. We always thought that Roswell or similar was the proximal cause of their entire conspiracy.'

Lucy Morgan shook her head.

'Can't be,' she said. 'You look at history and you see that it's littered with records like these. More to the point, Sumerian culture features a proto–language and script that has no known origins.'

'Really?' Amber Ryan asked. 'I thought they had something called cuneiform?'

'They did,' Lucy confirmed, 'but their language remains foreign and shows no resemblance to Indo–European, Semitic or any other language. The only true record we have of the Sumerians is from their successors, the Akkadians, who created a Sumerian–Akkadian dictionary that allowed us to decipher their records.'

'Islam contains similar beings,' Mitchell rumbled, 'the angels Harut and Marut, who descend to earth and are consumed by human frailties before being washed of their sins by god himself.'

'Common themes,' Jarvis echoed thoughtfully. 'Much of the work Ethan and Nicola did in this area during previous investigations showed links across entire continents that bridged ancient cultures that had never encountered each other; identical legends, events, the emergence of technologies.'

'So MJ–12 was interested in these Watchers,' Lopez said. 'That means that they must have considered them to be a reality, something tangible?'

'The general consensus that we reached at ARIES was that all of mankind's religious legends were in fact the memory of real events, distorted by time and the retelling across hundreds of generations,' Hellerman said, joining the conversation. 'I didn't believe any of it myself to begin with, but year after year there seems to be more mounting evidence suggesting that there is something in all of this, not least of all your discovery Lucy some years ago in the Negev Desert of Israel.'

'So what do we do about it?' Amber Ryan asked. 'Why are we going to Egypt?'

Lucy gestured to the images she had laid upon the table, and held one of them up.

'This is a picture of a stele dedicated to the Pharaoh Thutmose III,' she said. 'It was in part commissioned and designed by the scribe Tjaneni, a name that has come up several times in this investigation. Tjaneni was Thutmose III's greatest scribe and is known to historians for recording the Battle of Megiddo in 1457 BCE. The Tulli Manuscript, also coveted by the Vatican among others, is also likely to have been written by Tjaneni's hand around the same time and describes a remarkable encounter with what sounds very much like alien spaceships just days before the battle.'

Lillian picked up the story as Ethan listened.

'Tjaneni then abruptly disappears from the historical record, and nothing is heard from him again. The trouble with this is that he is known to have still been alive, so what could have happened to him to have him vanish from the records in such a way? It turns out that this image we found explains why he disappeared, and why the Russians are searching so intently for his tomb.'

Lucy then raised another image, and this time everybody gasped.

The hieroglyphic image she held was of four Egyptians, their wrists permanently attached to carrying rods suspended on their shoulders, and between them a large ornate box topped with two cherubim facing each other with their wings touching.

'That's the Ark of the Covenant!' Lopez exclaimed.

***

XXXVII

Lucy Morgan nodded.

'This is indeed the Ark of the Covenant, portrayed many centuries before the Hebrew Torah, or Old Testament, even existed.'

'Whoa, easy tiger,' Amber Ryan said. 'There's a few million Jews who'd beg to differ.'

Hellerman spoke up in Lucy's defense.

'The Ark was never a Hebrew legend, but an older Egyptian one adapted for their supposed historical account of their origins. The tablets that Ethan and Nicola obtained from the Vatican describe how it came to emerge into Egyptian lore. To say that it's explosive would probably be the greatest understatement ever uttered in the history of mankind, ever.'

'Why?' Mitchell asked.

'Because what Tjaneni found was powerful enough to change the world around him, and likely to him represented as great a threat to humanity then as nuclear war does now. He describes the discovery in a cave of an object of extreme power.'

Ethan leaned forward. 'Okay, now I get the Homeland's interest in keeping this to themselves. What else does it say?'

Hellerman focused on an image of the tablet and read directly from the Sumerian script.

'In the year twenty-two, on the third month of winter, sixth hour of the day, among the scribes of the House of Life it was found that a light from the previous day had fallen amid the deserts. The scribes visited the place where the sky had met the earth, and therein they discovered a brilliant light so vivid and bright that no man could look upon it and survive. Two of the scribes were lost to the strange and powerful creation, turned to dust and ash by its power, and the beings of light who left it behind were nowhere to be seen.'

'Beings of light,' Ethan echoed the description. 'Like you described before, how the gods were glowing beings that couldn't be looked upon, like Lucifer.'

'Exactly the same,' Hellerman agreed, 'although I suspect that it was the object itself that they left behind that glowed with such intensity, rather than the beings themselves. It's sometimes tough to translate Sumerian directly.'

Hellerman returned to his reading.

'The object was found in a chest that measured two and a half cubits by one and a half deep and one and a half wide. Its surface was covered with the finest gold, polished to a sheen as reflective as the surface of a still lake beneath a setting sun. Atop the box were two Cherubim, their wings meeting in the center, and the whole was born aloft on two rods held by four men.'

Ethan stared into the glowing coals for a moment and then he looked at Hellerman.

'Majestic Twelve were looking for the Ark.'

Hellerman nodded. 'That's what I thought, and it explains why the Russians are searching out here too and trying to beat us to the prize. From what I can understand from the inscriptions, Tjaneni travelled south from Saqqara to Karnak and from there to his death, vanishing into the desert with forty followers who died with him in order to protect a secret. It is from that Egyptian story that comes the later legend of the Lost Tribes of Israel wandering the deserts for years.'

'Israel would do anything to keep something like this buried,' Lopez pointed out. 'The state's existence is ultimately dependent on their historical capital of Jerusalem as described in the Bible.'

'Which is not a true history of the region,' Hellerman agreed. 'Israel and western Christians make much of the discovery of things like the Dead Sea Scrolls and other ancient documents revealing the early history of Christianity, but far older material such as this reveals the lack of historicity behind those scrolls. The Ark of the Covenant was supposedly sent down to Moses by God and contained the tablets upon which were written the Ten Commandments, of which we already know there were actually forty–two and that they were Egyptian. Even Moses' name is Egyptian, as in the Pharaohs Thutmoses and Ahmoses, and partially reveals from where the story of the Old Testament was derived: ancient Egypt.'

'The whole thing?' Lucy Morgan asked.

'Every word,' Hellerman confirmed. 'All of the creation legends, the gods and so on were borrowed from ancient Egypt by the Israelites and Hebrews when they created the Torah, or Old Testament, rewriting history to suit their own needs. All of the greatest legends such as the parting of the seas, the Exodus, the triumphant battle victories and even David and Goliath all come from the myths of older and more established civilizations. Israel, for instance, never has had a capital in Jerusalem. Their only historical capital city ever was Megiddo itself.'

Mitchell, who had remained ominously silent for now, spoke finally.

'I'll cancel my subscription to the God Channel when I get home.'

'The whole thing is a myth, borrowed from other older myths,' Hellerman confirmed, 'but this tablet describes in the witness's own hand the origin of those myths and the discovery, I think, of what we now know as the Ark of the Covenant.'

'I thought that the Ark was just something in Hollywood movies.'

'So do most people,' Hellerman enthused, 'and most people also assume that as per the Bible the Hebrews were sent the Ten Commandments by God, who then handed things over to Moses, who broke the tablets and put them into the Ark. From that moment on, the Ark supposedly represented the power of God Himself.'

Lillian picked up as Hellerman left off.

'The Bible describes the Ark as an object of unspeakable power that incinerates whole armies and lays waste to entire regions,' she said. 'The thing is, there's no mention of the object outside of the Old Testament unless you look at the much older civilization of ancient Egypt.'

'The Egyptians speak of it?' Mitchell asked, his expression as somber as ever.

'They do a lot more than that,' Hellerman replied. 'It exists in their texts, their art work and even their monuments long before the Hebrews had even borrowed the Phoenician script, which they used to write the Torah. Scholars have identified that the Ark was well known to the ancient Egyptians and you can see the Ark here in these hieroglyphs, which are especially interesting as they were found in the tomb of the world's most famous pharaoh, Tutankhamun.'

Ethan leaned closer and saw the famous icon of the two winged Cherubim facing each other, like angels, their wings touching at the tips.

'And this, found actually inside the tomb with the pharaoh,' Hellerman added as he switched to another image.

To Ethan's amazement, he saw the Ark itself in an old photograph taken of the tomb at the time it was first discovered in 1923. The Ark was sitting in Tutankhamun's tomb, its rods ready to be lifted once again, and atop it sat a carving of the Egyptian God, Anubis.

'Further images and engravings appear at the Egyptian temple at Medinet Habu,' Hellerman added, 'which was dedicated to the worship of the Ark. What's even more interesting is that Tutankhamun's father was Akhenaten.'

Dr Lucy Morgan's eyes widened.

'The sun god pharaoh,' she said, 'the king with the elongated skull.'

'The same,' Hellerman replied. 'Akhenaten abolished the old religions and introduced the worship of the sun itself, calling himself the son of the one true god and providing the foundations for the monotheistic religions of Christianity and, later, Islam. Ethan and Nicola have previously investigated Akhenaten as part of operations into the Incas in Peru, the connections to which I'll let you find out for yourself, but it's enough to say that Akhenaten was the most unusual of all the Pharaohs.'

Lillian gestured to the images scattered across the table before them.

'What brings us here now though is the fact that Egypt was the home of the Ark, and from what I've uncovered, that home was at the Giza plateau.'

It didn't take anybody long to figure out what Lillian meant.

'The pyramids?' Amber uttered. 'You're going out on a limb here, even after all we've seen.'

'Maybe,' Jarvis said, 'but bear with Lillian here because this is stuff that even I wouldn't have believed six months ago, and yet it's all in plain sight for anybody to see. The Pyramids of Giza, despite all claims to the contrary, show no signs of having been built by the Pharaonic civilization with whom they are most normally associated.'

Lucy Morgan shook her head.

'That's crap,' she shot back at him. 'We've found the tombs of the builders, the tools that they used, graffiti inside the pyramids made by the people who built the damned things!'

Hellerman levelled her with a calm gaze.

'We've found builder's tombs,' he agreed, 'but they contain no imagery or hieroglyphics associated with the pyramids, which would have been normal procedure for the Egyptians. They celebrated their achievements in their art. We've found tools, none of which conform to the construction of those megastructures, and no art or texts describing their construction or the techniques used. The graffiti is compelling, but given that the arts of tomb raiders are well known it's a bigger leap to assume they built the pyramids than to assume they were attempting to rob them. The words describe people, nothing more.'

Lucy shook her head, clearly irked, but she did not reply as Lillian went on.

'Egyptian scholars consider the great pyramids to be the work of their ancestors and they are proud of that heritage. Anything that suggests that the pyramids were built earlier than the Pharaonic era is rejected by them. Yet we have ample evidence that the Sphinx was already standing when the first Pharaoh's ruled the region in the First Dynasty and that so were the foundations at least of the pyramids.'

'What does all of that have to do with the Ark of the Covenant?' Ethan asked.

'We all know that there are pyramids all around the world,' Hellerman said, 'in almost every ancient culture. The word pyramid itself comes from the Greek "pyra", meaning fire or light, and the Greek "midos" meaning measures. The Great Pyramid of Khufu, the largest in the world, stood nearly five hundred feet tall with its gold capstone and is built from two and a half million blocks of stone, some weighing as much as seventy tons. It is built with a precision that is truly unrivalled, and is orientated to the four cardinal points of the compass. The casing stones were placed with an accuracy of five one thousands of an inch. The mortar used is of an unknown origin and cannot be reproduced even with today's technology. Worst of all for patriotic Egyptians, no hieroglyphics or writings have been found anywhere inside the pyramid that conform to its construction. And that is where the Ark comes in.'

'It does?' Lucy asked, feigning interest.

Hellerman ignored her dismissive tone as he continued.

'In what is called by Egyptologists "The King's Chamber", a red granite coffer was found. This is the only object found anywhere inside the pyramid. No Pharaoh's body, mummies or treasure chamber has ever been found to match the coffer. It was too large to fit through the passages, so it must have been put in place while the pyramid was under construction. Analysis of the coffer revealed that it was made with some sort of drill that used hard jewel bits and a drilling force of an incredible two tons. It was cut out of one block of solid granite. What interests me here is that the cubic capacity of the coffer coincides with the measurements of the Biblical chest of Moses, the Ark of the Covenant.'

Ethan felt a little twinge of excitement as he considered this.

'You think that the Ark was kept inside the Great Pyramid.'

Hellerman nodded.

'I think that it was originally inside that coffer, that is now mistakenly assumed to be the unused tomb of a Pharaoh. I mean, c'mon, the largest and most impressive megastructure tomb of all human history and they forget to put the dead King in it when he finally keels over?'

Lopez was smiling with intrigue. 'Anything else that supports this little theory?'

'Sure,' Lillian said, warming to her theme, 'the Biblical Book of Exodus records the Ark as being two and a half sacred cubits long by one and a half high and wide. The volume of the Ark in cubic inches matches the volume of the pyramid's cubic inches, an important symbolic coincidence if nothing else. Then there's the sheer size of the pyramid complex itself, designed as though to be visible even from space and with the three main pyramids originally cloaked in white stone with golden caps, in the sunlight they would shine as bright as stars on the surface of the earth, and especially so at dawn and dusk when the setting sun would light only the golden capstones.'

'Which would match the stars of Orion's belt if viewed from space,' Ethan recalled.

'The pyramids were built for a reason,' Hellerman insisted. 'Nobody would build something so immense without a good reason, and there is not a shred of evidence actually connecting them to the ancient Egyptians, other than the fact that they're in a country that was later to become Egypt.'

'And how does the Sphinx tie in with that?' Lucy Morgan asked.

'It's age,' Hellerman replied. 'The weathering on the Sphinx suggests it withstood intense rainfall, something that had not occurred in the Nile Delta for many thousands of years before the Pharaonic dynasties began. Some of the larger limestone blocks show disproportional weathering to the others at Giza. The bottom few courses of Khafre's pyramid are built of cyclopean blocks, and The Osireion at Abydos in ancient Greece also has unmarked cyclopean masonry and is associated with the earliest dynasties. But the clincher for me is that salt encrustations an inch thick were found inside the great pyramid when it was opened, and were found to be consistent with sea salt deposits common after floods.'

Ethan thought back to the description of the Sphinx and intense weather erosion consistent with torrential rain.

'That would make the pyramids at least as old as the Sphinx, right?'

Hellerman shrugged. 'No other way around it.'

'But the pyramids have been consistently dated to around five thousand years ago,' Lucy Morgan argued.

'Again entirely true, but you cannot rely on carbon dating for stone,' Hellerman pointed out. 'It works well with many materials but not all.'

'The data was taken from pollen seeds and spores found inside the pyramids,' Lucy countered.

'Precisely!' Hellerman said. 'Not from the pyramids themselves. Grave robbers entered the pyramids throughout Egyptian history and would have contaminated the otherwise sealed buildings time and again, carrying pollen and spores in with them. No dating from a pollen seed can be relied upon!'

Ethan looked up at the stars.

'What about the shafts inside the pyramids?' he asked. 'What were they for?'

'Most scholars believe that they aligned to specific stars,' Hellerman explained. 'The only true alignment that made any sense was one that followed the longitude of Perihelion at zero degrees. That last happened in 4,043 BCE, while the building of the Sphinx was calculated to be approximately 4,500 BCE, the last time that the constellation of Leo rose before the Sphinx itself.'

'Nearly seven thousand years ago,' Lopez said as she looked at Ethan, 'right about the time civilization first rose up in the fertile crescent. Those people were barely out of the hunter gatherer lifestyle.'

'Exactly my point,' Hellerman agreed. 'Whoever built the pyramids, no matter what exotic conspiracy theory you may believe, possessed technological abilities far beyond those traditionally ascribed to the people of the time. If the older dates are correct, then they exceed the oldest known dates of human civilization.'

Ethan thought for a moment.

'And if the Ark was placed inside the Great Pyramid way back then, and it was as powerful and significant as the Hebrews thought it was…'

'Then the Egyptians would have found it and revered it,' Hellerman agreed. 'It would have become a powerful weapon, just the kind of weapon that could allow pastoral desert nomads to grow into the world's first true superpower. The Egyptians, not the Hebrews, found and held the Ark aloft in battle, conquering all before them.'

Ethan looked at Lopez.

'And that's what Majestic Twelve were interested in: whatever the Ark really was.'

Lillian spoke with a sense of finality.

'Tjaneni records that he would bury the Ark with himself, that it was too powerful to remain in the hands of men. Of course we assume that to be the Great Pyramid, but as that is empty he must have gone elsewhere. We're going to need help to find out where he might have chosen to bury the ark, and for that we need the rest of the tablet decoded.'

Lucy Morgan sighed.

'I know somebody in Cairo who can help.'

'Then we move as fast as we can. If Elena is guiding the Russians, they're going to head out there as fast as they can.'

Mitchell moved across to Ethan's side and grabbed his shoulder in a vice–like grip.

'Don't go in there without first having a plan to get out again, like in Syria. There's likely a good reason that thing hasn't been seen for thousands of years. Tjaneni hid it so well to protect his own people as well as others, and that means that he was afraid of something.'

Ethan looked up at the big man and nodded.

'I'm afraid of something too,' he said. 'I'm afraid of whatever it is Tjaneni buried out there getting into the hands of people like Gregorie and Mishkin.'

***

XXXVIII

The Museum of Egyptian Antiquities,

Tahrir Square, Cairo

The museum was located on Meret Basha on the eastern banks of the Nile, just north of Tahrir Square, a handsome building fronted with fountains and stone sphinxes bustling with tourists. Ethan led the way, his features concealed behind sunglasses and a cheap tourist hat that he had found being hawked by an Egyptian vendor in one of Cairo's busy streets. The sun was beating down on the busy square as they made their way through the bustling crowds. Ethan walked with confidence into the museum and through the vast halls filled with Egyptian mummies, the ancient remains of Rameses II and the elaborate gold head mask of Tutankhamen attracting crowds of tourists, their cameras flashing as they photographed of the famous relics.

'Do you have any idea where he is?' Lopez asked.

Ethan saw the man he was looking for, working on an exhibit that looked like an ancient mummy encased in glass.

'Dr El–Wari?'

The Egyptian man wearing spectacles and with receding black hair, his dark skin stark against his crisp white shirt, turned and his eyes widened as he recognized Ethan. Almost immediately his heart sank with his expression.

'Warner,' he said as though he had eaten something unpleasant and was seeking to spit it out. 'I thought I'd last seen you years ago.'

'Nice to see you again too,' Ethan replied. 'You helped Doctor Lucy Morgan a few years back and we need your help again.'

'If you're here to talk to me about aliens building the pyramids and contacting ancient Peruvian cultures I swear I'll mummify you and put you on display in this museum myself. Do you know how long it took me to re–establish my reputation here after what you and Lucy Morgan put me through and…'

'This way doctor,' Ethan said as he took El–Wari firmly by the arm and guided him toward a nearby access door.

Ethan hurried the Egyptologist through the access door into a quiet corridor, Lopez following them through and pulling the door shut behind them.

'We're here about a manuscript that was recorded during the reign of a Pharaoh, called the Tulli Manuscript.'

'Oh no,' El–Wari shook his head wearily and tried to push past Ethan. 'Take your questions to somebody else, please. I don't want anything to do with this, with any of you.'

'We're not interested in any ancient astronaut theories,' Ethan snapped as he pinned the academic in place against the wall as gently as he could. 'This is about children.'

'What?' El–Wari asked, confused.

'Trafficked children,' Lopez said from nearby as she kept watch on the door behind them. 'They're being abducted and smuggled out of Syria into Lebanon, and one or two of them ended up in Utah.'

El–Wari's collapsed helplessly. 'I don't understand. What does this have to do with me?'

'We found this on the wall of a Utah compound belonging to an apocalyptic cult,' Ethan said as he fished out the image of the hieroglyphics from his pocket and showed it to El–Wari. 'You recognize it?'

The Egyptologist scrutinized the image for a moment and nodded. 'Yes, I can read it, but what's it doing in Utah?'

Ethan released the old man as he replied.

'The cult had purchased a number of girls who had been smuggled out of Syria under the cover of a charity they operated,' he explained. 'They were being used because the cult believed that they were some kind of Egyptian Oracles.'

El–Wari offered Ethan a flat stare. 'Seriously. You abduct me into this hall to talk about oracles?'

'Girls are vanishing in large numbers and we think that the Russians are behind it,' Lopez explained. 'They're looking for the tomb of an Egyptian scribe named Tjaneni.'

El–Wari raised his hands in supplication. 'All right, but I still don't understand what this would have to do with abducted girls. The Tulli Manuscript alleges an encounter between ancient Egyptian peoples and some kind of unidentified flying objects, although I thought that the author was unknown. What does that have to do with oracles, if they even exist?'

'That's a longer story,' Lopez admitted. 'Just tell us what you do know.'

El–Wari sighed heavily.

'The scribe Tjaneni served under the Pharaoh Thutmose III, and then under his son, Amenhotep. The location of his tomb remains unknown, as does much about his later life.'

'Yeah, about that,' Ethan said as he took another image from his pocket and showed it to the Egyptologist. 'We think his disappearance may have something to do with this.'

El–Wari looked at the image of the Ark of the Covenant and baulked. 'Oh, please, no more. You think that is the Covenant Ark, no?'

'We know that the Ark was Egyptian in origin,' Ethan replied, 'and we know that the Russians are using the oracles to search for it.'

Doctor El–Wari pushed past Ethan angrily. 'I'll show you your damned Ark!'

The doctor stormed back out into the museum, forcing them to follow him, and he quickly stopped before a large glass cabinet. Within, mounted on dark blue velvet, stood an Ark with Anubis sitting atop the lid, the poles running through mounts at the Ark's base.

'This is the Ark of Anubis, found in the tomb of Tutankhamun over a century ago,' El–Wari seethed. 'As you can see, it has levelled no mountains or turned anybody here into a pillar of salt. There are no world governments sending in lethal agents to recover it either, or if they are they're not very good at their jobs as this artefact has been on display for about a hundred years!'

Lopez smiled sweetly at the Egyptologist. 'Probably not the one we're looking for, doc',' she said.

'Then I don't know how I can help you,' El–Wari replied miserably.

'It's Tjaneni's tomb we're after,' Ethan said, 'and we've got something to trade with you if you can help us.'

The Egyptologist looked up to the ceiling in hope. 'That you'll go away and never come back?'

'Yes,' Lopez replied as she unslung her rucksack from her shoulder, 'but better than that, you can have these.'

In one smooth motion she opened the sack and showed El–Wari the priceless tablets hidden inside. The Egyptian stared at them for a moment and then his eyes flew wide.

'Where did you...?'

'Don't ask,' Ethan said, 'just be reassured that they were being hidden to ensure the rest of the world would not learn about them. You get them for the museum, if you can translate the writing on the back.'

El–Wari ushered them through the museum to his office, which contained a large poster that had been laminated and framed on the wall. Upon it were dense ranks of hieroglyphs, each with a translation beneath them in both Greek and Latin that Ethan guessed had been taken from the famous Rosetta Stone, a granodiorite stele inscribed with a decree issued at Memphis, Egypt in 196 BCE on behalf of King Ptolemy V. The decree appeared in three scripts: Ancient Egyptian hieroglyphs, the Demotic script, and Ancient Greek, and had allowed linguists with a means to finally decode the mysterious Egyptian hieroglyphs.

Lopez placed the tablets carefully on the table as El–Wari examined them closely.

'These are exceedingly ancient,' he said in wonder, 'Tjaneni could not himself have created them. They must have been preserved.'

'Tjaneni is believed to have carved the inscriptions in the front of the tablets,' Ethan confirmed, 'but the rear facing script is much older.'

El–Wari frowned as he read the lines.

'The text is uncertain but I believe that part of it is referring to a tomb in Sqarra, that of the sage Ptah–Hotep.'

'Hellerman said that was where the hieroglyphics in Utah were copied from!' Lopez said to Ethan.

'Can you decipher the rest?' Ethan asked Doctor El-Wari.

'I only know one person who could reliably decipher the rest of this. His site is just a few miles south of the city.'

'Can you take us there?' Lopez asked.

'I cannot leave the museum,' El–Wari said, 'but the same expert in ancient texts is working at Saqarra right now. If you like I can call him and have you meet him there?'

***

XXXIX

A wave of blistering heat assaulted Ethan as he stepped out of the museum and into the street, the sun a fearsome flare sky in the flawless hard blue dome of the sky above.

'Here we go again, huh?'

Lopez moved alongside him outside the museum as they watched the bustle of people and battered vehicles fighting for space on the crowded streets and creating a din that was Egypt's capital city's signature.

'Let's get out of here,' he replied as he flagged down a taxi, a ramshackle white car that looked vaguely European in design and thus might possess air conditioning.

Ethan was aware that the head of the DIA had recently visited Cairo for two days, during which he had held talks on boosting military and security cooperation. Egypt's volatile political situation after that "Arab Spring" uprisings had calmed enough for the country to again become a valuable US ally and bulwark to the troubled north and east of the region.

Ethan climbed into the cab with Lopez, and their driver agreed in halting English to drive them the twenty or so miles south of Cairo to reach the Saqqara site. To Ethan's dismay the car had no air conditioning, the driver instead fighting his way through Cairo's intense traffic with all of the windows down, the horn blaring as he yelled in Arabic at virtually every other road user he encountered.

The heat wafted through the interior of the car, bringing with it the pungent scents of animals, vegetable stalls, unwashed bodies and sweet coffee.

'You sure know how to show a girl a good time,' Lopez smiled at him sweetly as the car lurched this way and that.

Ethan suppressed a smile as the driver finally broke free of the traffic and accelerated, allowing a blessed breeze to blast away the pungent odors as the car drove past the Giza plateau, the immense pyramids rising up into the smog–filled Cairo air. Ethan wondered not for the first time how on earth the ancient Egyptians had built such colossal structures. Although mainstream archeology had located what was believed to be the tombs of the builders themselves, there were no descriptions in those tombs of how they actually built the monuments. It was supposed by experts that ramps were built around the pyramids as they were constructed in order to haul the massive fifteen ton blocks from which the monuments' exterior was constructed. Yet, as pointed out by many, the ramps would have ended up being as big a construction project as the pyramids themselves.

'Doesn't make any sense,' he said out loud as he looked out at the site.

'I know,' Lopez replied, guessing what he was thinking. 'What's even more amazing is that they used to be covered in white stone, with a gold cap at the top.'

'You gonna tell me and the rest of the world how men built those things then?'

'The mistake you all make is that you assume men built them,' Lopez replied.

'You think that aliens did it?'

'No,' Lopez said as she loosened her shirt. 'Women. Historically, women have always done the hard work while men have passed the time fighting and hunting for dinner.'

Ethan shook his head as the car travelled on, eventually reaching the site of Saqqara. The driver pulled over as he was waved down by a portly Englishman dressed in shorts with a straw hat protecting him from the blistering sunshine.

Ethan paid the driver and climbed out with Lopez as the Englishman shook their hands profusely.

'Professor Benjamin Radford, University of Oxford, welcome to Saqqara. Doctor El-Wari said you'd be here and that you were both insane, so you're in good company.'

Radford was every inch the British scientist stranded in a foreign land, his skin red from sunburn, his eyes twinkling behind square-rimmed glasses below the brim of the straw hat and a red kerchief about his neck. Ethan figured that he could have showed up in Egypt in 1840 and not looked out of place.

'It's not every day that I get a call from the Defense Intelligence Agency,' Radford enthused. 'What is it that I can do for the Yanks out here?'

Ethan suppressed a smile as he replied.

'We need access to a particular tomb,' he explained, 'and we're told you're the man to show us.'

'I am indeed,' Radford replied as he led them along a dusty path toward a series of step-pyramids before them. 'I can guide you through any tomb you choose in this vast complex.'

'What is this place exactly?' Lopez asked.

'Saqqara is an ancient burial ground. The name is believed to be derived from the ancient Egyptian funerary god Sokar. The site served as the necropolis for the Ancient Egyptian capital Memphis, and features numerous pyramids including the world famous Step pyramid of Djoser which you can see over there.' Radford pointed to the irregular pyramid as they walked. 'It is the oldest complete stone building complex known in history, built during the Third Dynasty. This area was an important complex for non-royal burials and cult ceremonies for more than three thousand years.'

'So people of importance were buried here,' Ethan said.

'Many. Do you know the name of the tomb you're interested in?'

'The tomb of Ptah-Hotep,' Lopez said.

Ethan caught the look of uncertainty in the professor's eye as he looked at Lopez. 'Why would the great American government be interested in the tomb of a sage from the fifth dynasty?'

'It's a long story,' Lopez replied. 'Right now we just need to take a closer look at the tomb.'

Radford shrugged but said nothing more as he led them to a rock–cut tomb on the south east side of the complex known as a mastaba, which had signs in English and Arabic above the entrance, which was decorated with two pillars. The searing heat vanished instantly as Ethan followed Radford and Lopez into the darkness, as though the cool breath of the earth were whispering past them in the shadows.

'This is the mastaba of Ptah–Hotep,' Radford said, his voice eerily distorted inside the tomb.

Ethan followed Radford through a room filled with reliefs on the walls, then past two rooms on each side of a corridor until they reached a court surrounded by ten pillars. More rooms followed, Ethan now keeping a sharp lookout for the relief that they sought, passing a false door of some kind with an offering table before it.

'Most of these walls are decorated with reliefs,' Radford said, 'but mostly only the lower parts of the scenes are well preserved and…'

'I've got it,' Lopez said as she crouched down alongside one wall.

Ethan joined her and peered at the relief before them, recognizing instantly the shape of the alien figure they had been shown in Washington DC.

'What do you make of this?' Ethan asked Professor Radford.

Radford peered at the image for a moment before shrugging. 'Judging by the rest of the reliefs, it looks like a lotus flower in a vase that just happens to be vaguely reminiscent of an alien figure.'

'That's a stretch,' Lopez replied, 'and I'm a sceptic.'

'What is it that you're looking for here?' Radford asked. 'Why on earth would the American government be taking a mural such as this seriously in terms of extra–terrestrials?'

Ethan pulled an image from his pocket, taken at the site of the cult in Utah. He handed it to the professor and explained how they had discovered it.

'The artist is blind,' Ethan said. 'She claimed to have been channeling the thoughts or experiences of a sage named Ptah–Hotep.'

Radford humphed and handed the picture back. 'More likely she copied the picture from the Internet or similar.'

'She is blind,' Lopez reminded him. 'Tough call, don't you think?'

Radford blustered and waved her away. 'I don't believe in such mythical things as channeling and remote perception. I deal in facts.'

'Okay,' Lopez said. 'So, factually, how the hell did she draw this when blind, and also guide a Utah Sheriff out of a burning building and predict their imminent deaths accurately enough for the sheriff to avoid obstacles and save their lives?'

Radford stared at her for a long moment. 'Coincidence and good luck are remarkable bedfellows.'

'So are ignorance and bullsh…'

'Shouldn't we focus on what we do know for sure,' Ethan cut Lopez off. 'We did our homework professor. This isn't the only anomalous image on ancient Egyptian reliefs, is it?'

Before Radford could reply, Ethan handed him one image after another.

'A mural above a doorway in a temple in the Kush goldmines, which appears to show a rocket ship and people standing next to it as another craft flies overhead. Rows of hieroglyphics in ceiling beams of the three–thousand–year–old New Kingdom Temple at Abydos, dedicated to the god of the Egyptian pantheon, Osiris, perfectly depicting a modern helicopter, aircraft and hovercraft.'

Lopez stepped forward. 'And this,' she said, holding out another image they had collected from Hellerman before leaving Garrett's yacht. 'Supposedly the mummy of an eight–month old unborn child but with almond eyes, an elongated skull and fingers twice as long as any baby's should be, found in the tomb of Tutankhamun and Ankhesenamun in the Valley of the Kings.'

'Which matches these remains found in Chile's Atacama Desert in 2003,' Ethan went on, 'a supposed fetus six inches tall that was DNA tested and found to actually be some six to eight years old, had only ten ribs, an elongated skull, almond shaped eyes and DNA that diverged from human by no less than nine per cent.'

Professor Radford held up his hands in supplication.

'Science doesn't know everything,' he admitted, 'but that's no reason to jump to such far–fetched conclusions.'

'All we're interested in is solving a case,' Lopez insisted. 'There is another icon on this relief, called the Eye of Horus.'

'A common icon in Egyptian lore,' Radford confirmed, 'often referred to as the All Seeing Eye.'

'The eye also appears on a stele that mentions the ancient Egyptian scribe, Tjaneni,' Ethan said.

'It appears in conjunction with many Egyptian figures,' Radford replied. 'I don't understand the significance you're placing in one individual's relation to the eye. Horus was a falcon–headed idol considered the king of all Egypt, the symbol of which was the pschent, a red and white crown of a particular shape associated with Horus.'

'From what we understand, Tjaneni is believed to have travelled south from Saqqara to Karnak and from there to his death, wandering in the desert with forty followers who entombed themselves with him in order to protect a secret. That secret is something to do with the Tulli Papyrus.'

Radford's eyes widened behind his spectacles as he finally understood what Ethan and Lopez were seeking.

'The Tulli Manuscript,' he echoed. 'El–Wari wasn't kidding when he said that you two had lost your minds.'

'We just want to know what the Eye of Horus means to you, what it meant to the Egyptians, and how it might connect to Tjaneni and the possible location of his tomb,' Ethan asked.

Radford sighed and used a kerchief to mop his forehead as he spoke.

'The Eye of Horus supposedly was a symbol of protection for Egyptians and was personified by the goddess Wadjet,' he explained. 'However, there is a school of thought that suggests that the eye is in fact a depiction of the pineal gland in the human brain.'

Lopez blinked. 'Say what now?'

'The Eye of Horus matches precisely in shape and form the human brain's thalamus, one of the most ancient and primal structures inside our brains. The organ translates all incoming signals from our senses, and some schools refer to this part of the brain as the "third eye", essential for things such as astral projection, remote viewing and so on. The Eye of Horus traces perfectly the form of the brain's corpus callosum, thalamus, Medulla Oblongata and hypothalamus.'

'How would the ancient Egyptians have possibly known about something like that?' Ethan asked.

'Precisely my question!' Radford asked. 'They were capable of basic surgery but nothing that might have exposed them to such a structure deep inside the human brain. They are said by most archeologists to believe that the heart was the repository of all human faculties, yet the Eye of Horus was also formed of six basic components, each referring to a different sense; smell, touch, taste, hearing, sight and thought. Clearly, they knew very well what the organ was for and believed that some seers, or oracles, could divine the future using the Eye of Horus as their guide.'

Lopez looked at Ethan. 'The Watchers, the Eye of Horus, oracles who can see the future, it all fits together somehow.'

Ethan nodded in agreement but he decided to get Radford back onto the task at hand.

'Can you tell us, from what's written on this tablet, where the tomb of Tjaneni might be found?' Ethan asked.

Radford looked at the images Lopez handed to him, reading intently with a furrowed brow before he spoke.

'Where on earth did you get this?'

'Long story,' Lopez said.

Radford looked down at the images as he spoke.

'The tablets speak of a canyon shaped like a crescent moon, named the Canyon of Horus for its similarity in shape to the All Seeing Eye,' he said, 'that lay in the direction of the setting sun when viewed from the Temple of Horus in Behdet.'

'Behdet? Ethan echoed. 'Where is that?'

'It's the ancient Egyptian name for Edfu, a small ancient settlement five hundred kilometers south of Cairo. If the scribe Tjaneni left clues to his tomb's location, then that would be the best place to look but there's nothing but desert out there for thousands of miles. I don't understand why so many people suddenly want to head out there?'

'What do you mean, *so many people*?' Lopez asked.

'There were some tourists here earlier, asking questions about the same location. Russians, I think.'

'They're ahead of us,' Ethan said.

'Anything else?' Lopez asked Radford.

'The mastaba or tomb was made in a wadi that "held the heavens in its palm",' Radford went on as he read the script, 'and was three ituru east of Edfu.'

'How far is that in miles?' Ethan asked, sensing that they were closing in on their target.

'About twenty–five miles,' Radford replied.

Ethan turned to Lopez. 'With satellite technology we could find that canyon in minutes.'

Lopez snatched the images from Radford and kissed him on the cheek.

'You're a star.'

Radford stared at her in bemusement. 'You're welcome.'

Lopez followed Ethan as they hurried away, Ethan dialing a number on a fresh and untraceable cell phone Jarvis had given him.

'We're ready,' he said as soon as Jarvis picked up the line. 'It's west of Edfu. We'll need Lucy and Hellerman, and Mitchell too.'

'Will do,' Jarvis agreed. 'We won't have time to muster a large force or desert vehicles but I'll have Mitchell leave now and meet you near Karnak. If you can get a ride out as far as you can into the desert, you could make it to the tomb before the Russians.'

'They'll need to assemble their men and equipment and get it all into the desert, and that takes time,' Ethan said. 'We need to leave now to beat them to it. Send Lucy and Hellerman too, and make sure Mitchell brings weapons and at least one GPS distress beacon in case we're compromised.'

Ethan shut the phone off and looked thoughtfully out to the south.

'The Russians will be on the same course if they've got information out of Elena,' Lopez said. 'They could have crossed the Sinai by now, might even be within a few miles of us.'

Ethan nodded.

'No time to waste. Let's go.'

***

XL

Thebes, Egypt,

1407 BCE

Tjaneni walked toward the great temple of Karnak, leaning upon his cane as he moved. The scent of the great deserts and the Nile filled the field of his awareness, the heat of the great sun high above and the sound of people toiling nearby as they heaved great blocks of stone in teams.

Tjaneni sensed but saw none of this, for his sight had long ago abandoned him. He could hear the small entourage of priests who followed him reverentially through the city of Waset toward the immense pillars of the Hypostyle Hall.

Tjaneni wore none of the traditional robes of the high priesthood, for his calling came from a far higher place and warranted absolute secrecy. A phalanx of the Pharaoh's most feared guards protected the small group as they moved between the pillars, citizens of the kingdom silently moving out of their way and whispering softly to each other. Tjaneni could not quite hear everything, but he could gain some sense of what was being said.

'Who are they?'

'What are they doing?'

'Why are they allowed to enter the dwelling of Amun–Ra and the God–King?'

Tjaneni felt the heat of the sun fade away slightly as the entourage moved into the shade offered by the vast pillars, a hundred and thirty–four of them arranged in sixteen rows. Some were over twenty rods tall with a diameter of three rods, and each weighed hundreds of tons: such was the power and knowledge of the kingdom, wrought and forged in the massive temples and fortresses they had learned to build.

Tjaneni led his priests through the pillars toward the Great Festival Hall, wherein resided the God–King himself, the Pharaoh Amenhotep. The late, great Thutmose III had been succeeded by his son after an incredible fifty–four–year reign. Amenhotep had grown into a wise and just ruler who, after so many seasons of war under his father's name, had brought peace to the Kingdoms. And that, it had turned out, was why Tjaneni had arrived at Karnak.

Tjaneni led his priests to the Festival Hall and inside. He could sense the air of expectation within, could hear the flaming torches lining the walls, could sense the presence of the King's guards and the scent of palm oil, fruits and woodsmoke.

Tjaneni paced his approach to the God–King perfectly despite his blindness, and he prostrated himself slowly before the Pharaoh. His priests helped him to his knees as they too got down before Amehotep.

'Tjaneni,' the pharaoh said in a soft, deep voice that sounded so much like his father's, 'rise and speak with me.'

Tjaneni rose weakly to his feet with the help of his aides, and then he motioned for them to leave. He heard them back away as the Pharaoh motioned for his own entourage to do the same. They retreated as a group until Tjaneni was alone with Amenhotep.

The younger man stood from his throne and moved to Tjaneni's side, and with one hand the God–King guided him to the throne.

'Sit, Tjaneni, for you need it more than I.'

There was no mockery in the tone, only the respect that a great King held for the scribe who had accompanied his father on so many wars and campaigns throughout his long reign.

Tjaneni sat gratefully, feeling almost blasphemous as he took the seat of the God–King. Amenhotep rested one hand on Tjaneni's shoulder as he spoke.

'It is done?'

Tjaneni nodded, and managed a tired smile. 'It is done.'

'The tomb is constructed?'

'The work is complete, and the builders even now are preparing the tomb for its final occupant,' Tjaneni assured the Pharaoh.

He heard Amenhotep release a brief sigh of relief. 'As ever, you have exceeded all that I and my father could have asked of you, wise old Tjaneni. Can your priesthood be trusted with what we know?'

'They shall take their knowledge with them into the underworld, my King,' Tjaneni promised, 'and return it whence it came, to the gods themselves.'

The Pharaoh nodded.

'Good,' he said, 'for it has become too dangerous to the Kingdom for men to know of its location or its power.'

Tjaneni nodded in agreement, not for the first time in awe of Amenhotep's wisdom and maturity in this, the most difficult decision in the history of the Kingdom and, perhaps, mankind itself.

Thutmose III, Amenhotep's father, had presided over the greatest series of military victories of any Pharaoh in the history of the Kingdom. He had created the largest empire Egypt had ever seen in no less than seventeen campaigns, and he had conquered from Niya in North Syria to the Fourth Cataract of the Nile in Nubia.

Much of the reason for that success now lay in a tightly sealed wooden crate born aloft by four chosen men of inscrutable courage, and the scribe Tjaneni who had led them across much of the world on Thutmose III's campaigns with a single object at their head.

The Ark.

When Tjaneni had first encountered the Ark it had taken the lives of two friends most dear to him, all those years ago in the caves near Megiddo. Tjaneni had not then understood the incredible power contained within the Ark, but word of it having incinerated two men who had simply dared to look upon it and almost killed Tjaneni spread quickly through the kindgom.

Under Tjaneni's guidance, Thutmose III's army had mounted the fearsome object onto rods and carried it away from the caves. That night, alone inside Thutmose III's royal tent but with an entire army watching in silence outside, Tjaneni had opened the Ark at the Pharaoh's bidding.

Despite the crushing fear he felt, Tjaneni had been surprised to find inside the Ark not the terrible fire of the gods he had expected, but instead stacks of tablets. Some were made from clay, but others were hewn from raw metal. Fearfully, Tjaneni had reached inside and again had been surprised to find them inscribed with hieroglyphics that were familiar enough that he could read them.

Tjaneni had read one, then another, and with a shock of supernatural proportions he had realized what the Ark was: information. Incredible information, almost frightening in its depth and breadth. In one stroke Tjaneni knew how to win the war against the King of Kadesh, how to quell the land of Canaan, how to build things that could never have been built before.

How to crush any civilization with an unstoppable force.

Days later, the army had marched upon King Kadesh's forces. During the immense Battle of Megiddo, the Ark was born aloft amid the Pharaoh's banners as the army routed the Canaanites in battle and laid siege to the city. Utterly defeated, the enemy had surrendered shortly after when the Pharaoh's army had smashed their way into the city and taken the spoils of Canaan.

Magnanimous in victory, Thutmose III had spared the city itself and its citizens, thus winning their gratitude and respect. From that day onward, the army had marched into battle with the Ark aloft before it and had never known defeat throughout the King's long reign. The legend of the Ark had spread across regions, to the extent that Asiatic armies had been known to flee upon sight of the golden Ark as it was unveiled from beneath a billowing purple veil and held aloft as the Pharaoh's forces charged into battle. Hushed, fearful whispers in many dialects of the Ark burning entire legions to a crisp, levelling mountains and laying waste to entire regions preceded the Pharaoh's army wherever it travelled until no King dared stand against Thutmose III.

Those days were long gone now, the Kingdom prosperous and unified, now led by a King with no fear of battle but no stomach for more war after a lifetime of conflict. Amenhotep released Tjaneni's shoulder and spoke softly.

'And nobody but the builders know the location of the shrine?'

'None,' Tjaneni confirmed, and from his robes he revealed two small clay tablets that he handed to the Pharaoh. 'This, oh king, is the location of the tomb and the only place it has been written.'

The Pharaoh took the tablets and concealed them beneath his own robes.

'And they know the consequences of this great trust I place in them?'

'They welcome it oh King and consider it an honor, as do I. Only one of our number, the elder Taiteh, shall walk away and into the deserts. He shall not return.'

Amenhotep took Tjaneni's hand and grasped it firmly.

'This power, it is too much for mortal men and even I fear it, fear what it means for our future for it is only a matter of time before the greed of men brings war to our doorstep. You know this, of how other Kings will covet it, fight wars to behold the ark of the Eye of Horus: it must disappear to prevent more bloodshed. Only the gods themselves were able to bring it here, and only the gods themselves can take it away again. It must remain unfound, buried for all of eternity if necessary. I will ensure that false words are spread of its location across the known world, rumors and whispers that will confound even the bravest and most determined hunter. Let no mortal man ever lay eyes upon it again, for it is not of this earth.'

Amenhotep stepped away from Tjaneni and together they walked around behind the throne. Although he could see almost nothing, his eyes long since blinded by cataracts due to his exposure to the Ark's fearsome power all those years before, Tjaneni knew when he was in the presence of the supernatural. He could sense the Ark before him, silently radiating its fearsome power.

The high priesthood had taken to engraving hieroglyphics into the Ark's golden walls, and the form of Anubis, God of the underworld, now crouched atop the lid, but otherwise the Ark was unchanged from when Tjaneni had first found it.

'Men will search the four corners of the globe for it,' he whispered as though he too could make the same prophecies that the great oracles could, 'will fight wars for it, spill blood just as we have spilt blood in their search for power. And all of it, to one day again reach this same decision.' He turned to Amenhotep. 'I only hope that a King of your stature makes that decision for them.'

'Go, Tjaneni,' Amenhotep said to the scribe, brushing off the compliment. 'Take your priests and wander into the deserts. Lead them to a safe place where they can never be found, and return the Ark to Horus. I will join you when the time comes, in the afterlife.'

Tjaneni turned and waved for the priests to join him once again.

'We shall depart after nightfall,' he promised, 'and leave no trace of our passing.'

The priests nodded, and Tjaneni addressed them as the Pharaoh and his guard left the Hall.

'You all know what is expected of us, the fate that awaits us,' he said. 'Our time has come, and our entire Kingdom depends on what we do next. We shall travel tonight with the Ark at our head and no army shall ever dare cross us, for our destination is a place where no mortal man can tread, and we shall ever after be lost to history.'

The priests murmured a soft response.

'Amun,' they whispered their traditional chant of acquiescence, the word meaning "hidden" or "invisible", for their work was that of the unknown.

Tjaneni stood by as he listened to the workers veil the Ark and prepare for the journey into the deserts to the west, and he wondered if some day, perhaps thousands of years in the future, men would somehow follow in his footsteps in search of people who had vanished into time itself.

***

XLI

Hierakonpolis,

Kon al–Ahmar

The desert air was cold as the first hint of sunrise appeared across the eastern horizon amid thin streamers cloud, the distant mountains glowing pink and orange and a chill wind whispering across the empty wastes.

Ethan crouched on a low hill and scanned the glowing horizon with his binoculars, searching for any sign of the Russians making their way toward the encampment using the blazing sunset as cover. Despite his best efforts he could see no sign of them, and with the dawn less than half an hour away he knew it would become equally difficult for the Russians to locate their camp in the immense darkness. With their Mil–Mi 24 Hind helicopter gunship out of action that left only ground–based detection methods, and in a desert this large the chances of their being located were reasonably low.

'See anything?'

Lopez crouched alongside him and he shook his head.

'I haven't seen any vehicle tracks yet so they're behind us somewhere. We need to stay dark for now.'

Lopez nodded and shivered, more than aware of the need to avoid giving their position away using any source of heat or light. They had used no open camp fires, Ethan and Mitchell instead digging and lighting a concealed fire–pit and filling it with rocks which, once heated, were used inside sleeping bags to keep them warm through the night. Mitchell had then put out the fire and covered it with sand, the heat from the trapped coals warming the sand beneath them during the long night.

'You always said you'd like to work in the field,' Ethan observed as he saw Hellerman working on a laptop.

Hellerman, shivering under a blanket now that the coals beneath them had cooled, winced.

'This wasn't what I had in mind,' he replied, his voice quivering. 'I'm hungry, cold and my laptop's almost out of juice. If I wasn't so damned excited about what we've got here I'd probably be in a bad mood. Are you sure we can't use the vehicles?'

Ethan shook his head as he kicked the dust at their feet.

'Two family saloons were never going to get far through this sand,' he replied, the cars hidden the previous afternoon in a wadi ten miles behind them, one of the engines already on the verge of overheating.

'Come on, let's get moving.'

Doctor Lucy Morgan's voice sounded unnaturally loud in the otherwise silent desert as they broke camp and began walking again. Ethan joined her with Lopez, Mitchell and the others following behind as they trudged through the pre–dawn darkness. To their left Ethan could see the dawn revealing distant hills that shielded them from the modern city of Nekhen, nestled alongside the Nile.

'This area would have been one of the oldest burial grounds ever constructed in Egypt,' Hellerman said as he glanced at the map Ethan held, 'but it's going to be tough to figure out exactly where the tomb is on foot even with the data we have.'

Ethan nodded as he looked around. The desert was barren, endless dunes and rock mesas, wadis and long–extinct rivers cutting through the terrain. It had taken modern archeologists hundreds of years to locate the tombs of even famous pharaohs in the Valley of the Kings – now they had perhaps an hour or two to achieve the same.

'Are you sure we've got enough terrain here to work with?' Lopez asked as they walked.

'We'll have to skyline ourselves to get enough elevation to see the surrounding area,' Ethan replied, 'but yes, I can put us right on Tjaneni's doorstep using the GPS locator Jarvis gave us.'

'Then all we have to do is figure out how to knock,' Lucy Morgan said from beside them. 'Most tombs were protected with doors of solid rock that weighed several tons, and we don't have the time to dig our way under or around them.'

Ethan rested his hand on the explosive charges in his backpack. 'You let us take care of the door.'

Lucy frowned. 'You'll be destroying the entrance to a priceless tomb that may contain artefacts of immense historical and archeological importance to…'

'Thanks for the lecture Doctor Jones,' Lopez interrupted, 'but if we don't get in there before our Russian friends arrive, there won't be anything left for you to pore over.'

Ethan said nothing more as the little group trudged through the endless deserts, the sky to the east growing swiftly brighter as they travelled. Here on the equator the sun rose with startling speed and set just as quickly. Ethan watched the terrain around him and waited until there was enough light for him to see the tips of the hills to their west bathed in golden sunlight before he made his move.

'It's time,' he said to Hellerman. 'Give me the map and the satellite images.'

Hellerman handed them over and Ethan turned and set off at a run for the slopes of the hills, following the flat terrain of the desiccated flood plain until he hit the slopes and began to climb. Beside him Lopez kept pace, Doctor Morgan trailing slightly as they scaled the low hills with frenzied steps until Ethan reached the peak of a flat–topped mesa. He turned and saw the brilliant sunrise searing the horizon to the east, and the distant greenery of the Nile and Edfu, the flood plain sprawling away beneath them toward the river.

Beyond, far on the horizon, he saw what looked like lines of dark cloud as though distant thunderstorms were rising up in the dawn.

'Are we there yet?' Doctor Morgan asked as she joined them breathlessly.

Ethan squatted down on the rocks and used a few small stones to pin both the satellite image and the map down before him, both of them orientated north.

'Okay,' he said, 'Tjaneni's tomb is supposedly concealed within a wadi to the west of the House of Life in Edfu, south of Luxor.'

'Radford said that the burial was made in a wadi that "held the heavens in its palm",' Lopez added, 'and was three ituru east of Edfu, or twenty thousand cubits.'

Ethan measured out from Edfu and with a pen drew a neat arc describing a thirty-kilometre radius from the city on the Nile. Then he leaned close and examined the various flood plains from the satellite image, searching for anything that might look like a hand or the palm of a hand. Within seconds he realized that he could see nothing that looked like either.

'I don't see anything,' he said.

'The Egyptians are not always to be taken literally in their descriptions,' Lucy said as she crouched alongside him. 'Think out of the box for a moment. The Egyptians wouldn't have had a map like this, so they would have described the terrain as they saw it.'

Ethan frowned at the map but he could not see anything out of the ordinary until Lopez suddenly pointed at the satellite map.

'There,' she said, 'it's right in front of us.'

Ethan peered at the spot and saw a perfectly ringed canyon, almost as though something had crashed down into the desert hills and forged an impact crater that opened on its north western side onto a vast and ancient river wadi.

'Brilliant,' Lucy Morgan said. 'It's not a hand shape on a map, but it would appear to hold the heavens in its palm if you were standing inside it looking up at the stars.'

'See?' Lopez nudged Ethan. 'I'm not just a pretty face, I have an amazing brain too.'

'And a head big enough to fit it in,' Ethan replied as he looked at the most prominent terrain features he could find around them, mainly Edfu itself and some high hills to the north. He drew several lines on the map corresponding to where they saw those features, and then pin-pointed their precise location.

'We're here, on this ridge at the mouth of the old river,' he said as he pointed at the map. 'The terrain feature Nicola identified is three kilometres away to the south west, directly up the river wadi.'

'We'd best move fast then,' Lucy Morgan said as she jumped up. 'The Russians won't be far behind us, and they'll locate us more easily in the day.'

Ethan looked out to the east again at the dark clouds that looked suddenly higher and more ominous than he had suspected, and almost immediately he spotted a smaller, closer cloud of disturbed dust and sand spiralling up from the desert, catching the rays of the rising sun. Ethan squinted at them, and in an instant he knew what they were. 'They're already coming,' he said as he pointed out across the flood plain. 'Let's move, now!'

*

Gregorie drove the jeep across the rugged desert terrain, having driven off the main highway a quarter mile back. The jeep's wheels churned the sand up around him, and in the mirrors he could see the five vehicles following him doing precisely the same, advertising their approach.

The risk was worth the reward. He knew that Warner and his entourage were by now on foot, poorly armed and heavily outnumbered. What was more, far out here in the lonely deserts and unsupported by the DIA, Gregorie could kill them and nobody would ever know.

'How long until we get there?!' Colonel Mishkin called above the wind buffeting the jeep as it careered across the deserts.

'The location is ten miles ahead of us, inside the hills,' Gregorie replied with mechanical efficiency. 'We will have to go in on foot.'

Mishkin nodded and then he grabbed a radio and spoke into it.

'Launch the drones, find them!'

Gregorie glanced in his mirror as they drove, and from behind them he saw one of the vehicles pull out of line into clear air. A large troop carrier, it was adorned with radio antennas along with two delta–winged drones mounted on the roof.

As Gregorie watched, the two drones spewed a thin stream of exhaust smoke and then rocketed into the air. Each was powered by a small jet turbine designed to carry them rapidly to altitude, from where they would glide on thermals before delivering their lethal payload.

'Drones airborne,' came the reply to Mishkin on the radio. 'If Warner and his people are out there, they won't be alive for much longer.'

Mishkin grinned as he gripped the radio. 'Fire upon identification,' he ordered.

The drones sailed over head, climbing into the brightening sky as the sound of their jet turbines was lost with increasing altitude. Out here in the uninhabited deserts, the canisters of lethal mustard gas would do their cruel work and then be dispersed to nothing by the endless desert winds.

***

XLII

'Almost there.'

Ethan led the team at a brutal pace through the broad valley, sheer cliffs of sandstone rising up either side of them but still some distance apart. The sun was well above the horizon now, the winds likewise whipping up and gusting as the temperature soared.

'I've got less than a mile,' Hellerman said from behind them as he scrutinized a GPS display. 'We should almost be able to see it by now.'

Ethan squinted ahead to where what had once been a broad river that had carved out the immense wadi turned to the left gently, the opposing sides of the valley closing in on them and funnelling the desert winds up the wadi. The rising heat of the vast plains beyond in the center of the deserts was drawing forth the cooler air nearer the Nile, and Ethan noticed a considerable acceleration of that wind as he walked, dust spiralling up off the desert floor around them and sweeping in angry vortexes against the canyon walls.

Ethan turned and looked back to the east and almost immediately he saw the strange haze hanging over the horizon, a bizarre orange glow in the light of the rising sun that seemed to swell before his very eyes.

Lopez noticed the direction of his gaze and turned to see the same thing.

'Dust storm,' she identified it immediately, 'and a big one too.'

Ethan cursed mentally as he realized that there was no possible way for them to get back to civilization before the huge storm swept in across the Nile and the deserts beyond.

'Keep moving,' he said as he heard what he assumed was the faint hum of the desert winds soaring toward them. 'We need to get into cover before that thing hits.'

He was about to turn and start walking faster when the hum of the storm changed note abruptly. Ethan hesitated, tilted his head up to look at the skies above as he realized that the brisk winds were carrying the sound of some kind of engine toward them.

Lopez too turned her head to the sky, but it was Mitchell who called the warning.

'Drones!'

The light of the low sun caught the edge of a small aircraft with a wing span that Ethan guessed was probably no more than four meters. A second identical machine followed the first, sweeping this way and that in the turbulent air.

'Get into cover!' Mitchell urged them.

Ethan frowned uncertainly. 'They're too small to be carrying ammunition,' he said

Lopez raced past him as she shouted above the growing winds.

'They don't need bombs to take us out!'

Ethan began running as he saw the two drones wheel over in the sky, their delta wings flashing as they suddenly dove directly toward him. The sky behind the drones was filling with a billowing wall of sandy colored cloud that stretched high into the atmosphere in vast golden veils as it advanced toward them.

Ethan saw the drones grow in size as they rushed down and he prepared to duck as they opened fire, but to his amazement they rushed overhead and soared back up into the sky once more.

'Where are they going?' Mitchell gasped as they ran.

The drones wheeled about again, and this time they descended more gently as though carefully lining up their targets. As Ethan watched, he saw a small object fall from each of the drones and then they turned sharply away and veered off to either side of the fleeing group.

The two objects hit the desert floor fifty meters behind where Ethan stood and immediately a cloud of yellow smoke burst from them and began drifting toward Ethan and his companions on the high winds, driven toward them by the storm.

'Landing zone smoke?' Hellerman hazarded.

'You think they're marking our position?' Lopez asked.

Ethan had never known yellow smoke to be used as an LZ marker before, and he felt a premonition of doom as he yelled out a warning.

'Gas! Get away from the clouds and stay away from the canyon walls!'

Ethan dashed to his right, heading out into the canyon wash as the billowing fog of acrid yellow smoke tumbled on the winds toward them in two dense streamers, the huge wall of cloud behind them now dense and dark. He saw Lopez scatter to his left, Hellerman close behind as Lucy Morgan ran hard to keep up with Ethan.

'It's mustard gas!' Mitchell shouted as they ran.

Ethan felt his guts convulse within him as he heard the warning. One of the most horrific of all chemical weapons, mustard gas was capable of inflicting horrendous burns on human skin, blisters the size of melons and life–long injuries including blindness. Illegal in all but the most brutal of regimes, it had been deployed by both sides of the Syrian conflict to devastating effect.

'Get upwind of the canisters!' Ethan yelled as he saw the two drones repositioning for another sweep. 'Don't try to outrun it!'

The clouds of yellow gas tumbled on the wind as Ethan's group ran past them on one side while Lopez and the others maintained pace between the two streamers of gas. Ethan looked up into the sky and saw that the two drones were lining up to deliver the next canisters in between the existing ones, spreading the lethal toxin across the entire wadi and forcing Ethan and the others back toward the Russians.

'Where's the canyon we're looking for?!' Ethan yelled to Hellerman.

The scientist looked about them as he ran, and then he pointed to a large eroded gap in the canyon wall ahead and to their left.

'There, I can see it!'

Ethan looked over his shoulder, and there in the distance he could see the Russian convoy of jeeps and trucks closing rapidly on them, perhaps only a mile or two behind and like tiny black specks against the immense bulk of the advancing sand storm.

Ethan looked up again at the two drones and watched as they swooped in toward the group. There was still a faint stream of ugly sulfur drifting between Ethan and Lopez as the dispensers emptied their lethal cargo, cutting him off from them along with Mitchell and Lucy Morgan.

There was no way they could outrun the smoke and wind, and Ethan knew there was only one way to defeat the attack and sneak past.

'Cut back and around them as soon as they deploy the next canisters!' he yelled.

Mitchell understood immediately and prepared to change direction, Lucy keeping pace with the big man as the drones soared overhead. Ethan saw two freshly dropped canisters hit the desert floor and explode with clouds of lethal gas.

'Now!'

Ethan scrambled to a stop and turned back on his own path, sprinting upwind as the canisters bounced and tumbled toward him nearby. Mitchell and Lopez followed, running hard into the wind as specks of sand pummelled their faces like little ice picks scouring their skin.

Ethan saw the thick clouds of sulfur smoke rush past him from where the nearest canister had rolled to a halt, and he ran in a wide circle upwind of it before turning downwind again and sprinting in pursuit of Hellerman and the others. He checked behind him and saw Mitchell and Lucy Morgan following but tiring, and behind them the pursuing convoy of Russian military vehicles.

The huge clouds of billowing sand loomed over the sky in an apocalyptic wave of darkness, the brilliant sunshine to the east a blaze of light on one horizon as on the other the clouds reared up against the blue sky overhead. Instantly the temperature plummeted as Ethan ran, the wind cool now and the desert enveloped by deep shadow as it seemed night was about to fall once again. As Ethan looked behind him he could see men mounted on the back of the Russian jeeps with heavy weapons, still tiny against the vast storm.

'Stay in the middle of the wadi!' Ethan yelled to Hellerman ahead. 'Don't let them figure out where we're going!'

'They'll be on us within a minute and they'll shoot us dead!' Lucy Morgan replied.

Ethan looked behind him and smiled grimly, the storm's arrival both a curse and a blessing.

'No, they won't!'

*

'Faster!'

Colonel Mishkin yelled at Gregorie, but the soldier's boot was flat against the floor pan as he drove the jeep at its maximum speed across the desert.

'It will not go any faster!'

Mishkin scowled and leaped up into the rear of the jeep as he cocked the machine gun there and aimed it out across the deserts ahead to where he could see the fleeing Americans. He looked up and saw the apocalyptic cloud towering above him as if waiting to crash down upon them, and ahead the sky was a thin bright line of molten metal as though he were in a cave looking out across the deserts.

'They're not in range!' Gregorie shouted.

Mishkin ignored the soldier and took aim, and then he pulled hard on the trigger and the machine gun clattered and rattled as it spewed hot lead across the desert before them, tracer fire zipping like laser beams in the growing darkness.

*

Ethan heard the first rounds zip past by nearby and looked back to see tracer fire rocketing wildly across the desert in all directions as the Russian gunners opened up in an attempt to catch a lucky shot before they were consumed by the storm.

'Incoming!'

Ethan did not dodge left and right to evade the bullets, figuring that it was better to let the pursuing jeep's motion over the rough ground spoil the Russians' aim. Instead he kept running and hoped that the storm would swallow the Russians before they came within lethal range.

A salvo of shots clattered against the walls of the canyon to his left and he saw the huge crater–like canyon open up before him, a vast amphitheatre of solid rock carved as though by human hands from the hills.

Ethan looked behind him, saw more tracer fire flash toward him and heard the bullets smash into the desert floor as the jeep came within range, and then suddenly the Russian vehicles were swallowed by the storm and he lost sight of them even though the tracer fire still rocketed toward them out of the roiling storm.

'Now!' he yelled. 'Everybody into the crater!'

Ethan changed direction and sprinted across the wadi as he saw Hellerman and Lopez lead the way just ahead of him, clearing the weakening streamers of gas tumbling down the wadi. Lucy Morgan scrambled up over loose rubble and into the huge natural canyon with Mitchell close behind as Ethan sprinted up behind them and clambered up off the wadi floor.

'We need cover from the storm!' Lopez gasped, her chest heaving as she rested her hands breathlessly on her knees.

Ethan looked at the huge circular cliffs around them and shook his head as he saw no features that suggested a tomb entrance or even a human presence.

'I don't know where to go from here,' he admitted, 'other than we should get into the leeward side of the canyon real fast.'

Ethan jogged across the wide expanses of the canyon, the rest of the team laboring behind him as the storm arced over them like a gigantic wave and a deep darkness fell as the wind began to howl and particles of sand poured down upon them like glass rain.

'Get close into the wall,' Ethan yelled.

They huddled into the wall of the cliffs as the storm burst overhead and the bright dawn sky finally vanished, the features of the canyon lost as the visibility dropped to almost zero. Ethan squinted against the driving, swirling sand as he pulled a kerchief over his face and looked at Lucy.

'How are we going to find the entrance to the tomb in this?!' he yelled.

Lucy Morgan pulled something out of her pocket and held it out to him.

'Easy,' she replied, as though she'd known all along. 'We'll use this!'

***

XLIII

The entire basin of the crater was filled with a sandy fog of particles gusting like dirty brown rain that forced Ethan to shield his eyes. Beside him, Doctor Lucy Morgan crouched down and pulled out a small map upon which she orientated herself to the north.

'What's that going to do?' Lopez asked her, shouting to be heard above the gale screaming across the upper ridges of the crater.

'This formation wasn't caused by an asteroid impact,' Lucy shouted back. 'It was caused by erosion from the passage of water from the highlands to the west. The sand from the deserts then filled the void after the water was gone.'

Ethan frowned.

'Then the tomb could be under fifty feet of sand!'

Lucy shook her head. 'Tjaneni was buried some three and a half thousand years ago, so his tomb won't be against the far back wall of the formation, it'll be somewhere closer by!'

Lucy stood up and pointed across the vast formation, through the impenetrable veils of sand sweeping through the air.

'It's that way, two hundred forty meters!' she announced.

Ethan blinked. 'You're sure?'

As if in reply Lucy Morgan pulled the straps of her back pack closer about her shoulders and marched off into the swirling miasma of dust. Ethan and Lopez exchanged bemused glances, and then set off in pursuit with Hellerman and the rest of the team close behind.

'It won't take Ivan long to figure out where we've gone,' Lopez said as they marched, covering her face against the screaming wind. 'Those drones might have kept an eye on us long enough to know that we dodged the sulfur gas.'

Ethan nodded as he looked back to the north, toward the entrance to the formation.

'They probably already know where we're going if they have Elena with them,' he replied. 'The only thing protecting us now is this storm and we don't know how long it will last.'

Lopez reached down beneath her shirt and checked her pistol, tucked safely into her shoulder holster.

'Once they break through and find us, we'll have to hit them hard or they'll leave us out here to die. There's nobody coming out here to rescue us this time, you know that, right?'

Ethan didn't reply, more than aware that there would be no airstrikes or other fabulous American hardware coming to their aid. With the DIA officially out of the picture and Hellerman now stuck in the desert with them, they were on their own and the Russians would take every advantage of that.

'Let's just hope that Doctor Indiana Morgan here can get us out of the sh…'

'Sssh,' Ethan snapped, cutting her off as he raised a hand and listened.

To his right, beyond the swirling sands and the howl of the gale, he heard the faint rattle of an engine passing by at low speed. He pointed out to his right and looked at Lopez, who listened intently for a moment and then nodded in agreement.

'We need to disappear,' she said, 'fast.'

Ethan looked up to see Lucy Morgan waving them to follow her, and he hurried to the archeologist's side as they trudged west across the formation.

'It's this way,' Lucy said.

Ethan followed Lucy for some fifty yards or more, the scientist changing direction subtly as she scrutinized the compass in her hand. The sand and dust was gusting across the formation more violently than ever, the light dimming to almost as dark as night as Ethan heard the violent winds screaming across the turbulent sky above reach a new and frightening crescendo.

The little group hunkered down, shielding their faces from the vicious gale as Lucy reached a spot on the formation and crouched down.

'This is it!' she yelled above the roar of the wind. 'This is where the tomb is located!'

Ethan stared down at an entirely non–descript chunk of sand. With the exception of a slight rise in the level of the ground there was nothing to see, and the storm was now so bad that visibility was down to a few meters.

'How the hell would you know that?' Lopez demanded. 'There's nothing here!'

Lucy didn't reply as from her backpack she produced a small folding shovel and began pulling away mounds of sand. Ethan helped her along with the rest of the group as they burrowed down into countless centuries of accumulated sand.

To Ethan's amazement within a few moments Lucy's shovel began scraping against rocks buried three feet below the surface. As they worked feverishly so he could see the smooth, flat surface of cut rocks, too perfect to have been formed purely by nature.

Lucy hurried to find the outline of the rock, the sand rushing past in painful gusts as the tiny particles hammered against their faces. Ethan found a thin, dead straight crack in the rocks and followed it around, sweeping sand aside with his hands as the rest of the team worked around him. After a few minutes they were all standing on a large cut rock perhaps four feet square, wispy gusts of sand billowing past them. The stone was slanted by about forty–five degrees, like a door cut into the living rock.

'Now what?' Mitchell asked.

Lucy crouched down and examined the seal of the tomb, the gaps in the rock so tiny that it would not be possible to slip even a razor blade between them, never mind a crow bar or lever.

'We get creative!' she yelled back above the noisy gale.

Ethan looked over his shoulder into the dense, shadowy veils of the storm blasting past them. If the Russians were able to use the oracle to locate the tomb, they wouldn't be far behind.

'Whatever you've got in mind do it now,' Ethan said, 'before we're found!'

Lucy ordered everybody back from the tomb entrance as she began to work, and Ethan looked up and wondered how long the storm would last to conceal them from the Russian forces he felt sure were breathing down their necks.

*

Colonel Mishkin peered through the windscreen of the jeep, a permanent scowl twisting his features as he saw before them nothing but a dense veil of dust and sand beneath a darkened sky. The jeep's headlights penetrated only a few meters ahead of them, and he knew that Warner's team had been several hundred meters away when the storm had enveloped Mishkin's convoy.

'How much further?' he demanded irritably.

Gregorie stared directly ahead as he replied, the jeep driving slowly across the rugged terrain.

'We are in the vicinity of the group but they could have gone in any direction or even split up. We will not be able to track them until this storm has subsided, and even then there will be little to go on. The storm will erase any trace of their passing.'

Mishkin growled and then slammed a balled fist against the dashboard.

'Stop the convoy!'

Gregorie braked slowly to a halt in the middle of the storm as Mishkin pulled the hood of his smock over his head and clambered out of the jeep. He jogged back to the troop transporter and climbed up into the rear to see his soldiers sitting expectantly on benches either side of the vehicle, a girl pinned between them. Elena's skin was pale, her eyes closed and her body limp.

'Get her ready!' Mishkin snapped.

The Syrian, Akhmed was sitting beside Elena and he stared in disbelief at Mishkin. 'Ready for what?'

Mishkin's fists balled at his sides as he glared at the doctor. 'We have lost Warner and his people.'

'She is exhausted,' the doctor replied. 'There is nothing in this girl left to take.'

Mishkin took a single pace toward the doctor and swung a fist to crack across Akhmed's face. The doctor let out a whimper as he cowered away from the towering soldier.

'There is her life,' Mishkin growled back, 'and yours. If you value them, get her ready.'

The doctor reluctantly began fishing about in his kit for the Trans Cranial Stimulator as the soldiers gently lifted the girl from between them on the bench and lay her down in the center of the truck. Too weak to resist or even respond, Elena slumped at the doctor's feet as he set the device upon her head.

'This will kill her,' he snapped, his anger overcoming his fear. 'What use will she be if she doesn't survive?'

Mishkin glared down at them both as he drew a pistol. 'The question you should be asking, doctor, is what use will you be if she dies?'

The doctor tightened the straps on the cranial device and then connected it to a battery terminal. He waited for a few moments, and then leaned down beside the girl and said a name in a loud, clear voice.

'Ethan Warner!'

The doctor cranked the terminals and instantly the girl's weakened body shuddered as live electrical current swept through the TCS and bolted through her weary brain. Mishkin watched as the girl twitched and writhed, her sightless eyes rolling up into their sockets and her teeth clashing.

'Ethan Warner!' the doctor repeated, hoping against hope that she could hear him.

Elena's body convulsed and she let out a groan as her eyelids closed and she mumbled something that Mishkin couldn't quite hear above the storm winds buffeting the vehicle.

'Still open… Dove is low.'

'What did she say?' he demanded.

The doctor leaned closer to her, and squinted as he tried to focus on her words.

'The seal has been broken!' the doctor said as he repeated the girl's broken words. 'As above, so below!'

Mishkin thought for a moment.

'They are at the tomb?' he asked.

The doctor whispered to the girl and she replied as her body trembled and twitched.

'The true prize is within, not beyond!'

Mishkin frowned and then he stepped forward and leaned down as he rammed the pistol against the girl's head.

'Where are they?!' he roared, tired of the girl's mystic ramblings. 'Tell me where they are!'

The girl's eyes flew open and Mishkin saw a brief flash of defiance on Elena's exhausted face.

'They are within reach!'

The girl's body arched upward and quivered with a terrible finality and then she slumped onto the floorboards as the doctor tore the headset from her and touched his fingers to her neck. He waited for a few moments and then spoke softly.

'She is alive, but she will not survive another session.'

Mishkin whirled and yelled at the troops.

'Get outside and fan out!' he roared. 'The Americans are close by!'

The troops tumbled out of the vehicle and spread out as Mishkin turned his back on the doctor and jumped down onto the sand once more. He watched as his men vanished into the gloom that surrounded them, weapons in one hand and radios switched on. Although they were out of contact with the outside world, the signals were strong enough to burn through the storm at close range.

Mishkin waited for almost ten agonizing minutes before his radio crackled.

'General, we have them!'

***

THE GENESIS CYPHER

Dean Crawford

XLIV

Mishkin listened intently to the directions given him and then hurried away from the troop carrier, following a mini–compass set into the hilt of his combat knife. As he passed the jeep he ordered Gregorie to follow him.

The two men trudged through the brutal storm, heading directly south east on a magnetic heading. Although the compass seemed to be keeping them heading in a straight line, Mishkin could not help the feeling that he was being gently turned to the right.

He was about to call on the radio and get confirmation of the soldiers' positions when he saw a small group of them directly ahead. Mishkin hurried forward as the soldiers saw him coming and stood back.

Between them there was a small depression in the sand, and Mishkin could see instantly that there was a smooth stone block inside the depression that was rapidly filling with sand being blown in by the storm. He moved alongside it and peered down at the surface, which was perfectly smooth and devoid of any markings but for the Eye of Horus in relief in its center.

'They must have been here moments ago!' one of the soldiers shouted above the gale. 'But this stone hasn't moved, so they must have given up and fled. Maybe they heard us coming?'

Mishkin peered down at the stone and then up into the storm around them. It was perhaps possible that Warner and his people might have heard the vehicles approaching the area, but he doubted that they would have simply fled without even trying to open the tomb.

'To hell with them,' he decided finally. 'Blow this entrance open, right now!'

'Explosives could collapse the tunnels inside the tomb,' said one of the soldiers. 'We might not be able to get in.'

Mishkin grinned cruelly at the soldier. 'Then if Warner and his friends are inside, they will not be able to get out either. Hurry!'

The soldiers began to place explosive charges around the tomb entrance as Gregorie moved to Mishkin's side.

'If they are not inside the tomb, then where could they have gone?' the former soldier asked. 'The nearest town is miles away and they could not have passed us, and this storm could last for days so to travel further into the deserts would be suicide. Where could they be?'

Mishkin looked at the nearby tomb and then the desert around them, and he had no reply for Gregorie. Warner and his team had simply disappeared.

The soldiers suddenly leaped up and waved everybody back as one of them unreeled a detonator wire. Mishkin joined them as they fell back and away from the tomb, and then the soldier connected the detonator to the wire and twisted it downward.

A dull boom reverberated through the ground as the charges blasted the massive stone entrance. Mishkin followed his soldiers back to the tomb and could immediately see large chunks of angular rock poking out of the sand around the site where the entrance had been blasted clear.

Mishkin gripped his pistol and jogged up to the tomb and aimed down into its depths.

He hesitated as he saw only sand.

'What? Where is the entrance?!'

The soldiers gathered around the stone and stared down at it.

'There isn't one,' Gregorie said. 'The stone was just lying here.'

'But it bore the Eye of Horus!' Mishkin roared.

Gregorie shook his head.

'It was a deception, to discourage grave robbers. The real entrance must be somewhere else around here.'

Mishkin roared in frustration and screamed at the soldiers.

'Fan out! Find out where they've gone!'

*

'Take it easy.'

'It's not my fault, I can't see a damned thing in here.'

Ethan slowly lowered the small but heavy block of stone down behind them, cutting off the sandstorm outside, and leaned against the cool stone of a wall. The air was stale and deathly still after the roaring gales. The only light came from Doctor Lucy Morgan's cell phone screen that illuminated a tiny stone stairwell ahead of them in an unearthly blue glow, narrow steps descending into the darkness far below.

'How the hell did you know that first stone was a fake entrance?' he asked Lucy.

Lucy Morgan's ghostly face smiled back at him over her shoulder.

'The Egyptians often created multiple entrances to tombs when they built them to deter grave robbers,' she said. 'Putting the Eye of Horus seal on that other door would have convinced robbers they were onto something and caused a hell of a lot of work for them to lift or break it, only to reveal a fake entrance and deter them from trying again. I figured that the real entrance would be unmarked.'

Lopez frowned.

'I still don't get how you found either of them in the first place,' she said. 'They were buried under a meter of sand.'

Lucy led the way slowly down a flight of steps that descended into the darkness.

'Iron,' she replied. 'The Egyptians used various metals, usually scarce ones to adorn tombs, and often those metals were from meteorites. They used the iron to make clasps and knives and other tools. Out here, in the absence of any other metal, a tomb will produce just enough magnetism to swing a compass if you're close enough to it.'

Mitchell's voice rumbled in the darkness.

'That only led you to the fake entrance,' he pointed out.

'That was enough,' Lucy said. 'Egyptian tombs were often created using a small pyramid to mark the tomb, called a mastaba, which was built for those noble or wealthy enough to warrant one. Tjaneni ordered his tomb to be unremarkable and hard to locate, but it would still have needed walls and supports to be in place and it couldn't have been a large workforce or everybody would have known about the tomb.'

Lopez got it.

'So you scout about a bit more with the compass and home in on the next biggest signal.'

'That's about it,' Lucy replied. 'Besides, Tjaneni seems to have been a wily old goat. He would have created large and grand false entrances to fake tombs, but I felt he would have built a narrow, insignificant one for himself. Watch your step.'

The descent into the tomb was through a narrow stairwell, which was unilluminated but for the glow from Lucy's cell phone as they crept through the silence. Ethan felt the air cooling further as they descended, tainted with the odor of millennia old dust undisturbed since the time of the Pharaohs themselves.

The narrow steps finally reached a chamber that Lucy led them into, and for an instant they were plunged into darkness as Lucy switched the cell phone for a glow stick that she broke in half. Ethan saw the stick fill the chamber with a warm orange glow and was instantly taken aback.

They were standing inside a structure that was perhaps forty feet square, with the narrow stairwell behind them and a single doorway in front that was blocked with a gigantic rectangle of solid sandstone. The surface of the block was carved with the unmistakeable cartouche of the Pharaoh Amenhotep, and beneath it the smaller but no–less significant seal of the scribe, Tjaneni. Above all three was the Eye of Horus that watched over the tomb. Between them and the opposite wall were two rows of four massive columns that supported the ceiling, the walls covered in hieroglyphics.

'This is more like it,' Lopez said as she looked at Ethan. 'You think we can blast that door out while we hide in the stairwell?'

Ethan shook his head.

'We don't know how deep the block goes,' he replied. 'What charges we do have either won't affect it at all or they'll bring down the whole chamber.'

Lucy Morgan eased her way closer to the seal and crouched down before it. Ethan watched as her hands traced the outline of the cartouche and she whispered softly to herself, as though she were praying before a three-thousand-year old altar.

A sudden, deep boom reverberated through the chamber from behind them, and Ethan turned as one hand moved to the pistol at his side.

'The Russians, they're coming through,' Hellerman said nervously.

'They're blasting the door out,' Ethan confirmed. 'We've only got a few minutes before they get down here.'

Lucy ran her hand swiftly over the lines of hieroglyphics that surrounded them, carved in relief into the ancient sandstone walls.

'The tomb of Tjaneni,' she whispered, 'scribe to the God King Thutmose III, servant of the Kingdom of…'

Ethan listened as she hurried along the walls, tracing the lines of text and reading them as swiftly as he might have read a newspaper article. A few of her words leaped out at him: great power, feared King, immense treasures…

'Immense treasures?' Lopez enquired innocently.

'Treasure has more than one meaning in this sense,' Lucy replied as she worked.

'I like the meaning it has for me,' Lopez replied. 'Do tell more.'

Lucy worked her way around the chamber even as Ethan heard another deep blast from outside, and this time he heard the clatter of rock fragments spilling down the stairwell.

'We're almost out of time,' he urged her. 'They've found the right entrance.'

Lucy stepped back from the wall and stared up at the ceiling.

'They're coming through!' Lopez whispered harshly.

Ethan grabbed his pistol and turned toward the entrance to the chamber as he heard the seal being lifted and Russian voices yelling above the gale outside, and then heavy boots thumped onto the stone steps.

***

XLV

'Go, now!'

Colonel Mishkin grabbed the nearest soldier and shoved him down the ragged hole in the stone and sand that their charges had created, the gale gusting over the dark cavity as the other soldiers followed him in.

Gregorie shoved his way past all of them and vanished down into the darkness with an AK–47 cradled in his massive arms, eager to confront Warner and his team. Mishkin checked over his shoulder to ensure that nobody was following them through the savage gale and caught the gaze of three of his men.

'Guard the entrance!'

Mishkin turned and stepped down into the stairwell. The roar of the wind subsided as he descended into the darkness, his way illuminated by small glowing crushable spheres dropped by the troops ahead to guide the way without compromising night–vision in the gloomy conditions. Mishkin hurried down into the chamber, rows of pillars supporting the ceiling, and saw his men standing and looking at a gigantic door of solid sandstone on the far side of the chamber. The walls were covered with hieroglyphics that shimmered as though alive from the glowing spheres tossed liberally around the chamber.

'There's nobody here,' Gregorie said, now barely able to contain his frustration as he looked at the Colonel. 'Where the hell are they?'

Mishkin approached the huge door and looked at the seal of Tjaneni, the cartouche of the Pharaoh Amenhotep and the Eye of Horus confronting him once more.

'Who cares?' he said. 'This must be the entrance to the tomb. We can blast it out and see what's behind it.'

Gregorie moved to his side. 'They came this way. They were ahead of us. How can they have vanished into thin air?'

Mishkin looked at the towering soldier for a brief moment. 'Gregorie, are you scared?'

For a moment it seemed as though the huge soldier was about to reach out and crush Mishkin's skull with his bare hands. His jaw clenched and his gaze became as hard and cold as Siberian steel as he replied.

'I fear only losing our prize,' he growled. 'They have disappeared, and that can mean only one thing.'

Mishkin took a deep breath and swallowed his pride. He too was afraid of losing the very thing they had worked so hard and travelled so far to obtain. The power of logic revealed to him that there was only one possible solution to the puzzle.

'They found another way past the stone.'

Gregorie seemed to breathe a sigh of relief.

'We cannot chase them like this,' he insisted. 'We must use guile to defeat them.'

'How many ways out of here can there be?' Mishkin asked rhetorically.

'Dozens,' Gregorie replied. 'The Egyptian Tjaneni wanted to hide his prize well, for good reason.'

Mishkin turned to the soldiers and barked an order.

'Get the seismic detector and search the area,' he snapped. 'Find the hidden entrance and quickly! If I have to I'll blast Warner and his people to hell before I'll let them walk away with our prize!'

The soldiers dashed to carry out the order as Gregorie looked at the tomb surrounding them.

'The oracle is useless to us now,' he said. 'Warner has the scientist on his team, and she may be the only person able to reach the tomb.'

Mishkin peered at Gregorie. 'If they reach the ark first then they will hide behind its power! How will we achieve our goals then, Gregorie?'

'The object is not something out of a Hollywood movie, colonel,' Gregorie uttered. 'They will find it and when they do they will have to transport it out of here. How do you think they will be able to do that when they have no vehicles and their support from America has been cut off? Use the girl as leverage against them.'

Mishkin thought for a moment and then he nodded as they walked together out of the chamber and ascended the stairwell.

'Very well, Gregorie, when we find them we will follow and see where they lead us.'

*

The corridor was pitch black, a narrow, high fissure through the solid rock that allowed only a little light to filter out from the two glow sticks Ethan held in his hand as he followed Lucy. The entire team shuffled sideways through the passage, one wall at their backs and the other brushing against their chests.

'How did you even know this was here?' he asked Lucy as they shuffled along.

'I didn't,' she replied with a shrug, 'but the hieroglyphics told the story of Thutmose III's victories in battle and the riches he brought back to Egypt. That story was broken by a vertical line of hieroglyphics that was highly unusual, and only when I read them from top to bottom did I realize that they were concealing this passage.'

Ethan had helped her to pull several sandstone blocks out of the wall one by one, the blocks sealed only with loose mortar and a dried out paste that was probably made by the tomb builders from sand and water to conceal the joins in the brickwork. Once removed, the tiny fissure had been revealed travelling deeper into the tomb.

Ethan had hurried the rest of the team into the fissure, each of them carrying a single brick over their heads, and then he had followed them in and one by one replaced the bricks with a thin layer of sand between them, thus loosely sealing the entrance. They had waited in silence, barely breathing, as they had listened to the Russians discussing where they had gone before leaving the tomb outside.

'How long do you think they'll be fooled for?' Lucy asked as they moved.

'Not long,' Mitchell whispered from further down the line. 'They mentioned seismic instruments. They'll get a reading on this passage soon enough, and that will force them to look a little closer at the wall.'

Lucy kept moving, leading the team through the tiny corridor. Ethan knew from his mental map of their course into the tomb that they were heading through the canyon toward the crescent shaped cliffs, roughly south east. Although he could not know what awaited them, he was fairly certain that with the increased depth there could be little chance of an escape route to the south.

'If we find what we're looking for here,' he said, 'there's no way we can get it out again.'

'You're right,' Lopez replied, 'this fissure is too small to carry anything larger than a house brick out of here.'

'It doesn't matter,' Lucy said. 'Whatever Tjaneni hid in here, it's not coming out with us. He would have built this place to ensure that the only way to escape with the prize would be to excavate the entire tomb complex.'

Ethan reflected briefly that it would be possible only for Egypt itself to excavate the tomb, and that would be almost impossible to do without the media becoming aware of it. If there was indeed an object of considerable power and perhaps extra–terrestrial origin inside the Ark, then they could hardly extract it without somebody knowing something about it.

'There's an opening up ahead,' Lucy said.

Ethan kept moving, and as he did so he heard a distant, dull thump that shuddered through the walls and his own chest as though an earthquake were shaking the entire tomb.

'They've started,' Mitchell rumbled ominously. 'It will only take them a few minutes to find us now.'

Suddenly, the fissure ended and Ethan saw light bloom ahead as glow sticks were tossed by Lucy into another chamber. The sounds they made suggested a much wider cavity and he followed Lopez out of the fissure and into a colossal subterranean chamber.

The glow sticks were not quite powerful enough to illuminate the tomb in all of its glory, but Ethan could see immense pillars holding the roof aloft leading away from them in a double row. Vast, smooth walls were covered in a mixture of hieroglyphic representations of great battles, of sun gods and other Egyptian iconography drawn in large scale all around them, while between the images were enormous statues carved out of the rock of Thutmose III sitting with his hands on his knees staring out over the chamber, his son Amenhotep alongside him.

'Wow,' Lopez murmured, her voice echoing slightly in the silence.

On the flanking walls of the tomb were upright sarcophagi, huge stone tombs that lined the walls one after the other, each marked with a single cartouche.

Ethan looked naturally down the line of pillars dominating the chamber much as the rest of the team did, and there he saw a wide, low bank of steps that led up to a sort of altar. The faint glow of the sticks flickered and reflected off something that was standing upon the altar, and even in the low light Ethan knew instantly what he was looking at. The glow of polished gold was impossible to mistake for anything else.

It was Lucy who spoke, her voice soft as though to utter the words were itself a blasphemy that could provoke the wrath of the gods.

'The Ark of the Covenant.'

***

XLVI

Ethan took a pace closer and stared in awe as Mitchell cracked two more glow sticks and tossed them ahead into the chamber. They burst into life as they skittered across the smooth stones of the floor and their light flared off the sides of the Ark, illuminating it for the first time in thousands of years.

Ethan heard a faint gasp from Lucy as he saw the Ark glow as though aflame in the orange light. Its sides were of solid gold and the same size as they had expected it to be, just like the wooden Ark found in King Tutankhamun's tomb a century before.

Atop the Ark were two golden Cherubim, their wings touching each other, while embossed into the golden side of the Ark was a relief of Anubis, Egyptian God of the Underworld, the canine appearance obvious even from this distance. Ethan could see the rods used to hold the Ark aloft, the ornate edges of the Ark's lid and even the faint layer of dust that had accumulated upon it. All around the Ark's sides were reliefs of Egyptian gods: Horus, Amun–Ra, Osiris and others parading in a line with the Eye of Horus watching them from above.

Lopez turned to look at Ethan.

'Is this where we open it and tongues of flame and fire blast us all to hell?'

Lucy stepped closer to the Ark. 'There's no power of God in that thing,' she insisted as she climbed the steps toward it. 'It was never anything to do with Yawheh, the God of the Bible, and it exists only in the myths of Israel's Torah. The Ark is an Egyptian relic, remember?'

'Yes, doctor,' Lopez said as she flipped Lucy a salute. 'So what do we do now?'

Lucy climbed the steps toward the Ark and Ethan was struck by how incredible it looked from his perspective. Steven Spielberg had tried his hardest but his movie was still nowhere near the spectacle of seeing the Ark in all its glory, amid the orange glow and the shadowy confines of the incredible subterranean temple.

Lucy paused before the Ark and examined it.

'I'll need help to get the lid off. It must weigh a ton.'

Ethan and the others moved slowly up to the steps as Hellerman stared in wide–eyed wonder at the Ark.

'This is the first time that anybody has laid eyes on the Ark since it vanished thousands of years ago,' he said almost reverentially. 'Do you really think that we should be opening it here and now?'

'Whatever the Russians want is inside it,' Ethan pointed out, 'and it's also one of the artefacts that allegedly caused the government to form Majestic Twelve back in 1947. Whatever it is, we need to see it.'

Hellerman stepped back from the Ark, uncertainty writ large upon his features as he moved to stand alongside one of the giant pillars nearby.

'I don't know Ethan,' he said fearfully. 'We don't know what might happen.'

Ethan got his hands under the Ark's lid and prepared to lift as Mitchell stood the other side. Lucy Morgan and Lopez readied themselves at either end, and then Lucy braced herself and said a single word.

'Now.'

Ethan heaved upward with the rest of the team and the lid lifted an inch off the Ark. Then a deafening crash thundered through the room with enough force to cause Ethan to stumble to one side as a brilliant light flared around them, as though lightning had struck the interior of the tomb. The Ark's lid smashed back down as Ethan blinked, stars of white light flashing in his eyes.

Boots thundered against the ancient stone behind them and Ethan turned to see a dozen heavily armed Russian soldiers rush into the temple with their weapons raised and pointed toward them. Ethan saw Gregorie and Colonel Mishkin hurry into the temple behind their men, an exhausted young girl whom he recognized as the oracle Elena pinned between them, and then gaze upon the Ark for a moment with genuine surprise and wonder.

For the briefest of moments Ethan realized that despite their differences the Russians only wanted to find out what was inside the Ark as much as he did. All of the wars, the propaganda, the lies and the mistrust all melted away in the face of human curiosity and the wonder of discovery.

Colonel Mishkin's transparent joy at finally laying eyes upon the Ark suddenly vanished as he aimed a pistol at Ethan.

'My congratulations, Mister Warner, for ensuring that Russia will be for all time accredited for locating the long–lost Ark of the Covenant and repatriating it to the Motherland.'

Ethan glanced at Elena, pinned between the Russian soldiers, and he switched his aim to her.

'Without her you have nothing!' Ethan snapped.

Lopez leaped forward. 'Ethan, no!'

Mishkin hesitated for a moment, and then he sneered at Ethan. 'You and I both know that you're no cold blooded murderer, Warner. Take his weapon away, now!'

A soldier grabbed Ethan's pistol from his hand, Ethan not resisting as his bluff was called. He held his hands up and replied.

'The Ark's no more Russian than I am. It belongs here.'

'A noble sentiment,' Mishkin observed, 'but, as you Americans say, finders–keepers? Step away from the Ark, all of you!'

Ethan stepped down off the altar as the Russian troops surrounded the Ark. Gregorie walked up to Ethan and towered over him, his fists balled by his side.

'I have waited a long time for this moment, Warner,' he rumbled.

Ethan smiled back up at the Russian.

'You're gonna have to wait a bit longer, 'cause you won't be getting the Ark out of here.'

'We don't want the Ark,' Mishkin pointed out cheerfully. 'Who wants a fancy golden box anyway. It's *so* last millennia. We want what's inside it. Open it up!'

Ethan watched as the Russians heaved the Ark's ornate golden lid upward. The soldiers shuffled to one side and then lowered the lid onto the altar as they looked down as one into the Ark.

Mishkin and Gregorie hurried to the Ark, desperate to get a look inside. Ethan looked to his right and saw Hellerman still behind the large pillar. Protected from the Russian stun-grenades, he had remained out of sight. Ethan jerked his head toward the exit, and the scientist silently made his way toward the fissure like entrance to the tomb and vanished into the shadows.

Gregorie and Mishkin each reached inside the Ark, and as Ethan watched so each of them lifted out thick, heavy tablets of stone that were engraved with markings that looked like hieroglyphs but were somehow different.

'The Black Knight,' Lopez gasped in a whisper as she saw the tablets. 'That's the same writing that was around the rim of the satellite.'

Ethan nodded, saying nothing as the two Russians reverentially carried the two tablets away from the Ark and set them down alongside each other on the stone flags near where Ethan stood.

'Behold,' Mishkin said in awe, 'the real tablets that were broken and placed inside the Ark. It was not Moses who was a party to this moment in history when a man spoke with the gods, but the Pharaoh Thutmoses III. There, our ancestors encountered an intelligence that to them appeared to be god-like, and they recorded the event upon these stones.'

Mishkin looked up at Ethan and grinned cruelly.

'Of course now that we have them we no longer have a need for any of you, or the Ark.'

Mishkin shoved the exhausted oracle toward them and Mitchell caught her as she fell toward the stone flags. Ethan watched as Mishkin's men carefully packaged the tablets and packed them into a pair of Bergens. Gregorie moved again to face Ethan and this time he smiled.

'Goodbye, Mister Warner.'

The blow from Gregorie's fist hit Ethan deep in the belly and folded him over as the breath rushed from his lungs and his eyes bulged as though they were about to pop out of their sockets. Ethan dropped to his knees and gasped for air as Gregorie's boot landed on his shoulder and sent him sprawling across the dusty stone flags.

'You worked hard for the Ark,' Mishkin said, 'and thus I don't have the heart to take it from you. Therefore, I shall kill several birds with one stone and leave you here with it. Within a matter of minutes this entire place will be blasted back into history, and all of you with it.'

The Russian soldiers backed out of the temple toward the fissure, one by one leaving them alone in the Temple until the last had vanished. Ethan groaned as he held his belly in his arms.

'I wish he wouldn't keep doing that,' he wheezed, and then looked at Mitchell. 'Is she okay?'

Mitchell lifted Elena's frail body up. 'She's alive, but she's weak. We need to get her out of here.'

'They're going to bomb the tomb too,' Lopez reminded Ethan as she helped him to his feet. 'They'll probably seal up the entrance before they go and booby trap it from the other side. There's no way we can leave the same way we came in.'

Lucy turned to the Ark and dashed up to it, and then she gasped in amazement as she looked inside.

'My God,' she whispered.

Ethan frowned and moved up onto the altar alongside her, and then he looked down into the Ark and was as stunned as she was.

Inside was a mummy, the ancient remains of an Egyptian man. The arms were folded across the chest, but unlike most mummies that Ethan had seen the legs were tucked up against the body. Ethan figured that the pose had been necessary to ensure that the body fitted inside the confines of the Ark.

Lucy Morgan looked at the bone dry remains and her whispered exclamation echoed around the tomb.

'Tjaneni.'

Lopez moved to her side and looked down at the ancient corpse, still encased within the endless wrappings that protected the body within from the decay that would otherwise have turned it to dust over the thousands of years that had passed since.

'Looks like he figured the only way to be sure that the Ark wasn't located was to stay with it,' Lopez said.

Lucy nodded, her gaze fixed upon the scribe's form.

'It all makes sense now,' she said. 'Why the Ark disappeared so completely, why this tomb was never found. The people who built it worked from the outside in, and they sealed themselves in and never left.'

Ethan looked up at the stone sarcophagi all around the walls of the tomb, and he realized what she meant.

'The builders,' he said finally. 'It's not just Tjaneni who is in here, it's his entire team.'

Lucy stood back from the Ark of the Covenant and glanced at the statues around the walls.

'They're stone sarcophagi,' she said, 'each one a tomb for a builder.'

Ethan glanced again at the exit where Mishkin and his men had vanished.

'The tablet's are gone,' he said finally. 'Whatever is written on them is lost to the Russians. All we can hope for is that Hellerman can escape and get word out to Jarvis that we're trapped down here.'

Lucy nodded. 'Those tablets were priceless beyond measure, the most valuable historical artefact in human history. We're nothing without it.'

Lopez chuckled bitterly.

'Maybe we should embalm ourselves and borrow some of those coffins, 'cause we're in for a long stay down here with the rest of these guys.'

Ethan looked about desperately for some inspiration, for a way to escape the tomb. Mitchell was doing the same, searching the walls.

'If these builders entombed themselves, there's probably no other way out,' Mitchell pointed out. 'They wouldn't have needed one.'

Ethan frowned as a sudden thought hit him.

'Hold on. Tjaneni couldn't have mummified himself, right? How did he end up in here and all of the builders end up in stone coffins, if they were the only ones down here?'

Ethan looked at Lucy, who appeared suddenly stunned by the question. It was logical of course that the builders could not have entombed themselves after death: somebody must have finished the process of embalming the bodies and placing them in the stone coffins and the Ark, unless…

Lucy whirled to the Ark and hurried to it.

'The words of The Watchers,' she whispered to herself, 'heard from human skin.'

Ethan moved to her side, aware of her sudden excitement as she stared down at Tjaneni.

'What?' he asked.

Lucy seemed to shake with anticipation as she reached into her tool kit and produced a small metal hook.

'The watchers, the prophecy, the words they used,' she said. 'Were they Aisha's exact words?'

Lopez nodded. 'That's what she said.'

Lucy looked back at Tjaneni's remains and smiled. 'You sneaky old goat, you knew exactly what you were doing right to the end.'

Ethan frowned. 'What are you talking about?'

Lucy leaned over and peeled back a few layers of the linen entombing Tjaneni's remains.

'He deceived us right to the very end,' she said. 'He knew that if anybody came in here they'd be looking for the tablets, the commandments as we now know them, the Word of God. They would instinctively steal the tablets and probably the Ark, and the riches surrounding the tomb, but they would have no interest in the mummy itself.'

As Ethan watched, Lucy peeled back a few more layers of the linen, and there within he saw a corner of Tjaneni's shoulder appear. The flesh was visible, a dark brown in color and as dry as the desert sands that billowed still far above them. He could see Tjaneni's bones poking against the desiccated skin, and against the dark brown he could see black shapes.

Lopez peered into the Ark and she gasped again.

'It's that same text again,' she said, 'the same stuff that was on the tablet and the Black Knight!'

Lucy shook with excitement as she worked.

'The tablets are a ruse,' she said, 'the whole legend merely a deception. They're not the word of God. Tjaneni is. He had his entire body tattooed with it before he went to his grave.'

***

XLVII

The passages of the outer chamber were entirely black, the glow sticks having long since been extinguished and the Russians using helmet-mounted lights to illuminate their way.

Hellerman stood in utter silence, not daring even to breathe as he hid behind a pillar in the chamber and watched as the Russian soldiers milled about, waiting for their companions inside the main tomb.

There were two of them in the outer chamber, both heavily armed and pacing up and down as though bored. Hellerman was moving slowly to his left, hugging the back wall and staying in the shadows, picking his moments to move when neither of the two soldiers was facing him.

He knew that he could not call the DIA for support, for they would never come out here again for Ethan and Nicola even if they were told of the enormity of what had been discovered. Their only hope for survival was Jarvis and his team, but with Mitchell trapped on the inside Hellerman wasn't sure what would happen when he broke free of the tomb into the desert. He had no weapon and only the GPS unit on him, which he could activate to let Jarvis know their position.

Hellerman slipped along the back wall, one pace at a time, remaining as silent as he possibly could until he reached the foot of the stairwell. In the distance far above he could hear the faint roar of the storm raging across the deserts. He knew that Mishkin would have placed at least two further soldiers outside the tomb entrance to prevent anybody from escaping, but Hellerman didn't need to get entirely outside the tomb. All he needed to do was get close enough to the surface that the locator beacon would be able to transmit a signal strong enough for Jarvis to detect.

Hellerman watched the two soldiers and saw that their pacing provided no opportunity for him to escape the tomb. One or the other's helmet flash light was always pointing at the entrance to the tomb, both men coordinating their positions so that if anyone other than their comrades appeared inside the chamber there would be at least one gun pointing at them. Only the narrowness of the fissure and the deep shadows had allowed Hellerman to slip back into the chamber unnoticed.

Hellerman clasped the locator beacon tightly in his hand and gauged the distance to the stairwell, perhaps ten feet. It was possible that he could make it, cross the gap and launch himself up the stairwell, but it would be but a matter of moments before the elite soldiers caught him. With no means of concealing himself inside the narrow stairwell he would be hammered with bullets long before he could make it high enough to send the distress signal.

He turned and watched the two soldiers for a moment, wondering whether he could distract them with a tossed stone or other ploy, but their caution would probably ensure that they would check both exits regardless if they heard anything suspicious.

Nothing else for it then.

Hellerman reminded himself that Ethan and Nicola had faced death many times and come through safely, if a little beaten up. Now it was his turn. He took a deep, soft breath and filled his lungs as he prepared to make a dash for the stairwell. If he timed it just right, he might be able to get there while both soldiers were just turning and partially blocking each other's field of fire.

Time to go. Three, two, one…

A Russian voice called out from within the tomb beyond, that of Colonel Mishkin, and the two soldiers whirled to face him as the general's shadowy form came into view within the adjoining shaft on the far side of the chamber.

Hellerman dashed silently across the chamber and into the stairwell, with every pace feeling ever more certain that he would hear the terrifying crack of a gunshot or shouts of warning to those above. He ducked his head down as he hopped through the narrow entrance and then tip–toed up the stairwell and into utter blackness.

Nobody shouted. Nobody opened fire. Hellerman breathed a sigh of relief in the darkness and looked up the stairwell as he began to climb. The tomb entrance was a barely visible rectangle of faint light in the distance and he could hear the storm more clearly now. Puffs of cool air laden with sand gusted into his face as he climbed, and he pulled the locator beacon out of his pocket and prepared to switch it on.

He slowed as he reached the top of the stairwell, ready to confront whatever was awaiting him outside. He knew that the Russians would shoot him on sight, but he knew how important it was to be rescued as soon as possible. If Jarvis did not know where they were, they were as good as dead.

You're as good as dead.

Hellerman steeled himself once again as he decided upon a change of plan. He couldn't cower down here with the locator beacon, because sooner or later the Russians would come out of the tomb and then both he and the beacon would be switched off permanently. He could hear the storm outside, thick blankets of sand rushing past, visibility down to a few meters most likely.

Hellerman took another deep breath and focused on the rectangle of light above as he switched the beacon on. The device illuminated a red light on top, informing him that it could not transmit a full–strength signal. Hellerman began running, launched himself upward as he dashed for the light.

The sound of the storm grew intense, sand gusting down the steps in thick torrents as he climbed. The light grew a little brighter and he saw the shadowy, turbulent sky above filled with gusting sand. Hellerman took the last few steps at a full run, his thighs aching and his chest heaving as he ran, and he saw the locator beacon's signal light change from dull red to bright green as it caught a satellite signal.

Hellerman burst from the tomb in a rush of legs and a scream of defiance, waiting to hear the first gunshot as he swung his arm back and hurled the locator beacon up into the sky. He released it as soon as he figured it would soar away from him at a forty-five-degree angle, the scientist in him ensuring that the device would fly as far away as possible into the impenetrable storm.

The beacon spun as it arced away into the dense storm clouds and vanished, and then Hellerman felt something slam into his back with the force of a freight train. His breath caught in his throat and his eyes bulged as bright pain lanced up his spine and his legs gave way beneath him. Hellerman dropped to his knees in the sand and barely saw the heavy black boot that flashed before his vision and sent him sprawling onto the dust.

A shaven headed Russian soldier sneered down at him, the barrel of an AK–47 pressed so hard against Hellerman's cheek he thought it might punch right through as the Russian spoke above the roaring gale.

'Nice try, American,' he sneered, 'but if that beacon can be detected by someone outside of this storm, how long do you think it'll take us to find it from twenty meters away?'

Hellerman's guts plunged in dismay as he saw a Russian soldier jog up to them with the beacon held in his hand and a grim expression of amusement on his rugged features.

'Americans,' he spat, 'they're all such geniuses.'

Hellerman sighed as the Russian tucked the beacon into the pocket of his smock.

*

Mediterranean Sea

'We've got something.'

Jarvis heard Garrett's warning and hurried across to him as the yacht carved its way silently across the sparkling blue waters of the Mediterranean.

'It's not much,' Garrett said. 'I got about thirty seconds of signal coming out of the desert to the west of Edfu, just off the Nile.'

Jarvis looked at a radar scope but saw nothing until Garrett re-wound the feed and he saw a weak signal flickering in the deserts of Egypt.

'Do we have a signal verification?' he asked.

Garrett shook his head.

'That storm system is blocking a lot of the finer details,' Garrett said. 'The beacon should have transmitted the data but it's coming through scrambled. About all I can tell you is that the signal's signature matches that of the beacon type we gave Hellerman, and it's broadcasting the distress code.'

Jarvis nodded. 'And it's not far from where we would expect them to be. Any way that we can get in there?'

Garrett shook his head.

'Not a chance. That storm system is whipping up sandstorms a half mile high and hundreds of miles wide off the Sinai and plastering them across Egypt. We can get over it but we can't land in it.'

Jarvis reached for his cell phone.

'Getting over it might just be enough.'

***

XLVIII

'We've got to get out of here, right now!'

Doctor Lucy Morgan lifted Tjaneni's mummy out of the Ark and set it down on the stone flags of the temple. Ethan watched as they hurriedly unwrapped the corpse, each layer of linen revealing endless lines of bizarre hieroglyphic text written thousands of years previously by unknown hands.

As the mummified corpse of the ancient scribe was revealed, so Ethan saw that his entire body was covered in markings similar to those on the linen wrappings, tattooed into the man's skin until barely a clear spot remained.

Lopez paced up and down, agitated. 'We don't have time for this,' she said.

'This is the only reason we're here at all!' Lucy shot back. 'If we don't record this before we get out of here, then everything we have done will have been for nothing!'

Lopez shot Ethan a concerned look, but he knew he could not argue against Lucy Morgan once she had made her decision.

'She's right, Nicola,' he said finally. 'We've got to take that with us or this is all for nothing.' He looked at Lucy. 'I take it that you've figured out some way of getting out of here?'

Lucy smiled grimly as she laid out the linen in sheets before her on the stone flags.

'I'm working on it.'

'Great,' Lopez uttered as she raised her hands into the air in exasperation.

Ethan watched as Lucy began photographing both the linen wrappings and Tjaneni's corpse, the body as dry as bone and the skin stretched across the bones like brown sails pulled taut across a ship's masts. The scribe's lips were pulled back by age, exposing his yellowing teeth in a millennia-long grimace, and his eyes were black pits long since decayed.

'They believed in an afterlife, y'know?' Mitchell said as he looked down at the corpse, Elena still in his arms. 'They mummified themselves to preserve their bodies ready for when they met their gods, put their brains and hearts in jars, stuff like that.'

Lopez rolled her eyes. 'Yeah, didn't do him much good though did it? It's not as though he looks like he just walked out of a salon.'

'He doesn't look so bad for three thousand years old,' Ethan mused.

'Three and a half thousand,' Lucy corrected Ethan as she took photographs, moving hurriedly around the body.'

Ethan watched as Lucy finished her work, and then he looked at the corpse of the scribe and thought for a moment.

'You think there's anything else in there?' he asked Lucy.

Doctor Morgan shook her head. 'The Egyptians took everything out of the body and skull and placed them in preservation just like Aaron said. The body cavity will be empty.'

Ethan frowned as he looked at Tjaneni's remains, and then he took a pace forward and lifted his boot.

'Wait!' Lucy wailed.

'What?' Ethan asked. 'He's not going to be worried about this and if there's nothing inside we have nothing to lose, right?'

Lucy hesitated. 'Yes, but, it's priceless and it's his body. You can't just desecrate it like this.'

'She's right,' Lopez said as she moved alongside Ethan and gently eased him away from the corpse before she turned to stand over it. 'You need heels.'

With one vicious thump Lopez drove the heel of her boot through Tjaneni's chest like a spear through paper. The aged scribe's bones splintered like dry twigs as Lopez's boot smashed them inward, and almost immediately Lopez lost balance as her boot landed on something metallic.

Ethan looked down in surprise as Lopez stepped back and looked down into the dusty cavity she had created in the scribe's long–dead body, Lucy Morgan gasping in horror and turning away with one hand to her head.

Inside, Ethan could see a thick layer of dust and the back of Tjaneni's ribcage, the thick bones of the spinal column rising up toward the skull. There, resting against them, was a strange little golden object no bigger than Ethan's clenched fist, wrapped in ancient cloth tied tightly together.

'That's not normal for the Egyptians,' Lucy said as she recovered from her shock and bent down to lift the small object out.

Lopez offered her a sweet smile. 'Okay, I've done you a favor, how about you do us one and get us out of here?'

Lucy nodded absent–mindedly and jabbed a thumb over her shoulder. 'It's that way.'

'It's what now?' Ethan asked.

Lucy didn't look up as she replied while examining the box.

'The dust is thicker across the stone flags over there than in the rest of the tomb, which suggests that wind–blown dust and sand has accumulated more quickly there than elsewhere. Like you said before, Tjaneni and his comrades cannot have been the last people in this tomb as they could not have embalmed themselves, so therefore there must have been one other person here and there must be another way out.' She looked at Lopez. 'That person could not alone have sealed the tomb entrance, ergo, it's that way.'

Lopez managed a brief sneer as she marched across to the corner of the tomb and examined the wall. Almost immediately she spotted the same patch of thin plaster that Ethan could see as he walked across to join her.

'They covered up the cracks in this fissure like the other one,' Lopez said. 'Looks like a few spots of it have dried up and fallen out.'

Ethan could see tiny slivers in the wall plaster, holes leading into an unseen cavity beyond. He looked at the sand at their feet and could clearly see the slight mound created by thousands of years of sand from outside slowly accumulating inside the tomb from the endless deserts.

'The Russians will be nearby,' he said to Mitchell. 'If we get out and they see us, we're dead.'

'Best not to be seen then,' Mitchell advised.

*

Mediterranean Sea

Doug Jarvis watched as a monitor showed the location of the weak signal emitted by Hellerman's GPS locator, and Garrett hurried alongside him with an anxious look on his face.

'We just got a call from an operator called Helen who worked alongside Hellerman,' Garrett said. 'He gave her our details.'

'What did she say?' Jarvis asked.

Garrett sighed.

'Our last chance at maintaining any links within the DIA just got blown out of the water. ARIES has been officially shut down and all agents associated with the program were burned.'

Jarvis turned to look at Garrett. 'Burned?'

'Two agents died in Manila after they were exposed due to the support being cut off at a crucial moment in their operation,' Garrett explained. 'The local and even international media are reporting it as an unsolved homicide of two tourists. Another DIA operative is missing in Berlin, and three more in South America.'

Jarvis exhaled and briefly closed his eyes.

From behind them Lillian Cruz and Amber Ryan walked up and looked at the screen, which showed a map of the Egyptian coast overlaid with various airways and no–fly zones extending south from the capital, Cairo.

'What do we do now?' Garrett asked. 'There's no way that we can extract them from inside that storm cell.'

Jarvis thought for a long moment. His own granddaughter Lucy Morgan was on the ground with Ethan and Nicola and the team had been reported heading into the desert with Russian forces not far behind.

'How precise are the GPS coordinates from where the signal was received?'

'Accurate to within a meter or two,' Garrett confirmed, 'but we don't know the team's location now and we received that signal ten minutes ago.'

Jarvis scanned the monitor before him as though somehow the computer image could reveal to him some way of solving every problem they had at once. If he used a UAV to strike directly then he risked killing everybody and losing everything that they had achieved. If he didn't, the Russians would likely kill them all under the cover of the same storm and make off with everything. Either way, Jarvis lost.

'We can't win,' Jarvis said finally. 'Order the strike in, and make sure the drone is likewise destroyed in the attack.'

Garrett stared silently at Jarvis for a long moment. 'You'll kill them all.'

Jarvis remained calm despite the raw emotion churning within him.

'This isn't an easy business,' he whispered back, 'and there are impossible decisions to be made every day. If you're not up to them, Rhys, then perhaps this venture is not for you.'

Amber Ryan stepped forward.

'You said that we're not Majestic Twelve, Doug,' she pointed out. 'You said that we would be different. From what I've heard about them, the decision you're making now would fit right in with their plans.'

Jarvis stared at her, for once speechless.

'We have never been like them.'

'Good,' Amber said, 'then there must be another way.'

'We lose whatever we do.'

'So we lose,' Amber agreed. 'Better to lose and live than have the blood of people we care about on our hands for the rest of our lives, no?'

Jarvis clenched his fists as he looked at the screen one more time, his mind filled with conflicting voices both urging him and restraining him from firing the missile that would destroy the ancient tomb far out in Egypt's deserts.

Then, one loud voice overcame them all.

'Fire the missile!'

Jarvis whirled as he saw an exhausted Aisha stagger from inside the yacht, her head encased in a Trans Cranial Stimulator. Amber rushed to the girl's side as she collapsed on the deck, barely conscious.

'What have you done?' Amber whispered in horror.

Aisha gripped her hand and whispered with the last of her strength.

'Fire the missile, or we will all die.'

Amber saw the fear in Aisha's eyes and she turned to Jarvis. The old man considered his impossible dilemma one last time and then he dialed a number on his cell and spoke into it.

'Track the GPS signal. Fire, now.'

***

XLIX

'It's this way, keep moving!'

Ethan hefted the desiccated body of Tjaneni over his head, Lopez and Lucy Morgan leading the way with Mitchell carrying Elena. The darkness of the shaft was impenetrable and Ethan was moving more by feel than by the feeble light of Lucy Morgan's cell phone that shimmered and shook before them.

The shaft climbed upward, occasional steps tripping Ethan in the darkness, but he could hear the sound of the storm raging somewhere above their heads as the wind whistled through tiny gaps in the stone blocks from which the secret shaft had been built.

'This is going to bring us out to the south of the tomb entrance,' Lucy called back. 'If we're lucky, the storm will conceal us from the Russians!'

Ethan held out no hope that they would escape unnoticed, especially given their less-than-good luck of the day. The last thing he had expected to be doing was creeping through an underground tunnel with a two-thousand-year old corpse slung over his shoulder and a waiting army of Russian soldiers just outside.

Lucy's pace quickened as the shaft began to widen a little and Ethan somehow knew that they were reaching the end of the tunnel and that the tomb exit was somewhere just ahead. He could smell the ancient scent of the desert gusting on the breeze that touched his skin as they ascended a shallow incline and Lucy came to a halt.

Ethan could see that the shaft ended in a narrowing tip, and that the walls either side supported a vast slab of sandstone that probably weighed several tons.

'No way,' Lopez said. 'Nobody could lift that seal anhd get out of here.'

Lucy touched the wall beneath the seal and Ethan saw blackened stains on the stones, like ash or soot.

'They didn't lift the seal,' he said as he realized what must have happened. 'It was propped open with wooden blocks, which were then burned to let the seal close.'

'Well we're not getting out this way,' Lopez said as she stared at the vast seal. 'Whoever last passed this way must have sealed the tomb behind them.'

'She's right,' Lucy said, 'we need to blow the side out. Do we have any charges left?'

Ethan fumbled for his backpack and found a single charge. He handed it to Hellerman, who passed it forward to Mitchell.

'That's not enough to blow a rock that big,' Lopez pointed out.

'Get away from the entrance,' Mitchell ordered them as he turned and carefully handed Elena's limp body to Ethan, who had set Tjaneni's corpse down in the shaft behind them.

Lopez, Lucy and Ethan retreated with his unlikely cargo carried between them. Ethan saw Mitchell set the charge not against the stone covering the tomb exit but in the join where the wall met the block, which itself sat upon the sandstone bricks.

Ethan knew what Mitchell had in mind and he crouched down as he turned to look behind him.

'Stay low and cover your ears or your ear drums will burst. Cover Elena's too.'

Ethan pressed one hand over one ear and tucked the other against his shoulder even as he heard the first blast. He looked up in surprise but saw Mitchell still working on setting the charge.

'Incoming!'

Ethan hunched down lower with his other hand over Elena's ear, Lopez mirroring his action as he heard the blasts coming from behind them as the Russians set off their explosives. He felt the vibrations and then the weighty thump of the shockwaves thundering through the tomb and past him as the tomb behind them was shattered and the flames of destruction sought an escape.

'Any time now would be good!' Lopez shouted.

Mitchell set the charge and hurried back toward them, and Ethan squinted and ducked his head lower as he saw a brief red flash and then the charge exploded with a vivid flash and a blast of debris and shattered masonry blasted toward them.

Mitchell crouched down and shielded them from the worst of the blast with his sheer physical size in the narrow shaft. Ethan heard the sound of huge chunks of sandstone smashing down onto the tunnel floor ahead of them, and then Mitchell's voice booming.

'Go, now!'

Ethan picked Elena up as he followed Mitchell back up the shaft and saw in the faint light from the desert outside that the charge had neatly shattered the rearmost third of the sandstone tomb seal. The huge rock had collapsed inward and formed a neat ramp that led up and out of the tomb.

Mitchell hit the ramp at a run as explosions ripped through the tomb behind them. Ethan ran up the ramp and out into the blinding sandstorm with Elena, Lopez struggling along behind with Tjaneni's brittle remains over her shoulders as he turned and saw Lucy hurry out of the tomb. They staggered away from the shaft as Ethan saw a sudden glow illuminate it as though Hell itself were reaching out for them.

Ethan staggered to one side as a tongue of searing heat and flame roared from within the tomb far below them. The blasts thundered out into the storm, and to his left Ethan glimpsed through the storm the ground give way and sink in a neat depression as the tomb far below collapsed beneath the weight of countless thousands of tons of sand and rock, burying the Ark of the Covenant.

The flames vanished in a cloud of smoke and dust that was whipped away by the roiling winds. The desert was still entombed in the raging storm, the sky above as dark as night and flashing with brief flares of lightning as the mother of all thunderstorms raged through the heavens.

'Where to now?' Lopez yelled above the terrible din of the howling gale.

'Anywhere but here!'

Ethan, his eyes stinging and his skin battered by the sand, turned and saw the rear of the crater–like crescent formation. Deep recesses in the cliffs offered the only salvation he could see from the storm, and at once he set off for them with the rest of the team following behind him.

*

Mishkin sat in the cab of the truck, Gregorie behind him and satisfied grins on their faces as Gregorie pressed the button on his detonator and they heard the blasts reverberate from the desert behind them.

'And that is the last that anybody will ever see or hear of Ethan Warner again,' Mishkin said proudly.

Gregorie nodded as he opened the window of the cab and tossed the detonator out into the raging storm before he closed it again. Then he turned and looked at Hellerman, who sat nearby with his mouth gagged and his wrists manacled.

'What shall we do with this piece of trash?' he asked.

Mishkin did not even look back at Hellerman as he replied.

'Do what we do with all garbage, toss him out.'

Gregorie grinned at Hellerman as he cocked his pistol and then reached over and opened the truck door. Hellerman did not wait to be shot, instead he hurled himself out of the vehicle and crashed down onto the sand as the truck bounced and weaved, vanishing into the darkness. Gregorie fired once at the little man's disappearing and tumbling form, but he could not tell if his bullet found its mark.

He yanked the door shut once more.

'He won't survive out here,' Gregorie said. 'And we have the fabled tablets from the Ark of the Covenant anyway. Do we know what they say?'

Mishkin held the tablets in his hands and turned them to face Doctor Akhmed, who sat with them in the rear of the cab.

'Translate this,' he ordered as Gregorie pressed a pistol to his head. 'Quickly.'

The scientist looked down at the tablets and frowned as he read them.

'This is unspeakably ancient,' he said, 'but it's not possible.'

'What's not possible?' Mishkin pressed.

The scientist traced the lines of hieroglyphics as he voiced the words.

'He who is beholden to these words shall forever be denied the great truth, for none who shall hold them is worthy of the knowledge of the stars.'

Mishkin grabbed Akhmed's collar and yanked him forward. 'What the hell does that mean?'

The scientist stared back at the colonel fearfully as he traced a few more lines on the tablets and spoke in a feeble voice.

'The rest of the text is nothing but records of accounts and Egyptian folklore that I recognize from other studies,' he said. 'This isn't the information you were looking for. The tablets are…, a deception.'

Mishkin's voice exploded like a bomb in the cab. 'Turn around, find the tomb!'

Gregorie leaned over his seat and looked into the rear of the troop transporter.

'Locate the GPS beacon! Find them!'

One of the soldiers looked back at him, a fearful expression on his face. 'But we took the locator from the American.'

'Where is it?!' Gregorie demanded.

Another of the soldiers pulled the locator from the pocket of his camouflage fatigues and held it up to Gregorie. Even as he saw it, Gregorie heard a screeching sound as though some horrific bird of prey had soared down out of the raging storm to attack the vehicle. The huge Russian's face collapsed into blind hysteria and he opened his mouth to scream at the soldier.

'You useless fu…!'

The interior of the cab suddenly filled with a fearsome glow as though a sun had burst into life in their midst. Searing flame and heat blasted through the interior and incinerated every single person inside the cab. Gregorie's last thought was of the unspeakable pain that ripped through his body as he saw his soldiers disintegrate before him as though they had been turned to ash in an instant and blasted into a thousand pieces. Then the white hot heat that was melting the metal seat cradle beneath him burned through his eyeballs and his skull burst like an exploding grenade.

The UAV drone's missile hit the troop transporter at almost supersonic velocity and detonated directly inside the cab, incinerating everything in a blaze of heat and light so intense that for a moment the blast appeared on monitors across countless military installations as satellites detected the impact deep in the Egyptian desert.

***

L

Pentagon,

Washington DC

Lieutenant General Foxx walked through the corridors of the most famous military complex in the world, a slim folder under one arm and a determined expression on his features. Although he was not the highest ranking officer in the United States Army and rarely appeared in any official documents, that suited him just fine. Such was his security clearance and his power within the government that hiding in plain sight as an unremarkable infantry officer was the perfect cover.

Once, long ago, men in his position had worn black suits, ties and hats. They were tasked with ensuring that witnesses to unusual phenomena, especially UFO sightings, remained silent about their experience and were "discouraged" from reporting them either to the media or friends. Their visits to members of the public from the late 1940s onwards had resulted in them being labelled with a strange moniker: Men in Black.

Those days were long gone now, and instead it was preferred for ultra–covert operatives to remain tucked out of sight in what appeared to be menial roles within the regular military. Foxx's true role as an agent of a highly classified government organization was thus perfectly concealed from all but those who served alongside him.

The office he sought was likewise anonymous among the many hundreds of others that filled the Pentagon. Foxx reached the door and knocked three times with perfect rhythm.

'Enter.'

Foxx walked in and closed the door behind him. Inside was a small office with pictures on the walls of the residing officer's family and military service. A simple filing cabinet stood in one corner of the room and the desk was cluttered with suitably mundane paperwork.

'Please, sit.'

Foxx sat in the only other chair inside the room and opened his file. There was no preamble, no briefing – Foxx was there simply to file his report, verbally of course, and then destroy all evidence that the report ever existed.

'The location site was destroyed and all evidence contained within likewise lost or irreparably damaged. Egyptian forces did not detect the blast that destroyed the site due to the unusually powerful storm cell over the area at the time.'

'Who fired the projectiles that destroyed the site?' the officer demanded to know.

'Either Egypt, and they're lying about their lack of knowledge about what happened, or a third–party. We're looking into it at the moment.'

'ARIES?' the officer asked briskly without looking up from his paperwork.

'Shut down completely forty–eight hours ago,' Foxx replied. 'All staff have been reassigned, all projects closed and all agents suitably dealt with.'

Now, the officer looked up.

'Completely?'

'Completely,' Foxx assured him. 'The only agents outstanding from the list are Ethan Warner, Nicola Lopez and Joseph Hellerman. All three were at the site in Egypt when it was destroyed, and there have been no survivors reported as having been located at the site when it was searched this morning, local time after the storm blew through. Judging by the blast report and the extent of the damage to the site, it is believed that all three perished in the detonation.'

The officer nodded, satisfied.

'What artefacts were recovered from ARIES?'

'That is a list too long to recount here,' Foxx replied. 'However, their archives did reveal the extent of the knowledge they had acquired over the years and verified our need to shut the operation down as quickly as we did. They were close, sir. Very close.'

Foxx handed the officer a photograph. The vivid color image revealed an ancient skeleton, humanoid but taller and with a physiology far from human. Photographed inside a seven–thousand–year old tomb in southern Israel, the remains had been discovered several years before by a palaeontologist by the name of Doctor Lucy Morgan.

'Where is Morgan now?' the officer asked.

'Unknown, but last seen in the company of Warner and Lopez. It is considered probable that she perished with them.'

'And we possess these remains now?'

'Yes sir,' Foxx replied. 'They are concealed at Wright Patterson Air Force Base along with all other artefacts located at the ARIES site, and are awaiting transportation. There is however one artefact that appears to be missing, something that we have images of but are unsure of its origin.'

Foxx handed another image to his commanding officer, this time of a strange metallic sphere contained within a small transparent chamber.

'Data attached to the records suggests that this object was retrieved from the crash site of an artificial satellite code–named Black Knight. It was this recovery operation that convinced us that the DIA was getting too close to the truth and that we should take over.'

The officer nodded.

'Is it possible that one of the agency's staff could have smuggled this object out of the DIAC Building?'

Foxx thought for a moment. 'Highly unlikely, but nothing is truly impossible. We should operate on the assumption that the sphere is in circulation somewhere.'

'Jarvis,' the officer growled. 'He remains a loose end in the operation and one that we must close, Foxx, is that understood?'

'Perfectly, sir.'

'Good, then this brings the proceedings to an end. We will no longer have to concern ourselves with civilian DIA operatives within ARIES overreaching into our affairs. Focus your search now for Jarvis and his lackeys. They know the game they're in and the risks they're taking. Eliminate them as soon as you find them. Dismissed.'

Foxx stood, turned and marched from the office. He heard the sound of the file he had brought in with him being shredded even before he had closed the door.

*

Atlantic Ocean

Doug Jarvis stood on the deck of Garrett's yacht and listened to the waves crashing against the vessel's hull far below as it carved a path ever westward and away from Europe.

Out here, far from civilization, it was at least possible for him to feel comfortable again, to forget who he was and what he had become. Although he felt sure that he had never lost his humanity, he sometimes wondered what could have happened to the cheerful, wide-eyed with curiosity boy he had once been. In a world where the act of discovery was something not to be jubilantly shared with others but to be veiled and hidden even the purest of hearts could become twisted, poisoned by those who cared little for the future of mankind.

Jarvis held his hands behind his back and watched the waves flow by, as though time itself was leaving him behind. There was still so much to do and now so few who would wish to do it with him. Amber Ryan had not spoken to him since the drone's missile had taken the lives of those closest to them all, and even Lillian Cruz seemed more distant than ever. Garrett was also becoming reclusive, as though for the first time he had come to realize just what a dangerous world he had entered, where the lives of individuals were so often sacrificed for the greater good of the mission. Ethan and the team had not been heard from for forty-eight hours, and the chances of them having escaped the tremendous blasts that had incinerated the Russian convoy were slim in the extreme.

He was looking into those waves when Lillian Cruz walked onto the deck to join him, staring out over the sun now descending toward a horizon slit by horizontal black gashes of distant stratus clouds gathering to the west.

'It's not your fault,' she said simply. 'You did what you had to do.'

Jarvis shrugged.

'It's not like I can walk up to Aisha and say; it's your fault, you told me to do it.'

Lillian smiled softly as the wind whipped off the wild ocean and caressed her face.

'She's the one that can see into the future.'

'It was still my decision.'

Lillian turned to him.

'We all do what we do so that others don't have to. It's a weight on our shoulders but it shouldn't be blood on our hands. We did our best and so did you.'

Jarvis managed a smile of gratitude that only lasted a moment as Amber Ryan's voice cut into his ear.

'You bastard.'

Jarvis sighed and turned wearily to face Amber, and was surprised to see her smiling at him.

'You got away with it,' she said. 'Warner just called in. They made it.'

Jarvis gasped. 'They didn't.'

'Lucy's with them and they have something to show you.'

For the first time in what felt like a thousand years Jarvis felt tears spring unbidden into his eyes and he staggered sideways as one hand grabbed a safety rail for support. In an instant Lillian and Amber leaped forward and each took one of his arms.

Jarvis turned his head away from them, pain piercing the corners of his eyes and his chest fluttering as he replied in an unsteady voice.

'I'll be right there.'

The two women held him for a moment longer and then they moved away. Jarvis stood for a few moments and watched the sun setting in the distance, and then he gathered himself and turned as he walked toward the bridge.

Garrett and the rest of the team were waiting for him as he joined them, gathered around a large monitor that showed an image of Ethan Warner's face looking back at them. Jarvis could see Lopez in the background, and then most important of all he saw his granddaughter.

'Lucy,' was all he could utter.

'I'm fine,' she called, apparently in perfect health and smiling as she waved at him. 'Once again you have these two to thank for that, although I did save their assess once or twice myself!'

Ethan nodded.

'We couldn't have done it without her.'

'Good to see you again, Ethan. Where are you?' Jarvis asked. 'Why didn't you call in sooner?'

'We decided to lay low until we could get a secure line to you, just in case we got bombed again,' Lopez said hotly, her characteristic fiery Latino temper once again to the fore.'

Jarvis nodded.

'There was no other option. Since you disappeared, ARIES has been totally shut down and Nellis has been reassigned,' he informed them. 'Several agents lost their lives due to the intelligence shake up and if I hadn't split when I did I'd probably also have had a nasty accident.'

'Which is what the DIA thinks happened to you in the desert,' Amber said. 'Right now the DIA believes that you're dead.'

'They went for it?' Ethan asked.

'Intelligence chatter suggests so, and we sure thought that you'd been hit,' Garrett explained. 'The DIA will probably be watching your families for a while in case you show up, but you're no longer likely to be hunted. That means whatever you managed to retrieve from Egypt can be studied without interference.'

Jarvis looked expectantly at Lucy, and with her Hellerman held out a small object the size of a clenched fist.

'We have new toys,' Hellerman said. 'This was found inside the tomb of an Egyptian scribe called Tjaneni who died thousands of years ago. It's built from pure titanium, overlaid with gold.'

Jarvis leaned closer and saw that Hellerman was holding a beautifully formed Eye of Horus. Slowly, he opened it to reveal a perfectly spherical interior.

'Guess what I think goes in here,' Hellerman said.

Jarvis could already see that the spherical cavity was precisely the same size as the exotic liquid metal sphere Hellerman had taken with him when he had fled America.

'You'd better get out here as soon as you can,' Jarvis said. 'We'll arrange flights on private aircraft for you, and you'll transfer off part way to avoid customs.'

Ethan nodded and checked the laptop he was using.

'Our connection won't last much longer before we have to move again,' he said. 'We'll be in touch in precisely twelve hours. Be ready, because Lucy here has translated what our ancient Egyptian friends believed to literally be the Word of God.'

Jarvis leaned closer to the screen. 'What does it say?'

For the first time since he had employed Ethan and Nicola, it was she who got the last word in.

'You're going to have to see that to believe it.'

***

LI

Ilsa de Culebra,

Bahamas

Ethan stepped off the deck of a small fishing boat and onto the enormous white yacht's stern, the warm Caribbean sun glistening off crystalline blue waters all around. He turned, and with Lopez helped Elena onto the deck as from inside the yacht he saw familiar faces approaching them.

'About time!' Garrett said cheerfully as he shook Ethan's hand, and then looked at Elena. 'Welcome aboard, Elena.'

The girl smiled briefly, shyly, and stayed close to Lopez.

Rhys Garrett's yacht was anchored a hundred meters off a tiny uninhabited atoll called Cayo Tiburon, nestled in the heart of the British Virgin Islands. Ethan, Lopez and the rest of the team had travelled via a private vessel across the Atlantic, staying well clear of the Mediterranean to ensure that no links at all could be made between them and Garrett should the DIA spot them on their travels.

They had then jumped ship off the coast of Brazil and travelled north on one of Garrett's hired yachts before transferring to a flying boat that had landed in Antigua. Finally, the anonymous little fishing vessel had transported them across to Garrett's yacht.

Garrett turned to Hellerman.

'The Eye,' he said. 'Do you really think it links up with the artefact you found on the Black Knight?'

Hellerman nodded as he fished the beautifully crafted golden icon from his jacket, the object glinting in the sunlight. 'It's a perfect fit for the sphere.'

Jarvis walked out from the yacht's interior into the sunshine, and instantly Lucy dashed across to him and threw her arms about his neck. For the first time in a long time, Ethan was reminded that Jarvis too was a human being, and that Lucy held him in high regard.

'Is mom okay?' Lucy asked Jarvis.

'She's fine,' Jarvis promised, 'I didn't tell her anything and now I don't have to.'

Jarvis looked at the icon Hellerman was holding.

'We don't know what's going to happen when you try to put that sphere inside,' he warned.

'There's only one way to find out,' Lopez said as she grabbed the icon from Hellerman and tossed it to Jarvis. 'Shall we?'

Jarvis appeared amused by Lopez's business-like attitude as he turned and walked into the yacht. Ethan followed, and found himself walking alongside Elena as the other oracles joined them with Aisha at their head. In sharp contrast to how they had been found, the girls now looked refreshed, glowing with youth and vitality as they broke ranks and rushed to Elena's side in a group hug. Ethan saw Elena's caution melt away as she was held by the other girls, and she looked up in Ethan's general direction.

'We owe you our lives,' Elena said to him as they walked.

'We're even,' Ethan replied. 'And at least now you can live without having the Russians breathing down your necks. I'm sure Garrett will be able to pull some strings and get you citizenship and a new life far from Syria.'

Elena nodded.

'He will.'

Ethan looked down at her as a supernatural chill rippled up his spine. 'Do you see everything?'

'I see enough,' she replied, and for the first time Ethan saw her smile as she glanced briefly in the direction of his voice. 'Enough to know we're in safe hands here, with all of you.'

Ethan glanced over his shoulder. 'I'm not sure; have you ever seen Nicola drive?'

'Can it, Warner,' Lopez shot back.

Jarvis led them through the huge yacht to a lounge near the bow which was lined with deep cream carpets and vast leather couches, immense oval portholes looking out over the ocean outside.

Ethan couldn't help but marvel at the splendor surrounding them as Jarvis walked to the center of the lounge and Ethan noticed a rectangular, transparent box on a glass table between the couches. Inside the box was suspended the bizarre, revolving ball of liquid metal that Lopez and he had found in Antarctica on a previous mission, one that had cost the life of an FBI Agent and close friend.

Mitchell closed the door behind them, sealing them from the staff on the rest of the yacht as Garrett used a remote control to close blinds on the oval portholes, the sunlight streaming into the room muted to a soft glow.

'You got any idea how to go about this?' Jarvis asked Hellerman.

'As a matter of fact, I know precisely what to do.'

'How?' Garrett asked.

Doctor Lucy Morgan stepped forward with a laptop computer and set it on the desk alongside the magnetic chamber containing the sphere. The screen lit up, and Jarvis gasped as he saw an image of the corpse of Tjaneni before him.

From where he stood Ethan could see the complex tattoos that covered the Egyptian scribe's body, and across his chest the Eye of Horus, it's center directly over his heart.

'Wow, he got seriously inked,' Garrett exclaimed.

'Tjaneni's body was literally covered from head to foot with these tattoos,' Lucy explained. 'With the exception of the Eye of Horus, everything else is a mess and makes no sense. That is, until you use the writing on the wrappings and the tablets found inside the Ark to decode them.'

Jarvis frowned. 'I thought the tablets were lost with the Russians?'

Lucy nodded with a bright smile. 'And that is where being a scientist and diligent recorder of evidence comes in.'

Lucy changed the image of the corpse on the laptop screen to one of the tablets that the Russians had stolen from the tomb in Egypt. Although not a perfect image, Lucy had been able to surreptitiously photograph the tablets as they were removed by the Russians from Tjaneni's tomb.

'Hellerman was able to use graphics packages to enhance the image enough that we could read the Sumerian and hieroglyphic instructions, which were then used to decode the information contained on Tjaneni's body. What is says is pretty startling.'

Lucy stood back as Hellerman stepped forward and took the Eye of Horus icon from Jarvis. He moved across to the magnetic chamber as he opened the icon in his hand and held it inverted over the magnetic chamber, just inches above the lid.

Then, with one hand, he unclipped the chamber lid and flipped it off.

Ethan saw the sphere of liquid metal drop for an instant, and then as though drawn by some incredibly powerful force it shot up out of the chamber and slammed directly into the icon with enough force to drive Hellerman's arm upward.

The icon slammed shut in Hellerman's hand and he was hurled a pace backward as he released the icon in shock. The golden Eye of Horus reached head height and stopped, hovering in the air before them.

A silence pervaded the room.

'Now what?' Lopez asked.

Before anybody could reply, Ethan saw a dim glow begin to appear inside the icon's eye, like a point of starlight in an otherwise immensely dark universe. Slowly the light began to burn more brightly, shimmering with iridescent colors that began to flicker around the room.

'What's it doing?' Garrett asked, suddenly nervous.

Ethan realized that despite his own concerns he was more relaxed than Garrett. Over the years he and Lopez had witnessed so many extraordinary things that unless the Eye of Horus was about to disintegrate the yacht and everybody in it, they were likely in no danger at all.

He glanced to his right and to his amazement he saw Elena watching the light and smiling broadly. Beyond her, the other oracles were likewise smiling.

'What is it, Elena?' he asked.

Elena replied softly as though entranced by the spectacle, and almost before she spoke Ethan realized that she shouldn't even be aware that the icon was hovering in mid–air or emitting light at all.

'I can see it,' she said.

Ethan turned as from the Eye of Horus emerged tiny specks of light, glowing orbs that expanded away from the hovering artefact to fill the room. He saw them shimmer and rotate as they moved, passing through objects and out the other side as though the light that they consisted of was both solid and vacuous at the same time.

'Contained light energy,' Hellerman gasped. 'I've heard people report the phenomena in UFO sightings but I've never seen it actually realized before. If the Egyptians witnessed something like this, without a doubt they would have believed it to have been the work of their gods.'

As Ethan watched so the lights began to join together, blending in a graceful ballet of light in three dimensions, and all at once he saw images. He heard the gasps around him, heard his own as he saw vivid, brief flashes of lucidity amid the glowing sphere of expanding light. He saw the pyramids flicker into view, their three gigantic forms in the desert coated in brilliant white stone so bright he could barely look at it, and their tops capped with smaller pyramids of solid gold that shone like brilliant beacons on the daylight.

Further images appeared; pyramids in Peru, in Mexico, in India and in Europe, and as they appeared so he saw what appeared to be schematics overlaying them, complex geometric designs that looked surprisingly like blueprints that traced the outlines of countless megastructures around the world.

'Oh my God,' Lucy exclaimed over the silent display, 'now we know what the Ark really was: knowledge.'

Ethan saw immensely complicated diagrams that flickered in and out of view, of buildings and temples all built with the knowledge delivered to ancient peoples across the world and with which they had grown to become the world's first superpowers.

And then the images transformed grotesquely, the glory of massive megastructures collapsing into vivid, grim images of wars and battles, of clashing swords and colliding armies, of rivers running red with the blood of the fallen and of people starving in besieged cities.

Ethan saw the carnage that the information contained within the Ark had wrought by those who had wielded the knowledge that it contained, the destruction of weaker societies, the genocide of entire peoples across hundreds of years. And then he saw something that nobody had expected. Over the death and destruction loomed a vast deluge that crashed across entire regions, smashing them aside and burying them one by one. He saw cities swallowed, entire races swept from the face of the earth, and then an image that appeared with startling clarity before them all.

A vast city, built from concentric rings in a broad bay, the metropolis bigger than anything he had witnessed before and yet technologically advanced. To his amazement, the startling city was shaped precisely like the Eye of Horus, its great walls forming the eye itself on a scale so vast that it seemed as though it would be visible from space. As he watched, so even that sparkling jewel of society was crushed beneath the waves and vanished into the deep.

The sparkling, dazzling array of images collapsed before them into a glowing holographic image of a man and a woman, behind them the Eye of Horus, the All

Seeing Eye, watching them. Inside their brains he saw the eye appear again, this time as part of the human brain and as old as evolution itself. The eye suddenly shone with a brilliant light, causing Ethan to throw his hands up to shield his eyes, and then the entire display vanished and the room was plunged into darkness as the Eye of Horus icon hovering in the center of the room dropped down and clattered onto the glass table.

For a long time nobody moved, and then Garrett opened the blinds and sunlight shone into the room. Ethan looked around at his companions; Lopez, Mitchell, Jarvis, Hellerman, Lillian, Amy, Lucy, Garrett and the oracles, and then he realized that Elena was shielding her eyes from the bright sunlight, crouching slightly against the glare.

'You can see,' he said.

Elena, Aisha and the others looked around them in wonder as their new-found vision slowly adjusted to the brightness around them.

'What was that?' Lopez asked as she pointed at the icon now lying on the glass table.

'That was knowledge,' Lucy said as she moved across to the icon and picked it up. 'That was a memory, of how we came to be who and what we are. It's an instruction manual to build a civilization, and a record of who sent that information. This is what Majestic Twelve was searching for.'

Ethan recalled the vast city at the end of the images.

'And how to destroy one,' he said. 'There was a city, and a great flood that destroyed everything. What the hell have we walked into here?'

Jarvis replied as he watched Lucy examining the Eye of Horus.

'The origin of our species, of all species. That city was destroyed by a flood, and it's a flood recorded in every legend in every society on earth. The Eye of Horus is the Egyptian All Seeing Eye, and it just revealed to us what I think was not our emergence as a species, but our decline.'

'Our what?' Lopez asked.

'Our decline,' Lucy said in agreement with her grandfather as she continued to study the icon. 'We saw what we were supposed to be, what we once were. Everything that has come afterward is what we've managed on our own. I think that this record shows that we were once assisted by another species, a technologically advanced species, and that they abandoned us.'

Mitchell stepped forward. 'You're saying that our past was better than our present?'

Lucy nodded.

'I think that what we read in Tjaneni's tattoos revealed the origin of The Watchers on earth, and that the city we saw in those images was what we now refer to as *Atlantis*,' she said finally. 'Majestic Twelve were searching for it, and now we are too.'

***

Sign up to Dean Crawford's Newsletter and get a *FREE* book!

www.deancrawfordbooks.com

ABOUT THE AUTHOR

Dean Crawford is the author of over twenty novels, including the internationally published series of thrillers featuring *Ethan Warner*, a former United States Marine now employed by a government agency tasked with investigating unusual scientific phenomena. The novels have been *Sunday Times* paperback best-sellers and have gained the interest of major Hollywood production studios. He is also the enthusiastic author of many independently published novels.

Printed in Germany
by Amazon Distribution
GmbH, Leipzig